Eva Woods grew up in a small Irish village and now lives in London, where she dodges urban foxes and tuts at tourists on escalators. She runs the UK's first writing course for commercial novels and regularly teaches creative writing.

LANCASHIRE COUNTY LIBRARY

3011813774370 8

Also by Eva Woods

How to Be Happy

Eva Woods

SPHERE

First published in Great Britain in 2018 by Sphere

1 3 5 7 9 10 8 6 4 2

Copyright © Claire McGowan 2018

The moral right of the author has been asserted.

Words from *Back to the Future* (p. 126) © Robert Zemeckis and Bob Gale
Words from *Grease* (p. 165) © Allan Carr and Bronte Woodward,
based on the playbook by Jim Jacobs and Warren Casey

*All characters and events in this publication, other than those
clearly in the public domain, are fictitious and any resemblance
to real persons, living or dead, is purely coincidental.*

All rights reserved.
No part of this publication may be reproduced, stored in a
retrieval system, or transmitted, in any form or by any means, without
the prior permission in writing of the publisher, nor be otherwise circulated
in any form of binding or cover other than that in which it is published
and without a similar condition including this condition being
imposed on the subsequent purchaser.

A CIP catalogue record for this book
is available from the British Library.

ISBN 978-0-7515-6855-4

Typeset in Baskerville by M Rules
Printed and bound in Great Britain by
Clays Ltd, Elcograf S.p.A.

Papers used by Sphere are from well-managed forests
and other responsible sources.

MIX
Paper from
responsible sources
FSC® C104740

LANCASHIRE COUNTY LIBRARY	
3011813774370 8	
Askews & Holts	01-Nov-2018
AF	£13.99
HAC	

the lives we touch

Two hundred and fifty-three. That was how many people heard or saw Rosie Cooke step in front of the bus on a bright, cold morning in October, as it crossed a bridge spanning the grey, muddied waters of the Thames.

Another ten would have seen it, but they were so engrossed in their phones they didn't know anything was wrong until the traffic stopped and, for a moment in the beating heart of London, everything was still and quiet and terrible.

An office worker on the twenty-seventh floor of a skyscraper heard it as he sat at his desk, thinking about leaving his job before it crushed him, but turning over and over in his head the size of his mortgage and the children's school fees. He frowned at the sound of screeching brakes that carried all the way up to him, and then went back to his spreadsheets.

Three people on the bus that hit Rosie were late for work. Another missed an interview for a recruitment job she hadn't really wanted anyway, and decided she was going to go travelling to Brazil instead. There on the beach, caipirinha in hand, she would meet her future husband, Cristiano.

A woman stuck on the bridge, which was closed off for hours, had to stay late in the office to make up the time, and cancel a first date with the man she would have married, who six months from that day would have slammed her head against a wall when she shrank a jumper of his in the wash.

Twenty-three people missed their trains. Two got fired. One of the paramedics who answered the 999 call decided this was the final straw, and he was going to quit his job and retrain as an art therapist. In the crowd, a party of hens from Glasgow got entangled with a stag do from Cardiff, and went on a riotous night out in the West End, after which more than one monogrammed T-shirt ended up on the floor of a Premier Inn. A small child who saw the accident happen became so afraid of crossing the road that for the rest of his life he'd have to count to three before taking the plunge, and eventually move out of London to that Channel Island that has no cars on it. The driver of the bus would take early retirement, and move with his wife to the Costa del Sol, where he'd never get behind the wheel again. His wife, who had been thinking of leaving him, would decide to stay now that he seemed to need her more. She'd take her driving test and become very interested in vintage cars. Two young women on a different bus struck up a conversation after one burst into tears, and six months later would move in together. In two years' time, they'd be happily married and adopting a child from Romania. More than one person went home to their partner that night and held them a bit tighter, spoke a little more kindly, overlooked the dirty socks on the floor. At least one child was conceived as a result. As many as fourteen people decided to abandon their diets and have a biscuit when they reached the office (for the shock). The street cleaner who had to mop up the blood had a flashback to the war-torn country he'd fled, but got on with it anyway, because what choice did he have? The doctor who met the ambulance, newly in post and on hour twenty of a shift, locked herself in the loos to cry afterwards. The ripples from the accident spread out, across London, across the country, across the world, far into the future.

And as for Rosie, she knew nothing about any of this, because for several minutes in the ambulance she was actually clinically dead.

But she came back. In a fashion, anyway.

DAY ONE

Rosie

'. . . losing her. BP is falling . . . '

'Stats are very worrying. Where the hell's Andy?'

'. . . buggered off again . . . '

'. . . in front of a bus? Suicide watch?'

'Get the crash cart and page him now!'

How strange, she thought. She'd fallen asleep in front of an old episode of *ER*. She hadn't watched that since . . . she had no idea. What was stranger, though, was that hands were touching her. Gently, but in a professional, distant way. Someone held her wrist, and someone else kept pulling out bits of her hair. It hurt. *Ow*, she said. *Ow*. No words seemed to come out of her mouth. She tried to open her eyes but they felt stuck shut. Her face felt . . . gritty. That was strange. Had she blacked out? *What's happening?*

A strange bright light was shining through her eyelids, as if someone was interrogating her. She tried to move away from it, cover her face, but her arms didn't move. And breathing was so hard. As if someone was sitting on her chest, some small but very heavy person. Danny DeVito maybe. *What the hell?* For a moment, with great effort, she forced her eyes open a crack. This wasn't her room. It was too bright, and there were plastic curtains, and on the other side of them another bed and something happening on it. It took her brain a while to figure out what it was. A man in motorbike leathers, but his chest was open and red. People in masks pulling on him, packing things into him, attaching tubes and wires. *What's going on?* She thought for a second she could see his heart beating, right there open to the air, and a surge of panic went through her. *Is he . . . ? Am I watching someone die?*

The man had longish fair hair, and just for a split second his eyes, bright green, opened and he looked right at her. Her heart jumped in terror and her eyes fell shut of their own accord, like shutters slamming down.

'. . . responsive. Call Dr Khan and have her transferred to the ICU.'

Now someone was tapping her eyelids. How very rude these people were. 'Rosie? Rosie, can you hear me?'

Yes, *Rosie*, that was her name. Her name was Rosie and she was . . . how old? She couldn't seem to remember any more. Where was she? Why did everything hurt? *What the hell's going on?*

'Rosie, you're in the hospital. You've had an accident. A bus hit you but you've been very lucky, you're still with us.'

A bus had *hit* her? *It's the drivers*, she said. *They drive like maniacs, have you seen them?* But again the words had no sound. Her

6

mouth was frozen. And how could she be lucky if a bus had hit her? What were these people on about? Who were they?

'... said a name in the ambulance – Luke? Rosie, who's Luke? Is he your husband?'

Husband. Did she have one? She didn't know. She didn't even know how old she was. Trying to remember hurt her head, and it was so comfortable in the bed she was lying on. Like a cloud. A cloud that was carrying her away from all this noise and brightness and pain and these strange people touching her. That was it, go to sleep and when she woke up again this would all be over. A cascade of untethered memories whirled through her mind as she sank, like watching a stranger's home videos. A grassy meadow, running over it as fast as her legs would carry her, white Clark's sandals flapping ... a fair-haired man on a beach, turning to her and saying something ... standing on a stage in blinding lights, an unseen audience furiously clapping for her ...

'Rosie? She's going under! Damn it, page Andy again!'

Rosie, she told herself firmly, as she slipped under again. *I am Rosie and I am ... I don't know who I am.*

Daisy

Daisy had never quite come to terms with the fact she couldn't speed up time. As a child, she'd lie awake impatiently every night once December came, counting down the days to Christmas. What kind of stupid world was it where time always moved at the same pace?

Now she was a grown-up, and she knew the sad truth.

Nothing went faster or slower because you needed it to. The Tube still dawdled between stations. Train doors took an eternity to open. People milled about on escalators like lost sheep. She cannoned off them, fighting her way out of the Tube station and up into the light. 'Excuse me ... excuse me ... SORRY, CAN I GET PAST!' Offended looks. Mutterings. For once, she didn't care. God, it had taken nearly an hour to get there. She'd run for the train on hearing the news, but was there a quicker route? No, a taxi would have sat in traffic for ages. There had been no way to get there faster, short of, say, a helicopter.

Had they taken Rosie in a helicopter? No, the hospital was so close to where it happened, the next street over. The best place to get hit by a bus, if there was such a thing.

Her feet felt weird. She looked down as she stumbled towards the signs for the hospital. Her shoes were on the wrong feet. She fought the urge to stop and change them round, dodging her way through the crowds. Everything was all wrong. She hadn't done any of her leaving-the-house checks, hadn't picked up any clean clothes in case she was stuck there overnight, didn't have her make-up bag or water bottle or the work she had to do today. She tried to reset her brain, tell it she wasn't going to get that report done. She wouldn't be in the office today at all. Bollocks, she had to text Maura. Her boss would be livid – she hated last-minute absences, especially in a week with a big pitch looming. But who could argue with *my sister just got hit by a bus*?

A nasty ball formed in her throat and she tried to swallow it down. She'd asked her mother, on the phone, 'But what do they mean, hit by a bus? Hit a little bit – like clipped by the wing mirror? Or hit a lot?'

'I don't know!' Her mother's voice had ricocheted around the line. 'She's out cold, they said. You have to go there now, Daisy. It'll take me hours on the train. And I don't have anyone to look after Mopsy and there's nowhere to park at the station and . . . Oh God, what if she's badly hurt?'

'I'll go,' Daisy had said, already pulling on her coat. 'I'll go right now.'

She had now reached the hospital, all fifteen floors of it, full of illness and suffering and death. She found she'd ground to a halt, her mixed-up shoes rooted to the pavement. What would she find inside? It sounded pretty serious, being hit by a bus. What if Rosie was dying right now, while she stood on the street dithering?

Rosie never dithered. She just decided to do something, and then did it. *You're always so careful, Daisy*, her mother had said, at the engagement party. *That's what I most admire about you, darling.* But thinking of the party brought up jagged, uncomfortable feelings, and she pushed them down. Would that be Daisy's last memory of Rosie, in her leather jacket and ripped jeans, red curls wild and untamed over her shoulders? What would she look like now after . . . after?

Daisy dragged her feet forward, as if detaching them from chewing gum stuck to the pavement. The hospital was bright and modern inside, with an M&S on the ground floor, not what she'd expected. She found the lift and got in beside two handsome young doctors in blue scrubs, talking loudly about nephritis, whatever that was. The doors opened and she rushed out into Intensive Care.

This place was more like she'd expected. Swift feet, beeping machines, a hot and oppressive atmosphere. Someone was crying in the waiting room, the jagged sobs like a bassline to the rest of the noise. She found the reception desk, which had a harried-looking young man behind it, with a tragus piercing and tattoos all up one arm.

'Um, hi, I think my sister is here? Rosie Cooke?' *Is it a question or a statement, Daisy?* she imagined Maura saying.

He consulted the computer and she saw him suddenly focus on her. Her stomach dropped away. Waiting for him to say, *I'm very sorry but . . .*

He called over a young woman in scrubs. Nurse, doctor? How did you tell who did what job? It was impossible. They all dressed the same. She heard him mutter the words, ' . . . bus jumper . . . ' What did that mean? *Jumper?*

The woman's face was calm and unreadable. 'Will you come with me please, Miss Cooke?'

She went. A horrible thought was crystallising in her mind, as she realised she'd feared this all along. Even before her mum's phone call. For years. Since Rosie was fifteen, really, and Daisy was only twelve, this precise worry had been at the back of her thoughts, every time the phone rang and an unexpected voice was on the other end.

Had Rosie done this to herself?

Rosie

Rosie opened her eyes. Except she didn't, because her eyes, like her voice, apparently no longer worked on command. *Come on, guys, open! After everything we've been through together! I'm sorry I forgot to wear sunglasses all those times and never take my mascara off. Please . . . move?*

10

A tiny crack of light opened up. She found herself in a private room, and with her was a small woman she recognised as her grandmother, sitting in a plastic orange chair, knitting. Which was weird, because she was pretty sure her grandma didn't know how to knit. God had invented M&S for a reason, she always said. See, that was a memory. 'Grandma?' she tried. It was so strange. She was sure she'd spoken the word, but the two doctors standing by her bed didn't seem to notice, carrying on their mutterings about BP this and systolic that like people going 'rhubarb, rhubarb' in the back of a bad am-dram production. They seemed ... muted, somehow. Not quite real.

Her grandma said, 'Rosie, love. What have you done to yourself then?'

'I ... really don't know.'

Her grandma got up, leaving the knitting on the chair. It was in some kind of lurid pink wool, and the shape of it was odd. Was it for a four-legged baby? Rosie's head hurt. 'Hmm, yes,' said her grandma, peering knowledgably at the chart on the bottom of Rosie's bed. The doctors did not turn around or even seem to notice the small woman in the navy drip-dry slacks. It was very strange, like watching two videos superimposed on top of each other. 'Massive head trauma. That explains it. You've got retrograde amnesia, I expect.'

'What?'

'I watched a lot of medical dramas after your granddad died, love.'

'Why am I ...? Why don't I know who I am?'

'You're Rosie. Rosie Cooke.'

Rosie Cooke. Two names. That was twice the information she'd had before. Progress. 'And you're my grandma.' She knew that, somehow, deep in herself.

'Course I am, love.'

Was this her mum's mother or her dad's? Who were her mum and dad? Oh God. There was so much she couldn't recall it was scary to think about it, like when you look under the sofa cushions and it's so filthy the only thing to do is put them back and try to forget.

Was that a memory? Was she the kind of person who didn't clean under their sofa cushions? 'Do you know what happened to me? Does it say on that chart?'

'Sorry, love. Just says some complicated stuff they never covered on *Grey's Anatomy.* But it's OK. They're helping you. See, they're giving you something, a nice drug. I tell you, I wish they'd had all this when I was your age. Two kiddies and only a slug of brandy to get me through!'

Rosie focused hard. OK. A hospital room, white, sterile-looking. Two doctors hanging over her, in white coats and scrubs. A young Asian guy and a blonde girl with fresh peach-like skin that looked good even paired with blue scrubs and no sleep. She tried hard to hear what they were saying. *Ears! Guys, you need to come through for me too, OK? Sorry about that infected piercing. That was my bad.*

She found she was able to make it out if she listened with all her might, like a station on a badly tuned radio. The girl was saying, '. . . should use the restraints really. It's protocol.'

'Come on, Zara. She's hardly going anywhere. She can't even open her eyes. I wonder what made her do it.'

Do what?

'The family are on their way. And I guess the police will want to ask questions. Hey, maybe she was pushed.'

'You watch too much *CSI*.'

'It's all they ever have on in the doctors' lounge.'

Yes, she could hear, but nothing helpful. Pushed how? Down something or under something? She tried hard to speak. 'Hello, can you tell me why I'm here?' Nothing. 'You can hear me, Grandma, can't you?'

'If you say so, dear.' She'd gone back to her knitting now, holding it up to the light. 'What do you think? Will he like it?'

'Who?'

'Filou, of course. Who d'you think it was for, a four-legged baby?'

'No,' said Rosie quickly. Filou was . . . 'Your dog!' She had him in her mind, suddenly, a yappy little pug. Filou had come back to her memory, slotting into place like a jigsaw piece. Surely the rest would come back too. It would all be fine. No need to panic just because right now she couldn't remember who she was.

'That's right. See, you'll get there, love. You just need to give yourself time to heal. It was a nasty accident, by the sounds of it.'

'A bus hit me.' She frowned, remembering the moment she'd been awake before. The lights, the pain, the man with his chest open and his green eyes looking right at her. Had that been real?

Grandma sucked her teeth. 'A bus! How did that happen, then?'

Rosie tried to take stock of her body, searching for clues. There was something on her mouth, tape of some kind, a tube in her throat and going down the back of her nose.

There were so many sore places she had to move through them, cataloguing. Head. Left ankle. Right knee. Bum. Back. Shoulder. Both hands burning like fire. Arm. Ribs. And her nose felt wrong too. 'I don't remember,' she said, frustrated. 'I don't know what happened!' Questions crowded her head. How had she got here? Who was she? Why had she said the name *Luke*?

'Look, here's Daisy. Maybe she'll know more.'

Who was Daisy? How had her grandma got here first? And why was she wearing slippers and a cardigan? Wasn't she in a care home somewhere? Devon? Yes, Devon. Had she busted out of her home and ridden here on a sit-on lawnmower, like that man in that film?

When had Rosie seen that film? No idea. She realised there was a noise in the room. A sort of dry, rasping sound, like when you tried to squeeze the last bit of shampoo from the bottle in the shower. The noise was coming from a young woman who stood in the doorway, with sensible shoes, A-line skirt, and an old-lady handbag. There was something weird about her feet that Rosie couldn't quite put her finger on. A diamond engagement ring, too big for her, sparkled on one hand. The woman was sobbing, leaning against the doorway of the room for support. The girl doctor was speaking to her in low, cool tones, hands in the pocket of her white coat. She strained to listen. ' . . . sustained massive head trauma. There was an intracranial bleed which we've managed to stop for now, and we've put in a drain, which explains the shaved hair.'

They shaved my hair! Dammit, didn't someone tell them my ears are too big to pull off a crop?

The woman in the doorway was still crying, gasping for breath. 'But how did it happen? How could she walk in front of a *bus*? Oh God.'

Rosie had a bad feeling. 'Grandma? Who's that? Why do I feel . . . ? Why does it make me feel terrible that she's crying?'

'That's Daisy, love. Your sister.'

I have a sister? But as Grandma said the word it all came flooding back, Daisy, Daisy, Daisy. Daisy a tiny baby in a cheesecloth blanket, so light on Rosie's knee. Daisy in a graduation robe, refusing to throw her mortarboard in case it hit someone. Daisy climbing into Rosie's bed with a nightmare, a small child, scratching her with toenails and hogging the covers. Daisy, a teenager, stealing Rosie's Rimmel Heather Shimmer lipstick but feeling so guilty she bought her a new one. A million index cards slamming into place in the filing cabinets of her brain, making her wince. Every memory stamped with *Daisy*. Daisy laughing, Daisy crying, Daisy screaming, 'God, Rosie, you're so selfish . . . '

Oh. 'We had some kind of fight? I . . . I can't remember why.'

'You will. You have to. Anyway, look, she's here, she's crying. She still cares.'

What did that mean, *you have to*? She looked up and saw Grandma was starting to recede, fade and grow smaller somehow. 'Wait! Please don't leave me. There're so many things I don't understand!'

But the old woman was gone, and so was her knitting for Filou. Who, now that Rosie had remembered him, she seemed to recall had been around when she was small and scared of him. How long did pugs live? How old was she now, for that matter? A grown-up, surely. Daisy, who was apparently her

15

sister, looked to be about thirty, despite being dressed like a sixty-something librarian.

Something else had been bothering her too, hovering around the edge of her vision like a bothersome fly. 'The thing is, Grandma,' she said, out loud – although the doctors and her sister didn't seem to hear – 'didn't you die too? Like, years ago?' And as she thought about it the memory was there – Grandma waxy and cold in her coffin, Rosie crying in a church pew wearing a too-tight grey dress from Jane Norman. Yes, she was almost sure that her grandmother, who had just been here chatting to her and knitting a jumper for a long-gone dog, was dead.

What the hell is going on?

Daisy

Deep breaths, deep breaths. She tried to remember Maura's advice from the time she'd cried in her annual appraisal. *Daisy lacks confidence and that killer instinct we require in our partners. Perhaps she would be more suited to a support post.* Her boss had watched her coolly across the desk as Daisy sniffed and hiccupped. 'Put your emotions aside, Daisy. Just bury them deep down.'

She tried to picture an empty pit, a spade beside it and a pile of soil, somewhere to shove these feelings in and forget about them, but it just made her think of gravesides, which brought up a lot of memories she really didn't want to relive, and panic seized her once again, squeezing her insides in an iron fist. Rosie had been hit by a bus. A *bus.* One of those gigantic red double-decker ones, tall as a building.

She tried to make sense of what the doctor was saying, that composed young woman who was likely younger than Daisy herself. Rosie had been thrown up in the air, and landed and hit her head on the road, but luckily – luckily! – the accident had happened only metres from the hospital, and she'd been whisked into A&E as soon as was humanly possible. 'She suffered a cardiac arrest on the way,' the doctor recited, as calm as a cold-caller trying to sell mobile phone insurance. 'We were able to restart her heart and stabilise her, for now at least.'

Daisy grasped at the words, which seemed to slide out of her hands like bars of soap. 'You mean . . . her heart stopped? She died?'

'Well, only technically.'

Daisy was stunned into silence. Dying, even if it was just for a few seconds and only technical, still seemed quite bad. A lot to deal with on a Tuesday morning when she'd been making her breakfast smoothie. Christ, she hadn't washed the blender, Gary would do his nut, and . . .

You sound just like Mum. That's what Rosie would say. Daisy was obsessing over small details, unable to take in the huge ones. The blender, and its washed or unwashed state, was not important right now. She hadn't even told Gary yet, just run out of the house with her shoes on the wrong feet. He'd left at six, as always, to get into the office and pick off the best clients before anyone else did. He had no idea Rosie was lying here, broken into bits with deep red scrapes all over her pale skin, her hair matted with dirt and blood and a patch of it shaved off, her leg in a cast. The machines around her, the tubes trailing out of her body. She was in a coma, the doctor had said. 'Will she wake up?' Daisy asked. 'Can she hear us?'

She saw the momentary pucker on the doctor's smooth face. 'We can't be sure. I'm sorry.'

'So . . . what will happen?'

The doctor hesitated. 'We have about three days before we have to take out the nasal and breathing tubes and put in something more permanent. Hopefully she'll wake up in that time. If she doesn't . . . Well, there will be decisions to make.'

'What does that mean?'

'You should discuss it with your parents, Miss Cooke. Excuse me now. Dr Agarwal?' And she went, ponytail swinging, accompanied by the more sympathetic-looking male doctor, who at least had a kind smile. Daisy was left alone with her comatose sister. Slowly, she approached her. Rosie's face was blank, a tube hanging out of her mouth. Daisy reached out to touch her hand – it was cold and limp.

'Rosie?' she tried. 'Can you hear me?' Nothing. Her sister seemed *gone* somehow. Not asleep, just not there any more. The last words she'd said to her weighed heavy in Daisy's mouth. *You're so selfish . . .*

This was all crazy. It was almost ten, a time when she'd normally be crouched at her desk inputting numbers, or drinking her fifth coffee of the morning, or meeting with clients. Instead, she was at her sister's bedside, while outside other relatives sat around in various states of worry or boredom or fear, and across the screen of a silent TV, the gibberish-like subtitles on a property show informed them whether Gareth and Gwen from Swansea had made a profit on the four-bed semi they'd bought at auction. Nothing made sense.

Her phone buzzed – she was squeezing it tight in her hand,

leaving smeary fingerprints on the screen. Mum. *Arriving Paddington now.* She would be here soon. It was a terrible thing, but for a moment Daisy was actually glad Rosie was in a coma. At least that way Rosie and their mother couldn't get into yet another fight.

Rosie

She missed oblivion. Letting her dry eyes close, getting sucked into the darkness. No name, no aching body, no million questions battering her head like moths around a porch light. What was going on? She was seeing dead people now? How? Rosie didn't believe in ghosts, or in life after death. Ever since Petey, she'd decided there couldn't be a God who would be as cruel as that.

Wait. Who was Petey? Rosie prodded that area of her memory, like an empty socket in a gum. The name brought a flood of feelings – sadness, fear, deep, deep love – and two clear images. A blue wall with yellow ducklings painted on. And a woman crying hysterically, her head in her hands. Nothing else.

You're hallucinating, she told herself firmly. *They said you had massive head trauma. Your brain is probably in a right state. You're imagining things – like your dead grandma, for a start.* Yes, that made sense. Her synapses were just a bit . . . scrambled. Either that or she'd been wrong about the whole afterlife thing. It was probably too late to hedge her bets now, if so. She had to just hope that the massive-fight-with-sister thing was a blip and she was actually an OK person.

Rosie looked around the now-empty room. Daisy had gone out, wiping her face and clutching her phone, and Rosie was still trying to make sense of what the doctors had said. Three days to wake up, or she might never come back. But she *was* awake, wasn't she? Couldn't they see that? She couldn't move her neck, which seemed to be in some kind of brace, and could only lift her eyelids a crack, so all she could see was the stained ceiling, some old pipes hanging from it, and the door out into the corridor, where people passed like swooping birds, flashes of navy and green and white, efficient voices and footsteps and clipboards and stethoscopes and trolleys. Everything moving while she lay, unable to lift a finger.

'What do I do?' she said, though no sound came out. 'Am I going to wake up?' She wondered if her grandma was still about. Her dead grandma. What was going on? 'Is anyone there?'

'Hello!' said an irritating shrill voice. 'It's me, Rosie!'

Rosie knew that voice. She had a thorough rummage through her brain to try to find it. It was filed somewhere under 'voices, irritating' and cross-referenced with 'friends, primary school'. But . . . it couldn't be. *'Melissa?'*

Sure enough, a teenage girl was standing at the end of her bed, dressed in a too-big maroon school uniform, frizzy dark hair sticking out in all directions, smeary glasses. 'Hi! It's me! Gosh, we haven't seen each other, since, what, 1994?'

Melissa had highlighter pen on the collar of her pale pink shirt. Rosie was trying hard to recall facts about her. 'We were at primary school together? We were friends?' Yes, that was right. The files in her head marked 'Melissa', though incomplete, gave her a warm feeling. Painting their faces green with her watercolour set, only to find it wouldn't wash off; recording themselves singing 2 Unlimited songs into a Casio tape recorder; rearranging Rosie's living room into a *Gladiators*-style assault course . . . and then, like a pocket of cold water in the sea, a bad feeling took over. Had they stopped being friends? If they were the same age, why was she seeing Melissa as a teenager?

There was an obvious reason for that, but her mind shied away from it.

'We were friends, yeah, but then I moved away. My mum made me go to private school, because of all the bullying.' She said it matter-of-factly, as if Rosie would know what it meant. Another nasty sinkhole of feeling had opened up in her stomach, a twinge like a bad tooth that told her, *You don't want to remember this*. Her whole memory was like walking through quicksand. 'Didn't help, though, in the long run. I mean, duh.' Melissa indicated her spectral body. If she was still a teenager, and Rosie was grown-up, that must mean . . .

'What . . . Um, Melissa, the thing is, my memory's a bit mixed up right now, and I can't really . . . Are you?'

'Dead? Oh yes. As a doornail.'

Rosie had so many questions, starting with: how had she died? Was that a rude question? Cautiously, she asked, 'Um, how long have you been . . . like this?'

'Oh, almost twenty years now. Time flies when you're dead.'

So Melissa had died in her teens. 'That's horrific. I'm so sorry. Melissa . . . do you . . . could you help me figure out what's happened to me? I know I've been in an accident, but I can't remember who I am or how it might have happened.'

'That's totally normal. I remember when it was me. Brains

get a bit upset when they're dying, or nearly dying, and they go into a panic. Plus, if you hit your head, all the information has sort of got jumbled up, like . . . '

'Sort of like knocked-over filing cabinets?' She was picturing her head strewn with scattered memories. A man with fair hair leaning in to kiss her . . . the same man smashing into her on the dodgems, the two of them laughing hysterically, Rosie's red hair streaming around her . . . Who was he?

'Filing cabinets, yeah. Oh, that is good. I'm going to steal that.' Melissa rolled up her ghostly shirtsleeve and produced a sparkly gel ghost pen from her ghost pocket, which she used to scribble a note on her ghost arm. Rosie felt faint. *What the hell is going on?* 'Here's the thing, Rosie. It happened to me as well. When you're in a coma, and your brain's been injured, it has to kind of reboot itself before you can wake up. Like a computer reset. I'm told computers really caught on after I died, who knew?'

Rosie was struggling to understand, on top of struggling with the whole fact that she was talking to a ghost/hallucination/whatever. 'But I *am* awake. I mean, I can hear things and see things – well, sometimes. I just can't speak, or move.' But that would come back, surely. Wouldn't it?

'I know. You're sort of . . . in-between. Like, everyone's life flashes before them when they die, right? That's happening to you too. You just . . . have the chance to still come back.'

'So what can I do? How do I wake up properly? The doctor said something about three days?'

'That's how long it takes for your brain to reset. So all you can do is try to remember why you're here. If your brain can make sense of things, it might start responding again and let you wake up. Now, sit back – well, you don't have a lot of choice about that, I'm afraid, hello, neck brace – and watch what your mind throws up.'

'What do you mean, what my mind throws up?'

Melissa looked sympathetic. 'Your memories are about to start coming back to you, Rosie. It's just what happens.'

'But that's good! That's what I need!'

'Well. They might not, like, come back in the right order. It might be a bit . . . confusing. And the memories that come – they might not be the ones you'd expect. Or that you really want to remember. But you need to look through them and remember who you are. Why this happened. Anyway, you'll see what I mean in a minute. Are you ready?'

'Wait! Ready for what?' Something was happening. The hospital room was fading, receding again, as if the real world was the ghostly one and Melissa the only real thing.

'It's starting,' said Melissa calmly. 'Just breathe, Rosie. Keep all hands inside the vehicle and restore tray tables to their upright position.'

'What?'

'Just a thing I'm trying. The first memory is coming now.'

But I don't understand! Rosie wanted to scream but her mouth was stopped up in this reality, and everything was spinning and blurring, and it made her want to puke, and was this death? Was she dying? Oh God.

There was light, a bright grey light. In front of her eyes, blurred like a distant memory, she saw what looked like a dial. Numbers, and the words: *day month year*. What was this? Was she . . . *travelling in time*? No. It wasn't possible. It was another hallucination, it had to be. The numbers flipped around, in a seemingly haphazard fashion, beyond her control, and then settled on the combination 17 10 2017. A date? Which was . . . crap, what year was it now? She remembered a glimpse of a calendar she'd caught in A&E, when they were wheeling her in from the ambulance. 2017. That was this year. That was a week ago. OK. This was going to help her make sense of what was going on. She took a deep breath and the world fell away.

17 October 2017 (One week ago)

When Rosie opened her eyes, she was somewhere else. A small, cramped room, with cheap IKEA furniture. What was IKEA? She waited for the gap in her brain that seemed to pop up when she thought of a word but couldn't remember its meaning. Instead, it was there waiting for her, all her associations for that word – *meatballs, row with Jack that time, allen keys, stress.*

Who was Jack? She didn't know. But other information was flooding back. She was remembering. 'This is my flat!' she said out loud.

'This is where you live?' said Melissa, from somewhere behind her.

Rosie jumped. 'You're here too?'

'Think of me as like your spirit guide.' Melissa was nosing among her DVD collection. 'Hey, I know all these! Don't you watch any recent TV shows? *Friends* ... ah, I love *Friends*. I was gutted I died before it ended, I never got to find out if Ross and Rachel made it.'

'Course they did. It's a show about happy endings. Not like real life.'

The room was as Rosie remembered, but shadowy somehow. A memory of the thing and not the thing. Melissa was looking at everything, opening drawers in the kitchen, peering under the coffee table, lifting up the colourful sofa cushions. There wasn't much to look at, actually. One room, a bed pushed into the corner, a two-seater sofa in front of a small cheap TV, a strip of kitchen against the wall. A door off to the side that Rosie knew was her bathroom, so small she was eternally afraid she'd slip and get wedged in there and die, as had happened in one news story she'd read (see, another memory!). Melissa heaved a sigh. 'I guess I thought it would be ... bigger. You know, in *St Elmo's Fire*, Demi Moore has that huge place.'

'Because she was a bond trader in the eighties!'

'And Monica and Rachel have a nice place in New York.'

'Rent control,' Rosie snapped. 'Also, fiction. Life's not like we thought it would be in the nineties, Melissa. Property costs a fortune and wages haven't gone up at all.'

'Oh. So no huge pink flats?'

'Not unless you're on coke and also working maybe as a call girl on the side.'

'Like in *Pretty Woman*?' Melissa's eyes widened. 'So romantic, that film.'

'Yes, well, wait till you discover feminism and it's ruined for you for ever. Turns out, paying her for sex: not that romantic after all.' Too late, she remembered Melissa would never discover anything, because she was dead. And yet here she was, talking to Rosie. It made no sense.

Melissa kicked the side of the sofa, releasing a cloud of dust. She coughed. 'I get what you're saying about houses being expensive, Rosie, and I'm fourteen so I don't really notice dirt, but isn't this kind of ... messy?'

Rosie looked around. The ghostly teen was right. It was a total tip. Why was she living like this? There were dirty dishes stacked all round the sink, and what looked like biscuit crumbs ground into the cheap velveteen sofa. Over the radiator, her underwear was drying, but it wasn't the fabulous lace and silk lingerie she'd imagined she'd have as a grown-up; it was washed out and holey and grey. Her heart sank. *I found my life again, but it sucks.*

Melissa was saying, 'I mean, where're your Magic Eye pictures? Your troll doll collection? There's not even a lava lamp. Disappointing.'

'Shhh.' Rosie could hear something. Footsteps, stomping up the stairs, and loud voices. 'Someone's coming!' She panicked. How could she explain being here, in her own flat, but with a teenage ghost who still thought lava lamps were the height of cool?

'It's OK,' said Melissa, calmly rummaging through a make-up bag. 'We're not really here. This is just a memory.'

As soon as she said that, Rosie understood. Of course it was a memory. It had taken place, as the dial suggested, a week ago.

The door burst open and into the shabby flat came – herself. Rosie stared, from her vantage point huddled against the radiator. She, her memory self, was wearing jeans with big rips in the knees, and Rosie heard a voice in her head: *Can't you buy clothes that don't have holes in them?* And she knew it was something her mother had said to her. No coat, though it was, as Rosie now knew, October. She was carrying a thin plastic bag with what looked like a Pot Noodle in it, and talking to someone behind her. 'Honestly, I'm fine. I just don't want to go out.'

She'd been followed in by a very skinny man in tight jeans and a T-shirt. His arms were covered in tattoos and his voice was whiny. 'But babe, you've not been out in, like, weeks, except, like, to the corner shop.' Was this Luke, the name she'd said in the ambulance? Surely not.

Real-life Rosie flopped onto the sofa, releasing more dust. 'I'm fine, Leo. I'm just . . . taking some time out.' Not Luke then. So who was he, and why had she said his name?

'Awww, Ro, I'm DJing tonight! I need to see a friendly face in the crowd!' The man she'd called Leo leaned against the wall, a self-pitying look on his narrow, pinched face. 'What do you say? Get your glad rags on, come out with me?' He looked around at the mess, staring right through Melissa, who was trying on a collection of long beaded necklaces that had been twisted round the handles of the chest of drawers.

Real-life Rosie scowled. 'How can I go out? You know I have no money. I don't have a job any more, do I?'

She'd been fired? Where from? What kind of mess was she in? She checked in her head but found she had no memory of what her job might be.

Leo crossed the room. His voice had softened, and he placed his hands on Real-life Rosie's shoulders. 'Come on, babe. You're having a shit time, I know. I've been there.'

'Leo, you've never even needed a job, let alone been unemployed. You have a trust fund.'

'But I get it. Look, I'll ask Dad to cut you some slack on the rent, OK? It's fine if you don't want to come to the warehouse party. Maybe we can just hang out a bit, chill, you know?' His voice had risen hopefully, and his hands had started massaging her back.

'He's talking about *sex*,' hissed Melissa, indignant. They didn't seem to hear her, luckily.

Now she was watching it, she could feel the memories settle back into place. Leo. Lived downstairs in a much bigger and nicer flat. Part-time DJ and beatboxer. Dad owned the building. Kept 'just popping by' to borrow milk and see if she needed any light bulbs changed or big spiders chased off. She hadn't done anything, had she? Not with Leo. She'd sworn not to, even on the nights when she felt so lonely, and she knew he was just downstairs listening to his terrible dubstep and practising beatboxing into a deodorant can, and sometimes she'd think, Why not? He's OK-looking, and he clearly likes me, even if he is a total idiot.

Her past self stared ahead, her eyes dull. Then she swallowed hard, and her voice changed too, became softer. 'Thanks, dude. Not tonight, though, yeah? I'm not feeling so good.'

Reluctantly, he removed his hands. 'OK. I need a spliff anyway to calm me down after all this drama.' Now he wasn't touching her, his eyes wandered over her flat. On top of the TV was a photo. The frame had been smashed and Rosie remembered that she kept meaning to get another one, but somehow never did. He picked it up, leaving smeary fingerprints on the glass. 'Your family? Who's the kid?'

Past Rosie sprang to her feet and practically grabbed it from him. 'Yes. Sorry, Leo, I've got stuff to do, would you mind . . . ?'

29

Once he was gone, Past Rosie closed the door, slid a bolt into place, and leaned against it with a juddering sigh. Rosie wanted to scream at herself, *You almost did it! What's the matter with you?* But she knew she had the answer to that question inside her, and that maybe she wasn't ready yet to hear it.

'This is my life,' she murmured, watching her other self cross the tiny room, and instead of washing the dishes or putting away the clothes that littered the floor, crawl into the bed with the not-too-clean duvet and pull it over her head. She still had her shoes on. 'How can this be my life?'

Melissa, being a teenager, couldn't hide her disappointment. 'You were so cool at school, you know? Rosie Cooke, netball captain. I thought for sure you'd be a top businesswoman with shoulder pads, living with Harrison Ford who'd be making your packed lunch for you.'

'Life isn't like the films, Mel,' she said sadly.

Melissa sighed and started unwinding the many strings of beads she'd twisted about herself. 'Well, we have to get back now anyway.'

'Back where?'

'Back to the future, Marty!' She snickered. 'I loved that film. We have to go back to your conscious mind, such as it is. This is just a memory you were seeing again.'

'But . . . why?' Rosie didn't understand. 'Why that one, out of all the memories I've ever had? Why a boring weekday afternoon, with Leo of all people?' She watched herself under the covers, only the slow rise and fall of her breath to show she was alive. Was that the point of this? To show her that, last week, she'd been miserable?

Melissa shrugged. 'Dunno. It's your brain directing all this. Come on.' She reached for Rosie's hand, the faintest touch, like walking through a heavy fog. 'Close your eyes, then open them again.'

Rosie did as she was told, hearing a whooshing sound like a plane coming in to land, and her stomach lurched unpleasantly. When she opened her eyes, she was back in the hospital bed, and Melissa was gone.

Rosie

She definitely wasn't dead. For one thing, she hurt all over, and she was pretty sure that didn't happen if you were dead. Her lungs felt heavy, and she heard some panicky sounds emanate from her chest. That was good too. She might not be able to speak out loud in this reality, but she was making some sounds. She was alive. And she wasn't alone. A woman was bending over her, about sixty, with well-styled ash-blonde hair. The smell of her perfume set off all kinds of complicated feelings in Rosie.

The woman was shouting, 'She's choking!'

The young female doctor (*Zara*, Rosie remembered) ran in again, checking Rosie's mouth with efficient care. 'When they wake up they usually try to reject the breathing tube. It's such an alien feeling. But she'll get used to it.'

'She's awake?'

'Not really. She may be coming back to some consciousness, though, which is a good sign.'

I'm here, Rosie said, inside her head. *I'm awake.* The real world seemed clearer this time, the edges sharper, like when you put on glasses.

The woman's stricken expression didn't ease. 'So . . . it was an accident? The bus, I mean?'

Dr Zara, who Rosie had nicknamed Posh Spice, had little time for this speculation. 'We don't know what happened. She stepped into the road, witnesses said.' Rosie would have gaped, had she been able to move her mouth. Was that true? She'd walked in front of it?

'Would someone not notice a bus driving towards them? An enormous red London bus? Could she have been on her phone or something?'

'Maybe. We do see a lot of accidents that way.' The doctor looped her stethoscope round her neck, tossing back her blonde ponytail. 'I'll be back later, Mrs Cooke.'

'Oh, no, it's . . . it's not . . . Please just call me Alison.'

Mrs Cooke. Alison. Rosie's mind reluctantly admitted what she'd known deep down in her bones as soon as she smelled the woman's perfume. This was her mother, the person who should love her most in the world. So why did it feel so hard to be here, alone in this room with her? Why was her chest heavy, not just with choking, but with painful feelings she couldn't even name, that made her want to get up from the bed and run?

The door opened and her mother leapt up, Rosie thought with some relief. It was Daisy. Her sister, Daisy. She had a sister and a mother. Did she also have a father, any other siblings? Rosie couldn't remember, and thinking about it was painful the way that pressing on a bruise is, so she stopped.

'How is she?' Daisy's glasses looked smeared and she'd acquired two paper cups.

'She choked before, trying to get the tube out. So she must be conscious of something at least.'

I'm here. I can hear you. But Rosie somehow knew that, even if she were conscious and awake and hadn't been hit by a bus, she'd not have very much to say to her mother and her sister. The sadness of that left an ache under her ribcage.

Daisy passed over one of the paper cups. 'Sorry. It's from a machine. I can go out and find some better stuff. I think there was a café . . . '

'It's OK, darling. I don't want one really. It's just . . . something to do with your hands. Where's Gary?'

'Oh, he . . . I haven't told him yet. I – he had a big meeting. I didn't want to worry him until we knew what was what. Mum . . . have you spoken to Rosie since . . . you know?'

Their mother raised the paper cup to her mouth, as if to hide it so she wouldn't have to speak. 'Not really. I – it's been difficult. Ruining your party like that.'

'I don't think she meant to.'

'She always does, though. One way or another.'

'Mum . . . '

'I know. I shouldn't say it, darling, but it's true, isn't it? I know I should have called her. But I just couldn't. Not after that.' Her voice was cracking, her face twisted.

Something squeezed at Daisy's face too, some emotion, sadness maybe, or guilt. She looked so tired, Rosie thought. Her sister was the healthy one here but she looked like you'd want to sit her down in a big chair with a mug of hot chocolate. In fact . . . hadn't Rosie done that, once? The memory was there, untethered from time. Cartoons on the TV. The scum on the milk from where she'd heated it up in the microwave, very carefully. Daisy's little face. *There now. Sit down and watch* Thundercats. *It's all going to be OK.* When was that? And had it all been OK?

No. She had the very strong feeling that, if it had, she wouldn't be in this bed now, with both her mother and her sister afraid to reach out and touch her.

'She looks awful,' their mother said, almost whispering. 'I just can't bear it.'

Hey! I can hear you, you know.

'The bruising. They said it would go down.'

'I mean underneath that. You can tell she's not been eating, hasn't brushed her hair in weeks, and those clothes she was wearing . . . they looked like *pyjamas.*' Her mother picked up Rosie's limp, unresponsive hand and examined it. 'And look at her nails. Bitten to the quick. What's happened to her, Daisy? Why was she even on that bridge, first thing in the morning? Is it because I . . . because of what I said to her?'

'Mum, I . . . I'm sure it isn't. We don't even know if she . . . It could have been an accident.'

'I should have called her. Why didn't I call her?'

Daisy reached out her free hand as if she might touch Rosie's foot, or move the blanket into place, but then she let it drop. 'Is there anything I can do? I could go to the shops, or . . . I don't know. Is there someone we should call?'

Her mother sighed. 'I suppose you already called *him.* Where is he?' Who were they talking about? The mysterious Luke?

'He has to get Scarlett from school first.'

'Oh, he does that now, does he? That's a change.'

'He was very upset.'

'He was always useless in a crisis. We need to be strong for Rosie, make plans. Get organised.'

'Tell me something I can do. I can't just sit here.' Daisy was mangling the paper cup in her hands.

'What about calling her friends? Is there anyone she's close to? Ingrid, maybe? They were always such good pals. Or that nice girl Caroline?'

'I'm not sure they're in touch still, Mum.'

'Oh. There must be someone you can think of?'

'Well . . . not really, no.'

Rosie was a little shocked at that. Wasn't your family supposed to think the best of you? Hers seemed to think she was unstable, ill-kempt, and had no friends.

Were they right?

'She'll need some things. Toiletries, clothes . . . I could go to her flat when he gets here?'

'That's a good idea. Some underwear and pyjamas maybe. You always want nice pyjamas when you're in them all day.'

Daisy looked happier already at the prospect of doing things, but then her phone rang. Guiltily, she seized it, turning to the wall and lowering her voice. 'Hi. Yeah. St Thomas's. Parking – um, I don't know, I'd have thought not.'

Rosie's mother rolled her eyes.

'ICU, yeah. They're . . . hopeful. Ish. She tried to cough out the breathing tube earlier and . . . Yeah, there's a tube, but I think that's kind of standard and . . . OK, OK. See you soon.'

She hung up. Their mother shook her head. 'What did I tell you? Useless.'

What was going on? What had happened to their family, and why weren't they speaking to her? Was there a memory that could explain it for her? She wondered if another denizen of the afterlife would show up to guide her through it.

'It's me this time,' said a kind, worried voice. 'I hope that's all right.'

Rosie tried to crane her neck, but couldn't, because of the brace. 'Hello?'

Now there was a figure at the bottom of her bed, right in the path of Daisy's pacing, but neither she nor their mother seemed to notice. The figure gave an awkward little wave. A middle-aged man in a tank top, with balding, mad-scientist hair and rimless glasses.

'Mr Malcolm?' Rosie squinted at him. Was it really her secondary school French and Drama teacher, standing there by her bed? Oh God.

'*Bonjour*! Yes, it's me.'

'Are you . . . ?'

'Oh yes. Pancreatic cancer, carried me off in a month. There was a special school assembly and some of the students even put their phones away for it. That was nice.'

'Gosh, I'm sorry. Was it like this for you?'

'Your life flashing before your eyes? Everyone has it, yes. Some for less time than others. A coma means you get more than most. Now, are you ready for your next memory?'

'What will it be?'

'I'm afraid I don't know, dear.'

With the arrival of Mr Malcolm, Rosie suddenly had access to a whole filing cabinet in her head marked 'School Memories'. So many of them, some she hadn't looked at in

36

years. The rubbery smell of the mats in the gym. The itchiness of her grey wool uniform, the feeling she was going to slip into a boredom coma (as opposed to this real one) in lessons, the haze of Impulse body spray in the girls' loos. She tried to remember who her friends had been at school. But the real world was starting to flicker and blur again, as if the light was broken.

She was going again. She was ... gone.

6 May 1999 (Eighteen years ago)

There was the spinning dial again. A sense of things happening around her, noise and light, but her vision intensely focused on the thing in front of her. Some kind of control panel? Numbers, whizzing around against a grey background. They settled once again into an order: 6 5 1999. She opened her eyes into a damp light. A large wet playing field, and some students in school uniform hanging about it. One of the three boys was smoking covertly, sneaking lots of glances over his shoulder. The two girls were a young Rosie and someone else. Rosie recognised the curtains haircuts of the boys and the friendship bracelets sported by her and her friend – it was the nineties, all right. She was also starting to remember what happened next.

She turned to the ghostly figure of Mr Malcolm, who was gazing nostalgically at the school in the distance. 'Ah, the old place. I spent thirty years working here, you know.'

'God, I'm so sorry. Can they . . . see us?'

'*Non, non, cherie.* It's only a memory. Just watch.'

Teen Rosie was all attitude and rippling red hair. She remembered that she'd hated it – battled every day against nicknames like Ginger Pubes and Period Head – but as an adult she could see it was beautiful. Pre-Raphaelite, not that she'd have known what that meant then. Something to do with the Ninja Turtles, she'd have guessed. The girl with her was someone Rosie now recognised. 'Oh my God, it's Angie! Angie, hi!' Angela Timmons, a cheery girl who fought a losing battle with her love for Jaffa Cakes and Curly Wurlys, who had three younger brothers, a blur of energy and smelly feet, whose mother was big and comforting and gave them cups of hot Ribena in the kitchen, whose father was benevolent and silent and brought home a different selection of chocolate bars every night when he returned from his taxi-driving job. Surely she and Angie were still friends. But she could find no memories in her head that suggested they were.

'She can't hear you,' whispered Mr Malcolm. '*Dommage.*'

'God, I haven't seen her since . . . um . . . I can't remember. Have I seen her since school?'

'Wait and see.'

Teen Rosie had contorted her body into a strange flamingo-like shape, with one foot propped up against the back of the mobile classroom where they were skulking. Her arm was thrown up above her head, posing like 'one of your French girls' – she would of course have seen *Titanic* four times already by then. 'Can I've a drag?' she said to the alpha boy. It was obvious which one he was. His face that bit more handsome and hard. A gold stud in one ear – the right one, of course.

The left one meant you were gay and you'd never live down a mistake like that.

She was remembering his name now, dropping into her head like a windfall apple: *Bryn Collins*. Dreamboat of Year 11.

'What am I doing?' she asked Mr Malcolm, who had stooped to examine some weeds on the edge of the playing field. 'With that boy?'

'Look, it's tansy, quite rare that. I think you're setting your cap at him, or whatever you kids said back then.'

'But . . . Angie liked him, didn't she?' She remembered now they had only gone to talk to the boys at Angie's request. They should have been in Drama class right then, in fact, Rosie's favourite.

'Her hand would suggest it, *oui*.'

The back of Angie's hand had a heart drawn on it, names scrawled in smudgy red ink, and she could barely look at Bryn. She stared at her feet in their Doc Martens instead. Rosie could almost hear what Angie was thinking, across the years. *Please, Rosie, don't flirt with him . . . you're so skinny and pretty and I've got spots and I'm too fat*. Angie's thoughts were practically the lyrics to 'Jolene' by Dolly Parton.

Bryn held out the cigarette, but instead of taking it, Teen Rosie leaned forward and grabbed his hand, raising it to her mouth to drag from the cigarette. She'd seen that in some film (perhaps also *Titanic*). The other boys – what were their names? She must have known back then – whooped, recognising the sexual current in the air. Angie's face crumpled.

Bryn was the kind of boy whose cool came from saying very little. He shrugged a shoulder in his bomber jacket. 'You wanna?'

Teen Rosie blinked. Bryn Collins, popular, sexy Bryn, wanted to get off with *her*? *Say no,* Rosie urged her past self. *Your friend likes him! Say no!* But instead, Teen Rosie blushed a little and tossed her long red hair. 'All right then.'

Angie gave a loud sob. One of the other boys – Steve Mills, that was his name! – half-heartedly said, 'I'll pull ya, if ya want.'

The other – Andy Franks! She was remembering it all now – just snickered.

Wisely, Angie fled. As she bolted across the yard she stopped and rummaged in her schoolbag, taking out a Curly Wurly, cramming it into her mouth in huge bites, her face covered in tears and chocolate. Rosie watched her leave, but instead of going after her, she followed Bryn a few metres away where, behind the bike shed, still in full view, he proceeded to suck at her face in the manner of the creature from *Alien* eating someone's brain.

'Jesus,' said Rosie, watching the memory unfold. 'That was a really bad thing for me to do. I guess Angie and I aren't friends now. I was one of *those* girls.'

'Looks that way,' Mr Malcolm agreed. *'Quelle horreur.* Well, I think this memory is finished now. Shall we return to the present?'

'But what was the point of that?' Rosie burst out. 'Showing me a time I was horrible, reminding me that I lost Angie as a friend – we were really good friends too! – and making me relive that horrible face-eating snog?'

'I don't know, dear.' Mr Malcolm had blushed at the word *snog.* 'Maybe your brain is choosing these memories for a reason. To help you work out something about your life, before it's too late. Remember, you only have three days.'

'But they've both been bad ones so far!'

'I'm sorry. Let's go back, dear. I think you have some more visitors. *Allons.*'

Rosie was blinking away tears, which despite this flat ghostly world she was in – the school in the distance distorted and shady, Mr Malcolm himself now see-through, just a voice and a vague sense of a body – felt very real. She felt the tears run over her face and drip down into her neck. This was awful. Being awake and in massive pain was surely better than this. Why didn't her brain want to relive good memories, like the time they won the Under-15 County Netball Championships, and her team-mates carried her on their shoulders into Assembly? Or the time in Greece, jumping off that cliff into the blue, blue sea? Or ... *Luke*, her mind whispered back, treacherously. Rosie shut it down, squashing it like she was slamming her hand over a fly. She wasn't sure what it meant, or who Luke was, but she definitely wasn't ready to think about it yet. She closed her eyes and came back to herself.

Rosie

Lights. Lights and noise, searing into her brain, making her want to curl up and hide. The hospital room. A small child was standing over her. 'Daddy! She's stopped crying now!'

Daddy?

Rosie could feel things – tears on her face. So those had been real. The ache in her feet, arms, lungs, head. That was real too, unfortunately. The small child – it was a girl, she thought – was peering down at her with interest, wearing what looked like a princess costume. That couldn't be right. Another dream/ghost/hallucination?

A man came into sight, looking harried and old, but dressed twenty years too young for him in khaki shorts and a straining polo shirt. 'Scarlett, be careful. Rosie's very poorly.'

'She was crying.'

'It's probably just her eyes watering. I don't think she can hear us.'

But I can! I can!

Scarlett had keener eyes than the adults. 'I think she can. She doesn't like the light being so bright. Can you turn it down, Daddy?'

Yes, that's true; thank you, Scarlett. Whoever you are.

'The doctors need it to see,' said the man, with that irritating grown-up adherence to authority that had enraged Rosie as a child. If she'd been able to open her eyes properly, she'd have rolled them conspiratorially at Scarlett. The man, whoever he was, was looking at Rosie as if she scared him. She could almost place him. It was on the tip of her tongue. The face she knew, but he was so much older, almost bald, and those stupid clothes . . .

'Dad!' said Daisy, coming in the door with yet more paper cups. 'You made it. Hi, Scarlett. Um . . . what are you wearing?'

'It was fancy-dress day at her school,' explained the man, taking one of the cups. 'Is that coffee?'

'Of a sort.'

Scarlett came over and gave Daisy a warm hug round the waist. 'Hi, Daisy. I'm sorry Rosie banged her head.'

Daisy had visibly crumpled at the hug, patting the nylon

43

back of the little girl's costume. 'The doctors think maybe she'll get better . . . we hope. Are you Elsa from *Frozen*?'

Scarlett sighed. She didn't seem like a princessy girl. She had short hair for a start, and sensible glasses. 'I wanted to be a dinosaur but Mummy said all the other girls were being princesses. It's so boring.'

Rosie was really warming to this kid. But wait, Daisy had said Dad. *Dad.* That meant . . .

Oh Lord. This try-hard older man with the young child was . . . Rosie's father.

Daisy

'Michael. You turned up.' Her mother's voice was as cold as ice-pops when she came back into the room and saw her ex-husband there.

'Alison. I came as soon as I could. I had to pick up Scarlett.' He indicated his other daughter. Daisy's heart ached for her mother. How could anyone handle this situation? 'God, she looks terrible. What have they said?'

'Is Rosie asleep?' said Scarlett, curiously. 'Will she sleep for a long long time?'

'She got hit on the head and it made her poorly.' Her mother's voice was stiff. *Hit on the head.* It didn't capture the horror of it, which Daisy felt she could see in the corner of her eye all the time. The screech of brakes. The thump. People screaming, gathering round, traffic stopped. Sirens. She could picture it so clearly, it was as if she'd been there.

'Oh. What's this tube for?'

'It helps her breathe.'

'She can't *breathe*?'

'Not very well, no.' Daisy could hear the strain in her mother's voice, and a swell of worry began in her stomach. Her parents hadn't been in the same room for years – not even at her engagement party – and added to all the anger, worry and fear sloshing around, this had to be handled carefully.

'Come away, Scarlett,' said her dad, stressed. 'Let's leave Rosie to rest. Does she know we're here?' He turned to her mother.

'They can't tell. It's possible.'

'I think she can,' said Scarlett confidently. 'Her eyes moved like she was waking up. *Why* did Rosie walk in front of the bus? Didn't she see it?'

Daisy's parents exchanged glances that were full of fear and something else. Guilt, maybe. Daisy read the room. 'Scarlett, why don't you pop outside? I'll give you my phone to play on.'

'Do you have Angry Birds?'

'No, but ... I'm sure you can find something. I'll get you a hot chocolate after.'

'With marshmallows?'

'If you want.'

'Did you know they're made from cows' hooves?'

'Um, no, I didn't. Please, Scar?' Daisy watched her leave, reluctantly taking a seat in the waiting room. It was too easy to imagine things being different, time unspooling back to when she and Rosie were small. Mum and Dad together. Dad not doing the school run at sixty, Mum not bitter, Rosie not under a bus ... but then Scarlett would not exist. And however painful the divorce had been, Daisy could not wish that. When her small sister was out of earshot, she turned to her

45

parents, summoning all the assertiveness Maura had tried to drum into her. 'The doctors need to talk to us. And after, we need to discuss what's going on with Rosie. Not just now. I mean for the past, like, thirty years. We have to talk about the reasons she's here in the first place.'

Rosie

'You're saying she might be conscious in there?'

'In a manner of speaking, yes.' Her parents and Daisy were talking to the two young doctors. The male one was speaking, the one Rosie had nicknamed Dr Chill. He had a soothing, laid-back voice, unlike the female doctor who spoke in brisk, jolly-hockey-sticks tones. Rosie's mother was wringing her hands and her father was nodding his head up and down like a Bobblehead toy. The space between them was painful. Daisy stood apart, her arms wrapped around herself so tightly her hands were white.

'So, she could still wake up?' Hope in her father's voice.

'It's possible. But her Glasgow Coma Scale scores aren't great, I'm sorry to say. She's a six.'

'Six out of what?'

'It goes from three up to fifteen.'

'And six is bad?'

'Dad,' murmured Daisy. 'Let them talk.'

The doctors exchanged looks. The female one took over. 'Well, it means she shows some signs of brain activity, can respond to some stimuli, like light shining in her eyes.' Brain activity. That was a strange way to describe, you know, being alive.

46

'Great! So she will wake up, then?'

'I'm sorry. It's not as simple as that.'

The male doctor went on. 'Sometimes people recover after a few days, or weeks, but sometimes they don't, and we don't always know why. The problem is that the longer she's in a coma, the worse it is for her body. Everything's atrophying. Being on a drip and catheter increases the risk of infection, a breathing tube can lead to pneumonia. In another two days she'll need a PEG feeding tube put in, as well as a tracheotomy. She'd have to be moved to long-term care. And there's always the risk her brain will swell or bleed again.'

Panic had seized Rosie's throat, where the breathing tube in question was so uncomfortably lodged. She was trying not to think about it, though it was maddening, the feeling of it. She didn't want her throat cut into. But was she ready to wake up, to face her family and explain about the bus . . . ?

She didn't remember about the bus. She didn't know why it had happened.

'What can we do?' Her mother's voice shook. 'How can we help her wake up?'

Dr Posh Spice said, in her brisk way: 'There are various techniques. Drugs and so on. Talking to her might also help, playing her favourite music, that kind of thing. It's possible her brain is still functioning, but has temporarily shut down some functions due to the trauma of the accident. Once it's recovered a little, it might respond better.'

'She's in there?' Her dad peered at her. *Yes, I'm here. I can hear you, talking about me.* 'Can she . . . hear us?'

'There's no way to tell. But even if she can it may not make

47

any sense to her. She could experience some of it as vivid dreams, or even hallucinations. It's worth trying, though.'

'We wanted to ask you something, actually.' Dr Chill consulted his notes. 'When they brought Rosie in, she was briefly conscious in the ambulance. She was saying a name. We think it might have been "Luke". Does that mean something to you?'

Rosie tensed (as much as she could). *Luke.* That name. It threatened to release a flood in her, a rainbow of emotions from brightest pink to darkest black. Who was he? A husband or boyfriend she'd forgotten about?

Her parents were shaking their heads blankly, Daisy too. 'No.' Not her husband then.

'Not a relative or . . . does she have a brother?'

Her family went rigid as rails. After a moment, her mother quietly said, 'No. But if it was a boyfriend, we wouldn't necessarily know. She doesn't tell me things.'

'She tells you more than me, Alison.'

'You might be surprised, Michael.' Their voices were so frosty, like a layer of ice on a pond. 'Daisy, do you know anything?'

Her sister was shaking her head. 'I . . . we weren't really talking either.'

'She could have been saying "look",' volunteered her father. 'You know, as in look out. Maybe . . . maybe she was warning someone else away from the bus and it got her instead.'

A tactful silence. Dr Chill said gently, 'Mr Cooke, I'm afraid the police have quite a lot of eyewitness testimony and it looked as if Rosie walked straight in front of it. So . . . if she does wake up, we need to think about putting her on suicide watch.'

Daisy gasped, and her mother seemed to sway on her feet. '*What?*' said her father, too loudly.

Suicide watch, what a strange phrase. Rosie imagined an actual watch on your wrist, one you could press when it all got too much. It would be too dangerous, something like that. Everyone felt at times like it was all too much. Would she have tried to kill herself? She'd have said no, of course not. But in this life she was learning about – where she wasn't speaking to her family, where she lived alone in a horrible flat – who knew? Who knew what she would have done?

'Oh,' said her mother, pressing a hand to her chest like she had indigestion. 'Oh, Rosie.'

Her father's voice was strangled. 'How can you stand there and suggest that she'd . . . that Rosie would . . . ? It was an *accident!*' Daisy put a hand on his arm.

'We know it's difficult,' said Dr Posh Spice, in the brisk tones of someone telling you an injection might sting a bit. 'I'm afraid you need to prepare yourselves for the chance that, even if Rosie does wake up, she may not be . . . as she was.'

'What does that mean?' said Daisy, sounding fearful.

'There are often cognitive defects with this kind of injury . . . severe neurological problems.'

'In English?' her father said, harassed. Her mother frowned at him.

Dr Chill took over, soothingly. 'Brain injuries can affect everything, unfortunately. Walking, talking, swallowing . . . being able to feed yourself . . . '

'She won't be able to *walk?*' Her mother sounded horrified. Rosie felt terror all through her body, leaden as it was. This was just temporary, wasn't it? She'd be able to do things again, like open her eyes and speak and move bits of her at will? Those things you took for granted, that everyone expected would just be there when they woke up in the morning.

'I'm afraid we just don't know. The point is that it's not as simple as "waking up".' Dr Posh Spice did air quotes.

'It was a very serious accident,' said Dr Chill. 'She cracked her skull on the road. One of her lungs collapsed and her leg is broken, as you know.' *Cracked. Collapsed.* Rosie did not like these words. They were talking about her head, not an egg carelessly dropped on the floor. But she was conscious! That had to be a good sign, didn't it? 'The brain swelled inside the skull, and it's a bit like . . . '

'Imagine a sponge cake in a tin that's too small,' supplied Dr Posh Spice. 'Rosie was very lucky it happened so near to the hospital.'

That word again: *lucky*. It was a strange choice in the circumstances.

Dr Chill consulted his clipboard. 'Is there anything else you can tell us about Rosie's health? Allergies, previous operations, that kind of thing?'

Her mother sounded close to tears. 'She's got a peanut allergy, she's blood type A, she fell out of a tree once and broke her wrist, er . . . '

'She cut off the top of her finger when she was a kid.'

'Yes, thanks for bringing that up, Mike.'

'I'm just telling them, Alison!'

'Er, that's OK, thank—'

'And it was all my fault, wasn't it? I was supposed to be looking after her, so blame me.'

'Really, sir, madam, it's—'

50

'All I know is it didn't happen on my watch.'

'Because you never had a watch! You were never there!'

From the corridor was a sudden commotion, a woman's voice shouting, 'Darryl! Darryl! Where is he?'

The two doctors exchanged a quick glance. Rosie saw it as if they spoke. *Your turn. I told them about the suicide thing.*

Argh. OK.

'Mr and Mrs Cooke,' began Dr Posh Spice.

'It's not Mrs Cooke. Not any more.'

'I'm sorry – we have to speak to the family of another patient.'

Thank God. Rosie wasn't sure she could listen to much more of this dire forecast on her future. Tears were pricking her unresponsive eyes again, and as she couldn't blink properly, they pooled and burned on her corneas, blurring out the world.

'Hey, don't cry,' said a voice. A man was leaning against the wall, in motorbike leathers. He was very handsome, with floppy honey-blond hair and a full, sexy mouth, tattoos peeking out over his neckline. 'Trust me, dying isn't something to cry about. It's living you have to worry about.'

'Um . . . who are you?' She knew him from somewhere, she was sure of it. Maybe he was her boyfriend. This could be Luke! Maybe she rode motorbikes too, her hair streaming out in the wind behind her as she laughed, carefree. Her poor shaved hair. But somehow, Rosie did not think this was true. 'I'm sure I've seen you . . . Oh! You're the guy from A and E?' Someone who'd been even more of a mess than she was. His chest had literally been open on the bed. But now look at him! Walking about and everything. Maybe they were just very good in this hospital. Maybe they'd fix her too.

'That's right. Darryl, hiya.'

'Rosie.' She was pleased she remembered her own name. 'I think your parents are looking for you. Are you OK?'

'Came off my bike taking the Elephant and Castle roundabout too fast, didn't I?'

'Oh. But . . . ' He'd not looked so good when they'd been opening him up on the bed in A&E, but here he was, upright and intact, seemingly chipper. There wasn't even blood on his white T-shirt. 'You look all right now.'

He laughed. 'I certainly feel like a new man.'

'So they fixed you? They're good?'

'I'm sorry, mate. No one's *that* good. I've gone, Rosie.'

A terrible thought was growing in her mind. 'You mean . . . ?'

'It's OK, you can say it. Yes, I'm dead. An ex-Darryl. I have ceased to exist!'

Rosie shuddered. Dead people certainly seemed pretty chilled about the fact of their own mortality. 'Oh my God, that's terrible. I'm so sorry.' Another dead person, just hanging out in her room, chatting to her. Her head ached.

He sighed. 'Terrible for my mum and dad, I guess. It's weird, but now I'm dead, I just can't feel anything, you know? Like, I know it must be crap, and they asked me a million times to get rid of the bike, and it kind of sucks I can't tell them I'm sorry, like, but I don't really *feel* it. I'm just glad the pain's all over.' Darryl's parents. Rosie winced for them. To be called here in the middle of a normal day, told their son was gone, shown his waxy dead body, the shell of him when only that morning he'd been alive, handsome, young. Maybe they'd even texted or called him today before it happened, said goodbye with no idea that it would be the last time. Or maybe they didn't talk much, just assumed there'd always be more time to say all the things that needed to be said.

'Do you . . . can you tell me what's going on? Why I can see you, and why I keep getting these memories? They've said . . . Darryl, they said that even if I wake up I might not be able to walk again, or talk, or . . . Is it true?'

'Honestly, I don't know, mate. I'm still adjusting to the whole "not being alive" thing. I just know I'm meant to come with you while you relive stuff. Close your eyes. It'll help with the tears too.'

'But your parents, they're——'

'Never mind about that, Rosie. Come on, time to go.'

She concentrated hard and eased her eyes fully shut, sealing up the crack where the world came in. The dial spun again, blurred and indistinct. 11 7 2005. Off she went.

11 July 2005 (Twelve years ago)

Rosie screwed her face up, and cautiously opened her eyes. The light was different again. Where was she? She peered around her at the beach she was on. White, warm sand, the water a deep green fading into navy. A faint cool breeze relieving the heat of the day, the sun just beginning to dissolve into the ocean in a puddle of Berocca orange. Of course, she remembered now – this was Crete. She'd come on holiday after uni, which meant she was twenty-one. It was late afternoon, her favourite time – having red hair and pale skin meant you had to avoid midday unless you wanted to crisp up like a roast potato. Grown-up Rosie watched her younger self as she came down the beach. 'God, I was slim.' She hadn't known it at the time, of course, but her legs were endless, her stomach flat. Rosie knew she'd hated her body back then, the pale milky skin – it was a time when sunbeds were all the rage – the cluster of freckles on her shoulders and nose, the long curly red hair no conditioner could untangle. But she'd been beautiful. How sad that she couldn't see it.

'Not bad, eh?' said Darryl's ghostly voice in her ear. 'I'd have probably chanced my arm with you. Course, I'd still have been sleeping off the hangover from the night before.'

'I'm surprised I'm not.' Rosie couldn't quite remember who she'd come on this holiday with, but she did recall that for the entire duration of it she'd felt seized with a bone-shaking panic that could only be eased by those massive bucket-sized cocktails they all drank. Her uni friends had training contracts lined up in law firms, office jobs, civil service exams. She had no idea what she was going to do. So she'd taken to sneaking away every day, while the others (who were they?) napped ahead of the night out, or spent hours blow-drying their hair in the tiny bathroom, overloading the European sockets in their apartment so the power always went off and the elderly owner shuffled round muttering in Greek at their extravagance.

Past Rosie spread a towel out on the sand and sat down, folding up her long pale legs, hugging them to herself. She looked soulful, like a girl in a film having an important epiphany about her life. Not like someone lost and scared who hadn't called their parents the whole time she'd been away. Not like someone who was seriously thinking of not travelling on with her friends (whoever they were), but instead just staying here on this beautiful island, listening to the waves every day, living off olives and salty feta, avoiding her problems. Avoiding growing up. What would be so wrong with that?

She was musing over her future when the Frisbee hit her on the head. A man was running up the beach to her. A gap-year type, in combat shorts and a Radiohead T-shirt, as tanned as she was pale. Fair hair that was shaggy and needed cutting. Gap-year bracelets round his strong wrists. Shocking blue eyes in a brown face. 'Oh God, I'm so sorry. I was throwing it for this dog, you see, and . . . '

'What, the dog's not got good aim?' Dazed, 2005 Rosie had still managed to sound funny. A barking beach stray was gambolling around her.

The man – a boy, really – said, 'I'm ashamed. To think I was even in the university Frisbee league.'

'That exists?' She was rubbing her head, sucking her stomach in under her shorts and bikini, though she hardly needed to.

'Oh sure. I could have gone all the way. Olympic Frisbee. Pro Frisbee. Are you hurt?'

'I'll live.'

He was standing over her, casting his shadow, awkward. 'Maybe I can buy you a drink to say sorry.' There was a taverna behind them, painted in jolly white and blue, serving Greek salads and chilled Cokes and fries laced with balsamic vinegar and good olive oil.

Say yes, Rosie urged her past self. She had said yes, surely? Past Rosie stood up, brushing sand off her long legs. 'That would be nice. Thank you. Um – I'm Rosie.'

He stuck out a hand, big and worn, warm from the sun. A traveller's hand. She remembered now that, as she took it, an electric charge had run down her spine, and she'd almost gasped, experiencing naked attraction for the first time in her life. But more than that, the fall of his fair hair and the curve of his smile seemed deeply familiar. She knew him, she was sure of it. This had been the start of something important.

What was his name? It was almost there, forming on her lips . . .

'I'll be having cider with Rosie then,' he said, blushing slightly at his own bad joke. 'Or rum and coke with Rosie, or whatever you're drinking. I'm Luke.'

Daisy

She was running. Down five flights of stairs, barely pausing for breath, out through the crowded hospital lobby and into the cold autumn air. She didn't even know where she was going, just that she had to get out of the hospital and away from what was happening around Rosie's bed. Her parents together were never a good combination, and although her mother was rigidly polite to Scarlett, the little girl was always a reminder that she'd been ditched, left for a younger model. That was how she saw it, anyway. The reality wasn't quite the cliché you'd imagine. When the doctors left, Daisy's head had been reeling with words – Glasgow Coma Scale, neurological problems, *suicide watch* – but she couldn't take them in. Her brain, normally so quick and efficient, processing facts and numbers, simply would not work.

'What did they mean?' she'd asked. It was as if she'd heard the words, loud and clear, but entirely failed to understand them.

Her mother had wrung her hands. 'Darling, they're saying . . . we have to be prepared for the worst.'

'Alison, that's not what they said at all! They said there was hope.'

'Hope doesn't mean the news is good, Mike. It just means they haven't totally given up. But she has a very serious injury. They're taking her for a scan soon, to see how much damage there is.'

'I just think it wouldn't hurt to be a bit positive . . .'

'We have to take this seriously! They said . . . we might have to make some tough decisions. In the next few days.'

'That's typical of you, Alison, always doom and gloom . . .'

Daisy had looked between her parents, helpless. This was all so familiar. Her mother and father, sniping, fighting. She caught in the middle. Rosie nowhere to be seen. Usually the cause of it.

She'd felt it all pressing on her – the hospital buzzing like a hive, the frenetic energy of it around Rosie's deathly stillness, and all the memories threatening to engulf her. The uselessness of just watching while the machines pumped fluids in and out of her sister, keeping her alive. She had to get away and do something to help. Try to find out what had happened, if Rosie had done this to herself. 'I . . . I'm going out.'

Now she slowed to a halt, realising her muscles and lungs, normally so obedient and well trained – she ran to work three mornings a week, before showering diligently and changing out of her lycra into sensible office clothes – had also stopped working, and she was possibly going to pass out. She leaned against the window of a café, waiting for the dizziness to pass. *Suicide watch*. The doctors thought Rosie had tried to kill herself.

'Hey, are you OK?' A man had appeared beside her from the café, in a black shirt with the sleeves rolled up.

'I . . .' Daisy opened her mouth to say *yes yes I'm fine* but instead, a large sob tore out of her. 'It's just . . . my sister!' The rest of what she might have said was drowned in tears.

The man was very kind. He sat her down on the bench outside the café, brought her out a cup of sweet tea – Daisy hated sweet tea, and Gary had made her swear off sugar pre-wedding, but the simple kindness almost broke her heart – then hunkered down beside her, concerned. 'From the hospital?'

'How did you know?' She sniffed, wiping her face on the back of her hand. She could hardly see his face through the blur of tears.

Tactfully, he passed her a napkin. 'Oh, a lot of people come in here when their relatives are sick. You sort of have that look about you.'

Was it branded over her skin, the sadness, the worry? 'It's my sister,' she sniffled, her breath hitching. 'She's had a bad accident.' If it was even an accident. *Suicide watch*. Rosie had stepped in front of the bus by herself.

'Shit, I'm so sorry. What have they said?'

'They're . . . hopeful, I think. I don't know. She's in a coma.' Daisy felt the word in her mouth, like a small heavy stone.

The guy said, 'Oh, that's nothing to worry about. Comas are ten a penny in that hospital, seriously they are. A coma, that's like . . . a normal Tuesday morning for them. Look, why don't you come in? I'll make you something to eat. On the house.'

Daisy looked at him properly. The swirl of a tattoo peeked out from under one shirtsleeve. Dark, straight glossy hair, slanting cheekbones. A kind face, she thought. It would have been lovely to follow him into the steamy-window warmth of the café and pour out all her worries, but she knew she couldn't. There wasn't time. 'Thank you. I'm just . . . I need to . . . there's something I have to do.' What she had to do was try to save her sister. If that was even possible now. She remembered the doctor saying, *If she doesn't wake up in three days* . . . Babbling her thanks to the man from the café, Daisy got up and continued on to the Tube station at a fast trot. She was going to Rosie's flat, to see if she could find a clue, any clue at all, about her sister's state of mind that morning.

Rosie

' . . . she's been unstable for years, Michael. Ever since you left. I just think you need to take some responsibility.' Out in the corridor, her parents were still arguing. A familiar sound – Rosie sensed she had a lot of files in her memory marked 'Mum and Dad, rowing'.

'Oh, give me a break, Alison. She was always like this. You seem to forget the suspensions, that terrible boyfriend, the fiasco with the school show!'

In the bed, Rosie cringed. She wondered was she actually dead and Hell was listening to your parents discuss whether or not you might have tried to kill yourself. Had she really been as bad as all that? She wished she'd stayed in the last memory, on the beach, feeling the sun on her skin and smelling the Factor 50 she always slathered on herself. Finally, a good memory. Luke. That was Luke. Why did that name make her heart race and her stomach drop? Why didn't her family know who he was? She remembered all the terrifying things the doctors had said. *Three days. Suicide watch.* What was going to happen?

'I haven't forgotten. How could I? I could hardly show my face at the Women's Institute that year.'

'Well then. Please don't blame me! I feel bad enough as it is. I never thought she'd do something like . . . I mean, are things really so bad with her?'

'I don't know. I . . . Well, we had a bit of a falling-out. We hadn't been speaking.'

'She never speaks to me either.'

'Mike. They've said that . . . in three days, if she hasn't . . . if there's no sign she's aware of things, she might never wake up. And then we have to make a decision. About . . . what to do.'

Her dad's voice was rough. 'She'll come round by then. I know she will. She *has* to.'

Her mother was crying again. 'Where did we go wrong with her, that she's ended up like this? Daisy seemed to cope.'

Their voices both softened at the mention of Daisy. Evidence, perhaps, that they weren't terrible parents after all. 'Hormones, maybe,' said her father vaguely. 'I don't know. I could never get through to her.'

Rosie's nose began to ache with tears. She looked around for another spiritual guide, or ghost, or dream, or whatever they were. Were any more dead people coming to give her wisdom? Darryl, Grandma, Mr Malcolm, Melissa . . . She tried to think if she knew anyone else who was dead. Both her granddads and her other grandma, but they were shadowy figures, gone when she was small. She couldn't imagine even recognising them if they popped up.

The door to her room opened a fraction. Someone was coming! Rosie waited expectantly. In came an older woman in an orange tabard, wheezing with the effort of walking. The other ghosts had just kind of . . . appeared. Materialised. Was this person real then? ''Iya, darlin'.'

'You can hear me?'

'My name's Dot. Rosie, isn't it? How you feelin', sweetheart?'

'Not so good, to be honest. But can you . . . ? Am I really talking to you? And who are you?' Admittedly, her brain was kind of mangled right now, but Rosie had no memory of ever knowing a Dot.

Her parents had not seemed to notice Dot going into the room past them, and were still bickering out in the corridor. Did that mean she was another ghostly visitor?

'What on earth are you wearing, anyway, Mike?'

'Carole bought it.'

'It's about ten years too young for you.'

'Dot,' Rosie tried, though she knew she wasn't really speaking out loud. 'I don't understand what's going on. Are you real? Have you come to take me away?'

'Not to worry, darlin'. You'll soon be better. I just know it.' And she patted Rosie's limp foot under the bedclothes, and bustled out again.

'But wait . . . are you . . . is there another memory coming up? I'm so confused!'

A voice said, 'Don't worry, lovie, it's me who has to do this one. We take turns.'

'Grandma,' said Rosie, relieved, as she spotted the small ghostly figure in the corner of the room. And was that . . . ? Yep, there was a ghostly pug with her, waddling about sniffing at things. Filou, back from the dead, or at least the depths of her memory. 'Do you know who that was?'

'No, sorry, darling. Eee, your mum and dad are really going at it, aren't they?'

'Yup. Grandma, what the— What on earth's going on with our family?' Grandma was her father's mother, she now remembered. Maybe she'd know what he'd been thinking when he'd spawned a small child. At his age!

'Well, your mum and dad had a few troubles over the years,' said Grandma, who was still knitting away furiously at the pink dog garment. 'You know, after . . . everything. Happens all the time. Course, it didn't in my day. You just put up with it, hid the sharp knives, smiled on the outside.'

'Yes, that sounds very healthy. So Dad and Mum are divorced?' She prodded her mind, trying to find the information, but it felt like such a jumble, the files scattered everywhere. 'Carole.' The name came from the depths of her brain-mush. 'Is that the name of my . . . stepmother?'

'That's right. She's not so bad, is Carole.'

'And she's the mum of . . . ?'

'Scarlett, yes. Though what kind of name that is, I don't know. *Fashionable*, I suppose.'

Rosie remembered now that 'fashionable' was the greatest insult her grandma could bestow. *Oh, your new jeans came ready-ripped? That's very . . . fashionable.* 'So I have a half-sister.' She tried to process everything she'd just learned. The child in the Elsa costume, that was her sister. (And what was *Frozen*? Was that something Rosie should know?) Her dad had left her mum for some mysterious woman called Carole, had had another child. But more pressingly, she had three days to wake up, to try to remember what had happened to her, why she'd walked in front of the bus. The doctors thought she'd meant to do it. But it must have been an accident, surely. She wouldn't have tried to kill herself, would she?

'Ready for another memory, lovie?'

Rosie knew she had to be. For some reason, reliving her life was the only way to find herself again, to remember, to wake up. At least the last one had been nice. There must be others in there of a time when everything was good. When she was very little, maybe. A time in, say, 1991. That year seemed significant for some reason. Maybe if she shut her eyes and tried really hard, she could control the strange time dial thing and go back to a happier time. Put things right again, even. Was that how it worked?

She pictured it, the numbers spinning on the grey. Everything blurring, a big noise in the background. She focused hard on the date. *1991. Take me there.*

1 July 1991 (Twenty-six years ago)

Rosie blinked. The light seemed different in this memory, brighter and softer both at once. Choosing the date seemed to have worked. She was in a room she recognised – the house she'd grown up in. The hallway, lined with framed pictures of her and Daisy as babies, her parents on their wedding day. You'd think, looking at them, that everyone was happy, a normal loving family. Rosie's eyes adjusted to the gloom and she saw in front of her a small girl knocking softly on a closed door. She was six or seven, maybe. She wore a *Flintstones* sweat-shirt and pale green jeans, her red hair in a swishy ponytail. It was her. It was Rosie as a kid.

'Lord, this is a long way back,' said her grandmother's voice, near her ear. 'Look at the dust on those pictures. Place needs a good clean.'

'What's going on?'

'You know what's going on, pet. It's ... the bad time.'

Rosie swallowed hard. Little Rosie knocked on the door

again. 'Mummy? Mummy, are you awake? Daisy's crying, Mummy. I think she wants some lunch.'

There was no answer. The little girl looked so small beside the door. She barely came up to the handle. Rosie watched as her younger self put an ear to the wood, listening hard. Nothing. She stood for a moment, then set her small shoulders with determination and marched into the kitchen. Present-day Rosie and Grandma followed, mere shadows.

A very young Daisy was standing on a stool and colouring something in with moody intensity. A sea of dark blue. She was only three or four here, was that normal? 'I'm hungry, Rosie.'

'I know, but Mummy's still sleeping.'

Daisy stabbed a crayon at her colouring. 'She's been sleeping all day! For ever and ever!'

'Where's Dad?' Rosie hissed to her grandmother. 'Why isn't he looking after us?'

'He's at work, pet. They didn't have the same type of parental leave back then. Different times. No harm came to you.'

'You really think that's true? Watch what happens next.' Rosie nodded at it. 'I remember this now.'

'I'll make our lunch,' declared Little Rosie confidently. 'I've seen Mummy do it. It's not that hard.' She stood on a chair and took out the bread from the bin, then went to the fridge for butter and ham. Then she opened a drawer and selected the biggest, sharpest knife in there. It was as long as her arm.

'Oh Lord,' said Grandma softly.

Little Rosie worked on the sandwiches, tongue poking out with effort. Butter on bread, that was easy enough. Slap the ham on top. *Just leave it*, Rosie was urging her younger self. *Eat it whole. Put the knife down!*

But there was no point. She knew how this memory ended. And she watched all over again as Little Rosie grasped the carving knife – not even a bread knife – and tried to cut the sandwiches into triangles, like Mummy did when she was awake, and sliced the top of her little finger right off. Rosie winced. She could feel it again, that slice of bright pain, the way the spongy white bread suddenly turned red. The tip of her finger sitting there on the table like a discarded plaster. For a moment, Little Rosie just stared at it in curiosity. Then Daisy began to howl. 'MUMMMMEEEE!'

Younger Rosie herself was dazed, just looking down at it with something like wonder. Older Rosie remembered that feeling. That the world was not as she'd thought. Your finger could come off. Your mother could forget about you. But now she came, staggering out from the bedroom like a zombie in her pyjamas. They had food crusted down the front and she hadn't brushed her hair in days. 'What did you do?' She seized Rosie by the arm. 'What did you do, you stupid girl!'

Rosie looked down now at the little white scar around the tip of her ghostly adult finger. They'd sewn it back on – it was quite common, apparently, for kids to lose bits of themselves – and she'd worn a bandage for a few weeks, which meant she couldn't help out with the school hamster, which was a more life-shattering event at seven than cutting a piece of your finger off. More than anything she'd never forgotten her mother's voice, hoarse and angry. *You stupid girl. You stupid, stupid girl.*

'There there, pet.' Grandma was holding out a ghostly handkerchief. 'Have a good blow.'

Rosie took it, surprised to feel cotton under her fingers. None of this was real. It was just a hallucination inside a memory. She was not really here. But . . . she could feel it again, the sadness and the fear. 'It wasn't fair,' she said thickly. 'I was only a kid.' Her eyes were filling again, as in the memory her mother lunged for the phone, screaming into it, and little Rosie just stood and bled into a puddle on the floor, and Daisy cried, and everything was awful.

'It's not real, love. You know that, don't you? It's just in your memory. You're remembering how you felt. Helpless and scared.'

'And angry,' Rosie said. 'Really angry at my mum.'

'I know, pet. But she was scared too. You can understand that, can't you, after everything?'

'I don't remember what "everything" is!' This was no good. She kept seeing memories, but she didn't understand what she was supposed to be learning from seeing herself cut off her finger. Wasn't that one for the mental waste-disposal? Leaving room instead for more memories of beaches, of Luke, of the warmth of his skin . . .

'Come on, let's get you back. Looks like something's happening.' Grandma held out her arthritic hand, and the world came back as the memory dissolved.

Rosie

Rosie woke up and she was . . . buried.

Above her eyes, just inches away, was a curved hard surface. Oh God. Was she dead? If only she could move any part of herself. *Come on, foot, move! I'm sorry I crammed you into all*

68

those uncomfortable shoes. If we get out of this, I promise, it's pedicures and Birkenstocks all the way. She remembered what the doctors had said. Even if she did wake up, she might not be able to walk. But no, that couldn't be true. After several moments of straining, her foot twitched very slightly – a victory! But even that tiny movement made her toes hit against something. Her entire body was encased in this thing – what was it?

A coffin, her mind whispered. *You died during that memory. You're buried.*

Panic surged through her, although she knew it was stupid. She hadn't been under long enough for that. Had three days really passed?

A morgue drawer, then. Locked in, on ice with the corpses. *But I'm not dead! I'm not dead!*

They don't know that. Maybe they pulled the plug. Thought it was kinder than keeping you alive, locked in yourself, not able to eat or talk or even scratch your nose.

Rosie's breath began to hitch. *Get me out! Get me out!* But she couldn't move. That tiny twitch of her foot had worn her out, taken an effort of will akin to climbing Mount Snowdon (when had she done that?). She tried again, but the foot lay there limply against the side of the coffin/morgue drawer/ whatever it was, like a dead fish that had nothing to do with her. *Help. Help! I'm NOT DEAD. I'M NOT DEAD.*

Oh God. She was trapped in this thing, she couldn't breathe, she couldn't even push her way out, she was trapped and she was going to die here and . . .

Light began to dazzle her eyes. She was moving. Not by herself, but some kind of mechanism was pulling her out into a harsh clinical light. 'Rosie. Rosie, are you OK?' The pretty posh doctor was standing over her, looking concerned. She spoke to someone over her shoulder, ponytail whipping. 'She was in distress. Her heart rate went through the roof.'

'You think she knew where she was?' The voice belonged to the other young doctor, the boy.

'I don't know. Rosie? You're safe, I promise. We just gave you an MRI. It can feel a bit scary if you're claustrophobic, but you're out now. We just had to look at your brain, that's all.'

Rosie tried to react. Make a noise, move something, but she was back to nothing. The other doctor came over. He had a Twix sticking out of the white pocket of his coat. 'Anything?'

'Hm. No. But I'm sure she was aware of her surroundings. Anything on the scan?'

'Yeah, some activity in the memory centres, then suddenly boom – a massive flood of cortisol and the elevated heart rate.' They both stared down at her again. 'You think she can hear us?'

'Maybe. It doesn't mean she'll wake up, of course. Or that she's even aware.' She bent over, so Rosie could smell her faint perfume. Jo Malone Bluebell. 'Rosie? If you can hear us, I know it's frightening not being able to move. These things take a while sometimes. You need to heal. If you can communicate with us in any way, try, OK? We'll be watching.'

The foot twitch had clearly gone unnoticed. Rosie wasn't sure how long it would take her to work up to another one. They were wheeling her out now, into the hospital corridor with its hushed energy, the rush of people with purposeful important jobs, healing and diagnosing and helping and comforting with that particular NHS brand of brisk kindness. And there was Rosie, helping no one, causing nothing but pain to her family, helpless on this trolley. Overhead, the bright lights looked like the midday sun. Rosie was pushed back into her room and efficiently hooked back up to her tubes and drips and monitors. She could sense her parents in the background, but couldn't turn her head.

'What did you see?' Her mother. Anxious, hovering.

'There's definitely some brain activity.' Pretty doctor. 'But we can't be sure what it means. Do try to talk to her. If she hears your voices and maybe her favourite songs – if some friends stop by to talk to her, read to her, that sort of thing – it may well help to switch her brain back on.'

If only they knew, Rosie thought. The voices of her family made her want to hide deep in herself and never come out. They might have more luck playing her *Loose Women* all day instead. After all, if her family struggled to communicate when she was awake, how would they manage to chat to her comatose body?

Daisy

She sat on the Tube, looking around her as if her eyes were suddenly raw and open to the world. All these people, heads down on their phones, music leaking from headphones. What secret sadnesses were they carrying? *My sister's in a coma*, she said to herself, trying it out for size. *My sister got hit by a bus.* There was something almost comical about that, and she wouldn't be able to bear it if people laughed when she told them. If Rosie died because of a stupid accident. She could just imagine what Gary might say: *Typical Rosie. Off in Rosie*

World. Perhaps that was why it was now lunchtime and she still hadn't told him about it.

Was it even an accident? *My sister walked in front of a bus. My sister tried to kill herself.* No one would laugh at that. But she couldn't believe it. She wouldn't. She stayed on the Tube, clanking and blessedly noisy, drowning out all thoughts, then got out at Angel and walked slowly along Upper Street, past the antique shops and chain restaurants. Rosie had liked it here, she knew. The area was buzzy, and there were so many cafés and shops and bars that she never had to sit in her flat alone. Daisy knew that sometimes Rosie felt the walls pressing in on her, crushing her, and she just had to get outside, fill her ears with music and chatter, anything to escape herself.

She stopped outside a narrow doorway between an estate agent's and an organic bakery, and let herself in using the keys from Rosie's bag. It had been untouched by the accident, thrown clear. Her clothes were so hopelessly bloodstained they'd have to be burned as medical waste. Daisy shuddered at the thought. Rosie's flat was up three flights of stairs, dusty and dirty. The hallway was littered with junk mail addressed to long-gone people. Something lonely about it, living with these ghosts. As Daisy went up the stairs, the door of the flat below Rosie's opened, revealing a man in tracksuit bottoms and a fraying polo shirt with a gilet on top, a Maori tattoo looping around his arm, though he was extremely white. A blast of weed emanated from the flat behind him, along with some banging dubstep. 'I thought you were Rosie. She's not been in all morning.'

'I'm her sister. Um – she's had an accident, I'm afraid. She's in hospital. I'm here to get some things.' And also to have a snoop in her sister's flat, and see if she could find any clues, anything at all, as to what had happened.

His reaction was slow (drugs, thought Daisy, who'd seen the same look on the faces of many City traders) but gradually his forehead creased. 'An accident?'

'Yes, she . . . um, she was hit by a bus.' She paused. 'They think . . . maybe she did it on purpose.' Hoping he'd say, *God no, Rosie would never do a thing like that.*

'Oh. You know, she did seem kind of down lately . . . '

Daisy's heart began to race.

' . . . not sleeping, doesn't want to come out, that sort of thing. And her hair's been all, like . . . ' He twiddled a hand above his own, indicating tangles. 'Like she doesn't brush it any more, you know. So . . . did she? Do it?'

'I don't know. I . . . sorry, I need to get her things.' Daisy couldn't talk about that. She had to keep moving, keep doing things. She called back: 'That stuff will fry your brain, you know. It's giving you a fifty per cent chance of developing psychosis.' Then, feeling bad – it wasn't his fault Rosie was in a coma – she fumbled the key in the lock and went inside. Who was that guy? She really hoped Rosie hadn't gone there. She knew the type – confident but paper-thin, a rumour of a person rather than the real thing. He reminded her a little of Jack, in fact. Thank God that hadn't lasted.

Daisy leaned her back against the door and looked around Rosie's flat. A square of kitchen, the tiles dirty and unwashed dishes piled up, fruit flies buzzing round a bowl of rotting bananas. On top of the dusty TV was a picture Daisy recognised, a crack in the glass. But she couldn't look at that, not right now. 'Oh Rosie,' she murmured, 'how can you live like this?' She thought briefly of the house she shared with Gary in Beckenham. Barely even London, Rosie had scoffed at the time. Gary wanted to move even further out, to Guildford perhaps. Get a three-bed with a garage. 'Start a family,' as he insisted on describing it. They were ready. They had matching plates, house plants that didn't die, a barbecue set. They were grown-ups. They went to B&Q on weekends. And here was Rosie, three years older, living like a student.

Daisy tentatively opened a drawer in the tallboy, looking for pyjamas. That was the main thing for hospital, wasn't it? But the only ones she could find were old and washed out – she could remember Rosie having them one far-off Christmas – or dirty with encrusted toothpaste. In the small bathroom, which had creeping mould up the tiles, she found a bent-looking toothbrush and some squeezed-out shampoo. This wouldn't do. Daisy left everything where it was, and instead picked up a few books and CDs she knew were her sister's favourites. As she stuffed them into a Tesco bag she noticed something on the coffee table, among the dirty plates and magazines. A piece of lined paper. Her heart stopped. *A suicide note.* But no, it looked like a list of names, some crossed out and scribbled over. Daisy peered at it.

Mel. Angie. Serge. Dave. Caz. Ingrid. Mum. Daisy. Dad. Carole. Mr Malcolm. Ella. Luke.

Her own name? Why?

And then: *Luke.* The name Rosie had said before slipping under. If this Luke was so important to her sister, why on earth had Daisy never heard of him? She looked around one last time at the squalid little flat. 'Oh Rosie,' she said to herself. 'I wish I'd known. I wish you'd talked to me.'

But it was too late for that, and so, being a practical kind of person, Daisy took the list, locked the door carefully behind her, and went back down the noisy bustling street to find some shops.

Rosie

'How you holding up there, Ro-Ro?'

Rosie's eyes flickered, taking in the hospital room, the buzz of life outside it. Melissa was in front of her, eternally fourteen. Except she wasn't there at all, was she? She was dead. Ghosts weren't real. You couldn't travel in space and time and relive past days of your life. All of this was just . . . some kind of mad hallucination.

She was almost sure of that.

'I'm OK, I guess. Though I wish they wouldn't keep talking about whether there's any brain function. Especially when I'm desperately trying to make contact and I can't.'

'Oh yeah, I remember how it was for me. Not much fun.'

'God, Melissa, I'm so sorry that you . . . died.' She wanted to ask how it had happened, but found that she couldn't. Did she already know, but just couldn't remember?

Melissa flapped her hands. 'Don't be. It's not so bad. There's a few of us younger ones, what with cancer and suicide and young men coming off motorbikes.'

'You've met Darryl then.'

'Only just.' She giggled. 'He's *dreamy.*'

Rosie didn't think she could cope with the hallucination/ghost/whatever of a long-dead childhood schoolmate having

75

a crush on her recently dead A&E roommate. She'd never get used to the casual attitude her dead visitors displayed to their own lack of aliveness. 'Melissa, I . . . They said if I don't wake up in three days, I might never. But I don't know how to. Is there a way to wake yourself up from a coma?'

'I don't know, sorry, Ro-Ro. When it was me people kept talking to me, playing me music and so on. That's supposed to help. But in the end I kind of . . . drifted away. And it wasn't bad, you know. It was peaceful.'

Same thing Darryl had said. Was that what she'd hoped for when she stepped in front of that bus? Peace, and an end to pain? She didn't know. 'So why am I having these memories?'

'I don't know. I think your brain is trying to figure something out.'

'When's it going to end, though? Will I just do this for ever?' Panic began to rise in her chest again at the idea of being trapped in this body for the rest of her life, withering away while her mind leapfrogged from memory to memory. All bad so far. Except for the beach one. That had been nice. A warm feeling spread through her, thinking of it. 'When I was brought in they said I was muttering a name: Luke. Well, I remembered who Luke is.'

'Uh huh,' said Melissa non-committally.

'It was a happy memory! The beach, the sunset, the two of us . . . Finally something good in there. I was starting to despair of my brain. Luke and I were together, right? I feel sure of it. We had to be, after we met like that.'

'Well. How about you just wait and see? I've come to take you back again. Ready?'

'Another memory? Yeah, I'm ready.' Already she was

hoping to see Luke again, if only in her mind. The curves of his face felt somehow settled in her. She knew it was one she'd looked at many times. Maybe they were even together now. Maybe the numbers on the dial were wrong, and that sordid flat had actually been a long time ago, and he and she were in love and owned a cottage somewhere and went to farmers' markets on weekends and . . . But now her vision was blurring again, the sound of the same noise rising in her ears, the spinning dial before her: 1 12 2010.

1 December 2010 (Seven years ago)

Breathe in. Eyes open. It was like surfacing from underwater, the memory bursting onto her senses, somehow more real than the 'real' world she'd left behind. She could feel the cold air that blasted in from the street and the warm fug of the bar on her skin. The clank of glasses and bubbles of laughter. The smell of beer – post-smoking ban, of course. One of her favourite cocktails of sounds and smells, and a low glow of candles – she was in a pub. 'Where am I? I mean, old me?' She and Melissa moved like ghosts through the crowd. She was the interloper here. None of this was real.

'There you are.' Melissa nodded at the door, where sure enough Past Rosie was crashing in, a wide smile on her face. Cheery red hat, black coat, extra-long scarf.

'I remember that scarf,' she said nostalgically. 'Mum hated it. She was convinced I'd get tangled up and sucked under a bus – well, I guess she was sort of right about that. So, what's this memory, then?' She searched her jumbled filing cabinets, imagining overflowing manila folders, alphabetical dividers. There were hundreds of memories marked 'Pub visits'. Rosie Cooke had clearly spent a lot of her life in such establishments. She watched her past self, glowing with seasonal warmth, pick her way across the crowded room to a leather sofa in the corner. A man stood up from it. Tall, sandy hair. Chunky grey cardigan, navy cords, the kind of clothes Rosie really liked on a man and—

'It's Luke!' It really was him. Paler than on their beach meeting, his hair shorter, his clothes less summery, but it was him. 'God, he looks even better like this.' How old would he have been then? Assuming he was the same age as her, and she was in her early thirties: twenty-six, something like that? So young still.

'Wow, he's sooooo cute!' gasped Melissa. 'This is exciting, isn't it? I never got to go to a pub while I was alive.' Because she'd died at fourteen, her life cut short, never to marry or grow up or go to university or even have a drink. How had she died? Had Rosie known about it? So many questions.

'Pay attention, Ro, it's important.'

OK. She was in a pub, meeting Luke ... Vague memories surfaced. A back-and-forth email exchange on dates and places, the subject heading 'Welcome Back Chrimbo drinks'. Some kind of party, a reunion, which had taken months to arrange. But why had she and Luke not arrived together? Who was being welcomed back, and where from? She watched her past self pause on seeing him, and a long glance go between the two of them. Then they were hugging as if they hadn't seen each other in years. The kind of hug that goes on slightly too long, where you sneakily take in gulps of the other person's smell, breathing in their skin. She raised a hand to her cheek, remembering the feel of his thick wool cardy against it. 'So we're not together.'

'Doesn't look like it. Sorry.'

'Why not? What happened after we met on the beach?'

'I don't know, Ro. You need to see for yourself. Just watch.'

Disgruntled, she turned her attention back, trying to hear what they were saying. Luke was talking. That voice, low and deep, with a faint Middlesbrough accent, as if he was permanently trying to hold back a laugh. She knew she'd heard that voice a lot. She just knew it. Maybe this was when they got back together, five years of missing each other, the romance of Christmas . . .

Luke was saying, ' . . . just been talking about that time we went to the souk in Marrakesh, remember, and I accidentally almost bartered you away for a camel! Good times. I'm so glad you could come, Rosie.'

There was such warmth in the way he spoke to her. Was she watching a memory of how they got together? If so, why did her past self look so miserable, a frozen smile on her face?

Someone was hovering at Luke's elbow, an expectant smile on their lips. A young woman, petite and neat, with waist-length shiny black hair and green eyes. Dressed elegantly in a black cashmere dress and knee-length boots. Rosie remembered what she was wearing under her coat: a Christmas jumper with sprouts on it. She'd felt so stupid she'd kept her coat on all night and sweated right down her back. The girl put her hand on Luke's shoulder – Present-day Rosie was shocked by how much she wanted to dive over there and knock it away – and murmured something in his ear.

Luke stopped his story. 'Sorry, of course, sweetheart. Rosie, I'd like you to meet my fiancée.'

Rosie

Rosie gasped out of the memory. Out of the cosy pub, away from Luke and that girl. *Sweetheart. Fiancée.* What was the point of that? To show her that, on top of living in a craphole and being estranged from her family, she'd had to watch as the love of her life married someone else?

Was he the love of her life? He must be, if she'd had his name in her mouth when they pulled her back from death. Maybe he hadn't married that girl after all. Maybe it was just the moment in a romcom where a hilarious misunderstanding keeps the lovers apart for twenty minutes, only for them to sort it all out by the end. But Rosie knew that, in real life, people often didn't work things out. That it was all too easy to find the person you were meant to be with, and then just let them slip away.

The door opened and her parents came into her room, looking tired and with the after-tang of bickering in the air. 'All I said was a second opinion can't hurt. That doctor looks about twelve. I wouldn't trust her to give me a hot-stone massage.'

'Come on, Alison. They're doing the best they can. They said we had to talk to her.'

Her mother gazed down at her, pulling on the sleeves of her cashmere top. 'How I can talk to her? She's unconscious. They should be doing actual medical things! Surgery, drugs! Not ... chatting.'

'Let me try.' Her father stood self-consciously at the end of her bed and cleared his throat. 'Hello, Rosie, it's Mike. Um. Dad. I hope you can hear me in there . . . I'm here with your mum, but don't worry, we haven't killed each other yet, ha ha.' Death stare from her mum. He cleared his throat again. 'Um, Rosie, we just want you to know that, um, we love you very much. Right, Alison?'

Her mother sighed. 'This is ridiculous.'

'I know things haven't always been easy . . . and I'm sorry for those words we had when Scarlett was born. I was a bit, er, sleep-deprived. No joke having a newborn in your fifties, I can tell you.' Even if Rosie had been awake, she'd have treated that apology with stony contempt. Perhaps he could tell. 'Er, we know things were hard too when you were younger—'

'Stop saying we,' her mother interrupted. 'There is no "we", Mike, not since you went off with that woman.'

'Please, Alison. It's Scarlett's mum you're talking about.'

'She can't hear me. She's busy with some Grumpy Birds thing, or whatever it is. Anyway, I don't see why she shouldn't know the truth – her mother stole a married man away from his wife, his children.'

'A wife who hadn't looked at me in years!'

Rosie wished she could seal up her ears. Not another row. She'd heard so many of these over the years, the words flung like darts, but usually she could storm out or slam a door or threaten to run away. Daisy's approach had always been to make herself very small and quiet, retreating to her room with a book and putting Westlife on her Walkman. Now, helpless, Rosie just had to lie and listen. This would be a great time for another flashback. She looked around hopefully but there were no deceased companions in evidence. No Darryl, no Melissa, no Mr Malcolm, no Grandma. No Dot – whoever she was.

'For God's sake, Mike, you're pathetic. Still defending your-self, when Rosie's lying here in bits!' Rosie watched her mother turn away, arms folded, trying hard not to cry. All this had happened years ago, surely – how could she still be so upset?

But then again, Rosie had never forgiven him either, had she? It was Daisy who said, *We have to go and see him. He's our dad, we can't just cast him off.* Daisy who sent birthday cards and bought Scarlett Christmas presents and dutifully took Gary round for Sunday lunch.

Gary. Oh God, she'd forgotten all about him, but there was his name in her mind. That was the name of Daisy's fiancé. Her sister was getting married. And Rosie was ... not happy for her. Why? She was afraid to probe too deeply, afraid that it might be yet another thing she didn't want to know.

'Are you ready for another memory, dearie?' said her grandma's voice. Rosie looked over, and there she was in the orange seat, knitting away. There was Filou, collapsed on the floor with the sheer effort of breathing, as Rosie remembered him. Poor Filou.

'I think so. But, Grandma – I'm worried it won't be a nice one. So far they're nearly all horrible. Don't I have any good memories?'

'Course you do, love, but these are the ones your brain wants you to look at, for some reason.' She nodded to her son and his ex-wife, hissing insults at each other with their lips curled back and teeth gritted. 'Got to be better than listening to this pair, anyway.'

'True. Are you coming with me?'

'Course I am.' She patted the pocket of her cardigan. 'Brought some sherbet lemons along for the ride too. Let's go.'

Rosie shut her eyes as the sounds of her parents fighting faded blessedly away and again the noise swelled in her ears and the dial swum in front of them. The numbers settled on 18 4 2010. Same year as that pub, Luke and his girl, but earlier. 'Grandma?' She panicked slightly, as the world blurred and spun.

'I'm here, love. Let yourself go.'

18 April 2010 (Seven years ago)

'We have to go,' Daisy insisted. 'She's our sister.' They were sitting on a country bus on a wet grey day, already dark outside, the swish of the tyres filling the air. Daisy looked only slightly different than in the present day – her hair a little longer, her handbag a different old-lady one. She was wearing a fleece and baggy jeans. At this time, Rosie knew, doing some quick calculations, her sister would have been just twenty-three. Just finished her law training course – oh, another memory. Daisy was a lawyer. Sensible, engaged, and with a good job. Rosie was getting the distinct feeling that she and her sister were not that alike. She, as observed by herself from a seat right behind, was wearing open-toed shoeboots, useless in the rain, and a long fringed skirt. Clearly, she'd been aiming at boho chic, but instead she looked like Jessie from *Toy Story*. 'She's not our sister,' she was saying. 'Urgh. It's disgusting. Dad's ancient to have a new baby.'

Daisy stared out of the bus window at the rain. 'This

weather. Do you remember that time in the caravan in Wales?'

Rosie groaned. 'God, it didn't stop pouring once! All we did was hang out in the rec centre and play board games with the pieces missing.'

'You snogged that boy from Pontypridd behind the loo block.'

'Hywel. Urgh. And Mum and Dad were—' Rosie stopped, narrowed her eyes at her sister. 'Very good, Little Miss Reverse Psychology. I know they were nightmarish together. It doesn't mean I want to meet his replacement kid.'

'Come on. It can't be worse than a caravan in Wales in the rain.'

'Wanna bet? At least I got really good at Scrabble on that holiday. And I learned the Welsh for kissing with tongues, though I really wish I hadn't.'

They got off the bus at a rain-soaked stop by the side of the road, nothing around except a cluster of dreary bungalows. A ghostly Grandma and Present-day Rosie followed behind. Past Rosie wrapped her arms around her inadequate jacket and huddled under the bus shelter, while Daisy did up the hood of her sensible anorak. 'Where is he, anyway? He was meant to be here.'

'Give him a minute.'

'This sucks. They live in Hicksville.'

Daisy just sighed. 'Look, there he is.' A car was drawing up – the impractical Jaguar their father had bought not long after the divorce.

'He'll have to change that now,' said Rosie, with some satisfaction. 'Baby puke all over the leather.'

The sisters trudged to the car in the rain, and Rosie went to follow. Grandma put up a hand to stop her. 'No need for that, love. Just close your eyes.'

She did so, doubtfully, and when she opened them the patter of the rain had stopped, and she was inside a cosy identikit living room, with chain-store furniture and a sofa probably bought in the DFS sale, pictures in Perspex cubes everywhere, the kind photographers in shopping malls shoot against portable white backgrounds. Rosie realised her lip was curling in sympathy with her past self, who was standing rigid in front of the mantelpiece, the hem of her skirt dripping onto the cream carpet. An anxious-looking woman was hovering, in black polyester trousers and a floral top. Her frosted-pink lipstick, which didn't suit her, was smeared on her teeth. Rosie gaped. 'That's Carole? But she looks like ... a bank manager.' She'd been picturing some kind of femme fatale.

Grandma was inspecting the mantelpiece for dust, and seemed satisfied with what she found. 'Close. She's a finance officer. Met your dad at an accounting conference in Swindon.'

So this was the floozy her dad had left her mother for. A forty-something in Next's finest. In this memory, Carole was nervously offering tea, or coffee, or wine, or beer, or spirits – she said 'spirits' like a temperance preacher – and putting out little bowls of crisps and olives. Daisy was dutifully munching, though Rosie knew she didn't even like olives. There was nowhere to put the stones, so Rosie watched her sister rummage through her own handbag – not dissimilar to Carole's – and wrap them up neatly in a tissue. Oh, Daisy. So neat, so polite. Whereas Past Rosie was clearly boiling over with rage.

'Won't you have a seat, love?' pleaded her dad. 'We can

have a nice drink and a chat – I got that wine you like, that Spanish stuff?'

'I don't want any wine.' But she sat down, perching on the arm of a sofa as if she might run away at any moment. 'Where is she then?'

'Scarlett?' Carole's nervous face creased with love at the name. 'She's having her nap. Would you like a little peep at her?'

They traipsed up the stairs, also lined with photos, including lots of Daisy and Rosie, and into a baby's room that was like an explosion of pink. Frills, flowers, hearts, teddies. In a flouncy cot, a baby was stretched out in deep sleep. Rosie and her past self hung back in the door, but she could remember how it felt – a gut-punch of jealousy, sadness, and strange sudden tears coming to her eyes at the sight of this little baby. Daisy said all the right things, of course. 'She's beautiful, Carole. Hello, Scarlett. We're your big sisters.'

Carole was misty-eyed. 'I never thought I'd have one. Forty-three and four rounds of IVF. And now a little girl of my own!'

'Because you took someone else's husband,' Rosie had muttered. Carole must have heard. There was a short awkward pause, the three of them crammed into Scarlett's room.

Carole said, 'It's very good of you to come, girls. I know it hasn't been easy, but I hope that you . . . that you'll see her as your little sister, like you said, Daisy.'

Daisy hugged her as Carole started to cry, murmuring soothing things. But all Rosie could think of was her own mother, weeping on the bathroom floor, staying in bed for weeks. That day years ago, the fear and the screaming. *Petey. Petey!* It wasn't fair. She pushed her way out of the baby's room and thundered downstairs, eyes blurred with tears, only to find her father on the sofa, his jolly expression sunk into one of exhaustion. *Good*, Rosie had thought with a stab of spite. *He's finding out what happens when you have a baby and you're actually around.*

'I know it's hard, Rosie love,' he said quietly. 'But will you please try? It's not her fault. Little Scarlett.'

What a stupid name. A name for a confident privileged little girl who rode ponies, and how could she ever be that with nervy Carole for a mother and their useless shared father? 'I know it's not her fault, Dad,' Rosie said, retrieving the wine he'd poured her and draining the glass in one. 'It's yours.'

Present-day Rosie, watching it all, winced again. Such a cruel thing to say, but she'd believed it, and afterwards, as his face crumpled, she had added privately to herself: *And mine. It's my fault too. All of it.*

She just wasn't entirely sure why.

Daisy

As Daisy closed the front door of her house, some of the engagement cards on the hall table drifted to the ground. She stooped to pick them up, feeling a twinge in her back. This was ridiculous. She was thirty, how could she already feel this tired and old? Gary appeared in the door to the living room, drying a glass with a tea towel. 'Might be time to put those away now,' he said, nodding to the cards.

'OK.' It had been two months. It felt like years.

Gary's face was caring. 'How is she?' She'd eventually called him on her way home, after returning to the hospital with bags full of new things for Rosie, finding her parents still fighting, and realising she needed some back-up.

'They seem sort of hopeful. She's made some sounds, responded to light – it's all . . . hopeful.' Mentally, she imagined scoring a red line through that sentence, like Maura would with her client reports. *Find a synonym for hopeful rather than repeating the same word, Daisy.* But she couldn't think of one.

'And did they say what *happened?*'

Daisy squatted to take off her shoes, leaning on the wall. Gary's lips pursed – the wallpaper had been very expensive. She took her hand away, balancing awkwardly instead. 'She walked in front of a bus.'

'You mean . . . '

'That's what they said. People saw her step right in front of it. They don't know if she just didn't see it or if she . . . ' Daisy felt her face crumple, an ugly grimace of pain, and her eyes fill with tears. 'I can't believe she would do it. On purpose. I just can't believe it.'

'Oh, hey, come on. Come and sit down.' He tidied her shoes onto the rack for her, then ushered her into the neat, cosy living room. The scented candles were lit, and the coffee table was dust-free, magazines stacked on it. Home. Daisy sank into an armchair and Gary perched on the sofa, gazing at her sadly. 'You don't know for sure?'

'No, but . . . I went to her flat. It's such a— God, she lives in a fleapit. It's horrible. And since Mum and I haven't really been speaking to her, you know . . . I think she might have been . . . unhappy.'

'Well, I hate to say it, but it's not surprising, is it? The way she was at the engagement party. I mean, *Dave*, for God's sake – he's not coming to the wedding, by the way, I've let the caterers know he's off the spreadsheet.'

Daisy slapped a palm to her head. 'The caterers! That was today. God, I totally forgot.'

'It's OK, I've rearranged. But we do need to decide soon. Chicken and Parma ham or beef Wellington? I've made a list of the pros and cons of each.'

Daisy stared up at him. They'd been living together for almost three years now, since meeting in the pub after work one Friday, her tired and freewheeling after a busy few days of contract law, him in his suit fresh from the management consultancy where he worked. A meaningless phrase which meant camping out in the offices of other firms and telling them everything they were doing wrong. She hadn't made it home in three days and was wearing knickers that still had the price tag on, bought in a hurried trip out of the office that morning. Then, Gary had just been an interesting stranger. Now, she knew every curve of his face, every item in his wardrobe. Today was Tuesday, so it was the blue and white striped shirt with the grey suit. His stomach hung slightly over the waistband of his trousers – they'd both agreed they would lose weight before the wedding. 'I can't think about the wedding when Rosie's in hospital,' she heard herself say.

'I know, babe, I know. Just saying, it's hardly out of character for her to do something ... unstable.' He finished off wiping the glass with a hard polish, holding it to the light to check for smears. Daisy recognised it as one she'd already washed and put away the night before. 'And when you think of it, walking in front of a bus, isn't that kind of selfish? I mean, what about the driver?'

Selfish. Unstable. Unhappy. Oh, Rosie. How did you get here? Daisy pushed herself to her feet. 'I might have a bath.'

'But I made dinner. Slimming World pasta. It'll get cold.'

'Sorry. Leave me some. I just ... I just need a bath.' She escaped up the stairs, into the white bathroom with the fake old-style claw-foot tub, the one they'd spent so long choosing in B&Q that time. They'd felt so grown-up, owning a house, paying to have the bathroom redone (though she'd had to shower at the gym for weeks). She'd felt like she'd achieved something, a life she could show to her parents and maybe allow them to stop worrying about at least one of their children.

As she ran the hot water into the bath, glugging in a good measure of the rose-scented oil her mother had got her for Christmas, which she normally kept for special occasions, Daisy took off her engagement ring and sat it on the side, where it sparkled and gleamed among the steam and bubbles. She was just overwrought. There was so much to do. Tomorrow, she had to get up early and call Maura, rearrange her work, explain she wasn't coming in again. Go to the hospital, referee her parents, hope there might be some change in Rosie. Try to find out what the note meant, what Rosie had been thinking when that bus hit her. She should really get out of the bath and do something useful.

But she stayed in there so long, just staring at the ceiling, that Gary was in bed when she got out, the lights ostentatiously off and her pyjamas left by the door in a neat pile. His back was already turned away from her. He was pathological about being asleep by nine. She bet Rosie hadn't been to bed by nine since she was at primary school. Rosie lived alone in a hovel, while Daisy lived in this all-mod-cons house with a garden and replica claw-foot bath, with Gary who cooked for her and would wake her in the morning with green tea, who she would soon marry and live with for the rest of her life. She was the lucky sister. Rosie was the one who'd walked in front of a bus. So why did Daisy feel a hollow gnawing its way into the base of her stomach?

She thought of the list of names she'd found in Rosie's flat, which was now slipped into a pocket of her handbag. What did it mean? Tomorrow, she would try to figure it out. She had to, because one day had already passed, and Rosie was still in a coma.

DAY TWO

Rosie

Time in hospital seemed to lose all meaning. The meagre light from the high window came and went, but the fluorescent bulbs burned constantly, and outside in the corridor there was always the sound of feet and beeps and hushed voices, occasionally rising to a shout or a run. It was night, she thought. One day run out already, and all she knew about her life was that it sucked. Did that mean she'd wanted to die? She'd walked in front of the bus on purpose? She only had two days to figure it all out, or she might never wake up.

'Hello, darlin'.' The door had opened and there was a vision in orange. Dot.

'Can you hear me?' Rosie tried. 'I mean, do you see that I'm ... awake?' *Are you dead* seemed a rather rude question to ask.

Dot bustled in, wobbling on her flat feet. She had short grey hair and a whiff of cigarettes about her, and she kept up a constant stream of chatter that was hard to interrupt. 'Let me see now.' She consulted the chart, pursing her lips. 'Oh dear, oh dear, that is a nasty one. Don't you worry, love, we've fixed all sorts in this hospital.'

'Have you? Do you think I'll ... will I get better?' Rosie wasn't even sure if she was speaking aloud or not.

'You'll be right as rain, my love, I know you will. You just sit tight and let that pretty head of yours heal. Now, let me see, what do we have here?' She tidied some paper cups from the bedside locker. 'Ooh, those are nice, aren't they?' Rosie's mother had put a vase of irises there, the deep purple and yellow lighting up the drab room. So she must believe, in some small part of her, that Rosie knew they were there. Or perhaps it was just blind hope.

'Dot? Can you ... can you tell me what's happening to me?'

Dot smoothed down her bedcover. 'It must be confusing, Rosie love, but we have it all in hand. You just get better, OK, darlin'? Now I have to go, but I'll be along to say hello again.'

'Dot? Dot, wait ... ' But she was gone.

Rosie wished she could sleep. Every part of her ached, from the soles of her feet to the crown of her head. But sleep brought memories, which threw her awake with her head racing and tears leaking from her eyes. Sleep brought no rest. She was alone for now, except for the nurses who passed, regular as clockwork, checking charts and adjusting her drips, their touch efficient and cold.

So. What had she learned so far about her life? Her family was fractured, and the love of her life (she knew Luke was that; she could feel her love for him carried beneath her solar plexus, as real and solid as a fist) had married someone else (probably), she'd been horrible to her stepmother and half-sister, and she lived in a nasty flat with a beatboxing drug-addled downstairs neighbour. Her parents were divorced, acrimoniously. Something had happened, something bad, when she was younger. The top of her finger ached, a ghostly memory of when she'd sliced it off. What other wounds was her body carrying, both physical and mental?

'This is fun, isn't it? All these memories.'

Rosie sighed as a ghostly apparition appeared in front of her in polyester maroon. 'Melissa. It's not that much fun for me, no.'

'But it's a real trip down memory lane!'

'Yes, if memory lane was haunted and full of potholes and feral foxes.'

Melissa chuckled. 'Oh Ro-Ro, such a joker. You could be on *Friends*. Ready for another memory? Let's go.' Melissa checked her Casio watch. She had fraying friendship bracelets all around one wrist. 'We're on day two now already. Time's running out, Rosie. Try to remember.'

'Remember what?' The hospital room began to fade around Rosie. The dial appeared, spinning drunkenly. 'Remember *what*?'

Too late. She was back there.

28 September 2017 (One month ago)

'It's actually a bit linked to *Friends,* this memory.'

'Oh?' That sounded better. Maybe she had a big group of loving mates after all, who'd show up at hospital any minute, bantering in-jokes back and forth.

'Ta da!'

Rosie looked around her. 'Right. So when you said it was like *Friends,* what you meant was, it's a memory about a coffee shop?'

'A coffee shop where you work! That's the dream, Rosie! Just like Rachel.'

'OK, well, it's not the dream once you're older than fourteen, Mel. So this is my job?' She gazed around her. A small, hip café, with gluten-free organic cakes arranged in piles, and a menu as long as the phone book. Brief bursts of memory were coming back to her – the rich smell of coffee, slicing into a pan of brownies warm and oozing from the oven, giggling at Serge when he had to wear a plastic hairnet over his beard . . .

(Who was Serge?) Each memory left a trail of different feelings, some happy, some sad, some dull, and then was gone like a speeding comet.

Melissa was gaping at the menu. 'I thought the only hot drinks that existed were coffee, tea and hot chocolate. What's cold brew?'

'It's . . . ' Rosie drew a blank. 'Sorry, I don't know either. You'd think I would, if I worked here. Oh look, there I am. Yikes, I look awful.'

Her uniform was a red polo shirt, the worst possible colour for her, and her gingery hair was bundled back, almost but not quite beaten into submission. She was behind the counter, and a large bearded man with tattoos was lecturing her. 'It's just not good enough, Rosie.'

Past Rosie said, 'What does it matter, Serge? It's all coffee.'

Serge – she remembered him now, her boss at the café, expert in krav maga, ran an ironic blog about fried chicken; oh God, she'd slept with him too, hadn't she, that one time when she was feeling particularly low? – gritted his teeth. 'Rosie! There is a big difference between Sumatran and Kenyan!'

'Which is . . . ?'

'Well, they're on entirely different continents, for a start. It's all about *terroir*. Provenance.'

'It's hot brown liquid, Serge. Which we charge a fiver for.'

'Shhh!' He looked around frantically, even though every single customer was plugged into headphones on their laptops and couldn't have heard. 'Honestly, Rosie – you're late all the time, you laughed when someone asked for a black decaf low coffee shot . . . '

'Water, that's what that is. Hot water. If they want to pay a fiver for that, then fair play to them.'

He shook his head. 'I don't think your heart is really in organically sourced coffee.'

'No. It's not. Sorry, Serge. I know you care about it, almost as much as you care about who's going to play the next Spider-Man, but I just ... can't.' Rosie was untying her apron. 'I need to stop kidding myself. I'm not an actress who makes coffee to pay the bills. I'm a barista, and a bad one at that. I think ... maybe I should try to get a proper job. Give up on the dream. I'm sorry. I'll come to see your ska band sometime. Bye.'

Now Rosie was trying to piece it all together. 'So ... I quit?' She'd left her job a month ago, been holed up in that flat ever since, fallen out with her family ... What state of mind was she in when she walked into the path of that bus?

'Now, what'll happen next is you'll get headhunted for your dream job, and earn more than you ever did, just like Rachel.'

'See, Mel, what you're doing again there is mixing up American TV of the nineties with real life twenty years later. What happens nowadays if you quit a perfectly good job is you can't afford your rent and you end up on the street. Or back with your parents.' And if they weren't speaking to you, well, then what did you do? Rosie had a horrible feeling she would soon be finding out. 'What am I doing now?'

'You're getting out your phone. Isn't it amazing how everyone has one now? Maybe if I'd had a phone back then, I wouldn't have been so lonely.'

'I ... I'm not sure that's necessarily the case, Mel.' Rosie watched her past self leave the coffee shop, fishing out her phone and calling up Tinder, swiping her thumb over and over in a kind of fever. She knew what she was doing. Looking for company, anyone she could drag back to her nasty flat or meet in a scummy pub and drink with all night, anyone at all, just to not be alone with her thoughts. She remembered now. Some guy called . . . Ben? At least half the boys her age seemed to be called Ben, so that was a safe bet. They'd met at the huge Wetherspoons up the road, the one that smelled of stale beer and chips, and the next morning she'd woken up to see him curled in her small bed, smelling faintly of cigarettes and garlic, this man she barely knew at all, didn't even know his surname or how old he was, and realised this was not the way to cure the ache inside her. 'No,' she repeated sadly. 'Having a phone doesn't always make you less lonely. Not at all.'

'Shall we go back?' said Melissa. 'I think this one is over.'

'So, a whole memory about me stupidly leaving my stupid job then sleeping around. Great. This is soooo useful.'

'You sound just like Chandler,' said Melissa cheerfully, as the coffee shop and Serge and the gluten-free cakes and the hipster patrons all faded like smoke.

Daisy

'I'm sorry, Maura, I really am. It's just . . . she's in a coma, you know.'

Down the phone, Daisy heard her boss's deep sigh. She pictured Maura in her office, where she liked to position herself early to watch her employees arrive, pumping tiny hand weights in her suit and heels. 'They're a huge client for us. They have nearly seventy per cent of the UK paperclip market. That's not nothing, Daisy.'

'I know. I know. What can I do, though? She's my sister.' Was she really arguing about this? What a crazy job it was. Daisy had woken up late, haunted all night by dreams of buses slamming into people, brakes screeching. Now she was dashing round the house trying to find her shoes (and ideally put them on the right feet). Gary had already left, kissing her on the forehead after he'd zipped up his biking gear and mixed his kale smoothie. He'd cycle the five miles to his office, shower there, drink his smoothie, then tackle the day with his usual efficiency. She felt exhausted just thinking about it. 'I'll come by the hospital later,' he'd promised. 'As soon as the morning meeting's out of the way.' He'd left her a helpful checklist of things to do for the wedding. *Buttonholes. Dove release. Cupcake tower.* It all seemed so trivial.

Maura sighed again. 'I suppose I'll have to ask Mai to do the pitch.'

Mai, who got in even earlier than Maura; who never wore less than four-inch heels; who had shiny, lacquered nails. Daisy felt a spasm of fear. Mai would do a great job. Better than her, most likely. Something that Maura was bound to take note of during the next round of appraisals.

But Rosie was in a coma. 'I'm sorry,' she said more firmly. 'It can't be helped.'

'No, I suppose not.' Maura had not expressed any concern about Daisy's sister, or sympathy at what they were all going through. She was grooming Daisy for a leadership position, she said. *It's why I push you so hard, Daisy. I want you to reach your full potential.* Was that what you needed to succeed? Ruthless efficiency? Daisy wasn't sure she had it.

Before she left the house, she put the dishes in the dishwasher, wiped the counters and plumped the cushions in the living room. That way Gary wouldn't come home to any mess, which he hated. Then she put on her coat and determinedly left the house, later than usual. The day had a strange holiday feel to it, almost. As if something was going to change. She only hoped it wasn't for the worse.

At the hospital, her mother, who'd spent the night in the relatives' room, was standing rigid by the door, clutching her hands together so hard they were white. It was nine a.m., but she was in full make-up and subtly glinting jewellery, a cashmere jumper and little heeled boots. Daisy hadn't put on any make-up at all – it didn't seem right when her sister was lying there with cuts all over her poor face. 'Hi, Mum.'

'Darling!' Her mother was putting on her 'stranger' voice. 'Isn't this nice, Rosie's friend has come to see her.'

A woman was sitting in the chair beside Rosie, gazing down at her with that combination of discomfort and dismay that Daisy was beginning to recognise when people saw her sister's blank, pale face, covered in cuts and bruises. One of Rosie's acting friends, who she'd met once in a pub maybe, cigarette-thin, her hair in dreads, a beautiful sculpted face and multiple ear piercings – what was her name again?

Her mother said, 'Caroline, this is Rosie's sister. Are you sure I can't get you a drink, dear, or something to eat?' As if she was hosting them in her living room, not at Rosie's hospital bed. It was Caz, of course. One of the names on the list in Rosie's flat.

'No, thank you, Mrs Clarke.'

'Oh, call me Alison, dear. I saw you in that *Lear*, you know. You were wonderful.'

'Oh, thanks, I'm in a play at the Donmar right now, but, Christ! Rosie! What happened? Leo said something about a *bus?*'

Daisy said, 'We don't know. It hit her.' *The bus hit her.* A simple way of saying it, but there was so much to unpick in those four words. The bus hit her, yes, but did she walk in front of it?

Although Caz was simply dressed in jeans and a baggy grey top, she exuded a night-time glamour, an aura of glitter and smoke and worn-out dawns. Beside her, Daisy felt frumpy and plain. She said, 'It's really good of you to come, Caz. Do you . . . when did you last talk to Rosie? It's just we're trying to piece together what she was doing in the last few weeks.' Because Daisy hadn't spoken to her since the engagement party. The dull ache of shame was like heartburn in her chest.

'She left me a weird voicemail yesterday. But before that . . . well, to be honest, it's been a few months since we talked. When I got the part in this play, I think Rosie felt . . . bad.'

'Jealous?' Daisy offered.

Caz chewed her lip. 'Maybe. God, that sounds awful, I know. But it's unavoidable. You're always competing in this job, always being judged, even against your friends. I'd have understood a bit of jealousy. But she just stopped answering my texts. Didn't come to see the play, even when all our mates got tickets . . . I was a bit hurt, to be honest.'

'What did the voicemail say?' asked Daisy.

Caz sighed. 'Said she was sorry about what happened

between us. I . . . I didn't reply. I would have, probably, but – I needed a bit of time. But then Leo called me last night, before I went onstage. You know, her neighbour, he's sort of a mate. He said she'd been in an accident. I just felt so bad. If only I'd replied!' She buried her head in her hands, and it was a strange sensation, to realise other people were aching for Rosie too, not just her family. 'I was such a bitch to her. I knew she was finding it hard, me getting these parts, doing OK, and I didn't . . . I didn't try to make that easier for her. I didn't really try to understand. Oh, shit. I wish I could say sorry.'

A picture was building in Daisy's mind. Her sister, alone and isolated, not speaking to her family, estranged from her friends. Living in that horrible studio flat with the sleazy guy downstairs. Making a list of names, people she'd fallen out with . . . An idea occurred. 'Caz? Have you ever heard Rosie talk about someone called Luke?'

Caz thought about it. 'I don't think so, no.'

So why then was his name on Rosie's lips at the moment of impact? If he was so important to her, why had her family and friends no idea who he was?

Daisy had forgotten her mother was still there until a discreet cough reminded her. 'Caroline? It's so good of you to come, dear, but if you don't mind they said two visitors only, and we have Rosie's father coming soon. I'm terribly sorry.'

'Oh.' Caz, who still looked rather dazed, began to gather her parka and her tatty ethnic bag. 'Will you let me know if anything . . . if there's any change?' She bent over and unselfconsciously kissed Rosie's cold white cheek. 'Get better soon, babe, yeah. And I'm sorry for everything I – I'm just sorry, OK? I'll come back when I can.'

Rosie said nothing. Of course. Looking down at her fluttering eyelids, mauve with bruising, Daisy wondered if she could even hear them at all. She reached out a hand, tentatively, and touched her sister's, tracing the blue veins on the inside of the pale wrists. As her mother saw Caz to the door, she whispered, 'Oh Rosie, please wake up. Please?'

Rosie

Caz. Caz! I'm here. I can hear you. Caz!
Nothing. She couldn't so much as get a finger to twitch. *Come on, please? I know I've neglected you too, I never get manicures and I bite my nails and forget to use hand cream, but . . . please?* Nothing. It was torture, this, to lie there like a lump and listen to her family and friends talk about her, not be able to join in. Her body lay perfectly calm, immobile, while inside she raged like a storm. At least Caz still cared. Or was it just guilt, at how badly they'd fallen out? Because this was *Caz*, of course. Her best friend. How could Rosie have forgotten her?

'Are you remembering what happened with you two?' Mr Malcolm's voice crept into Rosie's ear.

'Sort of.' The edges of the memory were there, the overall feeling of it. And that feeling was . . . shame. 'Please, Mr Malcolm, I don't want to relive it. I know it was bad. I know I . . . I wasn't nice to her.'

'I'm sorry,' he said sympathetically, materialising in front of her. She could see Caz's retreating back through his spectral body. 'You don't get to choose the memories. That's not how it works.'

'Why do you all keep saying that?' Rosie said, irritated. 'How does it work?'

'Your brain's in a real muddle, so it's pulling out certain memories it thinks you need to see. Like your computer scanning its hard drive. Or like ... picking files up from the floor when you've knocked over the cabinet.'

'But why *these* memories? They're nearly all terrible! I ... I must be a horrible person. Is that what my brain's trying to tell me?' If everything about her life was so terrible, *could* she have tried to kill herself? She still didn't feel it was possible. But the memories were so bad.

'I don't know. I'm sorry.' He looked so sad, in his green tank top with the hole in it, that Rosie's heart ached.

'It's OK. If I have to do it, I have to. Let's go then.'

'Close your eyes.'

'Yeah, yeah, I know the drill by now.'

Dial. Spinning. Noise, blur. 20 4 2006. When was that? She couldn't remember.

The world was gone.

20 April 2006 (Eleven years ago)

The smell of the place always hit first, like a ghostly path into the memory. Here it was dust, and paper, and a slight undertone of feet. A theatre. Rosie's favourite smell in the world, ever since she was five and her mother took her and a small squirming Daisy to see a regional performance of *The Nutcracker*. Daisy had fallen asleep within minutes, but Rosie had watched, transfixed, determined that one day it would be her up there onstage. She looked around for her past self, and winced. 'That was when I had the fringe. God, it really did nothing for me.'

'You'd suit a nice bob, you know,' said Mr Malcolm, surprising her. 'Let people see your face more.'

'Oh. Do you think so?'

'Oh yes. Like that Amy Adams, you know.' He sighed. 'She is just *fabulous*.'

Past Rosie was crouched in a corner of the theatre, stretching her limbs and swallowing hard every few minutes. She wore her audition clothes, baggy jeans with holes in them and a vest top. Trying to be like the kids from *Fame*, and instead looking like a reject from New Kids on the Block. This was one of the cruellest things about being forced to relive your memories – realising all the terrible fashion choices you'd made along the way. As Now Rosie watched, hidden in shadows, a slim black girl approached, dumping a large tote bag on a chair beside her. She wore leggings and a big jumper and moved with a sort of innate focus, like all the best performers did.

'Not this shit again,' she declared, scanning Rosie quickly, her sharp South London accent in striking contrast to the grace of her movements, like a debutante at court. Sizing people up was what you did in these situations. *Is she taller? Is she prettier? Is she up for the same part?* The differences between her and Caz, not just skin colour but height and weight and style too, had always made it easier for them to be friends, because they likely wouldn't be up for the same roles. 'Cordelia?'

'Goneril.'

'Isn't that the worst name? Sounds like an STD. Old Willie really had issues with strong women, didn't he? You show a bit of gumption and it's all, like ... ' Here the girl rather startlingly cupped her breasts and declaimed: '"Come, ye spirits, unsex me here!" A bit much, methinks.'

'Gosh, she's wonderful,' said Mr Malcolm approvingly. 'If only we'd had her for that sixth-form production of the Scottish play, you know the one where I gave the lead to Janine Campbell, and she was five months pregnant by the time we went onstage? It made that scene a *lot* more disturbing.'

Rosie was watching as her past self blinked. Caz had that effect – you wrote her off as a small pixie thing, swathed in layers of jumpers and scarves and cardies (like many actors, she was terrified of getting ill), then she stood up straight and spoke and you were just mesmerised. She had 'it'. Whatever it was.

'Sorry.' Caz snapped back into her own self, peeling off her layers. 'Did the Scottish play last year on a tour of the Scottish Highlands. It's never really left me.'

'You played Lady M?'

'God, no. I played the second page from the left, and sometimes one of the dead Macduff kids. It's a tough old business, eh?'

'Sure is.' Past Rosie had thawed a bit, de-iced by Caz's warm charm. 'I'm Rosie.'

'Caroline Harper. Caz.'

'Good stage name.'

'Thanks. It's really Hazada – Portuguese.'

'I'm plain old Rosie Cooke. Sounds like a kitchen maid in a Dickens novel, doesn't it?' They smiled at each other, the flash of sudden friendship running between them, that immediate clicking that was just as powerful as attraction, and lasted far longer. Falling in friendship. Rosie tried to remember when she'd last done that. This was actually a nice memory. Soon they would do their audition pieces – Caz's Lady Macbeth, her own rendition of Juliet's 'Romeo' speech – and they'd both get the parts, because it was a truly terrible production with an insane director who wanted them all to do *King Lear* as if they were in an African military junta, and made them get into character by flinging buckets of fake blood at them and screaming, but it paid Equity rates and was Rosie's first proper acting job, plus she and Caz went to the pub every night afterwards and became best mates and it was all great.

'Time to go,' said Mr Malcolm regretfully.

'But it's not finished! I got the part! Caz and I became friends!'

'It seems this is going to be more of a . . . montage memory.'

'What?'

'Your brain's got impatient, I think. It wants to show you more. *Allons, cherie.*'

'But . . . but . . .' The memory was already dying around them, her younger more optimistic self fading, her friend disappearing, the smell of the theatre lost. The dial appeared again: 7 10 2007.

This memory flashed by. Past Rosie still asleep, even though the novelty alarm clock on her bedside table read after eleven. Caz storming into her room in an oversized fleece dressing gown and practically jumping on the bed. 'Rosie! Wake up!' Of course, they had shared a flat for years. How could she have forgotten that? She'd loved that place. High ceilings, cracked oak floors, and her bedroom looked out on a lovely leafy square in Islington.

'Huh?' Past Rosie was groggy. Rosie tried to remember why. Had she been out, starring in some exciting theatrical role? Then she spotted the uniform crumpled on the floor. No, she'd been working the late shift in a bar. Not only that, but there was a man's T-shirt lying there too. She'd brought someone home with her – not an unusual occurrence. Who? The file in her head marked 'Hook-ups, bad' was filled to bursting point.

'I got it. I got it!'

'Got what?' sleeping Rosie mumbled.

Caz now began to bounce on the bed, her braids flying. 'I'm going to be Laura! In *The Glass Menagerie*!'

That made Past Rosie sit up. 'Oh! You got it?' This was a big deal. One of the leads in the revival of a Tennessee Williams play scheduled to start in a big theatre, with a Hollywood star as the male lead. Caz would be playing his sister, a shy and troubled girl. The role called for great nuance and range. Rosie remembered her feelings that morning: shock, initially. She hadn't thought Caz was in with a shot for the play, set as it was in the American deep south. Then: jealousy. Low self-esteem. *Why do I never get anything?*

'That's so great,' she said unconvincingly. 'Wow. You're going to be Andrew Yates's sister!'

'I know. God, I can't believe it. I can't believe it.' Caz was almost manic. She got up and whirled around the room, picking her way delicately over Rosie's discarded clothes. 'This is it, baby. The big break. And you'll be next. Did you hear back about Perdita?'

'Um, not yet.' That was a lie. One of the reasons she'd drunk so much and brought this guy back, whoever he was, was to drown her sorrows at receiving the form rejection email for the role. Panic had seized her. *Caz is going to make it big, and leave me behind, and she won't want to hang out with me, and Andrew Yates will fly her out to Hollywood to star in his next film, and I'll be all alone.*

The words that always seemed to echo in her head at low moments. *All alone. No good. Not good enough.*

You stupid, stupid girl.

In the memory, Caz stopped whirling and was looking at her friend with concern. 'Hey, you OK?'

'Oh, yeah, just drank too much rotgut in the Walkabout after work. And, er, Keith's in the shower.'

'Keith! Jesus, Rosie.'

'I know, I know, I said never again. I just ... I was drunk and a bit down. But it's so great about your role! I'm so pleased for you!'

'Poor you. Give Keith the boot-out and let's go down to Pablo's, get a big greasy breakfast. My treat. No more Equity minimum for me!'

Caz was so sweet and generous, so talented, and all Rosie could do was lie there feeling jealous, letting it eat away at her like a maggot in her stomach.

She heard Mr Malcolm's light tread behind her. 'Time to move on, Rosie.'

Rosie bit her lip. It was too sad to watch it all, from the brilliant beginnings of meeting Caz, remembering the fun they'd had living together, the dinner parties where they invited randoms they met in the street and plonked big pots of experimental stews down on the scrubbed wood table; the nights they stayed up, drinking cheap red wine until the dawn broke, setting out their future careers and the stardom that would surely beckon. 'I can't watch.' Seeing the memories again, her and Caz such good friends, and knowing it wasn't going to last.

'I'm sorry. It's the only way.'

She closed her eyes on her old bedroom – God, she'd loved that room! – on a time where she and Caz were still friends. She knew what was coming next.

*

The years skipped by. 3 5 2009. Caz had got engaged to an older theatre producer who wore tweed jackets and was so handsome Rosie couldn't look him in the eye when they spoke. She'd gone to the engagement party – in a hired-out restaurant, with champagne waiters, where Caz wore a green silk dress that cascaded down her slim body – alone, and spent the whole night skulking in corners as everyone else laughed with their partners (or so it seemed to her). Rosie could see her own eyes were red, though she couldn't remember what she'd been crying about. It was a strange feeling. She remembered how the loneliness had got too much for her, and she'd texted some random guy on her phone and gone round to his, spent the night shivering on the futon in the living room that was his bed, feeling terrible about herself the whole time.

18 11 2010. Caz's new play received a glowing review in the *Evening Standard*, with a glamorous shot of her in full Edwardian dress. Rosie had thrown it in the bin before retrieving it, covered in banana pulp and coffee grounds, ashamed of herself. Caz's sudden rise to fame seemed to coincide with a slow-down in Rosie's own career. After an initial strong start – second lead at the National, an ad for shampoo that paid a ridiculous amount – she hadn't had a paid acting role for eight months. The week before she'd played a polar bear in an avant-garde production about climate change. For payment she'd received a lukewarm half in the pub, after which the director had tried to grope her. But she had to try to be happy for Caz. After all, they were best friends. Weren't they?

12 4 2017. Earlier this year, when they were barely friends

any more. Rosie standing on the pavement outside a theatre, staring at a poster of Caz in yet another play, her face illuminated and beautiful, her cheekbones sharp as razors. Hearing the bell go inside, indicating it was about to start. Then slowly walking away, tossing the ticket into the bin.

25 8 2017. Just a few months ago. On this day Caz had strolled into the coffee shop where Rosie worked, fresh from a nearby lunch with someone Rosie recognised as a top theatre critic. She wore leather trousers and a tight silky top. Her skin glowed, her teeth gleamed. She was laughing at something the critic said, and when she got to the top of the queue, she asked Serge for a kale smoothie. Healthy, beautiful, successful, loved. Her engagement ring like an iceberg on her finger. And here was Rosie, the opposite of all those things. Caz hadn't even noticed her there, skulking in the steam from the coffee machine, just carried on out to the street on a cloud of laughter. And then of course Rosie had quit her job in the café and . . . who knew? Walked under a bus? Either way, she was having a pretty bad year. A pretty bad few years.

The dizzying whirl through places and dates was making her feel queasy. She turned back to Mr Malcolm, who was staring at Serge's topknot in fascination. 'Men wear buns now, do they? How wonderful.'

'Please. I've seen enough. I get the message – Caz and I fell out and it was my fault. Can I go back now? Back to the real world?'

'Are you sure, dear? You're in rather a lot of pain there.'

'It's better than this. This is torture.'

'OK then. Count to three then open your eyes again.'

Rosie

She did. The coffee shop faded – a ghostly smell of roasted beans in her nose – and she surfaced, choking and gasping at the tube in her throat. But no one noticed, though her room was full of people. They all had their backs to her. Rosie hurriedly counted: her mother, her father, Daisy, Scarlett – today in jeans and an *Octonauts* T-shirt – and Carole, in a flowery tunic and mum jeans, make-up inexpertly applied so that her unfashionable pink lipstick bled around her mouth. 'I'm sorry, Alison, it's just that Scarlett wanted to come back and . . .'

Rosie's mother snapped, 'She's only supposed to have two visitors at once. If you're here that means I can't be with her, or Daisy. And children are such germ carriers.'

'I washed my hands four times,' said Scarlett indignantly. Rosie saw Carole's hand curl protectively on her daughter's head.

'I'm so sorry for what you're going through, Alison, I really am. I'm here to help however I can.'

'You could help by not bringing a small child into the room. It's hardly fair on Scarlett either, is it?'

Scarlett scowled. 'I'm helping Rosie. I'm talking to her. Hello, Rosie, it's Scarlett, your sister. Well, sort of your sister. We're here in the hospital with you. I rode on a big red bus to get here. Um . . . sorry, maybe you don't want to hear about buses?'

'For God's sake, Mike, can't you stop this?'

Rosie wanted to block her ears at the sound of her mother's cold, angry tone. She wished she could intervene, shout out, *She's just scared, it makes her lash out*. But it wasn't fair to boot

Carole out. She could see now that her stepmother had only ever tried her best. And if the memory in the pub with Luke was anything to go by, someone being engaged or married didn't always mean you knew how to stop loving them.

But where was Luke now? Was it over between them, were they not even friends? He hadn't come to visit so far and no one seemed to know who he was, not even Caz, who'd been Rosie's best friend for years. Was he with his wife, if indeed he'd got married? She pushed the thought away and tried to communicate with Daisy, who was hanging back against the wall, looking miserable. *Look up, Daise*, she tried to say, via her barely open eyes. *I can hear everything. I'm reliving the worst moments of my life here, so it would be great if my hospital room wasn't filled with tension too. Daisy. Daise?*

For a moment, her sister looked straight at her. 'Everyone,' she said out loud, 'I think you should stop this. They said we had to talk to her, that our voices might bring her back. I don't think this is what they had in mind. And Mum's sort of right: it's not fair to talk like this in front of Scarlett.'

'I *did* wash my hands,' the little girl said again.

Her mother barrelled out the door, and the jagged sound of weeping could be heard from the corridor. Daisy closed her eyes briefly, then turned to her half-sister. 'I know you did, sweetheart. Mum's just scared and sad, the same way your mum would be if you were sick.'

Scarlett nodded. 'I understand. Can I keep talking to Rosie? Maybe I can play her a song on my phone?'

'That would be great.'

'Come on, you have to talk to her too. The doctors said.'

'Er, hi, Rosie. It's Daisy here.'

'She's your sister too,' stage-whispered Scarlett to Rosie. 'Your same-mum-and-dad sister.'

'Right, yes, um . . . we hope you get better soon, Rosie. We're all here for you and we . . . we want you to wake up.'

Thank God for Daisy, her patience and her kindness. But wait, weren't they also not speaking to each other? They'd always been close – at least, she thought so. What could have come between them so badly? Rosie sighed. When she woke up, things would be different. She'd spend more time with both her sisters, be kind to Carole, forgive her father. *If* she woke up, that was. Would she recover and get her life back, small and broken as it was? Or was this hair-raising montage of her worst ever days, her greatest mistakes and failures, the last thing she would experience before being gone for ever? Two days. That was all she had to figure out what had happened with this bus, and try to wake herself up before it was too late.

After forty minutes listening to tweeny-bopper tunes on Scarlett's tinny little phone speaker, Rosie was quite ready for another flashback, however traumatic. Who would be her guide this time? Her grandmother, her long-ago school friend, her old teacher, Dot – who she still hadn't identified – or a random guy who'd died alongside her in the hospital? She was surprised she knew so few people among the dead community.

But there's one more, isn't there?

Shh. Rosie pushed that thought far back into the jumbled filing cabinet of her brain.

'A random guy who died alongside you? That hurts, babe.'

'Hey, Darryl. Sorry.' Rosie was glad she was hallucinating

him – if that's what this was – before the terrible injury and not after. He'd looked less handsome with bone gleaming white through his skin and his beating heart visible in his chest. Poor Darryl.

'No feeling sorry for me, mate,' he said sternly, as if reading her mind. Although he was most likely *in* her mind. Wasn't he? 'I'm gone. I'm on, like, a different plane of existence.'

'What's it like ... afterwards?'

'Oh, it's cool. Everyone is so much more chilled than in life. They have a right laugh, looking down at all the dumb-ass stuff people do on earth. I think I'm gonna like it, being dead.'

Rosie was starting to feel a bit left out. Trust her to be alienated even by hallucinations from her own brain. If that's what they were. 'What's next? I've got to get away from this Justin Bieber-a-thon.'

Darryl looked fondly at Scarlett. 'She's a cute kid.'

'Yeah. I don't think I see her much. You know – the whole nasty divorce thing. I wish I had done now. She seems cool, despite her taste in music.' What if this was Rosie's punishment, to see all the ways she'd messed her life up and not be able to change it? 'Is there another fun memory coming? Maybe the time I dropped red ice-pop on my white palazzo pants on the school trip to Scarborough and everyone thought I'd got my period? Or is it always going to be ones where I do something awful?'

'Not always. Come on.'

She closed her eyes, and the sound of canned pop music faded, and the dial appeared. 26 12 1989. Another Christmas memory, then. Somehow she doubted it would be a merry one.

26 December 1989 (Twenty-eight years ago)

The smell of pine needles and woodsmoke. Twinkling lights, a real fire in the grate, a tree laden with baubles and tinsel, presents stacked beneath. Rosie found herself in a warm and welcoming room, Paul Daniels' Christmas show on the TV, which looked tiny and boxy now. She secreted herself behind the tree, although she knew they couldn't see her. 'They' were herself and Daisy, aged five-ish and two-ish, solemn in pyjamas on the sofa, little feet dangling. Daisy's were encased in puppy-dog slippers. Rosie's hair looked scarlet in the firelight. She turned to Darryl, hovering by the tree. 'I remember this. But this is a happy memory.'

'Well, thank goodness for that, eh, mate? Just watch.'

Their father – much younger, with all his hair, in an eighties sweatshirt – was pacing behind them. 'Now, girls, remember, a nice big welcome. We've got to show Mummy we have everything under control. No mention of the little fire from the Christmas lights, OK?'

The girls nodded solemnly. Little Rosie said, 'Daddy, can we say we had chicken nuggets for Christmas dinner?'

'No, darling. Let's not tell Mummy that.'

'Because she doesn't like chicken nuggets.'

'Right. So, big smiles and remember: don't mention the fire. Or the chicken nuggets.'

Little Rosie nodded. Daisy began to suck her thumb; it was past her bedtime. Their father went nervously to the door and led in their mother, carrying a white bundle in her arms. Rosie was, just for a second, knocked back in shock. Her mother looked so young. So happy. Her red hair, the same colour as Rosie's own, rippled and flamed. She'd been a sort of ashy blonde for so long Rosie had almost forgotten her natural shade. The deep grooves around her mouth were gone, and her back was straight, and she was ... smiling. 'Look at this! So Christmassy.'

'We decorated the tree, Mummy,' said Little Rosie.

'You did a fantastic job.' She eased in next to them on the sofa, and they crowded close to her. Rosie remembered this moment. The slight unease she'd felt for the previous week – meals at the wrong time and jumpers shrunk in the wash, Santa having for the first time ever forgotten to wrap the presents – was gone, and they were all home together and it was Christmas and there were mince pies in the kitchen that she thought she'd be allowed to eat. She'd already primed Daisy to ask, as she was younger and cuter. All of them there, and now there was one more. Their mother moved aside the cheese-cloth blanket in her arms. 'Girls, here's your little brother.'

They hung over the little face in the blanket, red and closed like a petal. Rosie remembered thinking he looked a bit like a squashed tomato. 'What's his name, Mummy?' said her younger self.

'Peter, like Granddad's name. Say hello.'

Little Rosie reached out hesitantly, and the baby grabbed her finger. On the other side, Daisy was also watching in her usual quiet way. 'Hello, Petey,' she pronounced, taking her thumb from her mouth. From then on, they'd always call him that.

'That's right, darling. He's littler than you, isn't he?'

Daisy looked to Rosie for confirmation that this was now the state of affairs. 'You're not the youngest now, Daisy,' she explained. 'Petey is.' The first time she said her brother's name. Their mother gathered all three of them in her arms, and from behind, their father stroked her hair back gently, to better see his family.

'It's all of us now,' said their mother, and Rosie remembered her voice, so full of happiness. 'Our family.'

'Mummy,' lisped Daisy, saying her first full sentence. 'The Christmas tree was on fire.'

Daisy

'She's smiling,' said Scarlett proudly.

Daisy looked up distractedly from her phone. Where was Gary? He promised he'd come soon. If he didn't, what did that say about him? She didn't want to think about that, so she needed him to get here asap. 'Maybe it's just an automatic thing, sweetheart.'

'No, really. Look.'

Daisy looked. It was true – a real Rosie-smile sat on her sister's face. One she hadn't seen for years.

'I think she likes my music,' said Scarlett, pressing play once again on One Direction's 'You Don't Know You're Beautiful'.

A knock at the door announced one of the young doctors, the boy one. Daisy couldn't think of him as a man; he looked like he'd only just started shaving. 'How's it going here?'

'I'm playing her music,' said Scarlett, beaming.

'A bit of the old One Direction, eh? Think that'll wake her?'

'If only to throw the phone out the window,' Daisy said quietly. 'Is everything OK, Doctor? My parents have just . . . I can fetch them if you want.' Her mother was off crying somewhere, she suspected, and her father had taken Carole to the canteen, trying to defuse the stand-off around Rosie's bed.

'I just wanted to give you this.' He fished around in his coat pocket and pulled out a small plastic bag with a phone inside. 'The police took it as part of their inquiries, but they've decided not to investigate further. Busy with all the murders and such, you know. It was thrown clear, apparently. Still works, amazingly.'

It was Rosie's phone. Daisy stared at it. Only a crack across it suggested it had been involved in a near-fatal accident. Even the phone was old and dented, a cheap model. 'She had it in her hand?'

'They think so. Wasn't in her bag with the rest of her stuff.'

'So that means . . . maybe she just wasn't looking, maybe she just stepped out?' Daisy could hear the hope in her own voice. You wouldn't have your phone in your hand if you were going to throw yourself under a bus. Would you?

He looked embarrassed. 'Maybe. If you know the passcode,

123

you could try and get some info off it – see who she texted last, where she was going, that kind of thing.'

Daisy took the plastic bag. She didn't know the passcode – yet another thing she didn't know about Rosie's life. But if she could get into the phone, maybe it would yield some answers and she could go to her parents and say, *Look, Rosie wasn't trying to kill herself, it was an accident.* Find a release for the anxiety that stretched taut between them, stinging like snapping elastic, or for the tight ball of dread under her own ribcage. Of course Rosie wouldn't do a thing like that. She wouldn't. And yet, as she watched her sister's sleeping face ripple with strange emotions, Daisy found that she was still not convinced.

Rosie

The Christmas memory had been so lovely. A feeling of being safe and warm and cherished, the excitement of presents and cake in the kitchen, the relief of having her mother back home safe with the new baby. Rosie was still smiling as the memory faded and the world came back, some awful tinny racket playing out of Scarlett's phone and Daisy in the doorway talking to the young male doctor. God, it was dull being in a coma.

'Hey, girl.'

Rosie looked up. Melissa had appeared beside her bed, grooving to Scarlett's music. She was still wearing her school uniform and had her hair in ill-advised pigtails. 'Hey.'

'This is some awesome disc-age. Rad.'

'Er, what are you on about, Mel?'

'Isn't that how people talk nowadays? I don't know, I only

124

had fourteen years on earth and I was tragically uncool for all of them.'

'I'm sure that's not true,' said Rosie, lying. 'Have you got another memory for me?'

'Yeah. Are you starting to remember what happened to you?'

'I don't know. It's like: when I first woke up I had nothing. I was all pure and clean. A blank slate. I didn't even know my own name. And now I'm – well, I don't really like what I'm seeing. It's all arguments and sadness and, you know, general badness.' Maybe she was a terrible person. She'd alienated everyone around her, so completely it was almost a strategy. 'Mel . . . am I horrible now?'

'I only know what you know, Ro-Ro.'

'Did you ever call me that in real life?'

'Sure I did. We were pals, for a while.'

Rosie sighed. 'I'm so sorry, Melissa. If I could go back, do it all over again, we'd totally still be friends.'

'Would we? Could we make friendships bracelets and discuss the plot of *My So-Called Life* and talk about boys we fancied?'

'Of course we could. Though you know that show got cancelled after one season.'

Melissa shook her head sadly. 'That sucks. But there's no do-overs in life, Ro-Ro. That's the sad truth. You can't change any of the things that have happened to you.'

'What's the point of this, then?'

'To change what comes next. If there is a next. To try and figure out if you want your life back or not. Anyway, shall we go? Time's a-ticking. Day two.' She looked at her Casio watch again. Rosie prepped herself for another memory. It was a bit like going under a wave when you learned to surf (but when had she learned to surf?). The first time was terrifying, salt water gushing into your eyes and nose and mouth, but then after a few gos you knew you wouldn't die, and you just got on with it.

'OK,' she said, squeezing her eyes shut. 'I'm ready. It'll be a relief to get away from this bloody music, to be honest.'

'I think it's bodacious,' said Melissa, wistfully glancing at the phone. 'We don't have tunes like that in the afterlife. Anyway, come on. Where we're going, we don't need roads! Man, I love that film.'

5 September 1991 (Twenty-six years ago)

The dial, the blur – mad as it seemed, Rosie was getting used to this. Imagine getting used to be being sparko in a hospital bed, while your family bickered over you and your only respite was reliving some of the worst moments of your life. She shuddered at the thought as she opened her eyes. The dial this time had said 5 9 1991. 'How can I remember the exact dates of these memories?' she said. 'I mean, I wouldn't be able to do that if you asked me.'

'It's all in there somewhere,' Melissa explained. They seemed to be in a playground, on tarmacked ground with hopscotch squares chalked onto it. 'Everything you've ever seen or heard or felt is in your brain. Like those computers you all have now – it's just about knowing how to retrieve it. Right now your memories are all muddled up and out of their proper places, so this is your brain putting them back in order, trying to make sense of everything.'

'And this is ... our old school.' Rosie looked about her.

She hadn't thought about this place in years, but the shape of it was disturbingly familiar, as if it had sat in her head all that time, just waiting. The low cream-coloured building, the little garden beside it, the football nets and cheerful brightly coloured monkey bars. Primary school. Where the world made sense, where what mattered most was what you'd brought in your packed lunch and who got top in the weekly spelling test. Rosie had been happy there, hadn't she? A ginger-haired Mary in the nativity play, the kind of little girl who had sleepovers and invited the whole class to her birthday party. 'But this isn't . . . '

Oh. She remembered now. In the corner of the playground, half-hidden behind the slide, a young Rosie was crouched down, crying hard. That sort of jagged sobbing you do as a child (and as an adult when things are really bad) where it's like falling down a hill and you can't draw breath and you're not sure you'll actually be able to stop. She was wearing her school uniform, and Rosie could see that her shirt had marker pen on it and her hair was wild and unbrushed. What had happened to that girl in the Christmas memory, so happy and loved?

'Hello.' Another little girl was approaching – funny-looking, wearing a school skirt so long it almost skimmed her ankles. Her hair was cropped close to her head like a helmet and she wore thick pink-rimmed NHS specs.

'That's me,' said Melissa.

'Oh. The short hair, that's . . . chic.'

'I had nits so my mum shaved my head,' she said matter-of-factly. 'Look, I'm going to talk to you. I must have been going out to the loos and seen you crying – remember, we had outdoor ones still at that school.'

'Hello,' said Young Melissa again, to Young Rosie. 'Are you OK?'

'F-fine,' stuttered Young Rosie.

'You're crying. Do you want me to get Miss Rogers?'

'No.'

'OK. Do you want half of my sandwich?'

At this, Young Rosie's weeping subsided for a moment as she glanced at what Melissa was holding – an uninspiring lump of grey bread with what looked like watercress sticking out. 'We were doing vegan that year,' the ghostly Melissa explained. 'I wasn't allowed sugar, or dairy, or salt.'

'No,' said Young Rosie, turning her nose up. Then, remembering her manners, 'No thank you.'

'What's the matter? Did you fall off the monkey bars? I did that last week.'

'No.' Rosie never fell off. She could do the whole thing on one hand, even.

'Did Jason Bryan call you smelly? He called me smelly this morning.'

'*No.*' Rosie knew, even at seven, that when Jason Bryan pulled her hair and made fun of her Barbie schoolbag, he was really saying something else entirely, and she'd already learned to laugh at him and flick her hair so he'd chase after her during Kiss Tag.

'What's the matter then?'

'I . . . I . . . ' Rosie was heaving big sobs. 'My mummy is . . . I don't know.' She must have been in a bad way to confide in weird Melissa. 'She's being weird.'

Melissa nodded wisely. 'Because of your brother?'

'I don't know. Yeah.'

'She's very sad, probably. My mummy was very sad when my daddy died, and she didn't brush my hair or make my lunch for a long time so I had to go and stay with my auntie, but now she's OK.'

Young Rosie raised her face up from her arms, swollen and red. 'H-how long? Before she was OK again?'

'Ooh, I don't know.' Melissa seemed to be pondering the nature of time. 'I think it was maybe from after Christmas until the summertime.'

'Oh.' An eternity when you were seven.

'What about your daddy, Rosie?'

'He's always at work. Even at night-times now. Or he goes away on, on, conferences.' She sounded out the word carefully. She wasn't sure what it meant, but it was a bad word, because it made her mother cry and lock herself in the room, and her dad stand outside shouting, *For Christ's sake, Alison, someone has to earn the money around here.*

Gently, Melissa reached down and patted Rosie with the hand that wasn't holding the sandwich. 'It will be OK, Ro-Ro. Can I call you Ro-Ro?'

'Er ... OK.' There was a noise – a bell ringing, and the beginning of a stampede, scraping chairs and running feet and banging doors.

'Breaktime,' said Melissa, in the tones of someone saying *execution time.*

'They bullied you,' said Rosie, remembering now. 'The other kids. They were mean to you?' Memories of hiding Melissa's clothes during swimming, putting a spider in her desk, throwing a ball at her head in the playground ... 'Not them. *Me.* I bullied you too?'

130

Melissa shrugged. 'Sometimes. You were only a kid.'

'But still, it's no excuse. Your dad had died! That's terrible, I'm so sorry. Is he . . . is he there with you? Like, in the afterlife?'

'It doesn't really work that way.'

Was anyone ever going to tell her how it *did* work? 'So what's the point of this memory? You were nice to me? Was I not nice back?' That would fit with all the other memories she'd seen, a parade of her own bad behaviour.

Younger Rosie had straightened up as the bell rang, wiping her face on the back of her hand. She hissed: 'Don't tell anybody I was crying, OK?' As soon as the first children streamed out the door, Rosie was loping over to them, hair bouncing, smile on her face, only her red eyes hinting that she'd been in such a state before. Melissa was left alone by the monkey bars, with her soggy vegan sandwich and ancient duffel coat. Then, just as Rosie's heart was sinking, she watched her younger self turn back. 'Do you want to come to my birthday party, Melissa?'

'Can I?' The other girl looked awestruck.

'Course you can. I'll get my mummy to phone your mummy. If she's not sleeping all the time.'

Current Rosie looked on. 'Did you come?'

'Oh, no. Mum wouldn't let me. She had some weird ideas about germs. But we did become friends. Even though you were way more popular than me.'

More memories were slotting into place. Round at Melissa's house, eating disgusting sugar-free vegan carrot cake, making a den in the back garden with two chairs and a duvet, playing skipping games and learning to ice skate together, hand in hand, on a school trip to the rink . . . 'But what happened?

Why did we lose touch?' Had Rosie known her old friend was dead? She must have done, or she wouldn't be seeing Melissa now. Assuming this was all a product of her disordered brain, of course.

'I moved away. It happens.'

'But we could have written, or phoned or . . .' Rosie trailed off. She had a feeling it was her fault they'd lost touch, and that she might be seeing that memory again soon too. 'I'm so sorry, Mel. I wish we'd stayed friends. You were . . . cool.'

Melissa burst out laughing. 'I wasn't cool, I was a weirdo. But that's OK. None of that matters once you're gone, you know.'

'What does matter?' It suddenly seemed very important that Rosie should know this. 'Does anything? Or do you just . . . stop?'

'It's the people whose lives you touched – that's what matters. Who remember you. The difference you made. That's the only way you live on.' Melissa looked again at her schoolgirl watch. 'Come on, Ro-Ro, time to get back.'

Rosie was silent as she shut her eyes, and the playground faded, and the bright lights of the ward fizzled into focus on her lids. The people whose lives you touched. Well, this was it for her, and it seemed she'd fallen out with all of them – her parents, her sister, her estranged friends. And maybe Luke too. *Luke.* Whatever had happened to him?

Daisy

Rosie's birthday. Her flat number. The start of her phone number. 1234. 0000. Daisy had tried all the four-number combinations she could think of, and nothing was letting her into the cracked phone. She'd already frozen it four times, and had to admit defeat. She was sure that her sister's secrets lurked on there, the reason she'd walked in front of that bus, where she'd been going that day. 'Rosie, what's your passcode? Can you, like, tap it out or something?'

Her sister didn't even move an eyelid. Daisy knew that, had she been conscious at all, she'd have knocked the phone right out of her hand. Rosie had always been private. Daisy looked at the wall clock: it was mid-morning already. Time ticking away, and Rosie still in a coma. She was supposed to be delivering a pitch now, on legal issues affecting the UK stationery business. No doubt Mai was handling it with aplomb. She was probably wearing the Jimmy Choo heels she'd got for eighty quid in the sale that time. Daisy never found anything good in the sales, just misshapen jumpers that, when she got home, didn't fit her at all and which she would keep, unworn, for three years before giving to a charity shop.

Her mother stuck her head into Rosie's room. Despite the lack of sleep, despite the raw, dry air of the hospital, she still looked flawless, her make-up like a smooth armour. Daisy could feel a cold sore starting up on her own face, and knew she had sandwich crumbs on her jumper. 'Gary's here.' Her mother's voice dipped on saying her future son-in-law's name. Approval. Relief. Daisy had chosen well; she would be looked after. So why did Daisy's own heart falter?

'Oh, great.' Unconvincing. 'He must have got out of work at last.'

'So good of him, when he's so busy.'

Daisy found snappy words in her mouth, the kind she usually pushed deep, deep down. 'He's a junior consultant working with a company that makes ball bearings, Mum, and my sister's in a coma. It's the least he can do.' He should have come sooner, she thought. Her mother was giving her a strange look.

'Oh darling. You aren't—'

But she didn't get to finish the sentence. Gary rounded the corner, talking loudly into his phone, the edges of his good wool coat flapping. He'd bought it in the January sales – something he was also good at – trying on what seemed like hundreds of different ones, researching price points online, putting everything into a spreadsheet, marching all the way across town to get it a fiver off. When Rosie saw it she'd said he looked like a football manager and after that Gary hadn't worn it for a week. 'Yeah, yeah, sorry, mate, I'll have to finish up now. Bit of an emergency our end. Let's touch base tomorrow, though, yeah? Thanks, fella.'

Since when had he said things like 'fella' and 'touch base'? Daisy made herself smile as he kissed her cheek.

'How is she?' he asked, in hushed tones.

'Oh, well – no change really. They've said we should keep talking to her, though.' Daisy had been trying, but it was so hard when Rosie didn't seem to hear her. Her mother was struggling to even try.

Gary stowed his phone in its holster – he actually wore a phone holster – as her mother came out to greet him. 'Alison. I'm so sorry.'

'Darling Gary. So good of you to come.' Her mother melted into tears again. 'It's been ... Oh, Gary!'

He took charge. 'Now, now, Alison, I'm sure she'll be fine. They've said there's still hope, yes? Let me go and find someone who knows what's going on. Hello. Hello!' He waved over the young male doctor, as if calling for a waiter. Daisy saw the doctor was in the same white coat with coffee stains as yesterday, now joined by what looked like a smear of jam. At least she hoped it was jam. Hadn't been home, clearly.

'I'm Gary Rudley, Rosie's future brother-in-law. What can you tell us about her condition, please?' Daisy cringed at the voice he was putting on, the corporate manager voice, the successful-young-man voice. Same one he'd used at the mortgage broker and the bathroom showroom.

The doctor blinked. 'Not much, sir. She's in a coma and all we can do is hope her brain wakes up from it.'

'But isn't there a treatment? I was reading—'

'We've given her all the treatment we can for now. It's down to her brain, and it depends how badly injured it is. We should know more in a day or two.'

'But—'

'Try talking to her. If she recognises your voice, it might help.' His tone was polite, but doubtful.

Gary huffed back. 'Honestly, the NHS is a shambles. Just talk to her – that's the best they can do?'

'They've saved Rosie's life,' Daisy pointed out. 'And he's been here all night. Don't be rude to him, Gary.'

His mouth fell open. 'I wasn't being rude.'

'Darling, you're just upset,' her mother chipped in nervously. 'Let's not fight. Gary's very good to come.'

Daisy made herself smile, a crooked unconvincing thing. 'Why don't we talk to her like he said?' Though whether Rosie would want to listen to Gary's stories about the ball-bearing account, she really didn't know.

Rosie

'Oh God,' she said – though only to herself. 'Gary's here.'

No one answered. Melissa had gone again, and she was alone in her bubble of 'real', the world outside seen as if through a plastic cover, blurred and muffled. Like zorbing, she thought. Though what was zorbing, and when had she ever done it? Hopefully the muffling effect would keep her soon-to-be brother-in-law (urgh) at some distance, because she wasn't sure she could handle Gary. Even though she couldn't grasp the details right now, she was quite certain that her sister's fiancé was a grade-A bore.

'So, Rosie,' he was saying, in a self-consciously caring voice, 'big day for me today. Would you believe I single-handedly sorted out the entire IT system for Harris and Harris partners? Huge firm, very prestigious. But let me tell you, the servers were an-ti-quated. They were still using Linux. Imagine.'

Rosie had no idea what Linux was. She searched her memory, but something told her she had never known what it was and would never care enough to find out.

'Goodness, is that an accountant visiting you?' said Mr Malcolm, materialising in his holey tank top.

'Oh, hi, Mr M. That's Gary. He is sort of an accountant. I think. Management consultancy. Means he goes into companies and tells them everything they're doing wrong, which is perfect for him because he spends his whole life doing that to Daisy too. And to me.' See, memories. Things slotting back into place. Another aspect of her life that was bad, or disappointing.

'I suppose you won't be wanting a Gary memory then, dear.'

'No. Please, he's right there. It would be too cruel to see him in my mind as well.'

'Well, let's see what we get this time. Are you ready? You have to try and remember more, dear. That's what will help you wake up.'

Rosie braced herself. Who knew what this memory would be? Tears, shouting, physical injury of some kind, or the overwhelming sense that she, Rosie Cooke, was just not a very nice person? 'I'm ready,' she said. It was still better than listening to Gary talk about servers.

2 June 2012 (Five years ago)

Dial. Blur. 2 6 2012. A date that meant nothing to Rosie. She opened her eyes and found herself in an office. Outside, a hot summer's day, and inside the torpor lay over people's backs like a heavy rug. The office was open plan and dingy, with about a dozen people hunched over bog-standard computers that would have been outdated even in 2012 (perhaps they needed to get Gary in). A few fans struggled helplessly with the hot air, pushing it aside without creating much change in the temperature. 'Well, this place is delightful.' It had every office cliché – a sink area in the corner where the stacked-up dirty dishes hid the plaintive notes about doing your washing-up, layers of grime on everything, people shutting themselves away under big headphones.

'You don't recognise it?' Mr Malcolm was reading the posters on the noticeboard about turning out lights and remembering to empty the dishwasher, plus one dog-eared jaunty one about coming to the company picnic.

'Should I?' Rosie was sure she'd never have been caught dead in such a drab place as this. What she'd seen of her life so far had been sad and often embarrassing, but at least it was dramatic. Not boring. She imagined that was something people might say at her funeral, if she didn't wake up from this coma. *Darling Rosie, at least she was never boring, you know?*

'There you are.' He pointed to a dark corner of the office, where someone had all but barricaded themselves into a corner desk. Red hair, black trousers and a polyester top with sweat stains. It was Rosie.

'Oh God.' Present-day Rosie scrunched up her face. 'I remember now. I temped here, that summer when I couldn't get any acting work and I needed some cash . . . Jesus, it was so dull.' Back-then Rosie was as apathetic as the rest of them, tapping at her dirty keyboard with all the enthusiasm of someone going to the gallows. She seemed to be working on some kind of spreadsheet, but Rosie had no memory of what the job had been. 'They sold something – what was it?'

'Lavatory seats, I believe,' said Mr Malcolm, pointing out an example of their wares, which was propped against the wall.

Rosie watched herself for a few moments, the blank-eyed stare and occasional twitch of her fingers as she keyed in a number. She looked miserable, drained of life. 'Why am I seeing this memory? It's totally boring.' What could this have to teach her?

She heard a discreet buzzing, and Past Rosie looked around furtively before sliding her phone out from beneath a pile of printouts. And suddenly her face lit up, all the life and joy and animation it had been missing flooding back to it. A message – but from who?

A short fussy woman in a red wool suit – the worst possible thing to wear in this weather; it made her look like a sweaty post box – was barrelling across the floor, and Past Rosie hurriedly hid the phone again. 'Ah, Rosie, can you print those accounts for me? Was that your phone I heard?'

'It's just the computer, Anthea,' Past Rosie lied smoothly. 'I'll do them now.'

'See that you do, please,' said Anthea, narrowing her eyes. Then in a burst she said, 'And can't you call maintenance about the heat? It's absolutely unbearable!'

Past Rosie went to the printer and jiggled her foot as bits of paper spewed out. Although Rosie could not recall this exact day – it hadn't been memorable, clearly – she knew what her past self would have been thinking. How had she ended up there, in that dingy dirty office with Anthea telling her what to do?

A man was approaching – overweight, huffing from the short walk to the printer from his desk, his stomach spilling out from between the buttons of his short-sleeved checked shirt. 'Hi, Rosie.'

'Oh. Hi.' She didn't remember this man at all, let alone his name.

'Printer working OK?'

Past Rosie cast a disinterested look at the pages coming out. 'I think so.'

'Cos if you need the toner changed, or the paper put in or anything, you can ask me. Me and this printer go way back.' He thumped the side of the machine affectionately, and it made a choking noise and the paper stopped rolling. A nasty crunching sound came out and the machine began to beep. 'Oh, crap. Sorry, Rosie.'

'Please ... clear ... paper jam,' said the machine in a mechanical voice.

'Can you fix it?' Rosie's happy expression was fading. 'Anthea wants these for her meeting.'

'Um ... um ... let me see.' Frantically, the man – what had his name been? – was opening flaps, pulling at bits of crumpled paper, getting ink all over his shirt and hands. 'Oh God, sorry, Rosie.'

Past Rosie's eyes strayed to the window, at the heavy gold sunshine that lay over London, the cool green shades of the trees in the park outside. She seemed to make some kind of decision. She laid a hand on the man's arm – he jumped – and said, 'Listen, it's OK. I'll send it to the desktop one, OK?'

'But Anthea—'

'She can wait. It can't be helped, can it?' Rosie remembered now that she had decided in that very moment to quit this job. That she wouldn't be spending another day there. This thought – plus whatever the message had been – had left her feeling unusually generous and relaxed. 'You know,' she said to the man, 'you can do a lot better than junior salesman. You're, like, the best person here. Don't let Anthea bully you, OK?' She moved off, gracing the man – Derek! That was his name! – with a smile. He sagged, a ball of anxiety and confusion, and slowly wiped his hand over his face, leaving an inky print.

Past Rosie went back to her desk, printed the documents on another machine, and picked up her phone. She smiled. Present-day Rosie craned over to see who the message was from. *Luke*, it said.

'I'm still in touch with him?' She turned to Mr Malcolm.

141

'That's what it looks like.'

'But . . . did he not get married after all then?'

'I'm sorry, *cherie*, I don't know.'

Her past self keyed out a message – *Actually I've managed to get out early, fancy a drink in the park??* – then picked up her cheap Primark bag and marched confidently to the door and out onto the street. No one stopped her. Once there she ducked into the first shop she found, a branch of Monsoon, and quickly selected a blue and white print dress with wide straps and a swishy skirt. She couldn't afford it, but had decided that didn't matter. In the changing rooms she peeled off her boring sweaty work clothes, shoved them in her bag, then almost danced out in the dress and asked the sales assistant to cut off the tag, taking out her Visa card with what Rosie now remembered had been over-optimistic confidence. But fate was on her side. The sale went through, the tag was removed and she was out into the sunshine in her new dress, undoing her sensible plait so her red hair rippled over her pale shoulders.

Rosie was able to follow her past self down Oxford Street towards Marble Arch and Hyde Park, and there, in one of the striped deckchairs you could hire, was a fair-haired man in sunglasses and cargo shorts, reading a paperback copy of *Shantaram*. Luke. It was Luke! Her heart soared to see him and she suddenly remembered exactly how it had felt to walk out of that office and see him there waiting for her, knowing they had the whole day to sit and talk, drink the gin-in-a-can he'd bought from Marks & Spencer. When he saw her he jumped up, a smile that matched hers spreading over his face. His T-shirt was an old, faded Radiohead one, and he had faint blond stubble on his cheeks. He held his hands wide in a ta-da gesture, indicating his cleverness in securing the chairs.

Past Rosie, who had stopped walking out of sheer happiness, began to move towards him, and she opened her mouth and said—

'Time to go back,' said Mr Malcolm. 'I'm afraid Gary's trying to talk to you.'

'Oh God, not him. Can't we stay here? I think something important might be about to . . .' Her and Luke. This was important, surely? Was this her memory trying to tell her they were together after all, that he loved her as much as she felt she loved him? But then why did her family not know who he was? 'Can we just stay, just a second? Please? I just . . . Look at me, I was happy!'

'Sorry, dear. Time to resurface.'

The park, and the sunshine, and her and Luke and the deckchairs were all fading. The sound of voices was rising. The lights above her head were coming into focus. 'No . . . wait . . .' Rosie tried. 'But Luke. Luke!'

She was back in the room.

Daisy

Daisy craned over Rosie's pale, slack face. 'Did she just say something!'

'I don't know. I maybe heard a noise. It didn't sound like a word.' Gary had already given up trying to talk to Rosie and was flicking through the magazines on her bedside locker, tossing grapes into his mouth.

Daisy was panicking. She was sure she'd heard a garbled hiss from her sister's throat. Was that a good sign or a bad one? If Rosie had spoken, did that mean she might wake up? Or did it mean she was hurting in there, unable to ask for help? 'I thought I heard her say "Luke".'

'Look? Look at what?' Gary gazed round at the small room. 'Not much to look at here, I must say. Still, Rosie never did make much sense.'

'Not look, *Luke*. You know, the name? Rosie? Rosie, did you try to say something? Talk to me, if you can, or move your hand, or just blink or something? If you know I'm here? Rosie?' She hooked her fingers into Rosie's cold ones, hoping to feel a squeeze or a touch or a flicker of some kind. Nothing. Her sister lay, utterly unmoving. Daisy wasn't sure if she'd heard anything at all. Was it just wishful thinking, desperately willing Rosie to wake up, or move or speak or anything at all? 'She said it earlier, in the ambulance. Or so the doctors said. Luke.'

He frowned. 'Who's Luke? Does she know anyone called that?'

'I don't know,' said Daisy, still watching Rosie's white, blank face. 'I really wish I did.'

Rosie

A conversation was going on over her body between her mother and her almost-brother-in-law. Urgh. The idea of being permanently related to Gary was unbearable. Maybe if she woke up she could tell Daisy she'd had some kind of vision that if she married him, he'd end up killing and eating her, or he'd get really fat and she'd have to crane-lift him out of the house one day, or ... But no. Her sister knew what he was like, and she had still, freely and deliberately, chosen to get engaged to him. To a man who insisted on re-balling his socks when she hadn't put them away in the manner he liked. To a man who always called his boss by his full name, 'my boss, Philip Cardew ACA', any time he mentioned his job; a man who insisted on going to sleep by nine p.m. every night and got annoyed if Rosie ever phoned after that. Daisy genuinely wanted to be this man's wife and have his horrible square-faced babies. She didn't know her sister at all. Now he seemed to be appointing himself as a medical authority on comas.

'I've been chatting to her for ages, Alison, and I can't see any change. I'm not convinced they're right about that.'

'Oh Gary, I know they said it might help, but ... I just feel silly. I don't think she can hear us.'

'That's what I think too, Alison. I'm sorry.'

Who died and made you Doogie Howser, M.D., thought Rosie, irritated. Being in a coma really made it hard to give snarky put-downs.

'Maybe she just wasn't interested in what you were saying,' said Daisy quietly.

Gary frowned. 'What did you say, Daise?'

'Nothing. I still think we should try to find out who Luke is. You know, the name she said.'

'Oh, darling. We don't even know if that's what she said. Have you ever heard her mention a Luke?'

'Well ... no.'

But I do, Rosie thought. *I do. I only wish I could remember exactly how.*

'You'll find out soon,' said Mel's voice in her ear. 'Ready for another memory?'

'Do I have any choice?'

'Not if you ever want to wake up.'

'Then lead on, Macduff. Not that that's the actual line.'

'Ooh, *Macbeth*. We were doing that at school before I died. Never did get to find out how it ended.'

'Not well,' said Rosie, as the world began to fade. 'About as well as my life, by the looks of things.'

21 May 2005 (Twelve years ago)

A small, grotty university kitchen. A chipped and stained table. Two students sitting on either side of it, elbows up, mugs of tea cupped in their hands, talking intently. One of them was Rosie, aged twenty-one, with purple streaks in her wild red hair, in a stripy sweater-dress and green tights. The other was her university friend Ingrid, who had shiny blonde hair and a Ralph Lauren jumper knotted over her shoulders. On the radio, the Darkness were singing about a Thing Called Love. They believed in it – at this time Rosie had not been sure that she did. Ingrid, she saw, was crying.

'Jeez, Rosie, this place is filthy too,' said Mel, looking about. 'There seems to be some kind of new species of mould growing in that saucepan.'

'Oh yeah, that was when we tried to make spinach vodka. We thought it would be healthy or something. What are we talking about?'

'Just listen.'

Ingrid was saying, 'I just can't believe it, Ro. Everything's booked for the holiday and then he just dumps me! I mean, what's wrong with me?'

'Literally nothing.' Rosie was remembering now. Her friend was blonde, pretty, confident, smart, and had impeccable manners. 'Sebastian's an idiot. As soon as he starts his job in the City he'll realise the only women he meets are lap-dancers and then he'll be sorry.'

'But I loved him!' Ingrid wailed. 'Whenever I looked at him my heart did flip-flops. I mean, you feel that way about Jack, don't you?'

'Sure,' said Past Rosie uncertainly. 'I mean . . . sometimes he does irritate me. When he insists on calling people "chap" or he gets upset about having mayonnaise in a sandwich.'

Ingrid sniffed. 'Ro, Jack loves you. He's a good one, believe me. Not like bloody Sebastian and his ski-instructor *harlot*.'

'Maybe you're right. I mean, we have been together two years, maybe this is normal.' Rosie remembered. Two whole years of university, when she could have been drinking shots and snogging random boys, had been spent in virtual cohabitation with her boyfriend, doing joint shops, watching pirated films on his laptop, and even visiting IKEA . . . Oh, of course. That was who Jack was. Her university boyfriend. Clearly, he wasn't on the scene in the present day, so what had happened? Maybe this memory would show her.

Past Rosie was watching her friend sob prettily into a hanky. 'And I was so looking forward to our trip. I can't go now, I'd just cramp your style. I'll have to get a job in Daddy's firm and, and, spend the summer in *Surrey*.'

'Listen, Ing . . . you should still come. Come travelling.'

Ingrid's head shot up. 'You mean it?'

'Of course. You and Jack get on, and it's not fair you can't go just because of bloody Sebastian. It's all paid for, isn't it?'

'Oh, Ro. You're such a good friend. But I couldn't! I'd just get in your way.'

'No, no.' Rosie could see her past self warming to this impulsive decision. 'To be honest, me and Jack might get on each other's nerves if it's just the two of us. It'd be good to have someone else there.'

Ingrid was sobbing again, this time with gratitude. 'I'll be the best travelling companion ever! Daddy knows someone with a yacht on Cos, maybe we can use that.'

Rosie patted her hand. 'Sure. And I bet you meet some sexy backpacker on the way, who'll help you forget all about stupid Sebastian. Shall I make us some hot chocolate with marshmallows?'

She was stirring the pan when a young man walked in, with floppy hair and his hands shoved into the pockets of a gilet. 'All right, ladies. Just scored a bloody *great* try.' Of course. This was Jack. Strange how she'd forgotten him, when she'd spent two years sleeping beside him in a single university bed. Why had they split up?

'Change of plan,' said Rosie. 'Ingrid and Sebastian are on the skids, so it's just the three of us travelling. That's OK, isn't it, babe? You didn't really like him anyway, after he sat on your head on the rugby pitch that time.'

She watched a strange expression pass over Jack's face, which at the time she hadn't really taken in or understood. 'Sure!' he said heartily, after a brief pause. 'Need me to punch him in the nuts for you, Ing?'

'Bless you, he'd grind you to a pulp,' she said, smiling. She raised her mug, which had the *Fifteen to One* logo on it – they were all massive fans, never missing an episode. 'Here's to our travels!'

'Our travels,' echoed Past Rosie and Jack.

'I asked her along,' said Rosie now. 'We went together, the three of us.' In hindsight, perhaps it was a bad sign that she and Jack were both so keen to have a buffer between them. 'But . . . what happened next?'

'You'll see. Gosh, I wish I'd got to go to uni. Boys! Drinks with umbrellas in! Intellectual debate! It must have been so sophisticated.'

'Er, yeah, if you mean Sambuca shots and dancing to S Club 7.'

It was coming back to Rosie now, those university years, falling asleep in lectures and dancing all night, curling up on Ingrid's bed with her collection of Winnie the Pooh soft toys. Halfway between children and adults. They'd been so close, despite the fact that Ingrid was a hundred times posher than Rosie and her mother was a Swiss countess. Another thing lost along the way. Had she fallen out with all her friends? Angie, and Melissa, and Caz, and Ingrid too? What was wrong with her? 'Am I . . . ? Are the memories trying to show me all the mistakes I made, so I can try to fix them? If I wake up?'

Melissa was non-committal. 'Only you know the answer, Ro-Ro.'

'But how will I know if I'm close, if none of you will *tell* me anything? It's kind of frustrating. Did I want to die? Have I messed my life up so much I don't even want it any more?'

150

'I don't know.'

'Well, neither do I! And it's already day two and I'm no closer to understanding – all I know is I've made so many mistakes. What if I can't figure it out, and I never wake up? Please, will you help me?' Tears were pooling in her dry eyes. Real or imaginary, she didn't know. 'What if I never remember?'

'Come on, Ro-Ro, don't get upset. Let's go back.'

Daisy

Daisy stared at the laptop she'd asked Gary to bring her from work. She was in the café over the road from the hospital, the one she'd had her mini-breakdown in front of, which had Wi-Fi, having muttered something about checking work emails. Gary did not seem to find anything strange about working while your sister was in a coma, but her mother had raised her well-groomed eyebrows. 'Surely they won't expect you to, darling, in the circumstances?'

'They have a big pitch coming up, Alison,' Gary had said seriously, and her mother deferred to him, as always. She did feel terrible leaving Rosie's bedside, but she also knew she had to. Maybe, if she could find out what had happened to her sister, she could help her wake up somehow.

The café was called Brief Encounters, and was mocked up as a 1940s train station buffet, complete with old-fashioned booths and chalk boards, retro condiments, and classic British snacks. She hadn't been able to face the hospital canteen, so she'd just walked out the door until this place appeared, its windows warm and steamy, its lights

151

welcoming. Daisy had connected to the Wi-Fi, but she wasn't going anywhere near her work emails. A large coffee and cheese sandwich sat beside her, both still untouched, as she Googled comas, and had learned that in over half of cases like Rosie's, the person never woke up. Even if they did, many were never the same again. Terrified, she switched out of it and went through her sister's Facebook friends, comparing them with the scribbled list of names she'd found in Rosie's flat. Maybe one of these people would know what she'd been doing on that bridge.

Caz. That was an easy one. They'd fallen out, she said. Rosie had tried to contact her yesterday and she hadn't answered. *Angie,* that was another obvious one. Angela Timmons had been Rosie's best friend at secondary school, and Daisy remembered hovering outside Rosie's room longing to be older, as the two of them giggled and tried on eye make-up and watched *Dawson's Creek.* Daisy typed the name into the search bar and scrolled down through the pictures that appeared. Angie either had no Facebook account – unlikely – or she'd got married and changed her name. But to what?

Daisy went back to the list. *Mum.* Well, that was a can of worms she wasn't ready to open. Who knew what things Rosie needed to say to their mother? It could take years. She skipped over her own name too, for the same reason, swallowing down all thoughts of the engagement party.

Ella was another name on the list. Daisy didn't remember ever hearing about an Ella, and Rosie's Facebook friends list also didn't reveal one. Without a surname, she moved on to the rest. Dave, that was easy, but she didn't want to think about him right now. Serge she didn't know, but as it was an unusual name, Facebook told her it was Rosie's boss at the coffee shop she worked in, who was also in a ska band called All Funked Up.

Mel was the next name. She tried to think if Rosie had a friend called that. A distant bell was ringing. A far-off impression of egg sandwiches and a too-long school skirt. That weird girl in Rosie's year. What had her name been? Smelly Melly. Weird Melissa. Melissa . . . Carter! That was it. Melissa Carter. Rosie had befriended the strange girl, and for years she'd come round to their house to play. She'd always been kind to Daisy, letting her join in their games even though Rosie would roll her eyes and say she was too little.

There was nothing on Facebook, so she quickly Googled Melissa Carter. An article from almost twenty years ago came up, from a local paper in Kent. *Teen dies in overdose.* Daisy stared at it, horrified. What a terrible story – the girl, who in the picture looked nerdy and bookish, not the type to even sneak cigarettes behind the bike sheds, had swallowed a bottle of sleeping pills in her bathroom at home, and never woken up. What would drive a fourteen-your-old to that? In the article it said she'd moved to Kent when she was eleven, which maybe explained why she and Rosie had lost touch. So why did Rosie have the name of a long-dead girl on her list?

'Can I get you something else?' Daisy jumped as the guy from behind the counter spoke near her elbow. He was clearing the nearby table, and nodding towards her untouched sandwich. 'If you didn't like it, I can make you something else. I do a mean bacon butty.'

Daisy blushed, remembering how she'd cried on him

yesterday. 'Oh! Thank you, sorry, I just got distracted.' She nibbled a bit to be polite, though her stomach felt leaden. 'Is that pesto?'

'Yeah,' he said proudly. 'I know it's not very *Brief Encounter*, but I like to add a little something extra. A twist on a classic.'

'It's good,' she said truthfully. 'I'm just not very hungry. I'm sorry.'

'How are things today, then?'

Oh dear, she'd hoped he might not remember. That maybe crying women were something he encountered on an hourly basis. 'Oh, you know.' She wondered how to explain the laptop. 'I'm not working. I just need to contact some of my sister's friends.'

'Nothing wrong with working,' he said, neatly stacking the cups and plates from the table. 'At times like this, you do whatever it takes to get through. Normal rules don't apply. I won't judge if you work or do nothing at all.'

'Thank you,' said Daisy gratefully. 'I'm not sure my boss would agree.'

'I know what you mean; my boss is a real slave-driver. I'm in here all hours. So if you ever need to chat . . . ' He somehow hoisted all the crockery in one hand and held out his other. It was strong and broad. 'Adam,' he said.

'Daisy. I'm sorry I didn't eat the sandwich. It's not the sand-wich's fault, honest.'

'It's not me, it's you, is what you're saying.' He raised his eyebrows. Daisy felt a smile spread over her face, before real-ity asserted itself like a bucket of cold water. Why was she flirting with a café guy when she was engaged and her sister was at death's door?

'Er, I better get back to the hospital,' she said quickly. 'There might be some change.'

'Here.' He scooted back behind the counter and, using tongs, selected a slice of Victoria sponge from the display on the counter, flipped it neatly into a brown paper bag. 'Take this. I insist. Everyone can always manage cake, even at the worst of times.'

'Oh, I couldn't . . . '

'Course you could. It's in my interests really, because once you taste it then you'll come back again and again and be my best customer.' He gave her a wide smile. Daisy felt it hook into her, dangerous, scary, and mumbling her thanks, she gathered up the laptop and stumbled out.

Rosie

' . . . so then Mr Cardew, that's Philip Cardew, ACA, said, "Gary, you'll go far in this business. I've never seen spreadsheets with this much detail!"'

'That's wonderful, Gary. So the promotion . . . ?'

'In the bank, Alison. At least, I'm almost ninety-nine per cent sure. I better go and call the office, in fact. Time waits for no man in management consultancy!'

Rosie rolled her eyes, and was gratified when they actually complied. *Thanks, guys!* No one noticed, however. Her mother was still fluttering adoringly at Gary, and Daisy had just wandered in, looking slightly dazed, carrying a small paper bag. *Hey, everyone, I'm here! I'm awake! I just can't speak to you!* Nothing. To them, it must look as if she was gone, absent, practically dead already. It was very frustrating.

'Where have you been?' their mother said suspiciously, as Gary ostentatiously went out to the corridor to make his phone call. (*'Phil! Fella!'*)

Daisy said, 'Nowhere. Do you want some cake?'

'Oh no, dear, have you any idea how many calories are in that?'

Daisy's hands crumpled the bag. 'How is she?'

'The same.' Their mother sighed. 'It's just so hard, not being able to do anything.'

'We should talk to her. Hi, Rosie. It's me. Daisy. Um . . . I'm here with Mum.'

'Do you really think she can hear you, darling?'

'I don't know. We have to try, though, don't we?'

'I just . . . it's so difficult. I'm so tired and worried.'

'I know. You could always go to ours and sleep for a bit if you wanted. Get some rest?'

'Thank you, darling. I should really go home, though – I need some more things, clothes and so on, and I have to sort Mopsy out, he does hate being left alone. I was thinking perhaps I'd check into a hotel. You know, it could be a while.'

'What do you mean?' Daisy frowned.

'Even if she does wake up, there's no guarantee she'll be . . . the same. She might need therapy, help to walk and talk again. She may not be herself.'

How rude! thought Rosie, indignant. *Of course I'm myself. I'm exactly the same. I just . . . can't move or speak.*

The thought of being trapped like this, alive and entirely herself, but inside the prison of a broken body, was so horrific that she blacked it out. It wouldn't come to that. She was sure. It wouldn't. Her memories would come back, and she would wake up, and everything would be OK. She would put right all the mistakes she'd made, which were playing out again inside her damaged brain.

Daisy was wrinkling up her forehead like she did when she was trying not to cry. 'But ... there's still hope. She might wake up. It's early days still.'

Their mother leaned in, pressing Daisy's arm. 'Darling, I hope you don't mind me asking, but is everything OK with you and Gary?'

'Of course it is. What do you mean?'

'Well, it's just ... you've been a little short with him, and you've seemed distracted even before this. The wedding's in six months and you haven't decided about the table plan or the menu choices or—'

'Mum!'

'I know, I know it's not important right now, but darling, I just had to ask if you were ...'

'What?'

Her mother looked wretched. Talking about feelings was not her style. 'If everything was all right.'

'It's fine. I'm just busy. I'm on the partnership track, Mum. I have a lot of responsibility.'

'And that's wonderful. But wouldn't you maybe think about ...?'

'What?'

'Well, once you're married, you might step back a little? Gary won't like it if you're always home at midnight, exhausted and crying, will he?'

Daisy gaped at her. 'But what else would I do?'

At this, their mother seemed to get cross. 'I don't understand this obsession with always having to *do* things. In my day, having children was enough to be getting on with. And now you have to be a CEO as well. Tell me how that's an improvement, darling.'

'But Mum, I don't have any children.'

'Not yet. But after the wedding . . . '

Rosie was sure she could see her sister shudder. It was torture to lie there listening to this conversation and not be able to crash into it, tell her mother it was 2017, for God's sake, and anyway her own homemaking ways hadn't been enough to stop her husband running off with a payroll clerk called Carole. Daisy's shoulders were sagging.

'Just think about it,' said their mother, lowering her voice and treating Daisy's arm to another squeeze. 'Here's Gary now. Be nice, darling. He'll look after you. And that counts for a lot, believe me. I'll just pop to the loo now you're back.'

She doesn't need looking after! Rosie shouted, inside her head, as their mother left the room. *She's fine, just fine.* But was she? Had Rosie any idea what was going on in her little sister's life? Their mother had mentioned crying, exhaustion. Rosie had a nasty feeling the answers were there, if she rooted around long enough in her disordered brain. But was she ready to find out?

Gary was back now. 'Mr Cardew says I'm much missed! I better go in tomorrow, Daise, is that OK?'

Daisy was blinking away tears. 'What? Oh, of course. There's not much we can do here anyway, except talk to her.'

'I tried that. I'm not convinced, I have to say.'

Rosie couldn't help but remember the last thing Gary had said to her before all this, hissed in her face outside that wine bar: *If you ask me, your family would be a lot better off without you, Rosie.* But try as she did, she couldn't make her face give him the stink-eye. She had to just lie there, placid and calm, while inside the rage ate away at her.

'What have you got there, Daise?'

'Oh, just a bit of cake. Want some?'

'Refined sugar? On a weekday?'

'Normal rules don't apply when someone's in hospital,' Daisy said, popping a piece in her mouth. 'Oh!'

'What?'

'Nothing. It's just really good cake.'

'Don't forget about the wedding. We promised we'd lose ten pounds each. That reminds me, I need to talk to you about the centrepieces. Mr Cardew said they had Sicilian lemons at theirs, so I wondered if—'

Daisy interrupted. 'Listen, I thought I might drive Mum home to Devon tonight. She needs to pick up a few things and sort out the cat. We could come back first thing tomorrow. Is that OK?'

Gary was frowning. 'But why do you have to go as well?'

'I just – I think Mum shouldn't be alone. And besides, there's some things . . . there's . . . Look, Gary, don't you think it's strange Rosie goes under a bus like this, when we haven't spoken in months?'

'You mean, you think she . . . ?'

'I don't know. I'd have said Rosie would never do that, but how would I know? I've basically cut her out of my life, and she's been living in that horrible little flat all alone, and her career's in the toilet and she seems to have fallen out with all her friends.'

Hey! Rosie tried to frown, and failed to move so much as a muscle. Dammit.

159

'What if it wasn't an accident?' Daisy went on, her voice low. 'I need to find out.'

'But will going to Devon help you with that?'

'I don't know. I just . . . have to check something, that's all. Can you be on call, if something . . . goes wrong? Talk to her, like they said?'

Gary sighed, rubbing his hands through his gelled hair. 'Of course. But I can't stay all night, I have an early start.'

'All right.' Daisy and Gary turned to stare at her. 'I wonder if she can even hear us at all,' Daisy sighed.

If only you knew, thought Rosie. *I can hear every word.* Although, now that she thought about it, she was very tired and it might be nice to rest a bit. It was clawing at her, exhaustion spreading through her body like the chill of deep water. What was Daisy going to do in Devon? What had she figured out?

She might know more than I do myself. That was Rosie's final thought before she suddenly blacked out altogether.

'Hello? Hello, is anyone here? Melissa? Darryl?'

Silence. Rosie was afraid. All through this terrible strange time, except for the moments between the bus hitting her and waking up in A&E, she'd been more or less conscious, moving in and out of her memories in a dreamlike state, seeing it all in a diaphanous blur. Now it was black. She could see nothing, hear nothing. Only the sucking silence of the inside of her head.

'Rosie?' said a voice.

Relief flooded her. She wasn't totally alone, then, here in the dark. 'Mr Malcolm, is that you?'

'Yes, dear.'

'I can't see! What's happening?'

'I don't know, dear. There may have been a change in your condition. You could be getting worse. You have to try and wake up, Rosie. Time is running out!'

'I'm trying! Wh-why are you here? Another memory?' The darkness, the silence, it was pressing her all over. *Am I dying?* Rosie kicked away from it, like a panicked swimmer trying to reach the surface of the ocean. Just to see something, to remember something, to hold on to a piece of who she was. 'I don't like this! Can we go away from here?'

'Of course, *cherie.*'

To Rosie's relief, the world began to clear again. The memory world, anyway. The dial read 17 9 1999. School. Back when things still made some kind of sense. Rosie seized on it, panicking, and off she went.

17 September 1999 (Eighteen years ago)

When she opened her eyes again she was in her old secondary school. She recognised it immediately from the smell of
rubber gym mats and dust. They said smell was the most powerful way to evoke memory, and Rosie would have to agree.
It was the assembly hall-slash-gym, shrouded in darkness and
lined with stackable seats, and a younger Rosie was standing
on the stage in a spotlight.

'Of course,' she said out loud. Not that they could hear her.
'The school play. What was it again?'

Mr Malcolm was there with her in the dark. *'Pirates of
Penzance.* A bit advanced, maybe, for schoolchildren, but it's
just so fabulous. *Magnifique!'*

'You directed it.'

'And you were the lead. Mabel. Gosh, I had ever so
much trouble getting the school board to agree to that
wave machine.'

'Didn't it rot through the floorboards?'

162

'Wonderful times,' said Mr Malcolm nostalgically. 'Totally worth it.'

Rosie focused on her past self, illuminated in the light. Pale, thin, her red hair flowing dramatically as she declaimed her lines. Then suddenly, Past Rosie ground to a halt and announced in her own, vaguely West Country accent, 'I can't do this.'

'That's not the line, Rosie.' This from Past Mr Malcolm, who was standing in the shadows near the front of house.

'Hey, there you are!'

Past Mr Malcolm didn't look much younger. He was the kind of man who must have been born wearing tank tops and with a bald patch. 'What's the matter, Rosie?' he asked her past self.

'I'm sorry. I can't do this.'

'The solo?'

'The whole thing. Act. Sing.' Past Rosie's shoulders were drooping, her face miserable. 'I have to . . . drop out.'

'But . . . what?' Mr Malcolm was bewildered, as well he might be. She'd fought off every other girl in the drama group to get this part, and had been rehearsing it for months. 'Rosie . . . are you having stage fright, is that it?'

'No. I just . . . What's the point of all this? Musical theatre. Dancing policemen. It's silly.' Past Rosie did not sound convinced, and no wonder; none of what she was saying was what she actually thought. So what was going on?

Mr Malcolm gave an audible gasp. 'But . . . you love musical theatre! You helped me organise the school trip to *Les Mis* last year!'

'Yeah, well, I've changed my mind. I'm into rap now.

Gangster rap. And this . . . ' Waving her arms to encompass the stage and the costumes and the lights, the troop of pirates and policemen behind her, awkwardly frozen mid-dance routine. 'This isn't my thing. I . . . I'm sorry.'

'But Rosie, we need you! You're the lead! You're the—' He choked on the last word: '*Star.*'

Rosie would kill to hear that now, when she often waited four hours just to audition for the chorus, but at fifteen she merely tossed her red hair, trying to look nonchalant and cool. 'I'm sorry, Mr M. I can't. Someone else will have to do it.'

'But there isn't—'

'Me! I can do it!' One of the pirates threw off their hat and peg leg.

Now Rosie groaned. 'Sarah Bloody Martin. She was my understudy.'

'I know it! I know every line!' Sarah Martin threw herself forward dramatically, adopting a theatrical pose, and launched into the song. 'Poooor Wand'ring ONE!' As she hit the high note, the lights on the ceiling vibrated alarmingly.

'That's why I wanted you,' said Mr Malcolm, the ghostly one, sadly. 'She had range but just no heart. Her voice was so harsh.'

'And I let you down,' said Rosie, watching her past self. 'I just walked out of the show? What on earth was I thinking?'

'Two days before curtain-up. What a to-do it was. Sarah was right, though, she did know every word. *Malheureusement.*'

And she'd been the toast of the school, Rosie could now remember, and gone to the Leavers' Dance with Drew McKinnon, the lazy-smiled semi-Goth who took all the male leads in the school plays, and now had a recurring role on

164

Hollyoaks. Though, now that she thought of it, she was pretty sure Drew was gay. And Rosie, what had she done? There was a big blank in her memory where the ball should have been. No dress, no date, no limo, no pictures. Had she missed her own Leavers' Dance?

'Why did I do it?' she asked, semi-rhetorically. 'Why would I walk out on a big role like that?'

As if to answer her question, the door at the back of the hall opened and in slunk a boy in a leather jacket, with jet-black hair and blue eyes that went right through your heart. The same one from the memory near the bike sheds. *Boy* was just about correct – he was sixteen – but he looked like a thirty-something playing a teenager in *Dawson's Creek*. Both Drew and Sarah paused in their romantic duet to stare at him. And as for Young Rosie, a quiver seemed to run right through her body. Her face, which had been twisted, as if she might cry, lit up, and she threw off the remnants of her costume, revealing ripped jeans and a tight black vest, like Sandy in *Grease*. *Tell me about it, stud.* Rosie noticed that her past self had new and painful-looking holes punched all through the cartilage of her ear, which seemed to be infected. She raised a hand to her own ghostly ear, feeling the bumps there. She had to put make-up over them for auditions now, and secretly she had always regretted getting them, though she would have undergone considerable amounts of torture before admitting that to her mother.

'I think that's why you dropped out,' whispered ghostly Mr Malcolm.

'Bryn,' Rosie said bleakly. So that was still ongoing. The School Bad Boy, the kind who shoved younger kids down toilets and set fire to science labs and already had a tattoo even though he wasn't legally old enough. Bryn thought some things were cool – fire, tats, booze – but most things were lame, and that included being the lead in the school play. And, it seemed, Rosie was pretending she thought so too. 'So I just quit. For a boy.'

Mr Malcolm sighed. 'It was such a shame. You were made for Gilbert and Sullivan, with your Titian hair. So very Pre-Raphaelite. Look at Past Me, I'm a wreck.'

As Young Rosie fled down the aisle and leapt at Bryn, her legs locking round his as her mouth suckered onto his like a remora fish, Sarah Martin declared, 'What an amateur. Drew, let's do this.' And the school band started up again and the lacklustre singing resumed. In the darkness of the hall, the younger Mr Malcolm took out a cotton hanky and shakily wiped his face. He looked devastated.

Rosie turned to his later incarnation. 'You . . . you really wanted me in the part? You weren't upset just because I left you in the lurch?'

'You were so good, Rosie. You had a softness, a vulnerability. It would have been wonderful. And the show was all I had. I was a lonely single teacher in a country school, with a cat and a sick mother in a nursing home. It meant so much to me.' He looked back at the door, where Rosie had disappeared. 'Not that I really blamed you. He had something, that Bryn boy. Bane of the teachers' lives, but still – he'd have been dazzling onstage.'

Something occurred to Rosie. 'Mr Malcolm . . . were you . . . eh?'

'Batting for the other team?'

'We just say gay now, usually.'

'I suppose. I never . . . found out, exactly.'

'You mean, you never . . . ?' It was strange to be discussing this with her old teacher, even though he was a) dead and b) a figment of her imagination.

'I was engaged to a woman when I was younger, but in those days you waited till marriage before you did . . . any of that business. She broke it off, of course, thank goodness. She's happily married now, several grandchildren – we sent Christmas cards while I was alive. And me, well, attitudes had changed so much. I was working my way up to maybe doing something about it . . . then I got ill. Cancer. And that was that. *Fin.* Not very much to show for a life, I know.'

Rosie bit her lip. They'd made fun of him at school, his shiny bald head, his smell of mothballs, the tweed jacket he wore every Monday, Wednesday and Thursday, his slight stutter when he had to tell anyone off. And all the while this man had had his own joys and sorrows and dreams, and his life had run itself out in obscurity. 'But you had so much impact, Mr Malcolm. You've got a former student who's on TV! And me, I did some acting, even if I didn't exactly . . . And Sarah Martin! She must be up to something high-powered these days.'

He smiled. 'She's at the Arts Council. Gives out grants and tells people where they're going wrong.'

'Sounds about right. And I bet you had hundreds of other students who were in your plays, who love music and drama even now because of you, or who got really good at French and went to work at the UN or something.'

'Do you think so?'

'Of course. I know I love it. Loved. Sorry, I don't know what tense to use.'

'But Rosie . . . you've given up acting, haven't you?'

'Um . . . no. Not exactly.'

'You haven't been to an audition in over a year. You've been applying for office jobs and thinking about training as a teacher. That sounds like giving up. And you were doing so well before. I followed your career, you know. Before I shuffled off.'

Rosie looked at the floor, where the ghostly markings for different sports looked like crime-scene diagrams. Mr Malcolm wasn't real, she had to remind herself. Anything he was telling her was something she already knew, in some deep recess of her mind. 'I . . . I lost my confidence. And Caz, that's my friend – or was – she's having this insane run of success.'

'You were jealous.'

'Yes. I know that's pathetic.'

'Rosie, I'm going to tell you what I told Sarah Martin when she came to me in tears because I'd given you the lead in *Pirates*. Just because someone gets an opportunity in life, it doesn't mean it's been taken away from you. It just means it was for them. Yours is out there somewhere. Your job is to find it.'

'And how did she take that?'

'Not well. Her mother came in to shout at me.'

Rosie smiled ruefully. 'I guess I really messed up. Then and now. I loved *Pirates*, too. I used to secretly listen to the soundtrack when Bryn wasn't about. I hid it inside an urban grime CD case. I'm so sorry, Mr M. What a stupid, selfish thing to do.'

Mr Malcolm looked at his ghostly watch. 'We better go back, dear. This has been a long epiphany for you. Rather exhausting, all those revelations.' The school, and Sarah Martin's harsh top notes, Drew McKinnon's louche posings, and all the pirates and policemen and ladies began to fade.

'Wait!' Rosie clutched the sleeve of his cardigan. 'I meant what I said. You were such an inspiration to me, you have no idea. I'm sorry I never told you that while you were alive.'

He chuckled. 'Nobody who teaches teenagers expects gratitude, Rosie dear. But *merci*.'

'Mr Malcolm ... will I get another chance? To go back to acting, I mean?' Rosie was afraid of what she was really asking. *Will I wake up? Will my life still be there or is it stopped, over, frozen in the terrible mess I made of it?*

'I don't know, dear. Let's go back now.'

Curtain down, lights, exit, pursued by a Bryn.

Daisy

'There was no need for you to drive me, darling. I'm perfectly capable of getting the train.'

'It's OK. There're some things in the house that might help Rosie, jog her memory, maybe.'

'I don't feel right leaving her by herself.' Her mother had been fidgeting the whole way in the car, checking her old Nokia phone every few minutes, fiddling with the heating, scratching at her arms. Daisy recognised the signs of anxiety. She also didn't like leaving Rosie – what if something happened while they were gone? And tomorrow would be day three – but she felt strongly that this was the way to help her sister. Rosie had written that list for a reason, and Daisy had to find out why those names were on it. Starting with Angie Timmons, who as it happened still lived in the village.

She said, 'I know. But it's just for the night, and Dad's there anyway.'

Her mother's face was stricken. 'I just don't know what to tell people. She walked in front of a bus! What would make her do a thing like that?'

'She fell in front of a bus,' Daisy corrected her. 'It's not the same thing.' But given the list of names, and what Caz had said about Rosie's message, was her mother closer to the truth? You didn't start contacting people from your past unless you were having some kind of life crisis. What if she'd been trying to make amends? Or say goodbye?

'Darling, don't drive so fast. We don't need another accident.'

'I'm five miles under the speed limit, Mum.' But she slowed down all the same. Thankfully the traffic was light, and it wouldn't take too long to reach the house. 'Honestly, Mum, she's got people with her. You need to look after yourself anyway. Let Dad do some of it.'

It was the right thing to say. Unlike Rosie, Daisy was very good at managing her mother. She'd had to be. 'It was like this when you were younger too. You don't remember, you were too little. But he was always away, at conferences, at the office – of course, we know now what he was really up to some of the time. I was very lonely. Especially after . . . everything.'

Daisy kept her eyes on the road. 'I know, Mum. It must have been very hard.'

'You'll find out. Wait till you have small ones and Gary's working late and you're sitting there alone night after night watching Open University films about the mining industry because it's the only thing on telly. At least you have that Netflix thingy, darling. Your generation has no idea of your advantages.'

Daisy didn't know how to explain that, to her, the idea of children seemed as distant and terrifying as the sun turning to a supernova. And especially having children with Gary. 'You know, Mum, just because we're getting married doesn't mean that'll happen right away . . . '

'Of course it will. Don't worry, darling, there's so much they can do nowadays.'

Sometimes Daisy wondered if her mother wilfully misunderstood her.

'Anyway, you're young. Sensible. You know time's ticking on and you've grabbed a good man, settled down.'

Was that what she'd done, grabbed him? As if the music had stopped in some game of Musical Chairs, and she'd seized on Gary as the most promising chair? Good prospects. Domesticated. What more did she want? 'I didn't mean because we couldn't have kids, Mum, I meant . . . maybe we'd wait.'

Her mother sighed. 'That's all you young people do. Wait to grow up, wait to settle down . . . Well, life doesn't always work that way, darling, and that's just a fact. Sometimes time runs out. I was only twenty-six when I had you, you know. And twenty-eight when—'

She stopped. The atmosphere in the car thickened into syrupy silence. Daisy held her breath. Now was the moment to discuss it. Be really open. Say what they truly felt. Talk about all the reasons Rosie might, just possibly, have fallen (or walked) in front of a giant London bus. 'Mum . . . '

Her mother leaned forward and turned the radio dial, letting out tinny music. 'Goodness, what a racket. Is that what they call pop nowadays?' And complaining about modern music took them over the brief hump, and all the way to the house.

Rosie

It was dark on the ward. Almost the end of her second day in a coma. Time running out. The lights were lowered, and outside evening was drawing in. Rosie was, for the first time all day, alone. Just her in the small room, and the beep of machines and the sound of hushed voices outside, nurses passing to and fro. At least she could see again, through the small crack in her eyelids, after that strange blip. That was some relief.

OK. Review what she knew so far. She was Rosie Cooke, aged mid-thirties-ish, from Devon, one uptight mother, one harassed father. One quiet sister who was, it seemed, three years younger, and one half-sister who was a lot younger and seemed like kind of a cool kid, despite her taste in music. She was single – but where was Luke? – and lived alone in a studio flat with a dodgy neighbour. Until recently she'd worked in a coffee shop and had for a number of years tried to be an actress.

And she'd hurt so many people. She'd been the worst daughter, sister, friend imaginable. She'd failed at everything. She'd lost touch with poor dead Melissa, let Mr Malcolm down, and neglected her grandma, and, well – she could hardly have been nicer to Darryl, seeing as they'd only met when his chest was being cracked open by a rib-spreader. But could she perhaps have communicated more kindness to him in that one look they'd shared?

'You're driving yourself mad,' Darryl commented. He was sitting in the chair beside her bed, flicking through the copy of the *Times Literary Supplement* her mother had brought. Rosie was in hospital with her brain smooshed and her mother still wanted her to have improving reading material.

'There's not much else to do here. Any chance you could use your ghostly powers to switch on *Escape to the Country*?'

'Mate, I'm not a ghost. And there's no time. We've got to go.'

'Maybe it'll be another memory with Luke?' She could hear the longing in her voice. 'I mean, that wasn't the last time I ever saw him, was it? In the park?' It couldn't have been. She could sense that the memories marked 'Luke' were in a huge towering filing cabinet, the doors secured with padlocks that were bulging under the strain. 'We were happy. We spent the day together. There must be more to our story. Can you show me that?'

'It doesn't work that way, sorry, mate. Come on.'

The world faded. The dial spun: 15 7 2005. She knew when that was. That summer. The one she'd met Luke. And for once she fell into her memory smiling.

15 July 2005 (Twelve years ago)

The first thing Rosie felt was sand under her feet. She inhaled deeply, smelling the sea and flowers and sizzling meat. It was a beach at night, a little harbour with boats bobbing in it, and further along the sand, a small taverna where the delicious meat smell was coming from. 'I know this,' she said. It was Crete. It was a few days after she'd met Luke on the beach. 'Where am I? Oh, there.'

Past Rosie was coming down the beach with her sandals in her hand, long bare legs in cut-off denims. Her hair was rippling down her back, a pink flower stuck over one ear, and despite her caution in the sun she had a soft glow all over. 'I look so happy.'

Of course she was. She was in Greece, a perfect sunny day fading into a beautiful warm night, the moon turning the calm sea to a silver mirror. She looked good, and she was on her way to meet the cute boy from the beach, a whole night with just the two of them. Plus, she was already slightly drunk from the bottle of toffee vodka she'd downed before leaving the holiday apartment.

She watched her past self almost dance across the sand, like in a Duran Duran song, and pause at the taverna to brush sand from her feet and put on her raffia sandals. When she saw Luke, her face almost split with smiling. Waiting for her at a table with a beer in front of him, his tanned arms resting on the checked table cloth. He wore a short-sleeved shirt and the bridge of his nose was slightly red. He too was grinning like an idiot. 'Hi!'

'Hi!'

'Just you tonight?'

'Oh, yeah, the others were a bit worse for wear. I hope that's OK?' Rosie still couldn't remember who she'd been on holiday with. Ingrid and Jack, maybe, based on the earlier memory. But if she had a boyfriend, why was she grinning at this new guy like an idiot?

'God, of course!' They could hardly look at each other without smiling.

Luke fumbled for a menu, written in tourist English, laminated with pictures of the food on it. But they were twenty-one. This passed for fancy. 'Um, what would you like? A fillet of turbo fish? Sounds racy.'

Rosie played along. 'I might go for the stack with pooper sauce.'

'It does not say that?'

'It does!' They giggled.

'You need a drink.' Luke looked round for the waiter. 'Er, *giasou* . . . '

'Yes,' the waiter said, bored. Past Rosie ordered some hideous concoction called a Malibu Sunrise, and when it came it was in a huge frosted glass with sparklers, straws and lurid pink liquid inside. They ordered food they wouldn't eat – too nervous, too excited – fried calamari and dolmades and pitta bread and tzatziki.

'So,' said Luke, when they were both a drink in and slightly less nervous. 'It's tomorrow, isn't it? Your flight to Morocco?'

'Yeah.' Past Rosie visibly drooped. 'Last leg of our trip, then it's back to rainy old Devon. My parents want me to temp while I find an office job in London. Mum thinks accountancy would be great for me.'

'But you don't?'

'God no. I . . .' She turned shy, afraid he might laugh. 'I want to go to drama school. I should have done it at uni, but Dad was worried it was a "soft" option.' *You've got to work out what you want to do with your life, Rosie!* Rosie didn't know what she wanted. Except she did, but she didn't think she could actually be an actress. You needed money for that, to tide you over in lean times. You needed contacts. And you had to be good. She'd starred in three shows at university, and after the last one, a production of *The Tempest*, the director had clutched both her hands and said, 'Rosie. You MUST go to drama school. Promise me.' And she'd laughed uncomfortably and gone to get drunk with the cast, but her heart had swelled up and up in her chest. Could she? Maybe she could. But she knew what her mother's face would look like when she said she wanted to go to drama school and she couldn't bear it. So instead of making a decision, she'd run away.

'So you did Business Studies instead?' He'd remembered. He'd been listening.

176

'You can't get much more different, right?'

'Did you act at school?' Luke was slurping down the last of his second beer. They all drank so much back then, free from worries about work or babysitters or getting the last train home.

'Yeah. I was meant to be the lead in something but I . . . I didn't in the end. Maybe it's too late now. That's what my parents say, anyway.'

Present-day Rosie winced. Poor Mr Malcolm. What a twat she'd been, dropping out of that play.

'Rosie, that's ridiculous,' said Luke hotly. She liked his passion. His fair hair flopped over his tanned face as he scowled. 'You can't be too old for anything in your twenties.'

'Except, maybe, wetting the bed.'

'A guy in my hostel did that last week. Too much raki.' They both laughed.

'You really think I should do it?' she said.

'If it's your passion.' He grew sombre for a minute. 'You and I both know, Rosie, that life is short.' Past Rosie put her hand shyly over his, and he gripped it, and Rosie remembered how that felt, her heart trying to beat its way out of her chest. But she couldn't remember what had happened to Luke. He'd lost someone? For that matter, what had happened to her?

He took another gulp of beer. 'When my dad was ill, he made me promise I wouldn't go into some crappy job just to make money, like he had. That I wouldn't settle down until I'd lived a bit, explored the world. So here I am, travelling on his dime.' Of course. She remembered now. His father had died when he was fourteen. He'd left Luke money in his will, which he'd stipulated had to be used for travel. She'd thought it was an amazing thing to do, one her own parents would never think of.

Past Rosie raised her cocktail solemnly. 'To your dad.'

'To Dad. And to living first.' They drank.

'So . . . where will you go after this?' she asked shyly.

'Oh, I don't know. I might check out Istanbul, get the ferry. Then volunteer in Africa, help build schools or something. That's the beauty of it. I've got no ties, I've got some cash, thanks to Dad, and I'll go where the road takes me.' *Oh, Luke.* She'd forgotten the exquisite confidence of young men, rushing into the world with open arms, sure that it would never hurt them.

'You don't think you might get . . . lonely?' said Past Rosie, faux-casual.

'I'll meet people on the way – the way I met you guys. Youth hostels, trains. It's all very friendly.'

Rosie tried again. 'But wouldn't it be nice if you had people with you? Some travel buddies?'

He still wasn't getting it. 'I guess, but Nick has to go back to start his job and . . . ' Finally, the penny dropped. 'You're not saying . . . ?'

'Well, we're sort of going the same way, aren't we?' Past Rosie laughed nervously, gulping half her cocktail. 'I mean, only if you want to.'

'The others wouldn't mind?'

'Oh no. Ingrid would love to have another person.'

He was watching her closely. 'Ingrid would?'

Rosie couldn't meet his eyes. 'Um, sure. We all would. It'd be fun!'

'Well . . . if you're sure . . . '

'You mean . . . '

'Yeah, why not? Let's travel together!'

They stared at each other, electrified with the hugeness of this step, and with the excitement of the world spread out in front of them. Past Rosie laughed. 'It's mad. We only just met!'

'But that's the beauty of travel. You make friends on the road, you have adventures . . . '

Friends. Past Rosie looked slightly crestfallen at that. 'I wouldn't want to cramp your style.'

He put his hand on hers again, strong and brown, the wrist twisted round with gap-year beads. 'Rosie, I'd love to come with you. It would be awesome.'

For a moment, it looked like they would kiss, there in the taverna with the Greek accordion music and the laminated menus and sunburned tourists. Rosie could remember the dizzy feeling of it, almost not wanting it to happen because it would end the delicious anticipation of the moment. Her head was tilted towards his. She could feel his breath on her cheek, smell his aftershave and the faint tang of suncream. Jack couldn't have been further from her thoughts. *Kiss me, for God's sake!* But they both chickened out, downed their drinks instead. 'Another round!' Rosie declared. 'To travel!'

'To adventure!'

'To the open road!'

'To Dad.' Luke suddenly had tears in his eyes. 'He'd have loved this. He'd have loved you.'

'Really?' Rosie was now tearful too. They were very drunk.

'Come on. Let's go for a walk on the beach. It's best at night.'

And that was where kissing happened. Had they kissed on the beach that night? Had she broken up with Jack?

Had she cheated on him? Or maybe they were already over. Enthusiastically, Past Rosie flung down her euros on the table and staggered after him along the sand, beer bottle in hand. The bored waiter came to clear their barely touched plates, and looked after them for a moment with an indulgent smile – ah, young people – before forgetting about them altogether.

But they hadn't got more than three steps when two figures materialised in front of them on the beach. A young woman, her face pink as a lobster, her hair sun-lightened, wearing a tight red bodycon dress and high heels that were sinking into the sand. And a young man, in a polo shirt and shorts, a jumper knotted about his shoulders. Both seemed effervescent, wide-eyed. They had, Rosie now realised, probably taken something back at the apartment. She'd been so naïve back then.

'There you are!' said Ingrid, latching onto to Luke, thread-ing her arm through his. 'Sorry I didn't come out earlier. Too many sambucas last night.'

'Oh,' said Rosie, looking between the newcomers. 'You felt better then?'

'Suddenly could eat a scabby donkey,' said Jack, putting his arm around Rosie. She winced as he pressed on her sunburn. 'All right, Luke mate?' He grasped the other boy's hand and pumped it hard. Luke also winced. 'Thanks for wining and dining my lady. I'm back on form now. What do you say we take these girls for some vino?'

'Sure,' said Luke unenthusiastically, and Rosie watched Ingrid lead him off, talking loudly about her family's ski chalet in Chamonix. Jack and Past Rosie followed. Her past self's face said it all: disappointment. Jealousy. What a mess.

'Oh,' said Now Rosie, watching it all fade. Why hadn't

she realised? She turned to Darryl. 'I was on holiday with Jack when I met Luke. Jack, my boyfriend. That's why we didn't ... why nothing happened? Did Luke get together with Ingrid instead? Is that why we fell out? Oh God, surely not. He was engaged to that other girl.' Poor dumped Ingrid, who after all had every right to flirt with the cute single boy they'd fallen in with on their travels. Whereas Rosie – Rosie who had a boyfriend – had no right at all. 'So what happened next?'

'Mate, you know what happened. It's all in there.'

'I don't! I can't remember. All I know is I think he got married. Not to me.' She didn't know why she felt ashamed saying this. Rosie screwed up her face, trying hard to pin down the memory of what happened next. It was darting round her head, always out of reach, like a fly when you try to scoop it out of an open window. She shook her head, frustrated. 'This isn't working! There's so much I still can't remember.'

She and Luke had been so happy then, on the Greek beach, talking and laughing. If you asked her what happy felt like, she would have chosen that night. But she hadn't been single. And Luke was no longer in her life, even as a friend? What had happened next? Rosie had a nasty feeling she was about to find out.

Daisy

'I suppose we should have some dinner.' Her mother looked vaguely round her kitchen. Daisy knew the fridge would only contain Slimming World meals and the cat's super-luxury food, much more expensive than what they'd had in the sandwiches in their school packed lunches. Mopsy, her mother's ancient and vengeful tabby, had shot under the cooker as soon as Daisy appeared. He hated Rosie and Daisy both, as if he knew they were rivals for Alison's undivided love.

'We could order a takeaway?'

'Darling, the calories!'

That made Daisy think of the boy in the café, the kind way he'd looked at her, the deftness of his movements flicking the cake into the bag for her. 'Rosie's in hospital, Mum. We have to keep our strength up.'

'Well, I suppose I could eat a Chinese maybe. Just something small. That black bean stuff. And some fried rice.'

This was Daisy's chance. 'I'll go and pick it up, it'll be quicker. You pack some things to take to London, then we'll eat and get some rest, OK?'

'OK.' This was a change, Daisy taking charge. As if the absence of Rosie, her argumentative, fiery presence, had left a gap for her sister to step into. As she picked up the car keys, there was a knock on the back door, and she opened it.

A man stood there, middle-aged, with distinguished grey hair and a quilted jacket.

'Oh hello, is Ali in?' he said. Ali, indeed. What was going on there?

Her mother looked flustered. 'Oh, John, hello. This is my daughter – eh, my other daughter. Daisy. John just moved in next door, darling.'

'Hello,' Daisy said, scoping John out. No wedding ring. Sixtyish, in good nick. A small bunch of roses in his hand, wrapped in tinfoil, obviously home-grown. And Mopsy had slunk out from his hiding place and was rubbing himself against the man's chinos. Mopsy, who hated everyone except Daisy's mum. Curious.

'How is she?' he asked sympathetically, as if he knew Rosie. Or had heard a lot about her.

Her mother shook her head. 'Not too good. We just came down to get some things. It's likely to be a long haul, I'm afraid.'

'Oh Ali, I'm so sorry.'

Her mother's eyes shone with tears. 'It's . . . it's very hard to see her like that.'

'Well, don't you worry about things here. I can water the garden, feed Mopsy, whatever you like. I've already got the key, after all.'

'Thank you, John. That's very kind of you.'

'I'll leave you to it. Just wanted to drop these over. I do hope she'll be all right.' He put the flowers on the side, and nodded and smiled at Daisy as he left.

'Er . . . the new neighbour,' her mother explained. She still looked flustered.

'He seems nice.'

'He has two boys about your age. His wife died last year, cancer, so hard. Wanted a change of scene. Has a nice chocolate lab, Lily, who Mopsy just hates. He sits on the fence and tries to scratch at the poor dog.' Excessive detail. Suspicious. Her mother's face had gone red.

'Well. I'll go and get the food then. I won't be long.'

'Get some spring rolls too, darling.'

'Spring rolls, got it.' She went to the door.

'Oh, and those prawn cracker thingies!'

Daisy smiled to herself slightly, wondering how long it had

been since her mother had let herself eat anything unhealthy. In the car, she sat and thought for a moment. She'd been to the Timmons' house a hundred times back in the day, dropping Rosie off, reluctantly picking her up. Could she remember where it was?

Turned out, she could. It was in what had once been the town's poorest council estate. Now the houses had all been sold off, and the drives were full of Audis and Golfs, children's scooters piled by the doors. Daisy went up the drive, feeling abashed. What would she say? *Hello, I'm looking for your daughter? I'm not selling anything!* Perhaps she should have messaged in advance.

The door was opened to a cacophony of sound, a TV blaring out and children fighting. 'God, would you two put a sock in— Oh! Hello?'

It was a woman – a young woman, Daisy could now see, despite the initial impression. Not much older than her. She wore a large floral top of the kind Carole favoured, and pyjama bottoms tucked into Uggs. She'd changed a lot since the nineties – but Daisy knew her all the same. She must have taken over her mother's house. 'Angie?'

Angie blinked. 'Yeah? Do I . . . ? Oh! You're Daisy, aren't you? Daisy Cooke?'

'Yeah. Sorry to just call round like this. Um. Could I have a quick word? It's important.'

Angie's front room was comfortable, if over-decorated. Daisy remembered it had smelled constantly of chips in the old days, but now the place was studded with scent reeds and candles, exuding a warm vanilla odour. Pictures of two chubby kids at various stages of growth, wedding shots. It was hard to believe that Angie and Rosie were the same age, and Rosie was living in that tiny studio flat. Daisy had said yes to tea, just for something to do with her hands, and it was too hot and she blew on it while Angie sat bewildered, a large glass of squash at her own feet. From the next room the noises of the kids went on. 'I don't understand,' said Angie. 'Rosie's in a coma?'

'Yes. They're hopeful, though, I think.' She could hear the lack of conviction in her voice. Were they even hopeful? So far Rosie had shown no sign of improvement.

'And you came to tell me?'

'Kind of. The thing is, Angie, I went to Rosie's flat. She'd written this list of names – some people I knew, some I'd never heard of. I think she must have done it right before she went out that day. You were on it. And as we're trying to find out what happened ... '

'I see. Well, she did ring me yesterday morning, if that's what you're asking.'

'She did?' Daisy's heart lurched.

'I thought it was a bit strange – we hadn't spoken since school, you know. Then she just calls, out of the blue.'

'What did she say?'

Angie looked embarrassed. 'I didn't pick up. I was busy with the kids, and you know ... no time in the mornings. And, well, we had a bit of a falling-out way back. Over a boy, as it happened. Bryn Collins. Don't know if you remember him, you'd have been too young maybe. Anyway, I liked him and Rosie went off with him. Silly girl stuff. But she wanted to say sorry. After twenty years!' Angie shook her head. 'I wish I'd answered the phone. I could have told her he was in prison, for a start.'

'He's in *prison*?'

'Oh yes. Beat his last two girlfriends black and blue, so he did. A real nasty piece of work.' Angie's face hardened. 'Tell you the truth, Rosie saved me from him. Fella like that, you need to be strong to stand up to him. And I wasn't. I'd have been crushed. Anyway, it all worked out fine. I ran away that day, sobbing my heart out, and his mate Steve came after me, offered me a bite of his Caramac. We've been together ever since.' She beamed. 'Almost twenty years, can you believe it? I've got a ten-year-old!'

'That's amazing.' And vaguely terrifying – Angie was only a few years older than Daisy. 'So ... you aren't angry with Rosie?'

'Oh no, water under the bridge. I'd planned to ring her back once I got a minute. I'm ever so sorry I didn't do it sooner.'

A thought occurred to Daisy. 'This Bryn – did Rosie go out with him for a while?' It seemed like something a sister should know, but Rosie had always been secretive.

Angie frowned. 'Long enough.'

'Oh.' Had he hurt her? Angie's silence felt heavy, and Daisy knew she couldn't ask any more. 'Well, thank you, Angie, that's been really helpful. I'm sorry to have disturbed you.'

'Not at all, love. I'd come and visit but I can't get up to London much these days. When she wakes up ... will you tell her there's nothing to forgive? Tell her ... it's thanks to her I'm happy, that I've got Steve and Jasmine and Harry. We'll go for a drink next time she's down. Cocktails at the George, only this time we'll be legal!'

As if his name had summoned him, a burly man with arms like hams opened the living-room door. Daisy vaguely recognised him from school, a few years above her. 'Hiya, love. All right?'

Angie smiled at him with fond affection. 'This is Daisy from down the road. Just calling in to say hi.'

'I better go,' said Daisy. 'Thanks, Angie.' She hadn't the heart to tell her it wasn't as simple as Rosie just waking up, good as new. That even if she did wake up, things might be very different.

So right before the accident, Rosie had been contacting the list of people she'd made. But once again, someone had not answered her call.

Did Bryn hit you too, Rosie? What were you hiding from us? Daisy sighed; the Chinese closed in ten minutes, so she'd better go and get her mum's prawn crackers, then speed back to Rosie's bedside. Her dad hadn't been in touch, so she could only assume things were fine, but the worry still clenched her stomach. *Why did you do it, Rosie? What were you up to?*

Rosie

Night had fallen on the hospital. Time was running out, day two was almost over, and still she didn't have an answer to the biggest question of all: *Was I trying to kill myself or not?* Outside, the spire of Big Ben was illuminated over the river. One of her favourite views, ever since she'd come to this city at twenty-one, all set for drama school.

Right. That was a definite memory. She'd felt for it and it

had been there, right where she left it. What a relief. So, she'd gone to drama school after all, as Luke had told her to. And before that, had she travelled with him and Jack and Ingrid? It was very frustrating, still finding gaps in your memory. Not knowing if you were the kind of person who, say, had ever worn jeggings. Or the kind of person who'd be in love with someone else's husband.

Her father had gone to sleep now, after spending hours by her bed, dutifully chatting to her about accountancy, and reading out bits of the paper. ('Ooh, look at this, Rosie, man grows biggest ever courgette!') Gary had looked in on her earlier, pushing the door aside while chatting the whole time on his phone, 'Course, course, mate. Let's run the numbers and see. We can move some of the surplus from K2 to K3 . . . ' Gibberish, basically. But Rosie had a nasty suspicion that this was how the adult world worked, all codes and targets and professional smiles, and she was lagging behind, with the job of a teenager, which she hadn't even managed to stick at. When she got out of here – if she got out – she was going to have to make some serious changes, starting with moving out of that horrible flat. It was exhausting just thinking about it.

Alone in the silence of the hospital – machines ticking softly around her, draining fluids, putting new fluids in, monitoring the beat of her heart – Rosie turned the questions over in her head. Why had she fallen out with her mother and sister? What the hell had happened to Luke, and why wasn't he at her bedside? Why was she reliving all these awful moments, and what could she do to make it better? If only someone could help her. These ghostly visitors, they were no good.

They could only tell her what she already knew. What if some memories never came back? *Luke. Luke. Come on, access memories of Luke.* She pictured clicking on a computer folder, holding the mouse down firmly. Nothing happened. The memories remained stubbornly elusive.

The door opened – God, not Gary again – and a nurse came in, the one who smelled of Germolene and didn't bother making chit-chat. Her hands were cool and efficient as they changed Rosie's catheter bag. Rosie would have thought this must be incredibly humiliating, to be peeing into a bag as an adult, but the nurses were so discreet and efficient about it that it was fine. She felt well looked after, in her body at least. The broken leg and bruised ribs would heal, her cuts and bruises would fade. Maybe her brain would even sort itself out. But the turmoil in her mind – the painful scrape of those terrible memories – she wasn't sure how long it would take to recover from that. She began to make a list in her head of people she had wronged. Angie, of course. Caz. Mr Malcolm, except he was dead. Had she known he was dead before this? She must have. Melissa, ditto. Her mother, she supposed. Her sister. But why? What had happened between them that they hadn't spoken in months? *Think, Rosie.* It wasn't easy to force yourself to relive a time when you'd behaved awfully, but she knew now it had to be done. The sooner she figured out what the lesson behind all this was, the sooner she might be able to wake up and take charge of her life. She could almost feel the memory inside her, sitting there, waiting to be relived. She wondered who would take her on this journey. 'Grandma?' she said cautiously.

'I'm here, darling.' There she was, a ghostly figure in a cardy, Filou on her lap, now dressed in the pink dog onesie she'd knitted him, and not looking very happy about it.

Rosie shut her eyes. The dial rolled round to a date just a few months ago: 1 8 2017.

1 August 2017 (Two months ago)

Success! She had managed to actually control her memory, and found herself now at her sister's engagement party. The noise level was high. There were about fifty people crammed into the room above a pub – Rosie remembered she'd been surprised Daisy and Gary had so many friends. She spotted herself loitering sulkily near the mini quiches, dressed in ripped jeans and an ironic Steps T-shirt. She stuck out like a caterpillar in the salad, as all Daisy's friends wore sensible shift dresses, ballet pumps, minimal make-up. Rosie could see that her past self was already drunk. She glanced around for Daisy. Her sister looked happy, smiling and displaying her ring to various friends and relatives, but if you knew her very well, you'd be able to see the tightening around her eyes. Because of Gary, Rosie had thought. Because she wasn't sure about him. But now she wondered if maybe it was in fact because of Daisy's unstable drunk sister.

Ghostly Grandma was picking over the buffet with unabashed

curiosity. 'Look at the size of those cocktail sausages. Tiny, they are. It weren't like that in my day.'

Grandma had loved a good get-together when she was alive. A chance to criticise the buffet food and catch up on family gossip.

'I have a feeling this might ... It might get a bit ... heated. I think it didn't go that well.'

'All the better. It's hard to have a good barney in the after-life, everyone just drifts about being serene all the time.'

Gary was holding court, a bottle of imported lager in his hand, talking loudly to his colleagues. She wouldn't have put it past him to throw this entire party just to impress his boss. 'So I took her to our favourite spot in the woods – that's the thing about Daise, she doesn't need fancy proposals or expensive trips abroad – and got down on one knee. Luckily I'd remembered to bring a tarpaulin! Didn't want to ruin my chinos.'

Urgh. Rosie tuned him out. 'He's the worst.'

'Seems a good catch to me, love. Solvent, all his own hair ... '

'But Daisy needs more than that. She needs someone ... adventurous, and lively, and open to the world.'

'That you or her you're talking about?' said Gran shrewdly, examining a wrapped prawn. 'Eee, party food's changed since my day. No hedgehog pineapple? No Black Forest gateau?' She passed a sausage to Filou, who was under the table.

'It's both of us. She's like me; she needs to not be boxed in.'

'But she's got a serious job and she's engaged at thirty with a mortgage and a set of barbecue tongs.'

Rosie sighed. It was true. What if she'd just been project-ing? What if Daisy really did want a dull, stable husband and a house in suburbia? 'I don't know how she can get married when she's seen the example Mum and Dad set. Look, he's not even here, Mum wouldn't allow it.'

'Your parents were happy for a time,' said Gran. 'Until all that. Not many couples could survive something like that, you know.'

Rosie couldn't really remember a time before 'all that', or even what 'all that' was. It seemed to sit on her childhood memories like a rock, crushing and shattering everything. 'Maybe we shouldn't watch the rest. I don't think I behaved all that well.'

Gran passed her a mini-sausage. 'It's not really me, love, you know. You don't need to worry.'

It was about to happen. She could see that a paunchy man in a *Star Wars* T-shirt had sidled up to her at the buffet table. He was casting covert looks at her, with her torn jeans and rippling red hair, as if she wasn't quite real. Past Rosie spotted him and downed the last of her drink. 'Hi.'

'Er, hiya.'

'Rosie. Sister of the bride-to-be. Huh.'

'Oh, yeah, we've met before actually. Dave. Gary's mate from school.'

'Dave.' Rosie's eyes flickered round the room, and her current self knew she was doing a calculation. There were no other single guys at this do except for some of Gary's work people, and they all looked like the type of guys who'd add you on LinkedIn after you'd spent the night with them. Speaking of Gary, he was about to make his speech, beaming, half-heartedly shushing the applause like he was running for President.

'Thanks, thanks. Daisy and I are so thrilled to have so many supportive friends and relations.' She bet he'd recorded exactly who was there, added it to some kind of friendship database.

'Three years ago I was in a bar, and there was this woman doing tequila shots, and she insisted I do one too. Well, who could resist a girl that buys you a drink? Though sadly it was something of a one-off as Daisy's now more than happy for me to pick up the bills!' Laughter. Both Past and Present Rosie winced. She knew fine well Daisy earned as much as Gary did, if not more. 'So . . . after a few years of dating and making sure she didn't have an actual drinking problem . . . I sensibly asked her to marry me and put a ring on it. I'm thrilled that Daisy Mary Cooke will, as of next year, be Mrs Gary Rudley.'

Past Rosie was miming retching. 'This is awful,' muttered Present Rosie. 'I'd forgotten that. Like she has no identity now – just his name! God, I hate him.'

'So, Daisy and I would like to thank you all for coming. Do stay for a cheeky wine or two with us – and otherwise we'll see you at the wedding!' He stood down, clasping Daisy to him and kissing her forehead, flushed with the success of his speech. Daisy looked rigid, her smile forced.

Present Rosie was still ranting to her imaginary grandma. 'How can Daisy stand all this patriarchal crap? I gave her *The Female Eunuch* when she was thirteen! I just don't understand it. Mrs Gary Rudley . . . I'm going to vom.'

'I think you already did,' said Grandma, pointing to where Past Rosie was hunched over one of the crisp bowls in the corner, shakily wiping her mouth.

Present Rosie winced. 'Oh yeah. God, I did puke, didn't I?'

'Right on top of the Hula Hoops, love. Shame to waste 'em.'

Rosie watched as her past self surreptitiously hid the bowl behind some curtains and sashayed, or attempted to sashay, back to Dave, who was looking horrified. 'Sorry about that. I guess their sickly sweet romance made me actually nauseous.'

'Um . . . do you want some water?'

'No water. Vodka!'

Dave went to the bar, fishing out a worn tenner from his tattered polyester wallet to pay for it. Rosie winced at that too. Had she made him buy her drinks? He didn't look rich. He came back with a drink – only for her – and she downed it again, a grim expression in her eyes. Then she made a beeline for her sister and Gary, parting the crowd with the strength of the booze fumes and her rage.

'Your speech.' She poked Gary in the chest. 'Bit presumptuous, no? What makes you think Daisy will take your name at all? She's got a career already.'

Daisy's face was frozen in fear. 'Rosie, please . . . '

Gary fake-laughed, tightening his hold on Daisy, so close a small slosh of wine jumped from her glass onto his shirt. 'Of course she'll take my name! It's what people do.'

'In medieval times, maybe. It's 2017, or haven't you noticed?'

'Well, I think it's nice – we'll be a family, a unit. She has to have the same name as our kids.'

'Newsflash, Gary, you don't have any kids.'

Dave was hovering anxiously behind. Their mother, hearing the commotion, swooped in. She murmured, 'Rosie, do lower your voice. You're like a foghorn.'

'I won't!' Drunkenly, she raised her finger again. Poke poke poke into Gary's chest. 'You seem to have it all figured out, Gaz.'

'Please don't call me Ga—'

'Put a ring on it, you said – like she's some kind of animal! – change her name, tie her to the kitchen sink having your babies, and give them all your name. Well, that's not what Daisy wants, OK.'

'How would you know what she wants?' Gary hissed. 'When was the last time you called her, or came to visit, or asked how she really was?'

'She's my sister. I know her.'

'You don't know her.' He turned to Dave. 'How much has she had to drink?'

That just enraged Rosie further. 'He's not my keeper! How dare you. You bloody sexist.'

There was a small choked sound, and the splash of more wine hitting the floor, glass shattering. Daisy had bolted from the room, crying. Gary moved to go after her, but Rosie rounded on him. 'Don't! She's *my* sister, I'll go.' She staggered out after Daisy, and Present Rosie followed, cringing. This was awful. As if someone had gone round and filmed all her most embarrassing moments and made them into a home movie. Like the world's worst episode of *You've Been Framed*. She remembered that Jeremy Beadle was dead too. Maybe he'd show up any minute and ask was she game for an after-death laugh.

Daisy was in the stairwell of the bar, biting her lip hard, her make-up already smudged with tears. Past Rosie tried: 'Hey, Daise—'

'Why must you spoil everything?'

Rosie stepped back, shocked at the rage of her mild-mannered little sister. 'I didn't mean—'

'Well, you did. It's my engagement party! And you're pissed, you've been sick on the crisps – don't think I didn't notice – and you're all over Dave, for God's sake, a guy you wouldn't spit on if you weren't trying to get at me . . . God, Rosie, you're so selfish!'

'I'm not trying to get at you, Daise! God, it's the opposite. I don't think you're happy, that's all.' She stepped forward; Daisy shrugged her off. 'When I see you with him, you're not yourself. Your eyes. They're all kind of tight and miserable. Why are you doing it? Just to make Mum happy? For someone to love you? Anyone would love you, Daise—'

'I'm not miserable. I'm happy! I'm getting married! You're the one who's miserable, Rosie, and you're trying to bring everyone else down with you!'

The door opened and the noise of the party rose and fell; their mother stepped out, shutting it behind her. She looked furious. 'Rosie, what on earth is wrong with you? Showing us up like that! What's going on?' She sniffed at her daughter. 'And you're drunk. Rosie, I think you need help.'

'You're the one who stopped Dad from coming to his own daughter's engagement party! You don't think that was kind of upsetting for Daisy too?'

Daisy stared at the floor.

Their mother's face hardened. 'I think you should leave. You're embarrassing yourself and us.'

'I just don't think Daisy should be marrying that guy. He's a prat. He won't make her happy.'

'He's a stable young man, with a good job, who won't let her down, unlike your father.'

'God, when will you stop blaming everything on Dad? Take some responsibility! What about what you did?'

'Oh!' Her mother's face tore into a sob. 'Oh, Rosie. How can you be so cruel?'

'*I'm* so cruel? What about—'

Daisy snapped. 'Will you just both stop it? I've spent my whole life listening to you two tear strips off each other. And this is my party. Stop ruining it!'

'Daisy!'

'Enough, Mum! Just go back inside.' Daisy turned to Rosie. 'Mum's right. You're drunk, you should go home. But don't take Dave with you, please. He's a sweet guy under all the *Star Wars* stuff. He doesn't need your drama.'

'What's going on out here?' It was Gary, of course, sticking his oar in.

Daisy sounded very tired. 'It's OK, I'm handling it.'

'Is she causing trouble again?'

'Just leave it, Gar. Come on. Your boss is here, let's go and smooth things over.'

Her mother and sister turned away from her, her mother wiping a shaking hand over her eyes, and closed the door behind them. Rosie was left alone on the stairs, shut out from the party. Gary hung back, staring at her.

'You've got something to say, I suppose?' she snarled.

'Don't think I'll put up with this kind of thing after the wedding, Rosie.'

'How fucking dare you, Gary? It's my family. It's nothing to do with you.'

He came close, hissing in her face. 'If you ask me, your family would be a lot better off without you, Rosie.' And he went back to the party, slamming the door, pasting on a smile.

As Rosie watched, her past self gave a long ragged sob and fled down the stairs, out onto the street. She remembered now that Dave had come after her, clumsily asking was she all right, and she'd dragged him home with her and— Oh, it was all a mess. A terrible, insoluble mess. And now she'd remembered, she couldn't even say sorry, because she was comatose in a hospital bed.

'Eeee,' was all Grandma had to say on the subject. 'It does take all sorts.'

Daisy

The village's sole Chinese takeaway did a roaring trade, and so did not have to bother with niceties such as non-laminated menus, environmental health ratings, or lighting that didn't make you lose all hope as soon as you entered. The man behind the counter was also definitely not Chinese. 'All right?'

'Yeah, hi. I'll have the beef in black bean sauce, the chicken chow mein, fried rice, spring rolls, prawn crackers . . . What?'

He was staring at her. Under his very dirty white uniform hat, his face was narrow and spotty. Early thirties, she thought. 'You're Rosie Cooke's sister, ain't you?'

'Er, yeah, I'm Daisy.'

'Thought you was. Andy, Andy Franks.'

'Hi. Were you friends?' Please God it was just friends, not another example of Rosie's famously terrible taste in men.

'Was mates with Bryn, you know, who she used to have that thing with.'

Daisy nodded, although she had only heard of this Bryn just minutes ago. 'I hear he's in prison.'

Andy's face hardened. 'Yeah. He were a bad lot. Took me a while to see it. Your Rosie, she were . . . Always hoped she'd ditch him. She were way too good for him. All that hair she had, like a princess or something, and in them school plays – she were right good. Did she make it, you know, at the acting? Always look out for her on *EastEnders* and that.'

Daisy hadn't the heart to tell him Rosie had given up acting, and was currently lying unconscious in a hospital bed. For this man, Rosie was forever a teenager, the beautiful live-wire she'd been back then. Of course, the thing about live wires was they were actually quite dangerous. 'Er, yeah, she's doing OK. I'll tell her you were asking after her.'

'There you go.' Andy slid over the warm, fragrant bag of food. 'Stuck a few spare ribs in and all.'

'Oh, that's really kind of you, thanks.'

'Tell 'er to look in and say hello when she's down.'

'I will.' Except Daisy had no idea if Rosie would ever set foot in this village again.

Despite pronouncing herself 'not very hungry', her mum had eaten three spring rolls and a generous helping of rice and beef in black bean sauce. Daisy was glad. There was something sad about this house, which had once held a family. The pathetic contents of the fridge, the single chair angled to the TV, her mother's glasses placed on top of her book. Ever since her father left, Daisy had been at pains to keep the peace, between him and her mother and also between Rosie and her parents (she hadn't done such a good job there). But she'd never really thought about how it was for her mum, left behind, sitting in her empty house while her ex-husband was off with another woman and a new child.

She checked the clock on the microwave. 'We should head off first thing in the morning, Mum. Shall I help you pack?'

'I'm fine, darling. If you want to find something to take for Rosie, there's some old toys and books in your room.'

'Oh, that's a good idea.'

'I still can't see it working, though. They need to be thinking about an operation, or some kind of medicine, not … *Chalet School* or whatever.'

'Well, it's worth a try. I'll take a look.'

Daisy trailed upstairs, running her fingers along the bumpy wallpaper. She and Rosie had often crept down these stairs at night as small children, listening to their parents talk in the kitchen, the warm hum of adult laughter. They'd picked off all the flocks with their childish fingers, driving Alison mad. Daisy and Rosie had shared a room then, in twin beds. They'd played a game they called Crocodile, jumping between the beds until they got in trouble. Some nights Rosie told her long involved stories, until she fell asleep. Daisy had been afraid of the dark. Rosie always said, *The dark is hugging you, Daise. It's like a big blanket wrapped around you. Nothing to be scared of.* And when it had all got scary for real, Rosie would get up and check under Daisy's bed or in the wardrobe. 'See, nothing here. No monsters.' And Daisy could remember her sister tucking her back in. 'I'll stay awake and keep guard. You sleep.'

Daisy could barely remember Petey being born, but she could just about recall the day he came back from hospital – the half-worried half-happy feeling that she was a big sister now. Had it been Christmas? She had a vague memory of lights and tinsel. And fire? Was that right?

Daisy paused now in the hallway and ran her fingers lightly over the door of the spare room. For a while after, she had not been sure what to call this room. If you said *Petey's room*, Mummy would cry and run out and everyone would look sad. Eventually they started calling it the spare room again, but Daisy always felt that second of alarm before saying the words. When Rosie hit her teens she demanded to move into it, which had caused another almighty row. 'It's not like he needs it, Mum!'

Daisy could hear her mother opening drawers in her own room, so she gently turned the handle and stepped in.

It looked totally different, of course. When her mother went away to get better that time, their father had stayed up all night grimly slapping paint over the blue walls, making them cream and bland. She remembered peering round the door, the fresh lemon smell of the paint. Mum had cried when she came back and saw it. *It's like he was never here. Is that what you want, Mike?*

For God's sake, Alison, I don't know what you want from me.

Now the room was a typical guest one – magnolia walls, blue carpet and bedspread. Throw pillows, pointless knick-knacks on the chest of drawers and bedside table. It hadn't been slept in for some time. Daisy realised it was ages since she'd visited. Work, she always said. Reports due. Pitches. But it wasn't a good enough excuse.

She touched the wall gently. Was that where the yellow ducks mural had been? Her mother had painted it. That was when she'd been fat and happy, of course. When Petey was on his way. Daisy could barely remember Petey, was the truth. A blob in a cot, always crying and taking their mother's attention away. When he'd gone she'd thought it was her fault, for not loving him enough, and she'd lain awake crying every night for weeks. Rosie would slip in beside her. 'Shh, Daisy. Grandma said God just wanted another little angel.'

'Then God is a big selfish poo!'

Rosie had fallen silent, trying to puzzle it out for herself. 'I know. It doesn't really seem fair.'

And it hadn't been. None of this was fair.

An enraged miaow interrupted her thoughts, and Daisy followed the smell of premium tuna to see Mopsy lurking under the bed, glaring malevolently. 'Yes, yes. I lived here before you did, you know. I'm going now.'

She slipped back out after the cat, closing the door behind her, just as she heard her mother's wavering voice from the bedroom, and was momentarily shocked at how old she sounded. Like a frail old woman. 'Daisy? I think I'll turn in. I want to head off early tomorrow.'

'OK. Night, Mum.' Tomorrow. Day three. Crunch time for Rosie. Daisy had to find out more about her sister's life, and fast.

Rosie

The ward was quiet. Rosie lay awake, dry-eyed beneath her heavy lids. She knew she must look serene to those watching, the nurses who passed every so often, industrious birds in their uniforms, with kind, efficient hands. Little did they know she was in turmoil. She'd got drunk and ruined her sister's engagement party. Shouted at her mum. Rejected her little half-sister, who seemed like an adorable kid. Lost her friends, screwed them over – Angie, Caz. And Luke. She'd lost Luke. She knew that, deep down. He'd have come, wouldn't he, if they were in touch. He'd be at her bedside right now, begging her to wake up.

'So what's the point?' she said, out loud, but not out loud. 'Is all this explaining why I wanted to kill myself? Did I walk in front of that bus on purpose, because I'd made such a mess of my life I couldn't go on any more?' It was a terrible thing, to not know if you'd tried to kill yourself. If it had been an accident, and you'd clung to your life with all your might as it was torn from you, like poor Darryl. Or if you'd let it go, throwing it up into the air like a captive bird.

What happened to me? How did I lose Luke? That night on the beach, the warm waves lapping and the cocktail flooding her veins, the smell of his tanned skin, the feel of his big capable hand resting on hers. That had been real. Had that maybe been the last time she was truly happy? Had the rest of her problems stemmed from there, a slow slide down until everything was ruined?

Rosie looked around her at the quiet, plain room. The rust stains from the water pipes which she'd already catalogued a hundred times. The switched-off TV that she wished she could turn on via mind control. The magazines her mother had left on her locker, tantalisingly out of reach. She had to try to wake up. And that meant facing everything, all the truth about what she'd done. 'I'm ready for another memory,' she called. 'Grandma? Darryl? Mr M? Mel? Dot? Can someone come, please?'

Silence. 'Is someone going to come and visit me?' she asked, to the empty air. Nothing. She sighed. 'Oh come on. I'll take any memory at all, I guess. Even though they mostly all suck.'

'That's good,' said Melissa, appearing by the bed, her frizzy hair sticking up. 'They mostly will all suck.'

'You look tired; is it night for you too?'

She yawned. 'I'm a teenager, remember. I'd sleep for twenty-four hours if no one got me up.'

'I used to be like that,' Rosie said nostalgically. 'Now I'm lucky if I get four hours.' Insomnia had plagued her for years, that almost-hysterical feeling of lying awake in the dark, listening to shouts and traffic outside her window, so sick of being herself that any kind of oblivion seemed better. Was that enough to make her walk under a bus?

'Do you remember when your sleep problems started?' said Melissa, reading her mind again. Reminding Rosie that the girl wasn't really there, she was just . . . a memory. A hallucination. Of a friend she hadn't even thought of in years. A friend who'd died without Rosie even noticing – or had she? She couldn't access the memories of how Melissa died.

'I guess it was . . . not long after that drink in London. With Luke.' She remembered the Christmas after the pub encounter, short grey days burning themselves out before Rosie staggered from bed, long nights in her mother's cold house, staring at the orange glow of the electric streetlight outside. Her father long gone, with a new baby. Finding out Luke was getting married. But from the park memory, he'd clearly still been in her life after that. So where was he now?

'Do you remember what happened between you two?' Melissa was gentle, but firm.

'No, but clearly I'm going to find out. I'm not going to like this memory much either, am I?'

'Sorry, Ro-Ro,' said Melissa, holding out her ink-stained ghostly hand. 'That's kind of the point of all this.'

Rosie knew now not to argue. She took her old friend's hand and closed her eyes, opened them. The hospital was gone; the dial was spinning. 28 2 2015. Several years after the park. She closed her eyes again. It was her last chance to remember, before dawn broke and she was onto day three.

28 February 2015 (Two years ago)

It was a hotel room. Anonymous, clean enough, with one of those stupid tiny kettles and bars of wrapped soap no bigger than a square of chocolate. Past Rosie was on the bed, regarding herself glumly in the mirror. She was in her underwear, the same kind of stuff they'd cut off her in A&E. M&S cotton, plain and functional.

'Ooh, free snacks!' Melissa was unwrapping a packet of chocolate biscuits from near the kettle. 'I never stayed in a hotel when I was alive, you know.'

'I don't remember this. What am I doing?'

Past Rosie suddenly got up, making an expression of annoyance in her throat, and pulled her jeans and jumper over the underwear, fluffing out her red hair. Her face looked pale and miserable. She went over the bathroom door and knocked on it gently. 'Are you OK?' she said tentatively.

The door opened a crack, letting out steam, and through it the hazy figure of a man in just a towel. 'Not really. I feel awful. You?'

'Well . . . no. I feel rotten too.'

'Christ, Rosie. I'm so sorry. I never meant for . . . God. This was a terrible idea.'

'Oh. I'm sorry.'

'I didn't mean . . . '

There was an awkward pause. 'I better go.' Rosie lunged for her shoes, fumbling on her socks, which had pictures of dinosaurs on them. Not the kind of thing you'd wear for a night of passion, surely. This was clearly the awkward morning after, but after what? And why was it *this* awkward?

'We should talk, though.'

'Should we?'

'I just need . . . God, this is all such a shock. I never expected . . . Give me some time?'

Rosie was buttoning her coat all wrong, hiding her face under her hair as if she might be about to cry. 'It's fine. I understand. I . . . I'll just go.'

'Rosie!' As she edged towards the door, the man came out of the bathroom after her. 'Can't we just . . . ? Christ.'

'Oh my God. It's Luke,' hissed Now Rosie to Melissa. And it was. The curve of his face, the width of his chest, his wet fair hair. Luke, who had been engaged to a tiny beautiful woman.

'Rosie! Rosie, wait!'

She turned briefly, her face contorted in tears. 'I'm sorry, Luke. It's not fair on her. For Charlie's sake, you need to at least try.' Then Past Rosie was gone, and Luke, dressed as he was just in a towel, clearly could not go after her. She watched her past self rush down the corridor of the cheap hotel, already in tears. Who was Charlie? Who was *her*, for that matter?

'What's going on?' Rosie turned to Mel.

'You know what's going on, Ro-Ro. This is all from your head.'

'Are we ... together?' Rosie's voice faltered. If they were, why were they here in a hotel? Why were they both looking so sad? And ... why did Luke have a wedding ring on his left hand?

'You know the answers to all those questions,' said Melissa helpfully, leaving spectral biscuits crumbs behind her.

Rosie didn't want to accept it – it couldn't be true, could it? – but the signs were all there for her to read. She and Luke were having an affair.

DAY THREE

Daisy

'What'll it be today then?' said Adam, smiling brightly despite the earliness of the hour.

Daisy was yawning, bleary-eyed. 'Oh, a latte please. Triple strength.'

They'd arrived at the hospital to find Rosie comatose, unchanged. Two days had ticked by with no improvement. They'd brought back old cassette tapes of Rosie's favourite bands, Ash and Take That and All Saints, her childhood stuffed rabbit, an old fraying poster with a very young Leonardo DiCaprio on it. All things she'd loved as a teenager, hoping to rouse some response in her brain, but it just underlined the fact they didn't know what Rosie loved nowadays. Or who. Daisy had gone out to get the strongest coffee she could find, and while she waited, she stared again at Rosie's locked phone, trying desperately to think what the code could be.

'Problems?' Daisy looked up to see Adam's keen dark eyes watching her as he frothed milk. 'You aren't some kind of international phone thief, are you?' he said easily.

'It's my sister's.' She realised that did sound strange. 'I just think she was maybe ... going through some stuff when she had her accident. That maybe she was on her way to meet someone. I want to know who that was.' Daisy couldn't explain why she was doing this. 'It's just so hard to sit and wait, you know? At least this way I can do something.'

'You've tried all the birthdays? People usually use a really obvious one.'

'Yeah. But it's not working.'

'May I?' He set down the milk jug and took the phone from her. Daisy felt his fingers brush her hand. He was angling the phone towards the lights. 'OK. First digit is maybe a two? Anyone's birthday start with that?' He laughed at her look of surprise. 'You just look at where on the screen is most smudged. Most people never clean those finger marks off.'

'Maybe *you're* some kind of international phone thief.'

'Nothing so exciting. I worked in Carphone Warehouse for two years before this place. You wouldn't believe how many people forget their own phone codes. Next one is six, I think.'

2 ... 6 ... Daisy frowned.

'Does that mean something do you?'

'Maybe. Can I ... ?'

She took back the phone, careful not to touch him this time, and typed in 2, 6, 1, 2. Then blinked in astonishment as the screen cleared, revealing rows of apps. 'It worked!' She let that sink in. Petey's birthday. 26 December. Rosie was using Petey's birthday as her phone code.

Adam took out a paper cup. 'Dunno why most people bother with codes, to be honest. Anyone can crack 'em if they know how.'

'Don't suppose you're any good with email passwords?'

He laughed. 'Those are easy. Most people have them written down on Post-its near their computers, or it's the same one for every account they have. Anyway, you've got into the phone now. Doesn't she use apps? Those are password free.'

'You're a genius. Coffee and cyber terrorism.'

'I try.' Adam flicked a tea towel over his shoulder and went back to the machine, humming over the sound of foaming milk. Daisy turned her attention to Rosie's phone, almost afraid of what she'd find there.

The texts were disappointing. Nothing that week except a circular from her phone company. Her browser history yielded a bit more – she'd searched for *Melissa Carter*, and for *Mr Malcolm teacher Coombe Bridge High*. Of course, he'd been on the list too. Daisy remembered him – the French and Drama teacher, a quiet and unassuming man, who shuffled about in old cardigans and blew his nose a lot. Rosie must not have known his first name. Teachers were just entities back then, and you never thought of them as being human. Daisy had dropped Drama as soon as she could but she remembered his excitement on learning she was Rosie Cooke's sister. 'Do you act, Daisy?'

'No, sir.'

'We must get you a try-out all the same. Rosie was just a wonderful performer.' Past tense, because by that stage her sister had stopped doing school plays altogether. Why was that? Daisy had obediently tried out for Mr Malcolm, and seen his furrowed brow at her leaden, mumbling recitation of Lady Macbeth's blood speech. She was more of a natural props handler, really. Rosie had evidently found something on Mr M, because one of the articles was an obituary on the school website for *Beloved Teacher Dies*. Oh, poor Mr M. Cancer. He couldn't have been that old.

Quickly, she checked the phone contacts, but there was no Luke. She hadn't expected there would be. And nothing on Rosie's Google search history about him either, no Facebook friends with that name, and without a surname she couldn't get much further. He was like a ghost. How could someone who'd had so much impact on her sister's life be unknown to those closest to her? There was also no one called Ella in the contacts or friends list or search history. No trace.

Unless you're not. Close to her, that is. You didn't know any of this, did you?

She shut down the nasty little voice in her head and moved on to the call history of the phone, not expecting to find much there. Nobody of their generation actually rang people, except their parents. No calls at all for the past few days, then a flurry on the day of the accident itself. Rosie ringing Caz and Angie, probably. Then another, at 6.45 a.m. Daisy stared down at it, recognising her own phone number.

Why would Rosie be up that early? Daisy tried to think. She hadn't seen a missed call from her sister that day, definitely not. She would have noticed it. Why, then? Where had she been at that time? In the shower, most likely. Staying under for an extra minute before she had to drag herself out and face the crushing terror of Maura.

'Here you go, triple latte. I make them with a dash of coconut milk, let me know what you think.' Adam was holding out her coffee.

'Thanks. Um ... can I ask you another quick phone question? If you find a missed call in your call list, but it never showed up on your screen, why would that be?'

His forehead puckered as he considered it. 'Someone must have seen the call come in and rejected it, I guess. That's the only explanation. Even if it got pocket-answered it would show up unless you manually hid it. Not you, then?'

Daisy's mind turned to two mornings ago. Herself in the shower. Gary in the bedroom knotting his tie. Her phone on the bedside table. 'No,' she said. 'Not me at all.'

Rosie

'Grandma? Is that you?'

'Yes, love. I'm here.' It was morning, after a long, dark, lonely night. The grey dawn came in her high windows. Day three. Hadn't they said they'd have to make hard decisions if she hadn't woken up by then? That if she didn't come back to herself today, the chances she ever would weren't good? They'd talked about feeding tubes, tracheotomies. Moving her to long-term care. The thought of it sent fear sloshing through Rosie, all the way up from her numb feet. She had to try to wake up. The sound of gently clacking knitting needles reached her ears, comforting her somewhat.

'What's going to happen now, Grandma?'

'Another memory, love.'

Of course. She couldn't face another bad one, reliving a day she'd done something bad, or hurt someone. Slept with someone's husband, even. This was the kind of person she was.

Gritty tears were in her eyes. In the real world, a nurse moved around her body, sponging and hooking and checking and emptying. The tears were wiped away like so much discharge. 'Grandma – what's this for? What's it going to achieve? If I wanted to ... if I didn't want to be here any more, and I walked in front of that bus, why did my brain try to bring me back? Why not just ... let me go, when I was dying there in A and E?'

'The body always wants to survive, love. No matter what. During the war, your great-uncle Colin, that was my brother, he was in the Japanese camps. It were a hard life and no mistake. Starving, halfway between life and death – he came back just skin and bone. But he didn't give up.'

Rosie said nothing. It made her feel even worse for being mired in her own petty problems, to hear about people who'd had Nazis and bombs and starvation to battle with. 'So why these memories? What's the point of them?'

'I don't rightly know, love. There's something you have to figure out for yourself. But you need to be quick about it.'

Rosie sighed. Maybe she was expecting too much from projections of her own disturbed mind. 'So there's no way out, unless I relive them?'

'That's right, love. Ready?'

'I don't think I have a choice.' Assuming, of course, she wanted to wake up. Assuming she hadn't stepped in front of that bus on purpose, wanting to end it all, fade peacefully away like her ghostly visitors had described. The truth was, Rosie didn't know. She braced herself as another memory approached. 2 10 1999. The dial, the noise, the blur. Time to lose herself again.

2 October 1999 (Eighteen years ago)

'What's that you're doing there?'

Teenage Rosie – fifteen going on forty – scowled at her grandma from behind a full face of make-up. 'I'm going out.'

In this memory, her grandma must have been about seventy. Not even that old, Rosie realised now, looking on as her adult self, but back then she'd seemed ancient, an old woman with grey hair and a twinset. Grandma wore a lemon cardigan draped over her shoulders, and in the living room behind her the TV was playing *Fifteen to One*. 'You're not going out, love, it's nearly dinnertime.'

Teenage Rosie had been trying to sneak out of the house, although it was almost dark outside. She folded her arms. 'I'm allowed to normally.'

'Are you? You won't mind if I ring your mum and check then, will you?' Grandma said easily. She'd raised two children herself; she was immune to teenage aggression.

'When was this?' said Now Rosie to Now Grandma – or

Dead Grandma or whatever she was, who was pottering around the hallway with interest. 'How come you're staying?'

'Look, I wonder what happened to that twinset when I went. Plenty of good wear left in it. It was after your dad left, love. Your mum wasn't coping too well, so she went to your Auntie Susan's, remember?'

Poor Mum. Poor Carole, too, to put up with years of crumbs from their table, meeting in shabby hotels off the motorway. Rosie realised this was the first time she'd ever felt sorry for Carole. She remembered herself in that hotel room with Luke, the shame and fear of it all.

'I came down to mind you and your sister. She was never any trouble, of course. It was all you.'

'Yeah, yeah, perfect little Daisy.' Through the open kitchen door, Daisy could be seen doing her homework at the table, in her grey school uniform. The good sister. Whereas Rosie, in her ripped black jeans and crayon-like eyeliner, hadn't done any homework at all and was planning to rendezvous in the park with some rather dodgy young men. This was after she'd fallen out with Angie, after she'd taken up with Bryn, after she'd ditched the school play because he didn't like her acting. The point where her life went one way instead of another, where it began to unravel.

'You can't make me stay in,' Past Rosie was now saying to her grandmother. 'What are you going to do, lock me up?'

Daisy was only pretending to do her homework. She looked up at that, biting her lip, worried.

'Rosie, pet,' said Past Grandma wearily, 'there's no need for this. I'm doing bangers and mash for tea, you love that.'

'I'm vegetarian now.'

'Well, Daisy and I got a nice film out of the video shop. *Circle of Friends.* You love that.'

'Boring. Why won't you just let me out!'

Grandma sighed deeply, admitting defeat. 'Be back by six.'

'Or what?' Present Rosie was mortified. How could she have been so rude to her sweet, wise grandmother?

'Or I'll come down to fetch you myself in my dressing gown and curlers.'

Checkmate. Rosie and her grandmother stared each other down in the hallway. Daisy listened from the kitchen, tense.

'Six o'clock.'

'Fine. God, this *family*.' Teen Rosie went out, slamming the door so the pictures in the hallway rattled.

'I'm sorry,' she said to her ghostly grandma now. 'I was awful. I don't know why.'

'You were young, pet. Young and angry. I wish you'd stayed home, though. That boy was no good for you.'

'Was it Bryn?'

Grandma nudged her. 'Follow and see.'

A blink, and she was on the street, walking behind her past self on the way to the park down the road. Teen Rosie stopped to apply yet more make-up from a small Boots 17 compact, then spray herself all over with Impulse O2. The synthetic sweetness gave Now Rosie a complicated feeling: part nostalgia, part sadness. Maybe nostalgia was always part sadness, always for something lost that you could never get back. The girl she used to be pushed open the small gate to the children's play park, now deserted, the shadows lengthening. Three boys sat around the slide, passing a bottle back and forth in a brown paper bag. White Lightning. Rosie ambled over, her eyes fixed somewhere beyond them at the swings, as if that was her intended destination. 'Hiya,' she said nonchalantly.

None of the boys answered for a moment, eyeing her like lazy lions would a gazelle. 'Ro,' said one of them laconically. It was Bryn. Even in the dark, even in his parka and with his curtains haircut, he was dazzling. Hot blue eyes and cheekbones cut with a microplane. Not that anyone in 1999 knew what a microplane was.

Rosie sat down on the grass, arranging her hoody under her. She must have been freezing, but not wearing a coat was somehow seen as alluring back then. 'Can I've some?' she asked nonchalantly.

Bryn passed the bottle, watching as she swigged it, trying not to gag. The boys went back to whatever they'd been talking about, which seemed to involve laughing and calling each other 'well gay'. Slowly, subtly, Rosie and Bryn drew away from the other two. The tension vibrating off Rosie was almost tangible. She wanted this boy to touch her, talk to her, own her, pay her attention. She'd do almost anything to get that. For just a crumb of affection. A pattern that was all too familiar from most of her relationships with men since. Either she desperately wanted what she couldn't have or she didn't want the person who wanted her. Stupid.

'Grandma . . . ' she began.

'Don't worry, love, seen it all before.'

Rosie still blushed for her past self. What an idiot she'd been, hanging around cold dark parks with dodgy boys instead of staying at home in her safe warm house with Wagon Wheels and *ER* on the TV.

'Oi.' Bryn jerked his head at his two minions. 'Give us a

minute, boys.' Obediently they left, with a snickering noise that Rosie remembered had made her feel excited and afraid all at once. 'C'mere.' He turned to Rosie, and took her hand, abandoning the bottle. She remembered she'd looked back at it, wondering if she should pick it up. Kids would play there in the morning, they might get hurt. But instead she just followed him blindly to the dark area under the trees, where you couldn't be seen from the road. And suddenly she remembered why this memory was so potent.

'Pretend I'm not here,' Grandma whispered. 'I'm not, you know. I'm dead these years and years.'

'I know, but . . . God.' No one wanted their grandma to see them losing their virginity under a bush in a playpark.

'Suppose it's too much to ask if you were being careful?'

'If you know everything I know, you'll already know I wasn't.'

'Eeeee,' said Grandma. 'That was right foolish, our Rosie.'

It was more than that. It was criminally stupid. From the bushes came rustlings, and unzippings, and heavy breathing, all moving far too fast to something that Past Rosie now wasn't sure she'd wanted – was she even ready? She wasn't even sixteen, it was against the law! – but then it was too late and there was a stifled yelp. It had hurt. She remembered it had hurt a lot.

'Oh deary me,' said Grandma.

The whole thing took about five minutes, and then Bryn was lighting a fag, and starting for home, leaving Rosie still with her jeans half-off. 'See ya,' he said.

'But . . . '

'What?'

'Um . . . ' Rosie hadn't known what to say. They'd had sex. He'd taken her virginity. Now he was just walking off, without even looking at her.

In the orange streetlight, his face was pale and cruel as carved marble. 'You're welcome.' That was what he'd said after doing that to her. *You're welcome.* Then he was gone.

Rosie watched her past self, a girl alone in the dark, struggling to pull up her jeans and underwear, wincing at the pain. Seeing blood and grass on her thighs, wondering how she would hide it from her grandma, who noticed a bit more than her parents seemed to. Biting her lip and trying not to cry. Realising she couldn't even tell Angie about this, her first time, as they weren't speaking. Getting to her feet, walking stiffly, and throwing her head back high. She wasn't going to show her grandmother that she'd been right, that boy was no good. The difference in how he'd been for months – *Rosie baby, you're so special, I just want to spend all my time with you instead of you always being at rehearsals* – was marked. He'd walked off. He'd just walked off. She couldn't take it in. So that meant . . . she was one of those stupid girls who believed a guy when he said he loved her?

Over the next two weeks, Rosie knew, she'd wait obsessively by the phone, doing her homework on the stairs in case it rang, and she'd hover by the bus stop and the park, but Bryn would never contact her again, and when they passed once on the high street, his arm round the neck of a giggling blonde girl, he would look right through her as if she didn't even exist. If only she'd said this or that, not said this, not said that. It would torment her, and her grades would slip even more, and the rows with her parents intensify, while at the same time

Daisy seemed to get smaller and quieter, taking up as little space as possible compared to her loud, difficult sister. Then she'd realise her period was late, and have to sneak into Boots and buy a test, and one of her mum's friends had been in there trying on perfume, and then she'd had to wee on the stick in the shopping centre toilets with an old woman outside banging on the door telling her to hurry up. What a mess she'd made.

'I should have listened to you, Grandma,' she said to the shadowy figure.

'Aye, grandmas always know best. But young people have to make mistakes. That's life.'

They watched as Teen Rosie walked off, arms wrapped round herself against the dark and cold, tears already turned icy on her face.

Daisy

She found Gary in the lobby of the hospital, phone in hand, and the rage broke inside her. All her fear and anger at Rosie being stuck here, her mother's unhappiness, Petey, all of it, came spurting out like a volcano.

Gary said, 'There you are. I'm off to work now. Could you pick up some soy milk on your way home? Oh and don't forget to look at the wedding playlist I sent over. We need to decide on "jazzy funk" or "funky jazz" for the drinks reception.'

Daisy spat, 'Why didn't you tell me Rosie called?'

He froze for a moment. 'What?'

'The morning of the accident. She rang me, didn't she?'

'Oh, er, I don't know.'

'There's a missed call in my list.' Daisy brandished her own phone and Rosie's, one in each hand. 'Look. A call from her phone to mine, only I never saw it on the screen. Why's that?'

'God, how should I know? You probably just didn't notice it.'

'Because it wasn't there. I haven't spoken to Rosie in months; don't you think I'd have noticed if I suddenly had a call from her?'

Gary sighed. She saw him roll his eyes, just a fraction, and her blood boiled over like an unattended pan on the stove. 'Oh, Daise. All she does is upset you. You had a big day ahead, you were already late, and you know what she's like. She'll have been up all night at some club, probably ringing up to have another drunken go at you. I didn't want that for you. I'd have told you about it that evening, when you weren't so stressed.'

Daisy just stared at him, speechless. 'You ... my God. You don't get to make those decisions for me, Gary!'

'Why not? I'll be your husband soon. I'm entitled to have a say over who we let into our lives.'

'She's my *sister.*'

'Your sister who ruined our party and embarrassed me in front of Mr Cardew. How do you think that made me feel? I could hardly look him in the eye the next day.'

'FUCK MR FUCKING CARDEW,' Daisy yelled, months of frustration bursting out of her, the long hours of waiting in hospital, the sleepless night in her old bedroom, shivering in her mother's unheated house and asking herself every five minutes: *Was Rosie trying to kill herself?*

Gary's face looked almost comically shocked. 'Daisy! Don't swear like that!'

'Why not? My sister's in a coma, why shouldn't I swear?'

'At me, your fiancé, who's only ever helped you and looked after you and—'

'I don't NEED LOOKING AFTER!' She didn't know where this voice was coming from, loud and enraged and so full of force Gary actually stepped back. 'Jesus Christ, do you hear yourself? It's not your business to interfere between me and my sister. She tried to ring me, and I didn't pick up, and next thing she's under a bus? What do you think that means, Gary?'

'I . . .'

'Yeah, well, thanks very much, you twat. You might have just killed her.'

'Daisy!'

'Why don't you just fuck off, Gary? Go on, get back to your precious spreadsheets and office bantz and tea rota. Rosie doesn't need you here and neither do I.'

And she turned and left him standing there, in his stupid suit, his stupid face mugging like a stupid goldfish.

Rosie

You saw a lot of things when you weren't technically conscious. Like the two young doctors, the way they bantered and bounced off each other, but also the way her tense shoulders relaxed when he came into the room, the way his eyes sought her out when she passed down the corridor outside, ponytail swinging. Like the way Gary and her sister always stood with a gap between them, and Gary never touched her or comforted her. The way he always angled his body to face whoever was speaking, something he'd probably learned in a wanky business skills workshop. The way, when she thought no one was watching, Daisy's face collapsed into little frowns and grimaces. The way her mother's face stiffened when their father arrived with Scarlett, a mask of disapproval hiding her real feeling – sadness. Jealousy. Rosie wished she could have caught at her mother's hand, said, *Mum, there's so much life left to you still, and you've got two daughters, and there's places to go and things to see and so much, just so much there for you.*

But who was she to talk? She'd had so much as well and she'd spent years festering in her horrible flat, stewing in guilt and jealousy. Maybe it was one of the curses of being human, that you could only realise what you had when you were in danger of losing it. The simple gift of being able to move your arms and legs, speak, open your eyes on command, dress yourself. Of being able to pick up the phone and tell people you were sorry, you'd messed up, beg for forgiveness. Feel the fresh air on your face. Turn over in bed. How could she have felt grateful for these things, when she'd never realised they could be taken away from her? And now she might never get them back. Day three. And she still couldn't speak or move or do anything on demand.

The young doctors had come into the room again. 'Hello, Rosie,' said the boy, leaning up to check her IV. The girl doctor squinted at Rosie.

'Do you think she can hear you?'

I can, I can! Please look, please see that I'm in here.

'There's a chance. She's GSC six, that's not awful.' Glasgow Coma Scale, it stood for. Rosie wished she had researched what it meant before all this.

'It's not great either. It's just . . . sometimes I wonder what the point is. The ones who are really far gone, you know. The brain injuries. The people they bring in from the nursing home who don't even know who they are, let alone why we're sticking tubes down their throat. It seems cruel.'

He watched her as she checked Rosie's read-outs, and he gently adjusted the sheets on the bed. 'Sometimes we have to hurt them to help them. You learn that on day one of med school.'

'But what if they'd rather we didn't? What if we just . . . let people go?'

He frowned. 'Zara! You're saying you'd help someone . . . end things?'

'Maybe. If they wanted me to. Let's be honest, the most likely thing is she was trying to kill herself anyway. Who are we to keep her here, if she doesn't want it?'

'You'd go to jail!'

'We took an oath, Praj! To help people. Sometimes helping them means helping them to die.' She whispered the last word in a fierce undertone.

'But how can they tell you that's what they want, if they can't speak?'

'I just know that, if it was me, I'd want to make the choice while I still could.' She shuddered slightly. 'I see coma patients, the way they are . . . getting their nappies changed, being fed through tubes, needing someone to help them just to turn over in bed, living for decades like that . . . I wouldn't want that. I'd want to be switched off, OK?'

He stared at her. 'Why are you telling me? I won't be the one deciding for you, will I?' They seemed to be talking about something else now. Zara's peaches-and-cream skin flushed, and she stared at the window. Rosie wanted to scream at her, *He loves you, can't you see? Just give him a sign!* But, just as in her memories, she was powerless to change anything.

'I'm talking about . . . hypothetically. Would you want to be like this? Trapped in your dying body?'

'She's not the worst. She's got hope. You saw the scans – she could still wake up.'

'But she hasn't. Barely a flicker in days now – you know she's running out of time. Later today we'll have to talk about moving her.'

She knew they were kind, and very young, and very tired, and doing their best for her, but it felt unusually cruel to talk about her over her own comatose body. From the corner of her eye, she saw the door opening, and a flash of orange lifted her heart. It was Dot, whoever she was. Kind, chatty Dot. Who Rosie was still not sure was alive or not. Once again, the doctors didn't seem to notice her slip in, this time with a yellow duster in her hand which she applied half-heartedly to the skirting board, clearly listening in.

Zara was saying, 'I sometimes think some hope is worse than none. Do you know what I mean? Families watch these films or hear these stories about people in comas who wake up after years, and they think that'll be them. So they sit and wait and hold on, while the person they loved is gone – long gone – and it's just a dying body they're talking to.'

'People do wake up sometimes.'

'Depends what you mean by wake. Would you want to be

228

conscious, and trapped in a paralysed body, not able to talk or feed yourself? People aren't always the same when they come back to us.'

He was silent for a moment. 'We shouldn't be talking like this in front of her. It's not right.'

She pulled herself together. 'I'm sorry, Rosie. If you can hear me. He's right. If you're in there . . . we're doing everything we can for you. Come on, we have rounds.'

Praj groaned. 'I'll never survive. I got exactly six minutes' sleep last night.'

'Suck it up, dude. I'll buy you a Twix.'

They left, and Dot came forward to Rosie's bed. 'Don't you listen to those two, my love. They might have letters after their names but I've seen plenty in your situation over the years. And you're going to be just fine.'

'Will I really? How do you know?'

'Trust Dot. I've seen worse off that woke up again, right as rain.' Gently, she smoothed down Rosie's hair. 'Eee, we could do with a shampoo, couldn't we? I'll have a word with the ward sister. Fix up that pretty face of yours, what do you say?'

It was true Rosie was feeling grotty. She hadn't brushed her teeth in days, and she was pretty sure there were still bits of road grit matted in her hair. 'Thank you, Dot. Can you hear me? And who are you – why can I see you if we've never met?' *Is this real? Are you dead or am I just hallucinating all of this or . . . ?* Rosie's head hurt trying to figure it out. She felt her eyes close, too heavy to stay open.

'You just rest. I know you can hear us in there. Get better and come back to us, love.'

Her words were as comforting as a hot bath, but Rosie didn't know if she believed them. Dr Posh Spice had been brutal in her honesty. Rosie felt oddly grateful, in a way. Although she of course wanted to believe that she'd get better, she'd be back to her old self soon, it seemed to undermine the seriousness of what had happened. That whatever happened now, her life had been split in two, and nothing was ever going to be the same again. That the old Rosie Cooke was, effectively, dead.

'How's it going, love?' Not Dot. Another voice.

'Oh hi, Grandma. You're still here then. I'm . . . well, I'm doing my best.'

She looked around her, straining her neck. 'Where is everyone? Aren't they supposed to be round my bedside, talking to me and singing "Kumbaya" or whatever?' Not that she had any right to expect it, after the way she'd behaved.

'Your dad's hiding outside the door there.' Grandma pointed with a knitting needle. She'd stuck around since the last memory, and Rosie was glad. She hadn't realised how much she'd missed this grey-haired woman with her crosswords and cardies and practical kindness. If only she could tell her that now, in real life. If only there was still time. But that's what death meant – no more time.

'That's typical. Never there when you need him.'

'That is my son you're talking about, love.'

'Sorry.' She sighed. 'It's kind of become a habit, blaming him for everything. For not being there, for leaving us with Mum.'

'I'll admit, love, he didn't handle it as well as he could. But he regrets it. Look, here he is now.'

230

Her father had snuck around the door, as if afraid some-one would catch him. It was surreal, watching him walk right past the ghostly form of his mother and sit down on the orange plastic chair. He stretched out a hand towards Rosie's limp one, then snatched it back and cleared his throat. 'Hello, Rosie. It's Dad. I don't know if you can hear me, or ... if you're in there at all. But they said to try. I—' His throat constricted. 'Love, I don't know what to say to you, and that's the truth. We're not close. Not since you were little. I know you think badly of me because of ... well, Carole, and Scarlett, and I don't entirely blame you, love, but ... well, all I can say is I was just trying to survive what happened. Like all of us.' He seized her hand sud-denly. Rosie could not move it, could not push him away or squeeze his back or give any sign she was listening intently to every word. 'Anyway, love, whether you can hear me or not, I just want to say ... I'm sorry. For any hurt you had. For anything that might have made you—' A loud sob. 'Did you do this to yourself, love? Why? Why would you want to do a thing like that?'

She would have loved to shout, *I didn't, Dad, it was just an accident*, but she couldn't speak, and anyway she still wasn't sure if that was the truth or not. She just had to lie there, unmoving, as her father cried in front of her for the first time she could ever remember. 'Gran?' she whispered. 'How did it happen, Mum and Dad's divorce?'

'You can remember it, love, if you try hard. If you're ready.'

There were still so many memories she couldn't access. Perhaps because she knew they must be the hardest ones, the most painful. But maybe she had to face them all, relive the worst moments, if she was ever going to wake up. 'All right. I'm ready.'

Rosie shut her damp eyes. She pictured the memory in her head. *Open it. I want to remember.* And she began to fade away. Away from the harsh bright lights and the ache in her bones and her father crying beside her, estranged from her, perhaps because of the memory she was about to relive. Just: away.

14 February 1998 (Nineteen years ago)

'Aw, Dad, we're watching that!'

'Sorry. I need to talk to you for a minute.' In this memory, Rosie was in the living room of her childhood home. She was a teenager, and wore Adidas bottoms and a vest top to sprawl in front of the TV on her stomach. Daisy was curled up in the armchair, already in her pyjamas. A typical Saturday night, cups of tea scattered around and the wrappers from Club bars screwed up about the sisters. Their dad, oddly nervous, had just stepped in front of them and turned off *Gladiators*.

'Oh,' said Rosie, watching her past self. 'This is when he told us.'

'That's right,' said Grandma, still knitting. 'If I'd known, I'd have given him a flea in the ear and no mistake. In your own home! With no warning! And on Valentine's Day too, oh dear, oh dear.'

'Would you have told him not to do it? If he'd asked?'

'I don't know, pet. When all's said and done, they weren't happy, your parents, were they?'

'Not since Petey, no.' The name still felt like glass in her mouth, though she was not really saying it, though none of this was real. 'Though I can't remember what that means, exactly.' She could feel the memory looming, a dark shape slowing taking form. 'I guess they weren't happy, no.'

'And he's happy now? With Carole?'

'God, I don't know. I never see them. And you're dead, so you can hardly know.'

'Less of your cheek please, miss. Just watch.'

In the memory, her father was pacing in front of the fire-place, and her mother was rigid in an armchair, make-up on, subtle jewellery, ironed white shirt. Daisy was in the chair still, but Rosie had jumped to her feet. She'd known there was something bad coming. If she didn't sit down, didn't listen, she could prolong it, maybe for ever.

'What's going on, Daddy?' Daisy said nervously.

'Rosie, will you sit down, please?' Her father was harassed.

Their mother cut in. 'Just say it, Mike. They deserve to know.'

Daisy and Rosie exchanged a quick panicked glance. Was one of them dying?

'I . . . ' Her father opened his mouth, and faltered. 'Girls . . . '

'Your father has met another woman, it seems, and so he'll be moving out and in with her.'

Daisy and Rosie gaped at their father. 'What?'

Their dad had aged before their eyes, haggard, ashamed. 'Girls, I'm sorry. It's just, your mother and me—'

'Don't you dare blame me, Mike.'

'No, no, it's just . . . I wanted a bit of happiness. Is that so bad?'

'You're moving in with her?' How like Daisy, to ascertain the facts, in a quiet voice, before flying off the handle. 'That means . . . you've known her for a while?'

'I . . . Well, yes, love. This was never meant to happen, but it has, and, well, Carole's not getting any younger and she—'

Rosie was on her feet, red hair bristling in rage. 'You're ancient, Dad! You can't have a girlfriend, that's disgusting!'

'It just . . . well, it just happened.' And Rosie had seen it. The flicker in her father's eye that told her that, no matter how painful this was for him, he was relieved, deep down. Released from a marriage that had never recovered from what happened. In love. A chance to make things right. Rosie had seen it and the bewildered little girl in her started to howl.

'You can't do this! You can't just leave us!'

'Rosie, love, you're a big girl now. Daisy too. And your mum . . . she agrees this is for the best.'

Oh, the iciness of her mother's voice. 'I hardly have much choice, Michael.'

'I'm sorry, OK? I wish it wasn't happening like this. But . . . it is. I'm sorry.'

Daisy had simply nodded, her hands laid flat on her knees. 'Right. OK. That's . . . I just need a while to process.' She'd already taken to speaking like the teens on *90210*, like someone twice her age.

Rosie had stared at her sister. 'Process? How can we process Dad cheating on Mum, and leaving her, at his age?'

Their dad pleaded, 'I still love you, both of you, and your mum and I—'

'Don't you dare, Mike . . . '

Rosie spat, 'You love us? Yeah, right. You've hardly been here for years. You just left us all to deal with it, while Mum went to pieces and we had no one looking after us. Now you're off to start another family you can destroy. Well done, Dad.' She began to storm out, throwing open the door to the hallway. Running, as was always her first instinct.

Her father blundered after her. 'Rosie – sweetheart – I wish you knew how much I loved you, both of you . . . '

'Yeah, well.' She spun on her feet, her face twisted in rage. 'Save it, Dad, because I hate you. I *hate* you.' And she seized the family photo off the wall in the hallway, the one from the day of Petey's birth – taken in this same room, when they'd all been so happy – and smashed it on the ground, before slamming out the front door. On the doormat, Rosie saw now, there was a pink-edged envelope addressed in childish handwriting, which got kicked aside and slid under the hall cabinet. And she remembered. 'That was from Melissa. We'd been writing to each other since she moved, but after this I just . . . didn't reply.' Current Rosie winced to herself. She'd stopped writing to her friend, and not long afterwards Melissa had died. 'God. I was awful.'

Grandma said, 'You were upset. You had a lot going on.'

'Yeah, but he's right. I shouldn't have taken it so hard. And he's my dad. Of course I don't hate him. I . . . Oh!' She gasped as, like popping open a canister inside her head, her mind was suddenly flooded with memories marked 'Dad, happy'. Suppressed for years because he'd dared to try to live his life. They came and came, all the lost days, crowding her head.

She was three, and her dad was scooping her up onto his shoulders, higher than a skyscraper, so she could pull leaves from the trees overhead . . .

She was seven and getting ready for school, and he was trying to plait her long red curls, sweating and muttering with the effort, while she offered the less than helpful commentary that *Mummy doesn't do it like that, Daddy* . . .

She was ten and Mary in the school nativity, despite having red hair, and she looked down after her big speech about there being no room at the inn and her dad was in the second row, crying his eyes out (so she had seen him cry before, she'd just forgotten, like she'd forgotten so many important moments of her life . . .).

She was sixteen and coming out of a teenage disco at two in the morning and her father was waiting in his Volvo, even though he didn't live with them any more, yawning to himself, Bryan Adams on the tape deck, and she slid into the warm interior of the car and he'd brought her a Caramac in case she was hungry . . .

She was eighteen and off to university, and he was hugging her on the pavement outside her halls of residence, having hauled seventeen bags of clothes and books and kettles and duvets up four flights of stairs, and he wasn't quite ready to say goodbye, to let her go, but she shrugged him off, eager for her new life to start . . .

She was in her twenties and standing beside him in church in a Jane Norman dress that was too tight, her hair straightened into submission, her dad's shoulders heaving. In front of them was a wooden coffin ('Mine,' said Grandma. 'I never did like mahogany, don't know what they were thinking.') and

Rosie put out her hand and took her dad's and they cried together . . .

She was twenty-six, and moving out of the flat she'd shared with Caz because Caz was getting married, and her dad was helping her lug all her stuff yet again, and awkwardly slipping her a cheque because 'I know it's hard to manage on your own', and she'd somehow taken offence and they'd ended up having another row . . .

And then her memories ran out because she'd blamed him for everything and done her best never to see him, Carole or Scarlett, except when she needed something. 'Oh. Poor Dad. Poor, poor Dad. And now I'm . . . Now he must be . . . Oh!'

Rosie wasn't sure if she was crying in the memory or for real, or both, but the pressure in her lungs increased, and she was gasping for air, racking sobs tearing through her. 'Grandma? I can't . . . I can't breathe!'

'Just try to wake up now, Rosie. *Wake up!*'

Daisy

She was still shaking when she got upstairs. She'd told Gary to fuck off. Gary, her fiancé! For a moment, she let herself imagine being without him, starting over – all those awful Tinder dates her friends went on. Going to weddings alone and sitting at the kids' table. Cancelling the venue and the church and the florist. She began to gasp for air, and for a moment she had to lean against the puke-coloured wall to gather herself. *What have I done?*

But no, it would be OK. Gary would understand. She hadn't slept. She was very stressed, that was all.

'You OK, love?' Her dad was sitting by Rosie's bed, leaning on his knees and staring at the floor. He looked as if he'd been crying.

Hastily, she pulled herself together. 'Hi, Dad. How is she?'

'No change. I've been talking to her but ... I don't know. Where's your young man?'

'Gone to work. As per usual.'

'I used to do that a lot too.'

'I know.' It was a theme her mother returned to often.

'Told myself someone had to earn the money, especially with your mother the way she was. And I suppose ... sometimes it's easier to be out of the house. With adults, where everything's kind of ... packaged up nice and clean. No one crying or making a mess or saying they hate you.'

'I know. It's OK, Dad.'

Her father looked at Rosie, who lay comatose, her body floppy and her face as pale as the sheets. 'It's not my place to say anything, Daisy ... God knows I haven't been around much ... '

'Dad, don't ... '

'And if Gary makes you happy, then great. But one thing I will say is that moments like this, seeing your daughter lying there in bed and not even able to help her, or comfort her, or know if she can hear you ... Well, moments like this you wish you'd left the office early all those times. Skipped the meeting. Turned the report in late. Gone to the school plays and ballet recitals ... She was always so good in the school plays, wasn't she?'

'Yeah.'

'I was ever so disappointed when she gave it up. Not disappointed in her – just felt that it wasn't fair somehow.'

'Fair?'

'Maybe if I'd been around more, if there hadn't been all that business with Carole, well – she might have stuck at it. Maybe she wouldn't be like this now.'

Daisy followed his gaze to the machines pumping Rosie's heart and blood and lungs. 'Who can say, Dad? I don't think it's any one person's fault. Rosie is just ... well, Rosie. She always was.'

'But everything that happened with ... '

Daisy couldn't bear to talk about it. Not now, the fight with Gary still fresh on her skin, the panic dissolving her bones. *What have I done?* 'Dad, come on, we have to stay positive. We have to talk to her, like the doctors said.'

'Right.' But they both stayed where they were, silent. 'She rang me,' her father said, so quietly Daisy almost missed it.

'Sorry?'

'On the day it ... the day. She rang my mobile. She never rings me. Not even birthdays or Christmas. Can't remember the last time.'

Daisy's heart began to hammer in her chest. 'What did she say?'

'I didn't answer. It was early, and you know how it is, getting Scarlett into her uniform and some breakfast down her, stopping to answer a hundred questions about how do fish breathe and do they think air is wet ... and, well. The last few times I spoke to your sister she called me some terrible names. I – I couldn't face it. I'd have rung her back later. Probably.'

'She called me too,' Daisy heard herself say. 'I didn't pick up either. I – well, it doesn't matter, but I missed the call.'

'Oh.' Her father's brow knitted together. 'She ring you often?'

'Nope. And not at seven in the morning. I ... we had a falling-out, at the engagement party.' She felt a sweep of embarrassment, recalling that she hadn't even invited her father. Her own dad.

He didn't seem to care about that. 'So if she rang you, and she rang me, and neither of us answered ... '

And then an hour later she was stepping into the path of a bus, her phone with its unanswered calls held in her outstretched hand. Daisy swallowed. 'Dad ... '

His fists tightened convulsively. 'What have I done? Is it my fault she ...? Oh Christ.'

Daisy wanted to say of course not, it didn't mean anything that Rosie had chosen the day of the accident to finally contact her family and friends after months – years, in her father's case. It was pure coincidence that later that same day she'd almost died. That she'd made a list of names, all so far people she needed to say sorry to. That could all be explained away. None of it meant for sure Rosie was trying to kill herself. But Daisy found that she could not say anything over the large shard of fear that had lodged itself in her throat.

Suddenly, Rosie made a sound. Not a good, positive, might-be-waking-up sound. A sound like she couldn't breathe, like she was screaming inside a vacuum and hardly any noise was coming out. Like the squeal of brakes and the cry of a child in pain and a hundred terrible noises all mixed up in one. Her father turned almost as pale as Rosie, whose lips were now tinged with blue. 'What's happening? Rosie, love, what's wrong?'

Daisy was already running for the door. 'Can someone come now, please! My sister can't breathe!'

Rosie

'It's OK. You're OK. I'm with you, Ro-Ro. Try to breathe.' Mel was there.

Doctors. Doing something near her throat. The feeling of choking, of drowning inside her own body. 'What's ... happening?' She knew she had not spoken out loud, that they could not hear her, that she could only speak to this ghost or hallucination or whatever, who was not even really there.

'What's happening?' she croaked.

'You're not getting enough oxygen. They said something about more bleeding in your brain.'

She tried to hear what they were saying, the two young doctors who held her life in their hands, but could not. The real world was nothing but blur and buzz and static, while her memories were so real she could not escape them. Through the glass doorway she could see her sister, her father, noticing how old he'd got. She hadn't seen him in over a year. Her dad who used to fix her bike and put plasters on her knee and do silly impressions of Zippy from *Rainbow*. She'd loved him, once. She still did. But maybe she would never get to tell him that.

A vague sense of urgent feet, of voices talking fast. 'Are they worried about me?' said Rosie, alarmed. 'Am I in a bad way?'

'You're slipping away, Ro-Ro. Come on, you have to try and wake up.'

'But I can't . . . I can't!' By her side, Dr Posh Spice was slipping a syringe into her IV. A warmth was spreading through her body, a fake chemical peace. Rosie tried to fight it, to stay in the world, but it was no use. All she knew was she had to try to remember everything. All the bad memories. All the reasons she had ended up here, in this hospital bed. She would never truly be ready for that, but there was no choice, and so she went.

21 August 2005 (Twelve years ago)

'Keep them closed!'

'OK, OK, I'm not peeking.' Past Rosie, giggling with excitement and nerves, with Luke's big hand over her eyes. She wore frayed denim shorts and a pink vest that clashed with the sunburn on her shoulders, and her hair was twisted up in braids to hold it off her neck. She remembered that moment so clearly – the roughness of his palm, the smell of cinnamon and the Origins mint shower gel he used, his breath hitting the back of her neck, damp with the heat of the marketplace. They were in Marrakesh, in the souk, the kind of place your eyes didn't know where to settle because everything you looked at was so beautiful and interesting: woven rugs, bright rainbow glass, copper wind chimes, carved wooden chess sets, and everywhere sacks of fragrant spices. Luke was holding her hand, and gently plunging it into a large bag of something brown and knobbly. Now Rosie, watching like a ghost from the dark, almost gasped as the sensory memory came back to her. The rough sacking, her fingers brushing against the spice . . . 'Cloves,' her past self said. 'Definitely cloves.'

'Not fair. That was an easy one.' Luke took his hand away.

'Your turn.' She was tall, but still had to reach up to put her own small hand, traces of picked-off red polish on the nails, over his eyes. Feeling the flicker of his eyelids under her palm, taking his hand and guiding it to another sack. He bent, sniffing.

'Is it saffron?'

'Very good. Did you know it's more valuable than gold, pound for pound?'

'So why do we bother buying gold jewellery, then? It'd mean more to propose with a ring of saffron strands, surely.' Luke had said it idly, leaning over a bag of cinnamon sticks, but Rosie's heart had begun to pound. It was a miracle she hadn't passed out during that month with him: the heat, the constantly held breath every time their hands brushed. The confusion and excitement and drama of it all. Nothing had happened, of course – she was still with Jack, even though, most days, he and Ingrid wanted to go clubbing till three, then sit by the pool and drink recovery vodkas, while she and Luke wanted to sightsee. They walked, and ate in cafés, and talked and talked and talked, her words trip-ping out of her mouth in her impatience to tell him things about her, find out things about him. It was so strange to remember all the times she'd sat with her mother over the dinner table, and been unable to summon up a single word to break the silence between them. She hardly felt like the same person at all.

But nothing had happened with Luke. It couldn't. She'd

been mired in doubt. Maybe he didn't like her that way. Maybe it would all end soon. What if Luke headed off to volunteer, as he'd planned, and she had to spend the rest of her life with Jack?

Melissa said, 'Pay attention, Ro-Ro.'

Her past self went to tuck her arm through Luke's – a friendly gesture, or what could be excused as one at least – but he pulled away. Luke was looking at her directly now, standing in the aisle of the bazaar, glaringly British with his sunburned nose and sensible trainers and khaki shorts, a smattering of gold hairs on his forearms. 'What?' she said nervously.

'Rosie, I . . . You're supposed to go home from here, right?'

'Yeah.' The flights had been booked months ago, before she'd even met Luke.

'And . . . after that, you'll be in London? With Jack?'

'I guess so. That's the plan, anyway. Find a job or . . . something.' Her voice sounded deeply unconvinced. Rosie wanted to scream at her past self. This was her chance. This was Luke opening himself up to her, trying to tell her something, and she just wasn't hearing it. 'Why?'

'I just . . .' He scuffed his trainers along the dusty ground of the market. 'I think you should do what makes you happy. Not what Jack wants, or what your parents want. If you want to be an actress, do it.'

'It's not as simple as—'

'But it is, Rosie. It is as simple as that.' He was looking at her so earnestly, this twenty-something boy, hardly grown out of his teenage lankiness. If only she'd been different, and braver, and known how to hear what he was saying, they might have been together all this time. Twelve years with Luke. The loss of it almost made her gasp. 'Life is so short. You're so young. Just . . . do what makes you happy, OK?'

Past Rosie was staring at her feet too now, at the chipped polish on her toes, which she'd applied weeks ago. Before she knew Luke existed. And now everything was different. 'What are you saying?' Her voice was barely audible over the sounds of the market.

'You know what. I just . . . It's time to make a decision. This . . . ' He gestured awkwardly at the space between them. 'It's going to end. You're going home. I'm going to volunteer. Is that what you really want? I mean, Jack's a good guy, but is he for you?'

'I . . . ' A long silence between them. *Say something. Tell him you feel it too.* But Past Rosie said nothing, and the moment had gone on a fraction too long. It was too late. 'Luke, I don't know. I . . . '

He stepped back, a blank, hurt look coming over his eyes. 'Right. I see.'

'I didn't mean . . . '

'I'm going back to the hostel,' he said, turning away. 'Are you coming?'

'You don't want tea and baklava?' Rosie loved it, the mint tea in the ornate cups, just the right amount of bitter cutting through the cloying sweetness of nuts and honey.

'No. Not today.' And he walked off, leaving her in the souk among all that colour and noise and smell.

Rosie's current self said, 'I let him go, didn't I? And he married someone else.' She'd lost him. But then why were they having an affair ten years later? Why couldn't she remember? The truth was, Rosie knew, that she did remember. It was all

247

in there, and she could access it if she tried hard enough. She just didn't want to. For a moment longer, she wanted to leave them as they were, young and happy, with the possibility of being together still alive. She sighed. 'I wanted to keep them. The nice memories of us.'

'The trouble with nice memories is they have to end sometime. No one can be happy always. Every day of your life, something will have been good and something bad. So. Shall we go?' Melissa dragged her on, efficient, and the bustling bazaar faded and she opened her eyes again on another scene. The same day, she knew. The dingy staircase of the youth hostel they were staying in, Arabic music blaring from the TV downstairs at the reception desk, a smell of incense and old tobacco smoke in the air. The halls echoing with slapping sandals and high youthful voices. It was evening, growing cool and fragrant. The call to prayer from the mosque had gone up, and Rosie had showered and changed into a long patterned dress. At this time, she would usually join her fellow travellers on the roof to drink beers, and later still fan out in search of grilled meat, and flatbread, and dancing, and maybe she would find more time to sit with Luke and talk to him, while the others got drunk. But not tonight. They had to sort things out, and Rosie had decided, while washing her hair in the gross communal showers, that she was going to take his advice. Because it was that simple, of course it was. She was twenty-one. Of course she could break up with Jack and carry on travelling with Luke rather than going home and working in some dingy office. She could do anything she wanted.

'But that's not what happened,' said Mel's voice. 'Is it?'

A nasty feeling was working its way up Rosie's legs. Not that these were her real legs; those were flopped on a hospital bed a thousand miles and twelve years from this moment. She knew what happened next. And she also knew one thing: it had been entirely her own fault.

The rooftop of their hostel. The warm night air, the bulk of the mosque just streets away, the city skyline and the birds that circled endlessly. The high keening of the call to prayer and the smell of incense. Her memories of Morocco came down to this: honey and nuts and olives for breakfast, music seeping out of taxi radios, a dry circling heat, and Luke. Luke beside her, walking down the hot bright streets. He was there, him and Ingrid, sitting on cushions around a low metal table, intricately carved. They were in a group of young people, Irish, Australian, French, Israeli ... Rosie could not remember any of their names. They were just people she'd spent one night drinking with, never to be seen again. Likely they were now back in their own countries, living their lives, perhaps married with kids, and if she died in her hospital bed, they would never even know or care. So many lives she had streamed through without touching.

Past Rosie was walking towards the group, a resolute expression on her face. At the same time, Jack was approaching from the bar, a beer in his hand, his face red with the heat. The four of them, her and Jack, and Ingrid and Luke, sitting so close together, converged like the points of a triangle. And as Rosie and Jack watched, Ingrid suddenly put her arms around Luke's neck and kissed him.

Her best friend. Her boyfriend. And the boy that, really, she actually loved. Why else would she feel like someone had

249

punched her in the stomach? But she had no right to be upset. Ingrid was single, Luke was single. Rosie was not single.

As Past Rosie looked up, she saw Jack standing beside her. And he was also staring at Luke and Ingrid, and he looked just like she felt – gutted. And suddenly it all made sense, and she turned and ran.

Jack caught up with her in the stairwell, which smelled of feet and cheap deodorant. 'Rosie!'

She turned, tears in her eyes. 'It's over, Jack. Isn't it? Why do we keep pretending?'

'What? I'm not pretending!'

'Oh, come on. I saw the way you looked at them. It's her you want. And you and me, it's not been good for months now, has it? Oh God, I'm sorry, Jack. I just . . . ' Rosie watched her past self grope for the words, to try to explain that she just didn't love him. That she was only twenty-one and there had to be more to life than sitting bored while he talked about skiing while coked off his head, or listening to him play maudlin songs on his acoustic guitar about the burden of having a trust fund. That she'd even heard sex might be something fun and exciting, rather than a chore she'd rather put off in favour of a hot bath and good book. 'I just . . . we're not happy, are we?'

'*I'm* happy,' he said unconvincingly.

'But we don't make each other laugh, or have fun together, or even get on that well.'

'Life's not about having fun, Rosie. You need to grow up a bit. I'll be starting at Goldman Sachs next year, it's a big responsibility. And we have plans – we've already got the lease on the Clapham flat. We can't just break up now!'

'But I'm only twenty-one! And I want to have fun, and try new things, not just get an office job and move to Clapham.'

'Yeah, well, it's dangerous to have no life plan. What do you want, to end up unemployed and alone in some studio flat?'

'I do have a plan.'

'Acting's not a real job, Rosie. Why don't you temp or do a law conversion course or something?'

'I'm sorry,' said Past Rosie miserably to Jack, 'I just want more. More than this. And you ... I think you want more too. Don't you? I really think it'll be best for both of us. I'm going home tomorrow. Alone.' She risked: 'You and Ingrid need to talk.'

He stared at her. 'You really are impossible, Rosie.'

Then Jack was marching away, back to join the group, and Past Rosie was wrapping her arms round herself, tears in her eyes.

'Well,' said Now Rosie. 'He wasn't wrong. I *am* all alone and unemployed in some studio flat. Is my memory trying to tell me I should have stayed with Jack, become a lawyer, got really good at skiing?'

'Just keep watching,' said Melissa, agog. 'Honestly, this is better than *Hollyoaks*.'

Because now Luke was there. 'Hey. Are you OK? I saw Jack come storming out.'

Past Rosie stared at the dirty floor of the staircase, making her voice cold. 'Fine. None of your business.'

Luke's face creased in confusion. 'Did I do something?'

'Other than stick your tongue down my friend's throat?'

Confusion was briefly replaced by annoyance. 'She kissed me. It's not ... Anyway, Ingrid and I are both single, Rosie. And you're not. Remember?'

'I am now.'

'Oh. Right. I'm . . . I'm sorry.' They looked at each other, and for a moment in that dirty stairwell, the future stretched ahead of them. The silence between them. The place it had felt too dangerous to go to, maybe because their emotions might overwhelm them. If only she'd been brave enough to say, *Hey, Luke, I'm in love with you, and I should have broken up with Jack months ago, but I'm a coward.* But what if he didn't feel the same? What if he preferred blonde, confident Ingrid to gawky red-headed Rosie? Ingrid, whose pretty face he'd just been sucking?

She hadn't been brave. Instead, she'd said, 'I'm going home tomorrow.'

'What?'

'I . . . it's time I grew up and settled down. So no more travelling for me. Back to my crappy old life.'

'I . . . Jesus, Rosie. Let's talk about this or something or . . .' If she'd let him carry on speaking, she could see it now, they could have gone on together. Been a couple. Seen the world.

But Past Rosie had shut down. Put her armour on. Easier than letting herself get hurt. 'I'm fine, Luke. You carry on with your plans.'

'So . . . it's our last night?' The hurt in his eyes. Why couldn't she see that? That he'd no interest in Ingrid? That Ingrid too had only been doing it to make a point, though not the one Rosie thought? 'I'm not going to see you again?'

'I guess not. I better go and pack.' And she'd gone to her uncomfortable bunk in the dorm, and cried for hours, and the next morning she'd left without saying goodbye to any of them, and Luke had gone on, bewildered, trying hard to forget about the girl he'd only known for a few weeks, finally fetching up in Thailand where he'd met an Australian girl and moved to Sydney with her, and they hadn't seen each other again for another five years, when Rosie had walked into that pub and there he was, with his beautiful fiancée, but all the same the thing that was between them didn't care about that, and so from this moment here, this decision, the rest of her life and Luke's life had been blown apart. Stupid Rosie. Stupid, stupid girl.

Daisy

'Ssh, Mum. It's OK. She's breathing again. It's OK.'

Her mother was doubled over on the green pleather seats of the waiting room, crying solidly, her chest rasping in and out like she could hardly breathe herself. She didn't even seem to notice or care that people were watching. Daisy couldn't bear it. Hearing her mother sob like this, it brought back too many memories of the bad time. She was three, and Mummy wouldn't get out of bed and Rosie was the one who walked her to nursery every day, hand in hand, and read her stories and made up different ones when she couldn't figure out all the words.

Her mother sucked in breath. 'Oh, Daisy. I can't lose her as well. I just can't.'

'I know, Mum, but you haven't. She's still here.'

'I heard them talking – if she doesn't wake up soon it's a very bad sign. She might live on for years like this, Daisy. We might never hear her voice again. Is that what she'd want? I don't think it is.'

She patted her mother's back ineffectually, trying desperately to think of something hopeful to say. 'People wake up from comas all the time. After years sometimes.'

'Oh darling, they might wake up, but that doesn't mean they're the same as before. Oh God. She's just like me, isn't she? After . . . after everything. The way I was, so depressed, staying in bed for weeks. They say it can be passed on. And now look. She's tried to . . . hurt herself. And I could have stopped it.' Her mascara was running now, leaving trails in the smooth mask of her make-up. 'It's my fault, darling. My fault she did this.'

Daisy sat back in the seat, which was broken and torn. Like everything here, including the people. 'What?'

'Rosie rang me that morning. Early. I found it on 1471 but I . . . I wasn't in, I missed the call.'

Daisy frowned. 'But . . . where were you?'

Her mother turned red. 'I was . . . Darling, I was next door. With . . . John.'

'Oh. Oh!'

'So, you see, she finally got up the courage to call, and I wasn't there, and so she must have decided to . . . '

'We don't know that she—'

'Oh, Daisy. Can't you see? The doctors think she did it. The police think so too. Everything points to it. She . . . she wanted to leave us. Oh, my poor Rosie. If only I could go back, Daisy, I would. I'd do everything differently. Everything. Since she was little. You've no idea how much I wish that.'

'Mum, she rang me too. And Dad. None of us picked up.' Daisy didn't say the rest of what she was thinking. Would that have been a reason, if you weren't in your right mind, to step under a bus? If you turned to your family and none of them answered? 'But we still don't know that she ... meant to.' It was there all the same, horrifying, in the doctors' eyes, in her mother's face, in the silences between them all. 'We have to hope, at least, don't we?'

'Of course, darling. No one is saying we can't hope. But if she does wake up, and she did this to herself, well ... we have to be prepared for the worst.'

Daisy got to her feet. She had to get out, find some air, think. 'I need to go and do something, Mum. Maybe I can find out something that'll help.' Although what, she didn't know. It wasn't as if she could actually speak to Rosie about her life, even if she was awake.

As she walked off, she thought what a strange thing it was her mother had said. When it came to Rosie, Daisy had been prepared for the worst for years now. Prepared for her to fall, and shatter. Trying to be the good girl, so at least her parents didn't have more worries. Living up to her namesake, the insignificant weed to her sister's bright, overblown bloom. And now it had happened, and Daisy was realising she'd had no idea about the truth of Rosie's life. No idea at all.

Rosie

She was back. Back to a reality she didn't want – helpless in a bed, estranged from family and friends, unemployed, a failure – and no Luke. She wondered how she hadn't felt it before. Of course they weren't together, of course she hadn't seen him in years. His absence was like a hole in her middle.

That happy, cinnamon-scented time with him had been just a brief burst. Her heart ached. Everything ached, from her feet to her head, but this was a different kind of pain. The pain of knowing you'd ruined your own life.

And there was her mother bending over her bed, lines of worry etched into her face. Finally talking to her. 'Rosie? Can you hear us? I know they said to talk to you but I just can't . . . I just don't feel you in there. Please, darling, if you can hear us, give us some sign!'

Yes, yes, I can hear all of this. I can see you and hear you and this is torture. But my memories are even worse. If only I could get away from myself. Escape . . . me.

Rosie seized on the thought, a clear shard of memory: she had thought this very thing before. Stepping in front of a bus, was that a very permanent way of escaping herself? Had it all just got too much, living with her mistakes day in day out?

'I think something's wrong.' Her dad's voice, worried. 'Rosie, love, do you know we're here? Can you say anything, or move a finger or anything?'

Say something. Make a noise. Any noise. With all her might, she strained every muscle in her body, finding a puff of air deep down in the bottom of her deflated lungs and trying to force it out of her slack mouth. AAAAAAHHHHHHHH.

Nothing. What would Mr Malcolm have said? *Come on, Rosie, enunciate. The lips, the teeth, the back of the throat.*

I'm here. I promise, I'm still here.

'Oh Mike, it's no good. She can't hear us. Rosie is . . . she's not here. We have to admit that.'

TRY, GODDAMMIT, TRY. *I'm here. I'm still here, and I don't want to die. I don't!*

The sound of her parents crying. 'Maybe this is . . . maybe this is what she wanted, Ali. Just to go.'

Rosie was exhausted. The effort it had cost her to try to speak was immense, worse than when she'd climbed that mountain in Wales that time (when?), and she still hadn't managed to do it. They thought she was already gone, dead inside a technically breathing body. And now – now, the black was reaching up to pull her down, the edges of the room fading and blurring. *No. I'm not ready. I'm not!* She focused on the faces of her father and mother – *please, I love you* – trying to cling to them like a life raft, but she was sinking back down, the waters overwhelming.

'Mike. Mike! Something's wrong! Rosie. ROSIE!'

Rosie was gone.

5 February 2011 (Six years ago)

'Well. That was a bit dramatic, wasn't it?' It was Darryl, his voice in her ear as the memory warmed to life.

'What happened? I didn't see any dials this time.'

'Dunno. You sort of blacked out. I mean, more so than usual. Mate, I think you're getting worse. They said this would happen, didn't they, that you'd have to go onto long-term life support. You need to try and wake up.'

'I am trying! Where are we?' The flat they were in was cosy and modern: wood flooring, colourful cushions, the radio playing low music. The kind of place Rosie would have liked to live, instead of that nasty little room she called home. She could see her past self standing by a window, looking out over the illuminated city. She wore a navy dress with a white collar, as if trying for a demure look. It didn't suit her and Rosie remembered it had shrunk in the wash, so she kept having to tug it down. In the living room of wherever this was stood several young people, twenty-something, the men in beards and lumberjack shirts, the women in skinny jeans and with flat, straightened hair, except for Rosie's, which curled and corkscrewed of its own accord. Who were these people? She counted: six including her. A dinner party, then. Two couples, and in the kitchen a woman she recognised. It was Luke's fiancée. Soon to be his wife – Rosie caught sight of a pile of hand-lettered invitations on the desk in the corner, in the process of being addressed. A hollow feeling settled in her stomach, and she could see that in the memory her past self was smiling with the kind of desperate jollity you only put on when your heart is breaking. Although she was in her own home, the fiancée was wearing leather trousers, enormous heels, and a loose floaty top. Her back was turned as she chopped something on the counter, and her hair was long and shiny. Rosie remembered how out of place she'd felt beside this seamless beauty, awkward, too tall, dressed once again in something ill-fitting and unfashionable.

And ... then, coming into the room with another man in tow, perhaps from answering the door, was Luke. He took her breath away, the beloved lines of his face. So why weren't they together? He wore a blue buttoned shirt that he seemed uncomfortable in, fiddling with the cuffs. Perhaps the fiancée had bought it (what was her name? Rosie's mind seemed to blank on it). And in the memory, Luke was walking straight to Rosie. She watched herself smile, tug down her dress. 'Hey!'

'Rosie, this is James from next door.' The other man wore a pink polo shirt, collar up, and chinos. Definitely not Rosie's type, not in a million years, but she shook hands gamely. Clearly, this was a set-up. She was remembering now. After the drinks in the pub at Christmas, the first time she'd seen Luke in over five years, and the shock of realising he was engaged, she'd been surprised to receive a message from the fiancée inviting her over for dinner. Perhaps it was that classic move, befriending the ex (though Rosie was not that, of course), neutralising the threat. And she'd gone because, clearly, the chance to be around Luke was worth the heartache of seeing him with someone else.

'So, then, Rosie,' said James, as Luke handed him a bottle of beer, 'how d'you know Luke and Ella?'

Ella! That was her name! Of course. Rosie watched as Luke and her past self fumbled over the answer to this question – how did they know each other? What were they to each other now? 'Er, you know, we met travelling years ago.'

'Thought you met Ella travelling, mate?'

'We did. Later on the same trip.' Ella came over, holding a plate in each hand. 'Shall we sit down?'

Rosie gaped at her. There was no mistaking the fullness under the floaty top. Her mind did the maths ... so they'd been engaged at Christmas, and that was two months ago ...

There was no denying it. Ella was pregnant.

'Hope you all like Thai food.' Ella was an effortless hostess as well as being glamorous. She'd not even broken a sweat serving up the pad thai with assorted side dishes. Taking her seat at the top of the trendy glass table, she put her hand over Luke's. 'It's our favourite. When we were out there we ate it all the time, didn't we, honeybunch?'

Honeybunch. Rosie could see herself beside Luke, opposite James, a rictus smile on her face. Of course, she remembered now. Luke had eventually fetched up in Asia after they parted, which was where he'd met Ella. That could have been Rosie, going round Thailand with him, eating spicy food that burned her mouth, riding on elephants (there were many photos on the wall, framed in a selection of shabby-chic frames no doubt sourced from vintage shops. Ella seemed the kind of woman who would source things rather than buy them). If only she'd been braver. If only she'd told him how she felt, taken that risk, opened up. But she hadn't. And here they were.

'Pad thai,' said Darryl, who'd been hovering, silent. 'That's got peanuts in, hasn't it?'

'Yeah. And I'm allergic.' She watched her past self, remembering now how she'd weighed up her mild childhood peanut allergy against the social faux pas of not eating Ella's dinner. *Don't do it, you idiot,* she urged herself, but it was no use. Past Rosie took a small bite, forcing it down her throat. It had been delicious, of course. Everything was done so well. There were little glass bowls of lime and coriander to sprinkle, matched Thai beers – Rosie had brought a not-expensive red wine, which she noticed Ella spirit away to the back of a dark cupboard – water in antique crystal jugs, some middle-of-the-road unthreatening music in the background. Mumford & Sons, she thought.

The other two couples – she had no idea what their names were, could not recall anything about them – seemed like faceless blurs. She remembered there was some vague chat about politics, the new coalition government, but Rosie had paid no heed, focusing instead on not spilling things down herself. Luke tried to get her and James chatting. 'So, Rosie's an actress.'

'Oh yeah?' James was attacking his pad thai. 'Been in anything I'd have seen?'

Rosie hated that question. How was she to know what people had seen? 'Um, mostly stage.'

'I never go to the theatre. Waste of money, isn't it? Your average theatre ticket, right, what is it? Twenty quid?'

'More, usually.' Rosie had set down her fork and was surreptitiously fanning her lips.

'Right, and I can stream films at home for free. Just need to know the right site.'

'You're talking about pirating?'

James winked. 'Well, who's it hurting, eh?'

'Oh, I don't know, just everyone who wrote and directed and acted in and made it? It's people like you taking money out of the industry.'

James was frowning. 'Easy, love. You should get a real job if you're worried about cash. Teaching, law, something like that. Everyone knows acting's not a proper job.'

Rosie scowled at him. 'I don't think it's fair that only posh kids can afford to do jobs in the arts. What about passion, and joy, and creating something meaningful? That shouldn't just be for rich people.' There was a short silence round the table, and to cover her embarrassment, Rosie took another bite of her treacherous dinner. 'Mm, it's lovely.'

'James is an estate agent,' Luke said, struggling on.

'Foxtons. Got my own car and everything, it's a sweet deal.'

'We're looking to buy, actually,' said Ella. Oh, how that 'we' had stung Rosie, a worse burn than the chilli in the food. 'Moving out of London, even. The prices are getting so crazy.'

'Oh yeah? Where?' There followed a long discussion about

house prices, which Rosie could not join in on. She seemed to be in some discomfort, drinking a large glass of water, swallowing with difficulty. Only Luke noticed.

'You OK?' he said, with concern, under the general hubbub.

Rosie was struggling to breathe now. 'Oh yeah, sorry, it's just—'

'Shit! You're allergic to peanuts! Oh my God, Rosie, I'm so sorry. What can we do?'

'I ... need a shot ...' She didn't carry an EpiPen, though she'd been advised to. No room for them in the stupid tiny handbags that were fashionable at the time. She just avoided peanuts and that seemed to work. Until now, when she'd voluntarily eaten a whole plate of them.

Luke was already leaping up from the table, grabbing his wallet and keys. 'I'll take you to hospital. Come on, it's only a few minutes away.'

She was waving him away with one hand, while clutching her throat with the other. 'Oh no, no, you're having ... party ... urgh ...'

'No arguments. Come on. I'll call a taxi.' He bundled her out the door, and the last thing Rosie saw was Ella's expression, as her fiancé left her dinner party with another woman. Albeit one who was red in the face and whose tongue had swollen to three times its normal size.

Then Darryl's ghostly hand was on her elbow, and the scene was dissolving, the light changing, and there were Rosie and Luke in a hospital cubicle, her with a breathing mask over her face, feeling very silly, while he sat beside her in the plastic chair. Around them the chaos of A&E on a Saturday night, drunks shouting and singing, machines bleeping. Same hospital she was in now, in fact, immobile in the bed six years on from this memory.

'I'm so sorry,' said Luke again. 'I remembered there was something, but then you used to love baklava, and that has nuts in ...'

'Different nuts,' she breathed, into her mask. 'Did you know ... a peanut ... 'snot actually a nut?'

'I did not know that. Always an education, being with you.'

Rosie took off the mask, and fluffed out her hair. She was feeling better after the shot they'd given her, and she'd be able to go home soon. 'I'm really sorry I ruined your dinner party. What an idiot, eh?'

'God, no, don't be, I was glad to get out of there. I can't believe she invited James. James! The guy would drive over his granny if it meant he got a parking spot for his stupid Foxtonsmobile.' She remembered that about Luke, his streak of social justice. Everyone had that in their twenties, of course, but his seemed to be surviving better than most. 'And the rest of them, Ella's work mates, this will sound horrible, but any time they come around I end up drinking too much just to stop myself slipping into a boredom coma.'

'How come you didn't invite any of your friends?'

'Oh, mine are all a bit scattered. Travelling or working overseas still. Like I always wanted to be. It's not exactly fighting the good fight, sitting at home writing articles.' She remembered now that Luke was a journalist, an expert on international development. Was he not happy, being back in the UK, about to be a dad?

Past Rosie waited. 'But a wedding, that's exciting, huh. And a baby! Big steps.'

Luke looked at the floor. 'Very big. It was all sort of . . . thrust upon us. You know, El wanted to live here and she'll be kicked out soon if we don't get married, so . . . '

Of course. Ella was Australian, they'd had to get married for the visa. If it hadn't been for the baby, Rosie might have felt some hope. But as it was, he was going to have a child, and that was that. She wouldn't have tried to steal away someone's husband, someone's dad, would she – not after what Carole had done to her own family? And yet there was that memory, her and Luke in the hotel together, four years from now.

'Luke?' said Past Rosie shyly. 'Now that we're both back, and we're in touch . . . it would be great to hang out again. You know, as friends.' There was no need to say that 'as friends', because they'd never actually been anything more, but Luke didn't question it. The small cubicle felt crowded, memories pushing them apart, unsaid words weighing heavy.

He didn't answer for a moment. Then he said, 'Of course. As friends.' And he took her hand, and squeezed it, in a way that was just about acceptable for one friend to another when the friend was in a hospital bed and a gown that gaped at the back.

'Come on,' said Darryl. 'Time to move on.'

'But can't I just—'

'Nope. Sorry, mate. Lots to see. Lots to remember. Let's go.'

Daisy

It was quite easy to track people down in the age of Facebook. People were harder to lose. Memories were almost impossible to forget when they popped up on your timeline, bright as the day you made them. Daisy had decided – she could not sit and wait a second longer, even if it meant leaving Rosie's bedside, even if people would judge her for it. She had to try to find out what had happened to her sister, and if that meant talking to everyone on Rosie's list, then she would do it. Maybe someone, one of these names on the list, would know the secret to why Rosie walked under the bus, and if Daisy found that out, then there was the slimmest chance she could wake her sister up. It wasn't much, but she had to take it. And time was slipping away.

Ingrid St Cloud, Rosie's university friend, posh and blonde but nice all the same. They'd stopped being friends some time back – why? Ingrid, who was a lawyer in a big international firm, was based near London Bridge, and Daisy easily talked her way in via her own legal credentials. When she told Ingrid why she was there, the other woman emitted a little scream, surprising Daisy. 'Omigod! Not Rosie!'

'I'm sorry. The doctors are hopeful but ... I thought you might like to know.'

'God, of course, of course. How utterly dreadful. You poor thing. Can I do anything?' She was already picking up her phone, the picture of efficiency in her black designer suit, red nails and lips, glossy blonde hair. 'You need food sent over? Accommodation?'

'No, no, Ingrid, thank you, it's just – did Rosie get in touch with you at all? In the last few days?'

Ingrid pursed her red lips. 'You know, now that I think about it, she did send me an email the other day. Haven't got round to replying yet, things are totally frantic, you know ... '

'Yeah. What did she say?'

'Well, it was rather strange. She said she was sorry we'd fallen out and it was all her fault! That was years back, and anyway, it was *my* fault really, considering I married Jack.'

'Jack? You mean ... '

'Yes, darling, I married Rosie's ex. Not very girl code, I know, but ... he's the one for me.' Ingrid tapped a framed photo on her desk, her and a preppy-looking guy on the ski slopes, two small children in bright ski suits hugging their legs. 'I was terribly sorry Rosie and I lost touch. I always thought she blamed me for it. Oh God! You don't think this has happened because ... ?'

'No, no, I'm sure it's nothing to do with that.' Not that she knew. Daisy stood up. She didn't have much time. 'I have to run now, but ... if Rosie comes through all this, will you get back in touch with her, please? I think ... I think she would like that.'

And she scarpered, leaving Ingrid's glossy mouth hanging open in surprise.

Next stop was Rosie's boss at the coffee shop, which Daisy was surprised to find empty. 'Serge,' he introduced himself, with a firm handshake that made Daisy wince. 'You're her sister?'

'Yes, I just wanted to let you know she was ill, in case ... She's not working here any more?'

'No, she quit a month back. Shit, that's terrible about her accident. I'm sorry.'

'And she sent you a message yesterday?'

'Yeah, just saying sorry for quitting, leaving me in the lurch. But it's all fine really.'

Daisy looked round. The counters were empty, the tables and chairs neatly stacked, the till lying open. 'You're closing down?'

'Yeah. Well, it was all because of Rosie, in a way. She gave me this big speech about how coffee wasn't her passion, and she had to do what she loved. I was pissed off at the time, but then I got to thinking . . . it's not my passion either. I mean, it's just coffee. Hot brown water. So I'm going to focus full time on my music. Put this place on the market.'

'Well, that's . . . that's great.' Daisy's mind was whirring. Follow your passion. That didn't sound like Rosie had been planning to kill herself. But on the other hand, why would she quit her job when she had nothing else to do?

'Don't suppose you know anyone who wants to buy a café business, do you?'

'Er . . . you know, I might. Let me take your number?'

Daisy ran on, place to place, person to person. Gary's mate Dave, the one Rosie had snogged at the engagement party, worked at a comic store in Covent Garden, and yes, he told her, standing behind the counter in a Flash T-shirt, he'd also had a message from Rosie saying sorry for her behaviour. 'I didn't reply, though,' he said, blushing. 'My girlfriend didn't want me to.'

'You have a *girlfriend* now?' Daisy gaped at him. 'Er, sorry. I just meant . . . '

'We met at Comic-Con. I guess it was because of Rosie, really. I never thought a girl would look at me, but then she did and she's so beautiful, you know. It made me think, maybe I did have something to offer, and then I met Sarah at the *Star*

Wars booth, and I just went for it. I hope Rosie will be OK. She didn't seem very happy that day.'

'No. I know she didn't. In her message, did she say anything else, any clues about what she was thinking?'

Dave looked baffled. 'Just that she was sorry and she'd post me back the *Star Wars* T-shirt I left at hers. It's limited edition, you see.'

'OK. Well, sorry, Dave, I have to run. Congratulations, and all that.' As Daisy stepped out onto the busy street, she wondered would she ever see Dave again, if she and Gary were over. But there was no time to pause and think about that now.

Rosie's flat. Might there be some clues there, something she'd missed? But when Daisy climbed the stairs, she saw the door was already open, and inside were Caz and Leo, on their knees scrubbing the kitchen floor. 'Oh!'

'Daisy!' Caz stood up, wiping her hands on her dungarees. She had a silk scarf over her hair, and looked like a woman in a catalogue. 'I hope you don't mind. We just had to do something. I was going mad at home, pacing about waiting for news. We thought we'd leave the place nice for her coming home, if she ...' Caz tailed off. If she came home at all. Because it wasn't guaranteed, of course. Nothing was.

'I asked my dad to have it redecorated,' Leo chipped in. 'Lick of paint, few repairs, new bits of furniture, that kind of thing.'

Daisy was stunned. 'That was kind of you.'

'Least I can do, mate.' He looked embarrassed, pulling on his beanie hat so it almost covered his face. 'Rosie's been a good friend to me. Brings me falafel when I'm coming down, reminds me to shower and that . . . and I kept trying to shag her. Er, sorry, I mean . . . make love to her. She deserves better than that.'

'That's OK,' said Daisy quickly.

'Nah, it's not OK. It's disrespectful, like. It's harassment.'

'Well, it's good that you—'

'She is well fit, though. Sorry.'

'Why don't you make Daisy some tea, Leo?' said Caz pointedly, rolling her eyes at Daisy.

'That's OK, I have to rush. But . . . thank you for doing this, both of you. I don't suppose you found anything while you were tidying – a note or a letter or . . . ' Daisy didn't really know what she was looking for. A sign. A clue. A clear description of who Luke was and how to find him. But they were both shaking their heads. Nothing.

A knock at the open door announced a man carrying a toolbox, with paint-stained combats and a pencil behind his ear. 'Hiya, I'm James. Painter and decorator?'

Leo pumped his hand enthusiastically. 'Wicked, thanks for coming so quickly, mate.'

Daisy moved to the door. 'I'll tell Rosie what you're doing. I'm sure she'd . . . she'll be pleased.'

'Rosie?' said the decorator, looking thoughtful. 'I met a girl called Rosie once, at a dinner party. She sent me off with a right flea in my ear about doing what you loved, being creative and all that. Next day I was in such a state I messed up at work, sold someone the wrong house, got fired. But I'm much happier now. Got my own business, freedom, work with my hands . . . '

'Right,' said Daisy, nonplussed. 'It's probably not the same Rosie, though.'

'No. Probably not. Now, where d'you want this lava lamp?'

Rosie

Briefly, she surfaced. The world was full of light and pain, and she had the impression of doctors working over her lifeless body, her parents in the background, faces pale and terrified. What was happening? *Move*, she urged herself. *Lift a finger or a toe or just blink your eye to show them you're still in there.* But she couldn't, and the darkness was already pulling her back under, to her memories, to the past. To the things she'd done her best to forget.

6 May 2011 (Six years ago)

'Where's this then?'

'Hello, dear.'

'Mr Malcolm! You're back.'

'Yes, dear. Can't you tell where you are?'

Rosie looked around. A lawn. A stately home. Giant Connect Four. Bunting. Women in high heels and floral dresses, pegged to the grass. Men in suits holding pints. 'Oh. A wedding. Is it . . . ?'

Rosie remembered now. Since the night of the dinner party, she'd seen Luke quite a lot. It hadn't gone the way of most London friendships, where you might see each other once a month if you were particularly close, or let meet-ups dribble away to nothing as work and distance got in the way. And he had a wedding to plan for. But they'd taken to meeting up during the day – Luke worked from home, and there was never much call for angry articles demanding that the government should pay more in overseas aid – having coffee, wandering by the river near where he and Ella lived in Pimlico, popping into the Tate to look at the paintings, gradually eking out the day until he had to dash home to make dinner and pretend he'd done some work that day. They were friends. As they'd been years ago, nothing more. Enough to invite her to the wedding, though. So here was Rosie, and her heart felt like the crushed raspberry in her glass of prosecco.

People were moving towards the house, being rounded up. She spotted herself, shivering slightly in a strapless turquoise dress she regretted wearing (really, if all this got sorted out she was hiring a personal shopper or something), clutching a wrap and bag and glass. On her own. She didn't know many of Luke and Ella's friends. James from next door, luckily, had not been invited. As she tottered inside in her poorly chosen heels, she realised what this was: the ceremony. She was now going to have to watch Luke get married.

She turned to Mr Malcolm, a ghostly form in his tank top, standing out among these polished young people. 'Do I have to? This was one of the most painful moments of my life.'

'I'm sorry, dear.'

So she gritted her teeth and watched it all, the medley of Adele songs, the reading from *The Owl and The Pussycat* (was this actually her memory of this wedding, or just a composite of every other one she'd been to in her life?), the vows. Oh God, the vows, as they held hands and looked at each other. Ella, of course, looked beautiful, so shiny and glamorous she didn't seem real. Her skin glowing, her dark hair swept up, the lace dress clinging to her curves and the swell of her baby bump. Luke was in a grey suit and waistcoat, with a blue tie to match the wedding colours.

'Will you all please rise?' said the registrar, and Rosie got shakily to her feet with everyone else, as Ella and Luke clasped hands. This was it, the moment they would actually be married. After this, she would have to put all thoughts of him away. She couldn't have feelings for a married man – she'd seen what her father's affair had done to their family. He'd have a baby soon, anyway. He wouldn't have time for her.

'I do,' said Luke. Rosie looked up from her feet, already swelling in the stupid shoes, knowing she had to watch even though it stabbed her inside. When she raised her eyes, she saw his gaze briefly flicker to her, just a moment, before looking away.

'He looked at me. During his vows! Did I . . . ? Was that real?'

'It seemed that way, yes.' Mr Malcolm beckoned her from where she was observing, the ghost at the feast. '*Allons, cherie.* There's just one more thing.'

The ceremony faded and dissolved, and the scene changed to the evening, everyone blurry and rumpled, drink flowing, people doing a conga round the dancefloor. Rosie was in the bar area, standing with a gin and tonic untouched in her hand, staring into space.

'Having a good time?'

Past Rosie turned to see Luke, and started, spilling some of her drink on her shoes. The groom had come to seek her out. It was like talking to the king. Luke was down to his waistcoat now, sleeves rolled up, a sheen of sweat on his forehead. She wanted to rest her head on his chest. 'Oh yeah, fantastic.' Past Rosie put on a bright unconvincing voice. 'Married, eh . . . Congratulations!'

'Oh, yeah. Hard to take in, really. Are you . . . you're OK?'

'Of course. Just having a breather, then I'll hit the dance-floor ...' She hadn't danced at all at that wedding, she remembered. Hard to when your heart was broken.

Luke suddenly laughed, a short abrupt sound. 'You know what's funny? I thought for sure you were married too. When I invited you to those Christmas drinks.'

She blinked. 'You did?'

'It sounds daft now. But I'm Facebook friends with Jack, and I saw he got married a few years back, but I never clicked on the photos because, well ... it doesn't matter why. So I thought he'd married you!'

'Oh God, no, he married *Ingrid*. Weird, huh?'

'Very weird. How did that happen?'

'Oh, it's just ... long story. I think they always liked each other, I just didn't see it. We're not really friends any more, sadly. I haven't seen her since ... Marrakesh.' At the mention of it, they both stepped back slightly. Rosie bit her lip and Luke frowned. Bad memories.

'Why's that?' he said. 'Were you upset about it?'

'No. Me and him, we were – well. It should have ended long ago. All I felt was that ... I wished I'd finished it much sooner. Before we went travelling. Before ...' *Before you*, was what she wanted to say. *Because then I would have been free and you would be marrying me today, not her.* But it was too late to say any of that.

Luke closed his eyes for a second. 'For Christ's sake. Rosie, I ...' Who knew what he'd been about to say to her? He hadn't said it, that was the point. There were things you just couldn't, that you had to keep locked up inside. Words like unexploded bombs.

For a moment they just stared at each other, as his wedding

went on around them, and then they were in each other's arms, in a crushing hug, his heart beating beside her ear, waves of heat coming off his body. She could smell his after-shave and a faint tang of sweat, taking her back to that day they'd met on the beach, and suddenly Rosie had tears in her eyes. She wiped them off surreptitiously on the back of her hand, smearing mascara.

'I'm so happy for you,' she lied. 'It's an amazing day. Go, find Ella. Dance with her.'

'OK.' Reluctantly – she could see now it had been reluctance, she hadn't imagined that – he went, and Rosie stood and watched him go.

Now, she waited to wake up, go back to her own aching body, but instead she didn't surface. 'Mr M?'

'Hold on, dear. There's a bit more, I'm afraid.'

And there was. As if the drawer in her memory marked 'Luke' had been forced open, images and facts and certainties flying through the air. '*Oh.*' A flood of it. She couldn't breathe. The pressure of all those memories hitting her cortex at once, like a hundred filing cabinets bursting open and their contents showering down on her.

Luke and her at a pub quiz, other people there in the background as dull blurs, feverishly hunched over the question paper, slapping a high-five when they got answers right . . .

Luke and her walking along the river near his flat, eating ice-cream cones though the coats and scarves said it was winter, and the sun sliced hard on the Thames and her chest hurt with laughing and the cold and she was happy, yes, happy . . .

Doing a crossword, in deep concentration, crammed into

276

the same seat of a train, her red hair hanging down over the table and brushing against his hand, which he didn't move away . . .

Karaoke, duetting on 'Islands in the Stream', his arm slung loose around her shoulders . . .

In a coffee shop, talking intently, Luke moving the sugar bowl and milk jug round the table to explain something (trade routes, she thought), the waitress, tired and bored, pointing out they'd closed ten minutes ago and kicking them out . . .

She and Luke in what looked like a hotel bar, him staring angrily into his beer, shoulders heaving. 'She lied to me, Rosie. How could she do this? How could she?' And Rosie's head reeling, trying to make sympathetic noises – what had Ella done? She couldn't remember. 'What should I do, Ro? You tell me. What should I do?'

What had she told him? She couldn't remember that either.

'We were friends,' Rosie said, poleaxed by the memories. 'Best friends, maybe, for a while. He came to me for advice about Ella, because I was his friend.'

'Yes. You were.'

Were. Past tense. She knew he was not her friend now, because her family hadn't heard of him. (Why? Had she kept it a secret from everyone, hidden how close they were getting? Had he done the same? Pretending all the while it was innocent, knowing deep down it wasn't? Seeing each other when Ella was at work, a daytime secret for the two of them?)

'So . . . what happened?' Rosie knew she wasn't ready to see it, not yet. The last day of her and Luke, whenever that had been. 'Did I tell him to work on it with her, or what? Did I tell him . . . I loved him?'

'I don't know, dear. But you were . . . something. You and him. Anyone can see that.'

Rosie was crying again. They had been something, something special. But whatever had happened between them, they weren't anything at all now.

Daisy

'Hey, it's you again.' Adam's smile was as warm as the air in his café, coffee-scented, the windows steamed up against the dreary day. It almost made Daisy cry. Comfort, she realised, was a very underrated thing. Gary would not understand that. He believed in cold showers and bracing walks and healthy, low-GI food. What she needed now was a long lie-down in a feather bed, with blankets and hot-water bottles, and tea and cake. Lots of cake.

'Yeah. I just . . . needed a break.' She'd been running round all day, talking to people, puzzling things out, and still she was no closer to the truth. Rosie was unconscious, it was dark outside already, and she might never wake up again.

He nodded in sympathy, as his quick hands stacked clean glasses. 'It happens. Can I get you something? Another latte?'

'Oh, no, thank you. I'll never sleep again if I do.' Not that she'd slept much the past few nights, lying awake worrying. The labyrinth of secrets Daisy was following her sister through. 'Do you ever get time off?' she said to Adam, watching him buzz about. She wasn't sure what made her ask the question. Did it sound like she was asking him out? She blushed, spinning her engagement ring on her finger.

She should call Gary. They needed to talk. Just … she couldn't face it right now. The fight with him seemed to have opened an abyss in her head. *Maybe I never loved him. Maybe I just wanted security, like Rosie said.* 'I mean, you always seem to be here.'

'Boss runs a pretty tight ship. Anyway, it's nice here. Talking to people, being around cakes, what's not to like?'

She surveyed the cakes on the counter, the swirls of raspberry and soft cracked icing and plump, generous sponge, like a pillow after a long day. 'Good point. I'll take a cake, please. In fact, I'll take two.'

He didn't judge. She'd known he wouldn't. 'Sugar is good for shock. Very wise.'

Daisy sat in the table by the window and, taking a deep breath, opened her laptop again. She felt a bit like a detective, piecing together her sister's last movements. Rosie had called Angie, and Caz, and Daisy herself, and her parents. She'd made a list of people that – what, she'd wronged in some way? She needed to make amends with? She'd discovered that two of them were dead. She'd left messages apologising to the rest. But Ella – who was Ella? And who was Luke?

'Everything OK?' Adam set down her cakes, along with a hot chocolate he'd made without being asked, drawing a leaf pattern on top. Imagine all that effort, just for something that would be destroyed in seconds. Making something nice, just for the sake of it.

Suddenly, she really needed to tell someone. 'Oh, it's just … I'm trying to find out what was going through my sister's mind before the accident. I found this list of names in her flat. Names. I thought it might … mean something. But there's a few of them I can't trace on her Facebook or phone or email. I even looked at her search history but there's nothing.'

'Have you tried the Facebook search bar?' He unfolded a napkin for her. 'If the names are people she looked at, it'll likely autofill to tell you who they are.'

'I never thought of that. God, you're brilliant. You should be a spy!'

'How do you know I'm not?' He spread his arms wide. 'This whole café thing could just be an elaborate cover.'

'Nah, you wouldn't be that good at making cakes if it was a cover.'

'See, that's how good I am. I trained as an actual pastry chef to cover my spying.'

Daisy laughed. She actually laughed, in the middle of all this pain and confusion. Immediately guilt descended, her face puckering into frowns, and she bit her lip. What was she doing, chatting to a nice man, laughing, making jokes, when Rosie was in a coma and she'd told Gary to fuck off? 'I . . . I'll try that then. Thanks.'

As he moved off, efficiently wiping tables, Daisy opened Facebook on Rosie's phone and typed in the name Ella. Her heart began to hammer as the app auto-filled it. *Ella Marchant*. A pretty name, a smart name. And Rosie had been searching for her. In the professional shot she looked glamorous and capable – full lips, dark glossy hair. The kind of person who, Daisy knew, Rosie would feel intimidated by. But she couldn't find any connections between them. They hadn't gone to the same university or worked in the same industry or anything like that. They had no mutual Facebook friends. How did Rosie know this woman?

Why had she been looking at her profile page, if they weren't friends?

An idea was forming in Daisy's stomach. She was trying to squash it down, because it wasn't a good one, but somehow, she just knew. She clicked on Ella's profile, scanning the public information, and there it was.

Married to Luke Marchant.

Luke. At last. In his profile shot, he was handsome, broad-shouldered, a bit beardy and hippyish the way Rosie liked. A radiance about him, his fair hair and tanned skin. Ella, the woman on Rosie's list, the glamorous beautiful woman, was married to the man whose name had been on her sister's lips as she clung to life. Luke was married.

Oh, Rosie. What have you done?

Rosie

Something different was happening. When she surfaced from her memories, it was only for a few seconds each time. Faces around her bed, voices calling urgently. But she couldn't stay, and she couldn't wake up. She just floated in the grey, the halfway, the in-between. The real world seemed to fade from her, as she clung until her fingers went white to these memories, these past days when she and Luke had been together.

10 October 2017 (Two weeks ago)

Another memory. She saw her past self walking up to the door of a small red-brick house, with a navy-blue front door and red roses growing round the windows. Past Rosie – only weeks ago – was standing there, as if psyching herself up to knock. She'd dressed up, in heeled boots and her hair pulled into a bun, make-up failing to mask the fact her face was white and her hands were shaking. As Rosie watched, her past self, trembling, knocked very quietly on the door, poised as if to run away.

'What am I . . . ? Oh.' The door had been opened, and Rosie remembered: this was Luke. It was Luke's house. He and Ella must have moved out of London as planned, bought a proper house. Behind him, she could see the bright green of a child's bike, with stabilisers and a bell. Of course. He was a dad. So what was she doing here, two years after she'd slept with him in that hotel?

She began to twist away, turn her back. 'Is anyone there? I don't want to see this, I don't want to relive this one.'

No answer. Was she alone in this memory?

'Hello? Are you there? Fine. I can wake up! I'm waking up now.' Rosie seized her left arm and pinched. Nothing. She was still in this dream, this memory, whatever it was, the dark crevice of her brain this had been hidden in. 'I . . . Oh God.' It was happening.

Luke's face went through various different emotions when he saw her on his doorstep, standing on the ironic mat that read: *You Again?* 'Rosie! What the hell . . . ?'

'I'm sorry!' Past Rosie was very close to tears. 'I . . . I just need to talk to you.'

'But . . . you said you didn't want to hear from me! You just disappeared!'

'I know, but . . . ' Rosie remembered now. After the incident in the hotel, she'd felt so terrible, overwhelmed with guilt. She had tried to stay away, deleting his emails and phone number. Because she knew the truth by then. She and Luke could pretend they were friends as much as they wanted, and carry on meeting for coffee, or a drink, just to talk, but things would always escalate. She could not be around him without wanting to touch him, put her hands on his chest and feel the beat of his heart. Even in this memory, standing shivering on his doorstep, she had been desperate to press her face against his, feel the rasp of his golden stubble under her hand, press her nose to his neck and breathe him in. 'I just . . . I'm in a really bad way, Luke, and I couldn't think who else to go to. There is no one else. I've . . . I've ruined it all. My entire life. I needed to see you . . . ' So Luke and Ella were still together? Whatever he'd been upset about, in that memory of her and him in the hotel bar, they must have got past it.

'So you just . . . showed up?'

'I . . . I didn't know what else to do. I knew she'd be at work.'

'Fucking hell, Rosie! I've been wanting to talk to you for two years, and now you just appear at my door? Come inside.' He seized her elbow, drawing her into the lovely house. Briefly she noted the photos in shabby-chic frames, the tasteful ornaments and knick-knacks which she remembered from the night of the dinner party in their old flat, when he'd taken her to hospital and held her hand. That memory was there too, bright and thrilling and cut through with shame.

Luke stood in his living room, running his hands through his fair hair. He wore grey tracksuit bottoms and a T-shirt, and she could see a line of golden skin in the gap where they didn't quite meet. She wanted to touch it so badly. He didn't offer her coffee or tea. 'Rosie, I know it's hard, but you can't be here. It's not fair to Ella. Things aren't . . . well, never mind that. I know you and I need to talk – God knows we do – but this isn't the way. I need to tell you . . . '

Ella. The name was like a knife in Rosie, even now. 'I had no choice, Luke! I . . . I need you.' And just like that, Rosie remembered why she'd come. About the weeks alone in her flat, sleeping only for snatched minutes here and there, only to dream about the past again, her mother shouting at her, her sister turning away. *You stupid, stupid girl.* She'd lost her job and her friends and failed at acting. A succession of dead-beat men dragged back to her flat, summoned by clicking and swiping at her phone, each one an attempt to stop the slow leak of loneliness in her life, and each one making it worse. She'd lost Luke. She'd lost everything. She was in a bad way.

And so, desperate, she'd found her feet carrying her here to his door, without thinking of the consequences if Ella saw her there. Oh God. She began to back away again, her shoulders pressing against the wall, except she wasn't really there, and the wall wasn't really there and this was all in the past, too late to do anything about.

Then, the key in the lock. Rosie's blood freezing in her veins – she remembered it exactly – and Luke freezing too with his hands on his head, and slowly, slowly, the door opening. Ella was beautiful. Even with the cold she'd come home from work nursing, her hair was shiny and glossy, her lips full. The little boy she was leading by the hand was also beautiful, with solemn eyes under a dark fringe. Charlie. Ella frowned. 'Rosie? What are you doing here?'

The little boy said, 'Daddy?'

Past Rosie was speechless. It could have been possible. They could have explained it away – she'd just popped round (miles away from where she lived) to ask Luke something or borrow something, they were friends after all, but neither she nor Luke was very good at lying. They weren't very good at affairs either, it seemed, if you could even call it that, the one time that they'd been together, both wracked with guilt and shame the whole time.

Luke's Adam's apple was working hard in his throat. 'Er . . . El . . . she just . . . '

Ella was not stupid. She slowly lowered the hand that was holding her keys, and looked between them, and Rosie then and Rosie now could see on her face that she knew.

Rosie ran. Her previous self sprinted for the door, barrelling past Ella and her son, Luke's son, sobs caught in her

285

throat, and her dream self was following, down the road, eyes already blind with tears. She was tearing towards the train station. The heel of her boot was worn down at the back. She wasn't looking, she was upset, she was going too fast. The road was uneven.

Present Rosie, helpless to stop any of these memories or change them, had to stand and watch as she tripped, tried to right herself and failed, and fell heavily into a heap on the road, weeping, the knees of both jeans torn open and the skin bleeding. She turned away, tears in her eyes, and felt a ghostly hand on her arm. 'Sorry, mate.'

'Darryl. You're here. This is ... this is the last time I saw him, right? Luke?'

She remembered it now. Luke had not come after her – arguing with Ella, no doubt, confessing it all, having it out with her. Despite what he'd done, he was not a liar. The betrayal had killed him. Rosie had lain on the ground for a few moments, dazed, then pulled herself slowly to her feet, wincing at the pain in her bruised knees and scraped palms. There was something deeply upsetting about having no one to help you up when you fell. She went on to the station, hobbling like an old woman, determined to get out of there as fast as possible. And she'd sat on the train, her face wet with tears, and gone back to her horrible flat and locked the door and begun to think about her life. All the people she'd let down. All the lives she'd ruined – and now Ella, and little Charlie too, had been hurt by her stupidity and selfishness. Luke was not hers, had never been hers. Why couldn't she just let him go, instead of clinging uselessly to things when there was no hope? He'd chosen Ella, clearly. Ella and Charlie. His son.

They'd worked things out. Sometimes she lied to herself, told herself he'd wanted to get in touch but didn't know her new number. When really she knew he had stayed with the life he already had, the nice house and beautiful wife and cute kid. Because that's what people did.

Darryl's ghostly hand was on her back. 'I'm sorry, mate. This is pretty heavy stuff.'

'Yeah. Well. My life is heavy stuff. I'm just getting to see the consequences of it.'

'Shall we go back?'

She nodded stiffly. Her current life – comatose in a hospital bed with her pee draining into a bag – was better than this, the shame, the pain. What would that do to a person? Would you get to the point, eventually, when going under a bus might seem preferable?

Rosie

Back in herself, her broken, useless body. Her fractured, functional mind. Trapped in her own memories, forced to see all the mistakes she'd made. Maybe this was hell. There were people in the room – her parents, the doctors – but they seemed so insubstantial. More like ghosts than the ghosts who visited her.

'Dude, what's up?'

Oh God. She wasn't in the mood for Melissa right now. Melissa belonged to a simpler time, where the worst thing Rosie had ever done was sneak an extra biscuit from the tin before dinner. Before all these many failures and mistakes.

'Mel, no one says dude any more. It's not 1993, OK? It's . . . things are very different now.'

Melissa, still in her crumpled school uniform, looked crestfallen. 'I know it's not been easy, Ro-Ro.'

'Er, that's an understatement. I've alienated all my family and friends, I'm unemployed, I've slept with a married man, oh, and I've been shagging any awful guy who showed me a crumb of affection, for years now.' She felt weird saying this to a teenager, even though she knew the teenager was just a figment of her imagination (or a ghost or . . . who knew). 'That's another thing, Mel. How come I see you like this? In my mind you should be ten, since that's the last time I saw you. And how come I know you're . . .'

'Dead?' she said cheerfully. 'You don't remember, I guess.'

'Remember what?'

'The list you made. People you wanted to contact to say sorry. I was on there. But you Googled me and found out I'd died. I guess you don't remember how either?'

'I . . . didn't like to ask.'

Melissa looked slightly sad for a moment. 'It was the bullying, you see.'

A cold feeling was rising up in Rosie's legs. That was interesting in itself, as she hadn't felt her legs since the accident, but right now all she could think about was this. 'You didn't . . .'

She shrugged. 'Maybe I didn't mean to. Maybe I just wanted to go away for a while, sleep, make it all be over. I was so lonely, so unhappy. I had no friends. My mum had these pills left over from when my dad died, so I just . . . yeah.'

Rosie felt sobs choke her throat. 'Oh God, Mel. I'm so sorry. I knew all this?'

'It was in the article you found. You knew I'd died and how it happened. Not why. You can never really know why. No one can.' Melissa glanced at the door. 'Your family, you know, they're wondering the same thing right now. If you stepped in front of that bus on purpose or it was just an accident. They want to believe you didn't mean it. But there's the list, you see.'

'Why did I write it?'

Melissa shrugged again. It was a uniquely teenage gesture, artless and careless, and it made Rosie's heart ache for her long-lost friend. If only she'd stayed in touch, could she have prevented this? Or was that the wrong way to think about it? Was everyone walking their own path through the wilderness, and all you could do was try to touch them as you passed? 'You know why, Rosie. Only you can know.'

'But I can't remember! Was I trying to make amends, or was I . . . saying goodbye?'

She could imagine that all too well. Alone in her sad flat, not speaking to her family or friends, the ache inside her from everything she'd lost – she could feel it now, gnawing at her – and the loss of Luke. She could see herself picking up a pen, writing down names, holding their faces in her mind, knowing she'd hurt them. Looking them up, finding out Melissa was dead. Probably she'd done the same with Mr Malcolm. The raw sting of guilt, of grief, of knowing it was too late.

She felt Melissa's hand in hers, the bitten nails, the scratch of a friendship bracelet. It felt real. Yet it was not real. She hadn't seen Melissa since they were both kids. She hadn't had a chance to say sorry, to do anything that might have helped keep Melissa from swallowing those tablets in the bathroom of her house. Maybe it would have been too late anyway. But she could have tried. 'There's no point thinking like this, Ro-Ro,' Melissa said kindly. 'I'm long gone. I don't exist any more. You don't need to say sorry to me. It's yourself you need to save now.'

'But ...'

'Come on. There's a few more things to see, and we don't have much time.'

'What do you mean we don't ...?'

The dark, the blur of grey light. The dial spinning. But Rosie already knew what she was going to see this time.

28 February 2015 (Two years ago)

Rosie's head hurt so much. Exploding with a lifetime's memories: every cup of tea, every kiss, every tear and every smile. 'Please ... I'm so tired. My head ... '

Melissa's voice was gentle. 'I know, Ro-Ro. It won't be long now. Just one more.'

This place, it was that hotel bar again. Luke ranting, semi-hysterical, tears shining in his eyes. 'He isn't mine, Rosie. Charlie isn't mine.'

She remembered now. Just the once. One time only, her and Luke. He'd been up in town for a conference, and she'd met him for a drink at his hotel. Stupid, in hindsight. How naïve they'd been. When she'd got there Luke was already drunk, on the verge of tears.

'What do you mean, he isn't yours?'

'She slept with someone else. Her ex, back in Sydney. She says she didn't know, she thought Charlie must be mine ... but then she saw him again last week. He's in London now. And she says Charlie . . . Charlie looks just like him! I guess maybe she always knew, or at least suspected. But now he's back.'

Rosie's head had been reeling. 'I'm so sorry. My God. What's going to happen?'

'I don't know. Charlie thinks I'm his dad, and I can't just abandon him. Jesus. How can we tell him? Poor kid.' He shuddered. 'You want to know the worst thing? It should have been you. I only married her for the baby, and because you'd left me. It was always you, Rosie.'

This was the moment. Rosie had watched Luke cry and storm, and she'd had the choice to be his friend or seize her chance for more, and she'd done the stupid thing. Because she couldn't bear to see him so upset. Because she'd give whatever comfort she could. So she'd leaned forward, pressed her mouth to his. The feel of his warm skin grazing hers, the golden hairs on his arms, his hands tightening on her back. His voice. *Oh God, Rosie.* Breaking with sadness, with years of holding this back. This was how it happened. Angry with Ella, overwhelmed by all the mistakes they'd made between them, the miles travelled away from where they'd started, and all in the wrong direction. Away from each other. So they'd gone upstairs, to that hotel room with the tiny wrapped soaps and too-small kettle, and she'd taken him in her arms, finally, his mouth on her, the weight of his body, the heat of his skin. But it was no good. He still had a family, a little boy who called him Daddy. Rosie would not be the one to break that up. So she'd run away, like she always did.

'Did you *do* it with him?' came Melissa's noisy voice in her ear, as in front of her she watched herself lean into Luke. No matter how many times she saw it, no matter how loud she tried to scream *stop, don't do it*, it would still happen. She could not change the past, only relive it, only see her mistakes again and again and again.

'Looks that way.'

'Urgh. Was it horrible?'

'No, it was . . . it was the best thing ever.' *Stupid Rosie, stupid, stupid girl.* And afterwards she'd cut off all contact with Luke, until she realised what a terrible mess she'd made of her life, just one bad decision after another, and two years later she'd gone to him, in a desperate last-ditch attempt to save herself, and there was Ella still with him and a voice in her head said he'd only slept with her to get back at his wife and . . . she'd run. Yet again.

'It's a bit like those Catherine Cooksons my mum used to read. A fallen woman coming to ruin.'

'Yeah, well, it's my actual life, so can we go now? I don't think I can handle any more of my Greatest Mistakes.' And her head hurt. God, it hurt.

'OK. Let's try and go back. But Rosie, there aren't many memories left. Once they've all come back, there's no reason for you not to wake up. So . . . try, please? You have to try.'

Daisy

There was no work information on Luke's public profile, and when she Googled him she found he was a freelance journalist. That would be no use for tracking him down. But Daisy had found out where Ella Marchant worked – only streets away – and now found herself walking there in a kind of daze.

She wasn't sure what she was doing. All she knew was she had to talk to this woman, learn the truth about Luke and why his was the one name Rosie had uttered when her life was draining away from her. She had the feeling it wasn't going to be a simple answer.

She waited outside the glass office block, shivering in the wind. This was stupid. Ella might be working late, or not even in today. It could be hours. *Go home, Daisy, you idiot. Go to your sister.* But she stayed. And eventually, after squinting hard at every woman who came out, she spotted one in an elegant camel coat, her glossy dark hair twisted into a French plait. She was tapping at her phone, one headphone in her ear. Her nails were dark red and shiny. Daisy stepped forward. 'Er . . . sorry, are you Ella?'

The woman frowned, as you would if a strange person accosted you outside your office. 'Yeah?' She had an Australian accent.

'Um . . . this is going to sound very weird . . . '

'Who are you?' Ella Marchant had a clear, ringing voice. Confident. Daisy felt her own fail in her throat. *Come on. For Rosie.*

'I'm . . . My name is Daisy Cooke. I'm Rosie's sister.'

'I don't have a lot of time.' Ella stared at her balefully over the cup of peppermint tea she'd reluctantly let Daisy buy her in a nearby Starbucks. It wasn't as nice as Adam's café. A cold breeze blew in from the door which banged open every few seconds, and it was full of people plugged into laptops, noises emanating from their headphones.

'I know. I'll be quick, I promise.' She'd already explained, haltingly, what had happened to Rosie and that she'd said the name Luke when she was brought in, and again when she'd almost woken up.

'She's really in a coma?'

'Yeah ... there was an accident two days ago. On Westminster Bridge.'

Ella pressed a red-tipped hand to her mouth. 'Jesus. That must have been what held my taxi up. Do they know what happened?'

Daisy shook her head, feeling her limp hair flop. 'No. They said she might have maybe ... that maybe she'd ... you know. But we don't know for sure.'

Ella Marchant was a decent person, you could tell, under all her gloss and toughness. She softened marginally. 'I'm sorry. But what is it you want from me?'

'Luke is ... your husband, yes?'

'Ex-husband. Or, he will be.'

'But on Facebook ...' Daisy blushed, revealing her own stalking.

'We haven't told our families yet. Not till it's all settled. But yeah, it's over.'

'I'm sorry.'

'Don't be. It was all a mistake, him and me. We tried, but ... there you go. I'm with someone new now.'

'Do you think it was him she meant, when she said the name Luke?'

'Probably.' Ella sighed, tapping her paper cup with one nail. 'Look, I take it you don't know anything about all this.'

'No. She never even mentioned a Luke.'

'They met travelling. Crete or somewhere. Then she went

home, out of the blue, they had some kind of falling-out, he travelled on, eventually ended up in Thailand where I met him, and we lived in Oz for a while. Anyway, a few years later we'd got engaged – I'd realised I was pregnant, and to live here I needed a visa – and came back, and we had these drinks. He invited Rosie along, as you do, old friends and so on. And I don't know . . . As soon as they saw each other . . . I mean, I was there. I saw it happen. There was just something between them.'

'Oh.' Her sister, in love with a married man.

'Anyway, later on he and I were having some . . . problems, and something did happen between them, and I found out, it all got messy, he promised to cut off contact so we could make it work, and that was that. Then the other week she turned up at the house. I think she got the wrong end of the stick – Luke and I were already splitting up at that point, only living together for the sake of our kid, but Rosie – well, she ran off. She was really upset.' *Our kid.* Luke was not only married but had a child.

'So . . . she doesn't know you've split up?'

'I don't know. I . . . it was kind of my fault, to be honest. Someone from my past, a guy, came to work in London. Someone I thought I'd never see again. He's . . . well, he's the father of my kid. I didn't know, I swear, not for sure, but . . . he is. So Luke and I . . . it's over. But it's fine. I'm fine.'

She probably was, Daisy thought. Ella seemed like a tough little nut, shiny, resilient. Not like Rosie at all.

'She didn't try to contact you?'

'Rosie? Not as far as I know. We only met a few times. At my engagement drinks, my wedding, a random dinner party, and when I found her in my house.' Ella's full mouth twisted in a parody of a smile. 'So, I don't think we'd have had much to talk about. She wouldn't have my number or anything.'

'Right.' So Rosie had not got as far as contacting Ella, or perhaps she'd chickened out. Did that mean she'd not been in touch with Luke either? There was nothing on the phone to suggest she'd called him. Just his name in her dying mouth.

Ella stirred, picked up her smart leather bag. 'I have to go. Sorry, Daisy.' Outside, Daisy could see a man waiting for her, in an expensive navy coat. He was holding a little boy by the hand. Seeing them together – same nose, same dark straight fringe – it was clear this man was the father of the child. Not Luke. How confusing. 'I'm sorry about your sister. I don't wish her ill, despite everything. Luke and I ... like I said, it was a mistake. We were too young, and I don't think he ever got over her leaving like that. Plus there was the baby and everything. But I'm not sure I can tell you anything that will help.'

'No. Thank you anyway.' She was gone, leaving her tea untouched, and Daisy looked around the too-bright café, realising it was dark outside, the third day of Rosie's coma almost running out, and she was still no closer to any answers.

Rosie

It was late now. Dark. She could hear rain pattering ineffectually against the high shatterproof window of her room, though she still could not turn her head to look. Her neck was still in a brace. Her leg in a cast. The catheter and drip still regulating her, in and out, in and out. She could see her parents by her bed, their heads bowed, faces anxious. Saying nothing, because nothing would help. Waiting.

Rosie had read stories of people who lay in a coma for years, decades even. How could you possibly live for years in your broken body, awake and alert but unmoving? How could anyone survive that?

But she knew that people could survive anything, carry around back-breaking loads for years. It was the curse as much as the gift of being human. Had she finally broken under hers? Was that why she was here?

'Hello?' she tried, knowing she made no sound in the world. Her lips were still frozen. Who would come to her next? Darryl, Melissa, Mr Malcolm, Grandma ... She had known these people were gone. That was why she saw them here, ghostly, dead. Too late for her apologies, too late for everything. They were only symbols, of all the things she'd loved and let go. Her family, her friends, her career. All the random people whose lives had intersected with hers, the butterfly-wing impact she'd had in her thirty-three years. It made sense that, in its fractured state, her brain would conjure them up as her guides to dying. Because she almost had. She had touched it, and pulled away, back into this confusing world of lights and beeps and gentle hands on her slack flesh. She had not died in the accident. But she still might. Her brain was trying to come to terms with that. The idea that everything inside it – every memory, every face, every smell and sight and sound – would be going with her, and all she'd leave behind would be people's memories of her. That was what it meant to be dead.

'I understand now,' she tried. 'I know you're not real but I . . . I'm lonely. Can someone come?'

Silence. Just the rain on the window, the slow rise and beep of her machines. Tethering her down to the earth, when otherwise she might gently float away. But then, Rosie got the sense she was not alone. It was a strange feeling. Comforting and exciting and scary all at once. Not a ghost, no. But it was hard to believe these were just hallucinations. She blinked her dry eyes – those worked, at least – and stared into the pool of light at the bottom of her bed. Someone was standing there. A child. Scarlett, maybe. But no, Scarlett was older, and real and noisy and breathing, like she could now see the living always were, blundering about, while the dead stood quietly, watching. It was all they could do.

This child was a little boy. A toddler, really, only just standing up on his own, wide-legged and stocky. He was dressed in jeans and a *Transformers* sweatshirt, the kind kids wore in the early nineties, when this boy had been alive. Rosie felt it all rush through her veins, along with the saline and painkillers and God knows what else they were pumping into her. Love. Terror. Guilt. 'Petey,' she whispered.

Petey said nothing back. He had never learned to talk, of course, not properly. He'd not even been two when he died. She could see in him her father's blue eyes, her mother's gingery hair, same as her own. His clear, unblemished skin. Her little brother. Finally returned to her. 'I knew you would,' she said. 'I knew you'd come back.'

3 April 1991 (Twenty-six years ago)

Rosie opened her eyes onto the past. Immediately her heart began to race and her breath came shallow and ragged in her chest. She knew this memory. She'd relived it over and over. If only it had been different. If only she could go back, do it over again, change things. And now she knew she could not, that this wasn't possible, she just had to stand here and watch it unfold. The very worst moment of all the bad moments that made up her life.

In the start of the memory, it was a good day, the first breath of summer in the air, warm enough to roll up your jeans and take off your jumper. Rosie knew the place. A park near their house in Devon, where they'd gone often as children. Before. Never after. Grass, and trees to hide behind, a van selling ice creams. And a stream, running along in a hollow just metres away.

There she was, in her favourite *Danger Mouse* top and her trainers with flowers on. There was Daisy, only three, cute and chubby still, her hair in pigtails, trying to make a chain of her namesake flower with her fat fingers. On a striped rug, their mother. It was a shock to see her once again, to realise how changed she had been by what happened next. Back then – *before* – she was a young woman, younger than Rosie was now. Her red hair was tied back with a wide yellow band, and she wore an embroidered sweatshirt and shorts. How pretty she was. Her legs were long and slim, her eyes laughing. Toddling about her – he'd only just learned to walk – was her youngest child. Peter. Petey, they all called him, since Daisy couldn't quite pronounce his name. A family of three children, all beautiful, all perfect. A loving husband who couldn't wait to race back from work to see them all, a warm and welcoming house, her youth, her health. In that moment, Alison Cooke must have thought she had it all.

Don't get up, Mum. Please just stay.

But as Rosie watched, her mother did get to her feet, dusting grass off her white shorts. 'I need the loo, Rosie; will you watch them just for a second?' Of course – she'd had three babies. Sometimes she just had to go, and there were public loos over by the gates. She could have taken the children with her, but they were happy, playing on the grass, and she didn't want to move them. She would only be a minute. Rosie knew her mother had also replayed this moment over and over, torturing herself, wishing she'd just held it in or gathered them all up and marched them home. Not let them out of her sight. But it was 1991. People left their kids then. And Rosie, though she was only young, was a responsible girl.

Rosie did not quite remember what happened next. She'd

never been able to. Had she taken it in, her mother telling her to watch Petey, or had she been engrossed in her own world, like her teachers always said at parents' evening? Imagining herself on a stage, in the spotlight, everyone clapping. The dresses she would wear when she was grown-up. The amazing flat she'd live in, just like in *Pretty Woman*, that nice film about the beautiful lady she'd seen five minutes of at her friend's house, which Mummy had said was 'highly unsuitable' (Rosie wasn't sure why). The boy she might marry, one day, who would look a bit like Scott from *Neighbours*. She'd been day-dreaming, helping Daisy poke holes in the stems of daisies, their fingers green and sticky, and she didn't know how long it had been before she'd thought to look up at Petey. He could hardly even walk. If you left him for a moment, he'd normally be right there when you came back.

But Young Rosie looked up, and her childhood ended, and the rest of her life was forever changed. Because Petey was gone. The next few seconds passed in a sweaty blur. She stood up, looking around in confusion. Where was he? Should she leave Daisy, who wouldn't be moved when she was enjoying something, and run after him? What if Daisy ran off too? Then her mother was racing across the grass, shrieking, and Rosie's eyes turned to the stream just a short walk, just a toddle, away and . . .

Now Rosie struggled again. The memory was fracturing around her. She didn't want to relive this. She didn't want this to have happened. 'Please, Petey. I don't want to . . . I'm sorry! I'm sorry I didn't watch you. I was . . . I was only little but it's no excuse. Oh God. I'm so sorry. Please don't make me watch it again.'

Something was happening. Her chest was burning, she couldn't breathe. Her dream body felt heavy, aching with pain, like her real body. The green grass, the bright day, her mother's screams, it was all dissolving. She looked down and Petey was no longer at her side. The real one or the one in her memory. Gone. The last time she'd ever seen him. '*Please*,' she said, but she didn't know who to, and she was wrenched into the light.

Daisy

Routine was a strange thing. For three years now, Daisy had walked up the stairs to her office every single day at eight a.m., keyed in the code to the door, walked past Reception to her desk. But somehow, today, going in so late, in her jeans and trainers, she saw it all with fresh eyes. The dust on the computer screens, the way her colleagues hunched, bleary-eyed, at their desks. Mai trying to retouch her make-up without anyone seeing – she'd probably been here all night again. The stale recycled air, the hermetically sealed windows over a city she never got to experience, the strip lighting. Why had she spent so much of her life here?

'Daisy!' Maura was beckoning from her office. She wore a black Prada suit and heels so high they made her knees buckle. Two other people were there too, a rectangular middle-aged woman and a slightly younger, almost spherical guy. New clients, Daisy assumed. 'There you are! This is Anthea and Derek from Flush With Success. They make loo seats. Very exciting.'

'Right, hi. I'm sorry I wasn't here, I've been dealing with a family emergency.'

Maura forced a caring expression onto her immobile face. 'That's right, how is ...?'

'Rosie. She's ... I don't know.'

'We used to have a Rosie with us, didn't we, Derek?' said the rectangular woman. 'Terribly flighty girl, didn't last five minutes. Rather left us in the lurch. Still, it showed me what I could accomplish by myself. Now I run the company, and Derek here's my partner. In more ways than one.' She brandished her left hand, wedding ring sparkling. 'Probably not the same Rosie, though.'

'No. Maura, can I ...?' Daisy beckoned to her boss, who came out and shut the glass door behind her. Instantly her frozen smile melted.

'Where the hell have you been? I was about to send out a search party.'

'I'm sorry. I was ... it's been a strange day. I had things to do.'

'Yes, well, I need you here. Mai's lost the report on the server. Can you redo it?'

Daisy blinked. 'My sister's in a coma. I haven't been thinking about the report.'

Maura frowned, deep furrows appearing in her Botoxed forehead. There was no facial toxin powerful enough to compete with the stress of this place. 'I'm afraid that's not good enough, Daisy. The report is your job.'

'But ... it's a family emergency!'

'Yes, and I gave you two days off for it, and she's not dying, is she?'

'Well, we hope not, but—'

'Exactly. There are limits to how much slack I can cut you. I was back in here myself the day after I had the twins.'

Yes, and you almost passed out in a meeting with a light bulb manufacturer. Suddenly she saw herself in ten years' time, in Maura's place. Not having slept properly in decades; seeing her kids, if she found time to have any, for half an hour each night. Commuting, eating Pret sandwiches at her desk, sucking up to rich tossers who wanted her to sort out the mess they'd made with their greed and carelessness. She drew in a deep breath, from the very soles of her (sensible, flat) shoes to the top of her head. 'I can't do this,' she heard herself say.

Maura was already on her BlackBerry, checking emails, not a second to spare. 'The report? You must remember some of what you wrote.'

'Not the stupid report . . . any of this. My sister almost died, Maura. She still might not wake up, or be able to walk or talk or . . . '

Maura massaged her temples. 'I don't know what you want me to say. I need that report, and it's your job to provide it. I don't think I'm asking too much here, Daisy.'

'It's not my job.'

'What? Of course it is!'

'No, it's not, because . . . ' Daisy took off her lanyard with her security pass. 'I quit, Maura.'

Finally some expression came to Maura's motionless face. 'You can't quit! People don't quit! If you've got another job lined up you still need to work your notice, do a hand-over . . . '

'I don't have another job lined up.'

'Well, you won't get a reference if you walk out now. You'll be finished in law.'

'I . . . ' She should care. She'd studied for years for this, gone to law school, clawed her way up, practically slept at the office. Her entire life, the wedding, the house, the astronomical mortgage, was based around keeping this job. It was terror of losing it all that got her up at six every day, sent her trotting to the packed train in painful shoes, kept her here long past dark every night. But Rosie had almost died. And that was all Daisy could think of. That if she spent any more time here, she might die too. 'I . . . I'm sorry, Maura. Bye.'

Rosie

Back in the room. Rosie had a glimpse of the bright hospital room around her, and her mother's face, older and lined in fear, hovering in the background, then suddenly she was choking, a line of burning pain down her throat into her lungs. *Help. Help! I can't breathe. I can't breathe!* The pain spread around her neck and shoulders, choking her in a band of red-hot agony. A small detached part of her thought: *Well, this is interesting; this is the worst pain I've ever experienced. Worse than knocking out my tooth on my roller skates (when was that?). Worse than chopping my finger off that time. Worse than losing Luke . . .*

But she didn't have time to dwell on that, because she was dying. She couldn't breathe and she was going to die. She could see her mother's mouth open, screaming, but not hear any sound, and then a team were through the door with a crash cart, paddles and latex gloves and lots of controlled, directed panic. The last thing Rosie saw before she blacked out was the ceiling above her, its damp stains like the drifting continents of the world.

Daisy

Daisy saw Adam right away as she tinkled open the door of the café, with its old-fashioned bell. He was clearing up for the day, humming along to the radio, which was playing a Bruno Mars song. There was something so neat about him, from the tips of his blue Converse to the top of his shiny black head. Not tall, but if they were standing opposite each other he'd have a few inches on her ... Hastily, she switched the thought off as he came towards her. He was always moving, drumming his fingers, whipping dishes away, foaming milk. This boss of his ought to know what an asset he had.

He saw her. 'Hey! I hoped you'd come back. I kept you the last slice of Battenberg.'

'Oh! Thank you.' How kind he was, she thought, taking the brown paper bag.

'Any luck?'

'Well, depends what you mean by luck.' She thought of the whole jumbled mass of clues. Rosie, calling everyone she knew. Rosie, out in the early-morning light, scarcely dressed. Rosie, her affair with Luke, the secrets she kept from her family. Stepping in front of that bus. 'I think, maybe ... she was trying to ... that she did do it. What we thought.' As she said it, unable to speak the actual word, tears rose up in her throat in a gasping sob. 'Oh! I can't ... I just can't take it in. But her life was such a mess, and no one was there for her, and the bus ... they saw her walk in front ... and ... I think we have to accept it. Oh God, I just keep thinking what I could have done differently. Taken her call. Rung her. Or just anything really, anything at all.'

He looked at her so kindly it broke her heart further. 'We're not responsible for other people's lives, Daisy. Only our own. I know it hurts, finding out all of this, but Rosie was on her own path. You can't know what was in her heart.'

She wiped her face, trying to get herself under control. 'Maybe. Anyway, I don't know what will happen now. If she wakes up, I guess we have to try to help her, as much as we can. Sort this mess out. If that's even possible.' She looked at her watch. 'It's late. I better go back. I just wanted to say thank you. You've helped me get through these few days. It would have been hell otherwise. I hope your boss knows they're lucky to have you.'

Adam smiled. 'You didn't spot it?'

'Spot what?'

'The name. Over the door. I'm the boss, Daisy – I own the place.'

'Oh! God, I'm sorry, I didn't twig at all. It's a brilliant café, I . . . I'll tell everyone to come and buy your cakes.'

'Daisy?' He was scratching his head awkwardly.

'Yeah?'

'I know this isn't really the time – in fact, it's the worst possible time really – but if you ever need to talk, maybe you can give me a call sometime? Or maybe we can meet up?'

'Oh? Er . . . '

'As soon as you walked in here the other day, I wanted to ask you out. A walk and a pint maybe. Or coffee, even though I spend the whole day making coffee and I can't even look at it outside of work or I want to throw up. Anything, really. I work here about twenty hours a day but maybe we can find some time. Three in the morning or something. When I do the market run. No pressure. I just ... I want to know what happens. How you are.'

For a moment, she teetered on the edge. On the one hand, being single again, moving out of the house, finding somewhere to live. Maybe having to stay in a nasty flat like Rosie's. No wedding, no house in Guildford with a garage and three bedrooms. Cancelling everything, having to tell her friends. The future wiped out. Life would be changed for ever. Her mother would be devastated.

But on the other hand, she'd probably get over it.

'The thing, is, Adam ...' Absently, she pushed back her hair with her left hand, the one with the sparkling ring, and he clocked it.

His face changed. 'Oh my God. I didn't notice. I'm so sorry.'

'What? Oh, no, no ...'

'What a numpty, eh? I thought maybe you were ... but I got it wrong. Jesus. Sorry.'

'Adam, you didn't get it wrong. I am engaged, yes. Though maybe not for much longer. I have some things to sort out.'

'I haven't got it totally wrong?'

'Not ... totally, no.'

'Oh.' The air had lightened between them. But ... she still had to sort things out with Gary! Her sister was still in a coma! Now was not the time for this. 'Um, do you mind if I just ... let you know? See how things go?'

'Of course! God, terrible timing, I know. I was just worried you'd step out the door and I'd never see you again. I only seem to meet people when their lives are falling apart, you see.'

'I have a feeling mine might be falling apart for a while yet. In a good way, if there is such a thing.'

'So . . .'

Just then, Daisy's phone rang. She pulled it out absently, not thinking about hospitals and medicines and death, but about the smell of coffee and the icing on cupcakes and the smile on Adam's face, which he was doing his best to suppress but not quite managing it. 'Mum? Mum, slow down, I can't . . .'

Daisy listened to what she was saying. She straightened up so quickly she knocked against a table and the cups on it almost fell. 'I'm coming. I'm not far.' She began hunting for her purse.

'What is it?' Adam was at her elbow, helping while she groped her arms into her coat.

'It's my sister, she, she, I don't know but something's happened. Some kind of crash. How much do I—'

'It's fine, Daisy. Just go!'

Rosie

The room again. But it was a different room, with brighter lights right above her, blinding like when you step into the spotlight on a stage. Her happy place, as she'd always thought of it, where she could be herself by being someone else. This wasn't a stage, but it was a kind of theatre. Here there was a smell of disinfectant and the noise of people coming and going, voices in the shadows around her. She could feel things happening to her body, something being rolled onto her legs – tights? – and a cap onto her hair, and then someone's gentle hand picking up hers and a voice saying, 'Rosie? I don't know if you can hear me, but if you can you'll feel a small prick now.'

How kind, to talk to her like she was still awake and functioning. The anaesthetist. The last one to touch you before you went under, sinking in the dark waters. And she felt it, quick and sharp, into her hand. 'If you can, Rosie, start to count.'

Other voices. 'She's been non-responsive for ten minutes now.'

'We better get in there and see what's happening. There may be a bleed.'

'. . . George assisting?'

'. . . in my parking space, really unacceptable . . . '

Rosie clung terrified to these scraps of the world, knowing she was about to be wiped out. She might die in this surgery, whatever it was, and never be able to say sorry to her mother or Daisy and all the people she'd ever loved, and Luke, *oh Luke, are we over? Will I never see you again?*

She felt a small hand in hers, and knew it was not real. 'Petey,' she croaked. There he was, her brother, in the same clothes he'd worn that day he'd drowned in the stream. In a few inches of water, on a bright sunny day, because she'd taken her eyes off him just for a minute. They hadn't even known he could toddle so fast. Petey didn't speak. He couldn't. He just looked at her, with his calm blue eyes, and squeezed her hand tight. He'd be where she was going. She knew that. 'Please . . . look after me?'

Everything was fading, breaking up. The world that had hurt her so much, the beautiful life she'd kicked to pieces, and how ironic, she could see now how good it had been, standing up on dusty stages, drinking coffee in her bed in the mornings, lying on the grass on sunny days, the faces of the people she loved, her sister, her parents, her friends, and Luke, always Luke. *So this is how it feels. If only I'd known.*

But no one can ever know until it happens. Otherwise we'd never get a thing done, poleaxed every minute by how beautiful our lives are, and how very short.

'I love you. I love you!' She forced the words through her dry lips, even though no sound came out, right before the anaesthetic kicked in and Rosie Cooke was switched off like a light bulb.

Daisy

She reached the room as Rosie was being wheeled out, gasping for breath, having raced up five flights of stairs to the ward. Rosie was pale and floppy on the bed, the doctors pushing her to the lift and one running with her IV. 'What happened?'

'There's something wrong with her brain.' Her mother was wringing her hands. 'It's swelling or bleeding or something in her skull, and she's not getting any air. They have to operate! Cutting into her brain! Oh God.'

'Will she be ...?' The word *OK* stuck in her throat. You weren't OK by very definition if you were being wheeled off for brain surgery, and the nurses and doctors were actually running with you, clearing the corridors and heading for the lifts up to the operating rooms.

'It's very bad, Daisy. I just wish ... I wish she could have woken up, even for a moment, so I could tell her I love her!' And their mother burst into loud, undignified tears.

Daisy watched for a moment, awkward. Then she went to her bag – she was the kind of person who always had tissues, of course. 'Here, Mum.'

Her mother pressed the balsam tissue to her face, shoulders shaking. 'It's my fault. I didn't even call her to see if she was OK. I was just so angry with her, and now look. I'm a terrible mother. It wasn't her fault what happened, not at all. She was only little. It was my fault, all mine. Oh, Rosie.'

Daisy reached around to pat her mother's shoulder. There was a lot to unpack in that. Where to start? 'Come on, Mum, don't cry.'

Just then they heard the sound of running feet in the corridor, and a man burst into the room. Fair-haired, in a navy knitted jumper, his blue eyes wild and staring. 'Oh! I'm sorry, I was looking for Rosie Cooke.' He took in the tears, the empty space where the bed had been. Daisy saw it in his eyes as clearly as if he'd spoken: *She's dead.*

He stumbled back. 'Oh God. Am I . . . ?'

'Oh my God,' she said. 'You're Luke.'

Rosie

Awake. Somewhere. Not hospital. Not the world, maybe. Somewhere . . . beyond. *In between.*

Rosie was only aware of a bright white light, so harsh and pure it hurt her eyes. She could see nothing, hear nothing. But suddenly she could remember . . . everything.

24 October 2017 (Two days ago)

Mel. Angie. Serge. Dave. Caz. Ingrid. Mum. Daisy. Dad. Carole. Mr Malcolm. Ella. Luke.

Rosie stared at the list she'd been up all night writing. A lot of names. A lot of people she'd wronged, that she needed to say sorry to. In the weeks since she'd quit her job and that disastrous visit to Luke's house, she'd at first spent a lot of time sitting in the flat feeling sorry for herself. Wishing she could speak to her family, too proud to call them first. Brooding over her life – all the turning points, all the wrong choices, all the places things had gone wrong. Falling out with Caz, and Angie, and Ingrid. Letting Luke go – time after time. Screaming at her mother and sister. Sleeping with a married man. Messing up, again and again.

She hadn't been sleeping. All night she would lie awake listening to voices and traffic from the road outside, until the window behind her cheap gauzy curtains lightened to grey and the birds started up. The doctor had given her pills,

314

but she'd stopped taking them, hating the feeling of wading through treacle. So they'd stockpiled. The silver packet was sitting on the table in front of her alongside the piece of paper with the names on it.

Rosie's head felt strangely clear, as if the insomnia had filled her bones with clean white fire. The long hours of the night over, watching a pink dawn break. Staring at that packet, the silver winking in the sun from the window, illuminating all the dust and mess of Rosie's flat. Of her life. None of it mattered. What mattered now was the rest of her life. If there was to be one. On the one hand, there was the mess she'd made of everything. Petey, Luke, Caz, her career, everything. The pills seemed to call to her from their shiny packet, the peace of it all. To just sleep, and not wake up. It was dangerous, how much she thought about it. On the other, how could she do that? To her parents, who'd already lost a child? To everyone who knew her? Would they care? There was only one way to find out. She'd contact them all. She'd say sorry. And then she'd decide what to do next.

She started with the easier ones, knowing she'd need to work up the courage. First, Caz did not pick up – understandable, perhaps. Ingrid, who she knew would be at her desk, did not reply to the email. They hadn't talked in years, of course. Understandable. Normal. Same with Angie, who was most likely doing the school run: Rosie knew from Facebook she had kids. But then her mother didn't answer the phone – her mother, who never went anywhere! Did she have caller ID, was she screening her own daughter? – and her father didn't either. Daisy had been a shock. She'd actually rejected the call, sending it to voicemail. Rosie's little sister, always so eager to please, so easy to win round with a hug or a Toffo, did not want to speak to her. The damage between them must lie deeper than Rosie had even thought. Mr Malcolm and Melissa, they were dead, the guilt of that lying heavy on her. Of being too late. Ella – she was too afraid to contact her. And then, aware that it was make or break, that everything was hanging on this, she'd called up an old email account, trying to remember the password with various failed attempts, resetting it. After that night in the hotel, she'd done her best to forget him, changing her own email address so his wouldn't be stored in there, deleting his number from her phone. But that morning, throwing caution to the wind with both hands, she'd opened the email account and there they were. Messages from Luke, sent every day since she'd run from his door. Sending his number. Asking her to call, to get in touch. To come and meet him at their old spot. Saying that he'd go there each day hoping to see her, that he understood sometimes you couldn't say these things in an email or over the phone, but only standing opposite each other in flesh and blood.

She didn't even stop to reply. She just picked up her phone and ran. If she'd been thinking straight – if she'd slept much at all in the past few weeks – she might have paused, answered, washed her hair, got dressed. As it was, she just went to him.

'My phone.' She remembered, now, alone in the bright white. It had been in her hand, and she'd been frantically typing out a message to him, saying she'd meet him there, she was on her way. Ready to say all the things she should have said to him years ago. That she'd always loved him, from the moment she'd seen him on that beach, all the way to Marrakesh, the years between seeing him in the pub, all those miserable snatched times together, then more years apart. She'd loved him for every second of every day she'd known him. And she was here, still, if he wanted her. She'd dropped the phone in her haste to get to him, knocked the battery out. Pieced it back together, half-walking, half-jogging over the bridge. The date and time had wiped themselves, as they always did when you took the battery out of her old, cheap phone, so error messages were coming up, and impatient, she'd tried to reset it as she hurried along. The dial. The numbers. Not time travel, nothing like that. Simply the last thing she had seen before the bus ploughed into her – numbers, a grey background, noise and light in the background. That could have been it for Rosie Cooke. She could have been killed. Instead, she'd been granted this extra time to come back to the world, a world she'd left messy and hurt, to her own body that was screaming in pain, to understand all the mistakes she'd made along the way. She had not been trying to kill herself. She had been trying to live.

'But I couldn't change it! I couldn't make a difference.' Rosie could see nothing, but she understood, somehow, she was not alone after all. People were here with her. Grandma. Darryl. Mr Malcolm. Melissa. And Petey. She would not be alone here, even if she could not come back to her life again. *The dark is hugging you.*

But her mother, her father. Daisy. Luke. Oh, Luke. If only she could have spoken to them one last time. If only love was enough to bring you back.

Daisy

Luke – she couldn't get over how handsome he was; really, he had a sort of *glow* about him – sat in the waiting room, head in his hands. 'I'm too late.'

'We don't know that. It's just … they've taken her for surgery.' Emergency brain surgery. That wasn't good. But for some reason Daisy felt she had to be optimistic for this man she'd never met before. Who her sister loved. 'So … Ella called you?'

'Yeah. She's … she's not a bad person. Her and I, we just didn't work.' Daisy was very aware of her mother in the background, looking puzzled. How to explain what she'd found out, who Ella was?

She said, 'Can you tell us what happened that day? You asked Rosie to meet you?' That was where her sister had been going, why she was up so early on that bright day. Luke had emailed her – to an old account, not the one linked to her phone – to say please come. Please come and meet me now, we have to talk. She would have been rushing, half-dressed, in her eagerness to see him. Not looking as she stepped into the road. Thinking only of him. Daisy had found the message in the drafts folder of Rosie's phone, where she hadn't thought to look before. She must have been writing it as the bus hit, knocking the phone from her hand, slamming into Rosie and changing her life, and all of their lives, for ever.

'I thought she just hadn't turned up again,' he explained. 'She never replied. Why would she, after what I did? Letting her run off that day, not chasing after her … I was ashamed.

I should never have married Ella, but there was the kid, you see. Well, he's not actually mine, as it turns out, but . . . he is, if you see what I mean. I couldn't just leave him. So I did what Rosie said. Tried again with Ella. But it's over now. I'll still be in Charlie's life, of course, but Ella and I . . . I wanted to contact Rosie, to tell her that, but she'd changed her number and email. So I thought that was her answer. Not replying, not being there any day I went. I thought she'd decided I was no good after all.'

'But she *was* coming.' Daisy could picture it all now. Rosie, her phone in her hand, trying to find the location or even maybe texting to say she was coming, please wait. Not looking where she was going. Stepping out, in expectation of seeing Luke again, and then the speed of the bus. 'She wasn't trying to . . . It was an accident. Mum, it was an accident!'

Her mother's face was set in hard lines. 'Daisy. Darling. It doesn't matter. Don't you see?'

And Daisy understood. Even if Rosie hadn't been trying to kill herself, if she'd stepped out by accident, not looking, rushing to meet Luke, then it didn't make a difference. She was going into surgery right now and they were opening up her brain. She might die anyway.

'Oh God.' Suddenly she understood. Rosie might die. Rosie was in the operating room right now, fighting for her life.

Rosie

'What's happening to me now?' she said, to the empty bright air.

319

'They're about to operate on you, dearie.' Grandma's voice. 'Your brain is bleeding, swelling up in your head, see.'

Mr Malcolm. 'They have to cut out a piece of your skull so it has somewhere to go. You're just slipping under now.'

'My – my skull?'

'No worries, mate.' Darryl. 'They do it all the time. They can close it up again, no bother. Let go, Rosie. Let them work.'

'We'll be right there with you,' said Melissa, sounding cheerful. Rosie didn't know why. They were cutting into her skull so her brain could come out – that didn't sound like much to be cheerful about.

'Grandma? Is . . . is Petey there?'

'Aye, pet, I have him.'

That was good. It was comforting to think Grandma had been looking after Petey all this time. She knew she didn't really believe this – she knew they were both just gone, vanished for ever – but it made her feel better all the same. 'Is he OK?'

'He's fine. We're all OK here. That's what happens . . . after. It's only in the world you have pain and accidents and people chopping your skull open.'

'Or your chest,' said Darryl darkly. 'You wouldn't believe how long it took to get those pecs, either.'

'Can I see?' Melissa said eagerly. Oh God. The voices of the dead were flirting in her subconscious. What kind of brain did she have that imagined these things in its dying moments? She realised why she'd hallucinated these ghostly companions for herself, as her brain clung to life, jumbled and terrified. The human mind could not imagine itself dead, switched off like a phone with its battery out. Which was what she was now, at least temporarily.

'Grandma?'

'We'll be here, love. You have to go now. Say goodbye to Petey.'

She felt a pressure in her arms, like the weight of a small boy, his sticky face pressed into her neck. His breath. But Petey had not breathed in nearly thirty years. She held him close. *I'm sorry. I'm so sorry.*

But she knew, though he didn't speak, that he didn't blame her for what had happened. The dead did not have time for blame. They were just gone.

She was panicking. 'Will you be here when I wake up? If I wake up? Will you be there if I don't?'

'I can't say, lovie. If you believe in things like that, I'll always be with you. But as to what you'll see and hear, I don't know.'

Wait. Wait! I'm not re— She went down, trying and failing to hold on to these last tattered remnants of herself. Of Rosie Cooke. Then she was just . . . nowhere.

Daisy

Time. Sometimes it crept along, the minute hand of the office clock seeming frozen. Sometimes it leapt and flew, and a year went by and she could barely think of anything she'd done with it. But this, sitting in the waiting room while Rosie had emergency brain surgery – this was a moment where she wanted time to both race ahead and freeze. On the one hand, if they stayed here for ever, Rosie was alive and there was hope. On the other, it was excruciating sitting there with the bad coffee and plastic leather seats that moulded to your bum, dwelling over and over on how Gary wasn't even there with her, how her parents sat with three chairs between them, and how Luke paced up and down, asking questions that no one knew how to answer. Her father kept stealing glances at him, and no wonder – they didn't exactly know how to explain who he was. He had offered to go, leave them to be just family – he had nice manners – but her mother had insisted he stay. Maybe to soften the jagged edges of all the broken things that lay between the three of them. So he was there, handsome in his navy jumper and grey jeans, working his hands over and over. Somewhere, at the bottom of Daisy's stomach, all that information was sitting ready to be sifted through. Rosie having an affair with a married man. Being in love with him for most of her adult life. She wondered would there ever be a good time to discuss all that. Her sister's secrets, spread out like her broken body, to be handled and poked by strangers. It wasn't right.

'How long did they say it would be?' her mother said. They'd lost all track of time now. It was somewhere deep into the night, dark outside, the overhead bulbs frazzling their eyes. The end of day three.

'Three hours at least. Maybe longer.' Right now, a few rooms away, people had their hands inside Rosie's head. They would have shaved a patch of her bright red curls and sawn her skull open. Daisy shuddered. How did doctors do it, get past the horror of cutting through skin and bone, opening up what should have stayed hidden for ever?

Luke stood up violently. 'This is my fault. If I hadn't . . . she wouldn't have . . . '

'We can't think like that,' said her mother. 'It was an

accident, that's all. Could have happened to any one of us, the way those drivers bomb along . . . '

The bus driver. Daisy had barely thought about him, dimly remembering the doctor saying the police weren't going to prosecute. Because it wasn't his fault Rosie had stepped into the road, not looking, fiddling with her phone. He wouldn't have had time to stop. At least she had been happy in the moment. Going to meet the love of her life.

'And where did you meet Rosie again?' said her father suspiciously.

'Crete. It was . . . a long time ago.' Luke stared at his hands. He had good hands, strong and broad. Daisy thought fleetingly of Gary's, which she'd always found unnaturally small. And where the hell was he? Was he gone for good, like she'd told him to? Was she not engaged any more? She'd pretty much agreed to go out with Adam, hadn't she? But she was still wearing her ring. Everything was so confusing.

'And you've seen her since then . . . ?'

Luke just shrugged, helpless. 'Mr Cooke, I don't think it's up to me to tell you the story. But I can say that I have always loved her. Always.' Luke was good at reading signals, it seemed. He motioned to the door. 'I, er . . . I'll just get us some teas. Give you all time to be together.' Polite. Thoughtful. Handsome. Why had Rosie ever let him go?

When he'd gone, her father also sprang to his feet. 'Bloody hospitals. Can't stand this. Reminds me of when Mum passed.'

'Your mother was old,' said Daisy's mother, slightly cross. 'She died playing bridge and drinking too much cream sherry. It wasn't like this.'

'And who's this chap that's suddenly turned up? Eh? Some random stranger?'

'Rosie said his name,' Daisy said, feeling the weight of the story press on her. 'I ... Dad, I think she'd want him here. OK? Mum asked him to stay.'

'Alison?'

'That's right, Mike. I let you have your wife and child here, didn't I, even though she's far too young to be exposed to a situation like this.'

'She's Rosie's sister.'

'Half-sister. And I can't imagine Rosie would want the woman who stole her father at her bedside. It was very insensitive of you, Mike. But then that's you all over. Selfish. You never thought of the impact you were having on Rosie.'

'Oh, here we go. And you did, when you took to your bed for months and left her and Daisy to their own devices? She cut her finger off, Alison!'

'It was grief, Mike! Not that you would understand that. You were never there!'

'I was working! Someone had to, since you'd given up functioning. And you never thought about how it was for me. I was grieving too, but I still had to keep going, put food on the table!'

Daisy bowed her head, listening to their angry voices buzz. What was this for Rosie to wake up to? A family who hated each other, fractured down the middle?

Shakily, she got to her feet. *Find your voice*, Maura always said, when she had to do presentations. *Don't mumble, Daisy. Put your words into the world.* 'Mum, Dad ... you need to stop this. I know you're both worried and you're sad over Petey, but still.'

They both reacted as if she'd slapped them. Petey's name had not been said out loud for years now.

'I know, I know, I said his name, but we have to talk about it. Our family is ... a disaster zone. No wonder Rosie's a mess. No wonder I'm ...' *About to marry someone I don't even like.* She swallowed. 'It was no one's fault, Petey. It was a terrible accident. Not Mum's fault, not Rosie's. And Mum, I know you were hurt Dad left, but it was years ago and he was just trying to be happy. It's not Scarlett's fault she was born. I wish you'd try and be happy too. That nice neighbour of yours ...'

'What's that?' said her dad, frowning.

Her mother wrung her hands awkwardly. 'He bought the Smiths' old place. John. He's ... well, he's my boyfriend.' A sob burst out. 'And I wish he was here with me, but I didn't think it was right, after I've been such a bitch about you and Carole!'

Daisy and her dad gaped. Finally, he said, 'Bought the Smiths' old place, eh? Done anything about that knotweed problem?'

'Well, yes, he's a wonderful gardener.'

'That's ... good.' He took a deep breath. 'Alison ... I know I did wrong, leaving you and the girls. I just ... I felt like I'd go under if I didn't get out. I was just trying for a bit of happiness. I ... I'd love it if you did the same, honestly I would.'

'I'm ... trying. I really am.'

Daisy couldn't believe she was hearing this.

'I'm sorry, Ali. What a mess, eh?'

'I'm sorry too. We mustn't blame ourselves too much. Not many could have got through ... what happened.' She turned to Daisy. 'Does Rosie really ...? She thinks I blame her for ... Petey?'

'Well, yeah, Mum. The guilt's been crushing her for years. You don't think that explains all this? You don't think that's why, when a handsome, lovely man like Luke wants her, she does her best to ruin it, because she thinks she doesn't deserve to be happy? Why she sabotages every friendship and opportunity she ever has?'

They were staring at her. 'Darling . . . '

'No, Mum. Both of you need to listen. If Rosie wakes up, we have to start again. Be a family, even if it's a family with some extra people in it. We have to try and love each other. Because Petey is gone but we're still here, and we have to try and live, and be happy, before it's too late.'

She turned. Luke was in the doorway, carrying four paper cups in his large hands. He must have heard most of it. Even the bit where she called him handsome and lovely. He blinked. 'Er . . . tea OK for everyone?'

Her parents took theirs with a big show of thanks, even her father, urging Luke to sit down and tell them about himself, and the awkward moment passed, and Daisy had said what she needed to. Her words had been folded back into the batter of their family. Could people change? Daisy had to believe it was possible. If her sister's brain getting crushed wasn't enough to heal their family, then nothing was. She just had to hope Rosie came back in order to see it.

Daisy rested her head against the wall, the dingy beige colour of it. Someone had come in to empty the bin, a grey-haired woman in an orange tabard. 'Mind if I get past you there, darlin'?'

'Oh! Yes, sorry.' She shuffled her chair, distracted. The small room with its old chairs, out-of-date magazines and posters about health scares was where they were going to live out the most significant moments of their family's history. She had a feeling that, bland as it was, she was going to be remembering it for the rest of her life.

'Don't you worry,' said the woman from the doorway – a cleaner, Daisy assumed, given she was flicking a duster half-heartedly over the chairs. 'She's going to be just fine. I know it. She's got people taking care of her. On this side and the other.'

Daisy looked up – what did she mean? – but the woman was already gone.

Rosie

Oh, her life. If only she'd known. It had been so beautiful. She could see that now her memories were back. Swinging between her parents' arms, Daisy a baby in her mum's tummy. Daisy a red bundle in a blanket, Rosie clambering on the hospital bed to see her new sister. Long car trips on holiday, inventing an elaborate game of I Spy crossed with wink murder. Primary school, and having the same *Sesame Street* lunchbox as Mel, sharing Monster Munch with her (Mel was only allowed carrot sticks). Teenagers, her and Angie, dancing round the room to the Spice Girls, practising dance routines. Rosie belting out the final song in the school production of *Blood Brothers*, the audience leaping to their feet in applause, Mr Malcolm in the wings with tears in his eyes, looking down to see both her parents there, proud faces smiling up. Her mother, a young woman, dancing her round and round the kitchen to Kylie Minogue, her red hair flying. Petey, his soft warm body snuggled up to hers in an armchair as she read him a story, *Where's Spot?* University, dancing like mad with Ingrid to S Club 7, jumping up and down, sweaty and joyful, flinging their arms around each other. She and Caz sitting at their cheap dining table, rings from red wine glasses all over it, the clock showing three a.m. and still so much to say to each other. And Luke, so many memories of Luke. Pressing her lips to his neck, the pulse of his blood. The smell of his skin on that beach, hot sand under her bare feet. Oh, Luke. And everyone. Her parents and Daisy and Caz and Ingrid and Angie and Mel and everyone she'd ever known. Everyone.

'My life,' she gasped. 'It was . . . it was so good. Why didn't I see? Why couldn't I?'

'No one can, darling,' Grandma said in her ear. 'Not till they're lying where you're lying. That's the heartbreak of it.'

'I wish I could tell them. I wish I could go back, do more with it. Make some kind of difference to the world.'

'Oh, pet, you did make a difference. Don't you see? That's what all this is for.'

'What?'

'All these memories. These lives you touched and you don't even know it. Angie, she'd have married that Bryn if it weren't for you. He'd have beaten her black and blue. You stopped that.'

'Not on purpose!'

'But even so. You made a difference.'

Darryl's voice said, 'Ingrid, that posh bird, she married your ex, and they've got two kids now. That would never have happened if not for you.'

'Oh . . . wouldn't it?' Her head was spinning.

Mr Malcolm. 'And your friend Caz, she only got that breakthrough role in the first place because you showed her the audition ad and ran lines with her, do you remember?'

'Oh . . . maybe.' Too many memories, exploding like a kaleidoscope. She couldn't grasp them, hold them in her hands.

Melissa now. 'Ella, she only came to the UK because she met Luke, because he was heartbroken over you. Her life's different because of you, Ro-Ro.'

'But my family, my parents . . . what I did to them . . . Petey would be alive if not for me!'

Grandma said, 'Petey would never have been born if not for you, love. Your dad didn't want a third, but your mum was so happy . . . she loved having you and Daisy so much, she wanted another, and you kept asking for a little brother. Remember?'

'Er . . . I don't know . . . '

'And if it weren't for Petey, your dad wouldn't have left, and Carole's life would be different too. Scarlett wouldn't be here. And think of all the things that kid's going to do with her life. Rule the world, most likely. All because of you. That's what you learn when you pass over, darling. None of us can exist without each other. And that's the truth.'

'But . . . what will happen now? Am I dying?'

'We can't say, pet.'

'I don't want to die! I know I thought about it, but I didn't. I decided to try and make things better instead. I was trying to come back from it, from rock bottom.'

'Are you sure?'

'I'm sure, I'm sure! I want my life back, crappy and broken and messy as it is. I want to fix things. I want . . . Please, I want to see Luke again, and my parents, and my sister – both my sisters . . . Please. *Please.* I don't want them thinking I tried to kill myself. I want to tell them what really happened. I want to go back.'

But maybe it was too late?

Daisy

'Hey.'

'Hey.'

Gary looked different somehow. Usually he wore his tie tight to his neck, so close it looked like it was cutting off his air supply, and he never took his suit jacket off if anyone could see. But now he sat in the hospital waiting room, in his shirt-sleeves, tie hanging loose, shirt crumpled, a paper cup in his hands and something resting on the seat beside him in a paper bag. 'Where've you been? Is that . . . cake?'

He shrugged. 'I . . . thought one bit wouldn't do any harm. Went to that café you're always in.'

'Oh yeah, it's good, isn't it?'

'Best Bakewell tart I ever had.' Gary sighed. 'Then I just walked about a bit. Thinking about – you know. Everything. Am I allowed to ask how she is?'

'She got through surgery. Now we just have to wait and see if she wakes up.'

'Oh.' He screwed up his face. 'You know, I never understood it, how things were with you and Rosie. I never had anyone else growing up, just Mum and Dad.' An adored only child born late to his parents, both now dead, Gary didn't

330

have much by way of family. It was perhaps one of the reasons he'd inserted himself so cosily into hers.

'She's my sister, Gar. It doesn't matter what she does, or how badly she behaves. If she's sick I come running. If she needs a kidney I'll be, like, slice here. That's just how it works. And you don't have the right to come between us. No one does.'

'I know that. I'm sorry for what I said about her. It was out of line.' He heaved another deep sigh. 'I've been put on disciplinary by Mr Cardew.'

'God! Why?'

'For taking the day off. He said only blood relatives, and even then they'd have to be at death's door.'

'She's in a coma! That *place*.'

'I know. But it's a good job. Good money.'

'That isn't everything.'

He looked sadly at his hands. He had cake crumbs on his shirt. 'Daise, what are we going to do? This wedding, it's costing a fortune.'

'I ...' Daisy sat down. It was now or never. Life or death. Stick or twist. 'Gar, I've been thinking.'

'Oh, Daise, no ...'

'Just let me say it.'

'Do you have to? Please don't.'

'Seeing Rosie like this, almost losing her ... it's made me think. What are we doing? The way we live ... up before dawn, on the train, back after dark, spending the weekends going to B&Q and painting the living room ... we're young. There're so many things we haven't done. Why are we in such a rush?'

'You don't want to get married any more.'

She opened her mouth to say of course she did, she just wanted to talk about it, but instead she said: 'No. I don't.'

'Not to me.'

'Not to anyone. For a while, anyway. I'm only thirty.'

'Do you love me, Daisy?' It wasn't something they asked each other, or said very often outside of Facebook.

'I . . . of course I'll always love you in a way, Gar. But – don't you think there must be more to life than this? Going to bed at nine with our pyjamas on, making sure to put on hand cream, floss our teeth, moisturise?'

'There's nothing wrong with flossing! It's important to look after your gums.'

She put a hand on his arm, felt him sag. 'I know it is. But . . . other things are important too. Like joy. Like love. Like . . . honesty. And I think, honestly, we're not in love with each other. Maybe we never were. I think we both just wanted that life. House, marriage, car, NutriBullet . . . all of that.'

Gary was quivering. She thought he might be about to cry. 'What will we do?'

Daisy sighed. 'I guess . . . I'll find somewhere to stay for a while. Maybe at Rosie's, if she's recovering. She'll need someone to cover the rent.' The idea was already there in her head, as if someone had dropped it there.

'You said it was a fleapit!'

'Well, it's been having some home improvements, as it happens.'

'You've got it all planned out, I see,' Gary said sadly.

'Not really. You just . . . you get a lot of clarity when someone might die.'

'We'll call the wedding off?'

'I think we better. It wouldn't be right, not with things how they are.'

'We'll lose the deposits.'

'I know. That just . . . can't be helped.'

He heaved another sigh. 'I'll have to update the spreadsheet.'

'I'm sorry.'

Gary got to his feet, brushing crumbs off himself. 'I know you think I don't care, but . . . will you let me know how it goes, with Rosie? I'm not sure it's right for me to be here if . . . well. But I do care. I hope she gets better. I should have been nicer to her.'

She stood up too. Incredibly, it seemed they were going to part like this, after so many years, in the waiting room of the hospital. All those nights she'd lain awake wondering if Gary was the one for her, realising how trapped she was with the wedding and the mortgage, and here it was just falling apart quietly, like a tapped Chocolate Orange. How easy things were, when you held them up against life and death. Against the battle Rosie was fighting, behind that door.

It was a shame she wasn't awake, really. Daisy was sure her sister would be happy to find out she and Gary were over.

Running feet. Her mother in the doorway, face ashen. 'Daisy. Come now.'

Rosie

Was this Heaven? Would she get in, after all the terrible things she'd done, the people she'd let down? Did she even believe in Heaven? It was certainly white, filled with a light so strong it hurt her eyes. Hands were holding hers, one on either side, and she no longer felt any pain in her head or lungs. Was this it? The peaceful end Darryl had talked about?

'Grandma?' she tried. Nothing. No ghostly visitors were with her now. Instead, she heard another voice, a young woman's voice. It was Zara, the doctor.

'Rosie? We've taken you off the ventilator, and we're going to see if you can breathe on your own, OK? We'll try three times and if she can't breathe we'll ... well, then we have to make some decisions.'

This was it. They'd patched up the bleed in her brain, but more damage might have been done. They were testing her, to see if there was any hope of her surviving. If she didn't manage to wake up now, that might be the end of her. *Come on, Rosie, breathe. Breathe! Just a little thing. Just in and out. Do it!*

Daisy

She would not have believed that every moment in her life, everything she'd ever gone through or thought or felt, could come to this: standing at a hospital bed, watching as doctors disconnected her sister's breathing tube. Rosie's face was pale and slack, her hands lying limp by her side. The polish on her nails was chipped. Daisy wished she'd thought to repaint them. Just one small act for her sister, to try to show her love, the pointless overflowing love that would have nowhere to go if Rosie did not manage to breathe.

The machines began to beep, and Daisy heard her mother

sob, and grim-faced and efficient Zara plugged the breathing tube back in. 'I'm sorry. We'll try two more times.'

Rosie

I can't breathe! I can't breathe! I can't—

The clutching panic eased as the blonde doctor hooked her up again and Rosie choked, and sucked in life-giving air. Was this it? If she couldn't breathe on her own, would she be like this for ever, trapped in her wasting body? Or would they just let her go, convinced she wasn't in there any more? She had two more chances to wake up, to come back to herself. To give her life, flawed as it was, one more try. *Please. Please, let me live.* But she didn't even know who she was talking to.

Daisy

Again, the disconnection of the tube, the agonised wait, the ticking of the clock. Watching Rosie's face turn blue and her chest stay stubbornly still, and the beeping and shrieking of the machines, and the reconnection, the calming.

'That didn't work either, I'm afraid,' said the doctor. 'We'll try again. One more time.'

And if that didn't work? Then what? She thought of everything she'd learned about her sister, the pain and loss she'd gone through, the unhappiness, her lonely life. Was it right to do this? Poke her full of tubes and needles, use machines to keep her heart pumping? Was it selfish to want her back, so they could try again with the mess they'd all made of loving her?

'Third attempt. Here we go.'

Rosie

Come on, Rosie. This is your last chance. When they switched the machine off, it was terrifying, like plunging her head beneath the waves. But she had to do it. She had to show she was alive. Not just that. That she *wanted* to live, to make her life better, to change things. To try again.

'Here we go, Rosie,' said the doctor in her calm professional voice. 'When I disconnect the tube, try your best to breathe for us.'

Panic. Choking. Fear. *Breathe, Rosie, breathe.* The simplest act, one she'd never even thought about before all this. Just the rising and falling of your chest. Nothing really, but everything too. Life. Hope. Because she wanted it, with all its pain and suffering and regret. She wanted her life back.

Taking everything she had, every ounce of sadness and hope and love, Rosie Cooke opened her mouth, and breathed in life.

Around her, everyone jumped back in shock.

'Did she . . . ?'

'Was that . . . ?'

'Rosie! Rosie, can you hear us?'

She flickered her eyelids experimentally – working. Light filtered in.

'Rosie! You're awake!' Faces beaming down at her, full of love. Was she dead? Being welcomed to the afterlife? She was pretty sure, however, that they would not play One Direction in Heaven.

'Scarlett, turn the music off!'

'It helped her wake up!'

'Well, maybe, but we have to be very quiet and gentle now. Rosie, love, are you there?' On one side, her mother, tears streaking her make-up. On the other her father, who looked as if he hadn't slept in days. Past them, there was Daisy, weeping, taking off her glasses to wipe them on her jumper. Carole, with her arms round a beaming Scarlett, who was holding her phone aloft. Her family. All around her. Also there was a tall grey-haired man with a kind face, who she didn't recognise. He had his arm around her mother. That was strange.

'Darling, do you know us?'

Come on, head. Just a little nod. Just for me?

'Oh, Mike. She knows us! She knows us!' Was she dreaming? Were her parents crying in each other's arms? Was her mother reaching out to bring Carole in, and the mysterious grey-haired man? Was Daisy stroking Scarlett's hair, who was looking baffled at the emotion all around her?

'Why's everyone crying? Rosie woke up, didn't she? She's OK?'

Her mother answered, finally speaking to Scarlett in kind, loving tones. 'Sweetheart, we're just happy. Because Rosie has come back to us, and we love her very much.'

Rosie nodded her head again, and slowly, like a dead weight, it responded. The effort left her exhausted, falling back on the bed, but finally she felt like she was driving her body again. Like she was back in it, not adrift in her mind somewhere. The real world seemed concrete, full of sharp edges and bright colours, no longer covered in that fine veil that seemed to separate her from the living. She was back.

Her parents drew away, tidying themselves up, sniffing and straightening, as if embarrassed at their spontaneous display of emotion. 'Darling,' said her mother tentatively, 'there's someone else here to see you. If you feel up to it?'

Rosie knew she looked a wreck. Her lips felt cracked and sore from the breathing tube, she hadn't washed in days, and her skin would be pasty and slack from lying in this bed.

There was someone in the door. Broad shoulders filling it. Light surrounding his fair hair like a halo. He was crying again. So sad they had made each other, both of them, but so happy too. Was that what love was? Going through the wringer for someone? He stepped into the room, coming closer, as if not sure she was really there.

'Hi, Rosie,' he said, swallowing down his tears to smile at her, like the sun coming out. 'It's you. It's really you.' He came towards her, clutching her hand in his big warm one. She felt a pulse between his thumb and forefinger. The life running through him. And she was alive too. And that meant anything was possible.

Rosie tried her hardest. *Come on, hand, please work. I promise I'll stop biting my nails and use lotion and get manicures all the time from now on. Just one tiny squeeze? Please?*

And, gathering all her strength, all the force of her love for him, she put all her might into it and managed to give his hand the faintest squeeze. It wasn't much. Barely there at all. But to Rosie, it was everything.

*

And all through the ward, there were smiles and some tears. The neurosurgeon who'd saved Rosie's life went home happy to her husband and children, and held them a little closer. Praj decided he would finally ask Zara out for a drink, because life was short, and sometimes miracles happened. The surgical nurse decided to stay on in her role, because there were good days now and again, days where you made a difference, and the following week she saved the life of a child who was choking to death on a pea. Dot – who really was a cleaner and really wasn't dead, just sometimes invisible because of what she did – smiled and nodded: she'd known it all along. The anaesthetist got promoted and was able to bring his brother over from Nigeria. Caz, weeping at the news of Rosie's recovery, gave the performance of her life that night, inspiring everyone in the theatre to be a little kinder and love a little more freely. Daisy thought about Adam's offer to meet up, and decided: why not? Happiness was in short supply, so you had to grab it while it passed through your hands and hold on tight. Scarlett decided she was going to become a brain surgeon when she grew up, if being a dinosaur hunter didn't work out for her. Rosie's mother had already made up her mind to ask John to move in with her and see if he couldn't work his magic on her rose bushes. Ella and her boyfriend would get married, now that Luke seemed OK and her guilt had eased, and have more beautiful shiny-haired babies. Charlie would be happy to have two dads, and two sets of toys. And as for Rosie and Luke, well, their story was definitely not over yet.

They say in our lives we'll meet something like eighty thousand people. Most of them just in passing, sitting beside them on a bus, buying a latte from them, overtaking them too fast on the motorway. Others will become friends, lovers, family. Some will stay in our lives for ever, and some will be swept away by the flow of life. But we touch all of these people in some way, tiny or huge, making more of a difference than any of us can imagine. Because, as Rosie's grandma had said, none of us can do it without each other. And even if she was, technically speaking, just a memory, it's what we leave behind us when we go, the way we live on in other people, that matters the most.

ACKNOWLEDGEMENTS

Thank you to everyone who helped whip this book into shape, especially my fantastic agent Diana Beaumont. I'd also like to thank everyone at Sphere and Harlequin US/Graydon House, especially Maddie West, Thalia Proctor, Margo Lipschultz, and Melanie Fried. And huge thanks as well to everyone who has been involved in copy edits, cover design, marketing, publicity, and more.

I've been truly overwhelmed by the messages I received about my previous book, *How To Be Happy*, so I'd like to say a huge thank you to everyone who read it and took the time to get in touch. I hope you enjoy this one too! I'd love to hear from you if you've read this book.

I'm on Twitter @inkstainsclaire, Instagram @evawoodsauthor, and online at www.evawoodsauthor.com. Drop me a line!

Lots of love,

Eva x